TO FORM A PASSAGE

ARTS OF SUBSTANCE - NOVEL 1

SHARON ROSE

ETERNAROSE PUBLISHING

Book Cover by: Kirk DouPonce, DogEared Designs

Edited by: B Squared Writer Coaching

ISBN: 978-1-948160-31-5

DEDICATION

To Elias,
May you always write fearlessly,
with hope spilling from the pages.

CONTENTS

CHAPTER I

L ight. Taken for granted aboveground. A rare commodity below. And few could deliver it.

Devron swept his forming sense down the polished shaft from the surface to the spreader he'd fashioned days ago. To those without a forming gift, the light shaft was just a pale circle in the cavern's dark ceiling. Faceted but cloudy, like a flawed diamond.

Ah, but Devron perceived what truly existed. The entire pure shaft twisted through dense rock from the surface to the thin opaque layer that remained above the spreader. He grinned, having saved this part for last, as always. With full understanding of every crystal within the layer—random, chaotic, distorting—he envisioned how they should align and commanded them.

They released, straightened, and rejoined.

Oh, that instant when light shot through the full shaft and drove back the darkness! Warmth radiated through him. Another perfect forming. Sunlight for their city-in-the-making. No matter how many crystals he polished, the wonder of it never grew old.

The conversations nearby paused as others looked up from the architectural drawings unrolled on a slab of rock. Mayor Borchel exhaled a long *Ah!* "Another shaft complete. Another shadow cancelled. Well placed, indeed, Alverlee!"

Devron's brother was already crossing the cavern floor to him, and a shade of annoyance passed over his features. With accustomed ease, he kept it from his voice as he answered the mayor over his shoulder. "My thanks for the compliment, but it would be nothing if Devron had not polished it."

"Yes, our thanks also to Devron and to the unknown polisher aboveground," the mayor conceded. "We realize that many bring your master plan to life and help finish the shafts you create. But really, Alverlee, you needn't be so reticent to accept the praise you deserve as chief former."

This, Alverlee did not bother to answer. He stopped beside Devron's reclining chair and squeezed his shoulder, uttering quiet words. "They don't understand, Dev, but I do. Well done!"

Devron's internal satisfaction carried him high, but he still welcomed the added bonus of Alverlee's praise. He'd learned long ago not to expect recognition from others. The most intricate gifts were the least valued among those of the Formers' Guild. He quirked the corner of his mouth in acknowledgment, finally resting against the extended back of his chair. Its tilt allowed him to face the cavern ceiling as he worked. Of course, his resting position looked identical to his working posture. The non-gifted never comprehended what it meant to *work* as a former. Oddly enough, he got more acknowledgment if he craned his neck while focusing his gift. Absurd!

He sensed his brother exploring the angles of the crystal shaft, savoring the practical art. The former aboveground—a polisher like Devron—was also still enjoying the symmetry they'd created. The three of them united in the appreciation of a true forming.

Alverlee might value the result, but only the polisher above savored the *doing* of it, as Devron did. Their connection...so intimate and yet so distant that Devron would never even know his name. But their delight in the work, their joint weariness, even the gratitude they shared...this, he knew.

Devron bestirred himself and drew upright enough to take Alverlee's hand and pull himself to his feet. Mayor Borchel was still talking with the others gathered around the drawings...something about extending the allowed building height.

With an upward glance, Alverlee muttered, "Unbelievable. I'd better nip that mistake."

As his brother strode off to rejoin them, Devron stretched muscles that had stiffened while he'd lain in motionless concentration. He bent to stretch his hamstrings, then twisted his torso, which brought his gaze to an approaching figure.

Fairlynn ascended the rough-hewn road from the original settlement. Her cane glistened with silvery and coppery hues. If one must use a cane, at least it should be beautiful. Two years had passed since she'd broken her hip, but though the medic former had knit the bone as best he could—well, nerves were hard to tame, after all. She would never be free of pain if that hip must bear her full weight. Not that a weak joint could hinder her kindness. Though she was Alverlee's wife, she stopped first to offer a jar of tea to Devron from the food basket she carried, for she never overlooked her bachelor brother-in-law.

He accepted it with a grateful smile and drank deep. She was no former, but as a streamer, she understood in part. Not what it meant to shift solid matter, but she knew that it took effort, just as it did for her to divert the waters to her will.

"You've finished another, haven't you?" Fairlynn asked.

He pointed to it in the dark, crystal-studded ceiling of the cavern. Most were dingy conglomerations, but the crystals he'd polished—they glowed like tiny suns. "That one, just now."

She squinted upward. "You prove our hopes yet again, Dev. Someday this chamber will be as bright as Welcia above." She handed him a pouch of dried fruit for a snack, then walked on to her husband.

What joy that would be—full daylight in this huge chamber. Still dim for now, but the sun's rays streamed through more than a dozen shafts. He could feel their obelisks rising a few feet above the distant surface, where the ground met the sky—a void he couldn't sense. Most of the peaks were only a few feet tall, but enough to capture sunlight for the belowground settlement of Jourendia. He and his brother had formed moon shafts, too. A rather different accomplishment, for they tracked the kingdom's official calendar rather than illuminating.

Devron tossed a handful of dried cherries and grapes from the pouch into his mouth and stretched his legs with a brisk walk around the planned town square. A small band practiced for the upcoming celebration. How different their instruments sounded in this vast cavern.

Their leader jogged over to meet him. After greeting Devron, she said, "One of our songwriters has an idea for the traditional half year anthem. In fact, a welcome of first light on the small moon's marker." She raised her brows with a hint of uncertainty. "But of course, we wouldn't want it to be awkward..."

"Ah, you're wondering if it's really going to light up." Fair question, for his and Alverlee's first attempt had failed. "I'm as certain as I can be before the shaft is proven."

She snapped a definitive nod. "We'll be ready."

Devron walked on as she hurried back to her musicians. Funny how the half year markers symbolized status—as though a city wasn't real until it had them. He munched another handful of dried fruit. That told him the season as well as moonlight on a marker since fresh fruit had not come through the tunnels in at least a month. By the sound of distant brays and clopping, a team of burros must be pulling another string of bins along the in-bound rail. Devron had helped to polish that rail back when his father was still alive. A dark job, that had been, carrying their light with them. Well worth the struggle, though. After widening the rough tunnel, leveling the floor, and installing the first transport rail, the small band of expansion settlers his father led had finally reached the lower cavern. How they had stared at its single natural crystal shaft, which gave them faint light from aboveground.

Devron smiled at the memory. They hadn't even known what day it was, but they'd celebrated Savoring Day all through the next passage of the sun over that dim crystal. The bond he and Alverlee had shared with their father still felt near when Devron drew this treasured recalling to mind.

Clatters and thumps commenced down the slope at the terminal station with its offloading pulleys and cranes. Devron paused for a moment, watching through the distant arch to the settlement as workers converged to haul goods. Probably more food for storage. Hopefully, some soil too. Now that the gem deposits had been tapped, it seemed a new family arrived every day. Plenty of rock here to build more houses, but soil for the rooftop gardens—*that* was harder to come by.

A salty breeze bore the ocean's scent through a distant gap. Invigorating. Devron resumed his energetic stride and returned to his chair, which he folded with a simple twist of its mechanism. He slung it over his shoulder and strode off to find a good viewing angle for the next shaft he wanted to work. A narrow light beam lay across one of the clock markings polished high on the eastern cavern wall. The afternoon was half gone, but enough time remained to carve a rudimentary matrix into the crystal.

He settled into his chair and examined a vein of raw quartz. Nature had been scanty, as it often was, so Alverlee had drawn more rough quartz to fill in the gaps. Devron studied it with his forming sense, determining the number of planes needed and their distance. He coaxed bonds to relax, letting rock behave almost as a liquid, and then relock their minuscule grains into the plane he asked of them. He began at the top, forming only the primary planes. A former above would find his pattern after the holiday and begin polishing out the cloudy material between the upper planes.

That would suffice for now. Devron stood to go and check the drawings before he designed the spreader facets. Usually, the location made little difference, but best to know if a low spot was planned between the three-story buildings that would someday be constructed. The mayor, architect, and various craft chiefs were still conferring around the drawings, his brother among them.

Alverlee jerked his head up and backstepped into a quick turn, his profile set in steady concentration.

Odd. Was he checking something within the surrounding stone?

He sidestepped farther from the group, and when Devron drew near, beads of sweat stood on Alverlee's upper lip. He snapped a soft demand. "Did you sense that?"

Sense what? Devron extended his awareness into the familiar stone in the direction that Alverlee gazed. "I think not. What am I looking for?"

Alverlee released a shuddering breath. "It was a long way off...probably beyond your range. Hard to describe. Almost like...like a thickening...more pressure within the crust itself." He swept his eyes in a slow circle, clearly searching out the other formers at work within the cavern.

Most showed no hint of surprise, but Bekta was striding toward them, a frown pushing her brow low. Alverlee hurried to meet her, away from the mayor's group, and Devron kept up.

"Did you sense that?" Alverlee demanded of Bekta, keeping his voice hushed.

"Sure did! Never felt anything like it in my life. Have you?"

Alverlee shook his head. "Any ideas of what it was?"

She squinted toward the source, fingering her long black braid. "I can't sense anything changing now, but I could swear the stone is denser. Off toward LourEstelle and maybe the access arches." She shifted her tone to deference. "Not that I've lived this far from the arches for very long."

"Well, I have," Alverlee murmured, "and there's never been any such...such a...thickening before. Can you place the location more precisely?"

She shook her head, skewing her lips. "I'll ask around among the boarders at dinner and see who else—" She lifted a brow as Alverlee's expression tensed.

"Do not speak of it openly." He seemed to force a pause, then resumed his natural calm. "Just tell me if any formers mention it to you. I'll not have this rumored around to spark fear in the non-formers. Especially with tomorrow's travel to Crysalan for Gifting Day."

Devron marveled at the change in Alverlee. Shaking and sweating one minute, firm confidence the next. How did he do it?

"But is it wise to travel?" Bekta asked. "What if it was a shift?"

"It didn't feel like that to me."

Her eyes rounded. "Have you actually felt a shift before?"

"We lived near the Weslin mines when I was young," Alverlee said. "I certainly felt *that* one."

Creeping chills wormed around Devron's collarbone—just as they had on that horrible day. He had only been a lad of five. Not gifted yet, but even he remembered the collapse that killed eleven miners. A friend's heart-shattering sobs had rocked his world, for her father was among those lost. The first true fear to ever spike through his young mind—might *his* father die? Even after all these years, dread still sank claws—still tightened his breath. His friend's tear-stained face now mirrored sweet little Perrie's. No! She was too young for such fears.

Bekta voiced the question that ever lingered around that long-ago tragedy. "I've always wished there was someone I could ask." Her brows drew up at the center. "Was it possible that a former caused that shift?"

Alverlee gave his standard answer. "I wasn't trained yet, but my father told us that *none* of the formers knew of the fault before the shift. It's true that a former sheared down a fresh drop of ore a few hours earlier, but that doesn't mean she caused the shift. Since she died with the miners, she couldn't have been aware of any risk of collapse." His teaching cadence laced his words. "We formers bear heavy responsibility. The safety of Dirklan rests upon us, but we are only responsible for what we *can* know and what we *can* do. Just as streamers do not make rivers flow, nor wind weavers control all weather, so formers do not control the entire crust of the planet. Only as much as Ellincreo has gifted to each of us."

Bekta accorded him the steady regard of a student attending to a master. Alverlee always had that presence about him.

"As for this thickening..." Alverlee tilted his head toward Devron. "The Crysalan chambers are within Devron's range, but he didn't sense any change. It must have been well beyond that. Too far off to trouble us here in Jourendia. In any case, I'll learn more when I reach Crysalan tomorrow. I will speak of it here when I have knowledge instead of guesses."

Bekta still looked shaken, but she dipped her head. "As you instruct, Chief Former." She returned to whatever had occupied her earlier, as Alverlee swept a gaze around the formers again.

Fairlynn approached from the fountain shaft, hewn a month ago. "Are you ready to head home, dear?"

Her sweet voice relaxed Alverlee's face as always. "I'm ready the moment you are." He took the basket from her and offered his arm, which she accepted, slipping her hand into the crook. A habit they had begun when she was injured. No longer necessary, but natural now.

Devron collected his folding chair and followed their stroll down the slope. A comfort to see his brother content in marriage this time. The way their heads tilted together in conversation...that fond gesture was never used in Alverlee's first marriage. Not in all seventeen years of it.

Devron caught up to them by the time they reached the house his father had built. Narrow and three stories tall, like all the houses constructed when Jourendia was only a settlement. By typical inheritance, it had passed to Alverlee and would eventually pass to his son, Kevenor, whose family resided on the upper floors.

Alverlee turned to Devron. "Join us for breakfast tomorrow."

Half invitation, half statement of the obvious, for the first meal began the holiday and they would journey together on the morrow. "Of course. Pleasant night."

"Pleasant night," the couple responded in unison as they opened their door.

Devron continued down the gradual slope of the thoroughfare toward the lake. As always, a dense murmur emanated from the short tunnel—endless ripples echoing around the circular lake chamber. One of several local waters that Fairlynn and the other streamers tended daily, though this one provided food rather than drink.

Devron neared his own abode, which he and his father had built when Devron approached manhood. Of average size, but bigger than he needed. His vague intent to marry had not survived the limited number of women or the strife that plagued his brother's first marriage.

He took a moment to slide his hand over the teal sheen he'd crafted upon his alloy door, then pushed it open and passed under the supporting arch into his welcome room. He propped his chair in the alcove beside the door. In the dim light filtering through the front windows, he turned the knob on the wall-mounted magnery lamp.

The glow intensified, revealing his couch and two chairs with matching blue cushions. When had they become so flat? He ran his fingers over the intricate relief work around the edge of his pedestal table. At least time couldn't damage his stone art. Two decades. Had anything changed here? A staircase climbed along the side wall, and shelves along the other held trinkets he sometimes fashioned for sale. What would the room look like if he had a wife?

Odd thought. Was this what happened when bachelors reached their fortieth year?

Devron crossed to the broad archway leading into the kitchen, opened his slow oven, and checked the meat. Not quite done—perfect timing. He stirred vegetables into the juices and closed it up again. Simple fare, but the savory scent made his mouth water. Besides, he always got a fine meal on the weekly Family Day in his brother's home. A bit noisy, but Alverlee's grandchildren were a blessing, after all. A wry smile twisted his lip. A blessing he preferred from a distance.

Alverlee, with his easy charm, was welcome to the little horde. He could as readily quiet dinner table racket as he could sway the city council, even now that it was filling with newcomers. Which made his reaction earlier...strange...if not downright unnerving.

Devron set out dishes, his mind still circling the perplexing event. What could have caused it? Rock did not suddenly change on its own. Streamers and wind weavers spoke of pressure variations, but formers—never. Yes, a former could discern that the pressure under Mount Estelle was greater than here, but the balance never changed.

Puzzling, yet what could be done about it? That was always the dilemma, but at least it wasn't his problem. He just had to make sure nothing fell from the ceiling while he polished crystals. And though he could feel every move when stone was harvested for construction or mining, it was up to Alverlee to approve excavations.

He'd been the perfect choice to lead Jourendia's segment of the Formers' Guild when their father died. His range was longer than Devron's, and he was a competent planner. Good looking too. The tallest of the brothers, with hair so black it shone, unlike Devron's dusky brown. Looks didn't matter, but they didn't hurt, either. His calm tongue mattered far more. The non-gifted couldn't tell a good former from a poor one, so they needed to hear confidence from the person they relied on. Alverlee's charisma was something Devron could never offer. Even if Alverlee erred in hiding this strange thickening event, he could make a convincing explanation for it later.

Devron let out a rueful snort as he found himself in the workshop behind his kitchen. Alverlee never got so lost in his thoughts that he went from one room to the next without realizing it. As always, this was the natural path of Devron's feet when his mind wandered. A place where no one's safety relied on him. He swept his loving gaze over metal arts in progress. His preferred form of *children.* This kind never bickered.

The music disc drew him. The alloy had been cast as a thin, shallow dome and mounted to the sounding board of imported wood. He tapped his knuckles against the metal. After an evening of polishing, the hollow *dong* now rang on key.

He perched on a low stool and began shaping the first strike pad, occasionally snapping a tuning fork and pressing it to the pad's anchor. Polishing an object so near—almost in his lap—was more like caressing it into shape. He formed and tapped until the note rang so true that the tuning fork caught the vibration and echoed it.

The pure tone relaxed him. How could a single chime be so beautiful? And only the beginning. He would fashion the metal to sound fifteen perfect notes, but he couldn't play music. Others would strike melodies from the disc to echo the myriad turnings of life. Adventure, longing, birth, mourning, love, joy, and countless others. The fulfillment of Ellincreo's desire, to be sure. These gifts he'd bestowed were never meant for his children to create in isolation. Only when they created together, did persistent beauty arise.

Devron's stomach growled, and he stood, giving the music disc one last look. It altered before his eyes! What was this that he saw? Separate panels sliding to overlap and open. No. Not possible! He squeezed his eyes tight and groped the disc to confirm its form. Still solid. He dared another look, his vision once again confirming its real shape.

He panted as his chest heaved. How disturbing! Of course, he always visualized what he would make before beginning work. But *never* did internal images seem to take on physical form. He rubbed his eyes, then raked his hair. What could this mean? The design of a new instrument?

No. Whatever it was had been silent. If anything, it would groan with friction. A mechanism for some purpose? Not that, either. The need came first, then he designed a device to fill that need.

He tried to recapture the image enough to study it in memory...but all he saw was his brother's face. The way he'd startled. His anxious frown as he stared toward the distant avenue into their land. The only access point into the belowground domain of Dirklan.

CHAPTER 2

When light was still golden from the sun's slant, Devron let himself through his brother's aqua-tinted door. Fairlynn's choice of color, for she had declared the pinkish-red of earlier years to be stressful.

"Uncle Dev!" Perrie shouted the instant he entered. At only four, she couldn't keep her eyes from the large travel bag he set beside the door. The way her lips pinched, she must have been warned not to ask about gifts. She grabbed his hand and tugged. "Breakfast is ready, and the travel cakes smell *sooo* good. Papa-Lee seasoned them from his special spice jar as his gift to the family." She dragged Devron toward the long table, which extended from the kitchen into the welcome room.

Colorful napkins were loosely tied around painted eggs in the center of each plate. Likely, there would be no traditional passing of them, for Devron could already feel the hurry. Quick motions. Banging pans. Voices crossing over each other, hardly making sense.

"Kevenor?" Crilla called to her husband, even as he ran down the stairs. Before he could answer, she commanded her eldest son, "Tebber, get your brother out from under my feet."

"Why do I gotta tend him?"

"Do it!" Kevenor said. "Perrie, go help." He paused at the bottom of the staircase and joined his father in welcoming Devron. "A joyous day to you, Uncle Dev."

Alverlee lowered his voice. "Have you heard anything among the formers?"

"I haven't talked with any since we parted yesterday." Devron met Kevenor's intent look. "Did you sense it?"

"Not really. Something weird, but so faint I assumed it must be a big ore drop a long way off." He hurried to his wife, for Crilla had demanded him again.

"Bekta stopped by late to tell me that no one else has mentioned it." Alverlee cocked a wry look toward the noisy kitchen. "There's enough fuss here already, so we're not speaking of it during the celebration."

Crilla threw her apron aside. "Father Alverlee, start the greetings please. Fairlynn, this is no time to slip away."

"We can wait for Mother Fairlynn," Kevenor said. Not exactly a correction of his wife, whose pitch had grown shrill, but close. He bent to pick up his youngest son, who had dragged himself upright against the legs of his high stool and was banging it against the table.

Fairlynn returned from her and Alverlee's bedroom beyond the kitchen, her hands behind her back. She cast a smiling glance to the children, who were on high alert for special treats.

Alverlee began the traditional greeting. "I offer thanks for the gift of my brother's presence at my table."

Devron responded with, "I offer thanks for the cheery welcome in Fairlynn's eyes."

They continued around, each person offering thanks for some small gift within another family member.

When it reached Devron's nephew, Kevenor spoke over the baby talk. "I'm thankful that Jojo is so hearty, and I'm sure all his babbling is thanks to his mother for preparing the first meal of Gifting Day."

Crilla, still in motion throughout the tradition, set the last plate of skilletbread on the table. "I offer thanks for the gift of a home in Father's house, and also thank Great Papa and Great Mama, who first made this house a home and passed it down to Father Alverlee." She pulled her chair out. "Tebber, stop poking your sister."

Alverlee concluded the greetings. "Let us break our fast in family's peace." He took his place at the head of the table. A good thing, for it was clear Crilla would sit down before the elders of the family if he didn't hurry it up.

At the opposite end of the table, Fairlynn whisked a jar from behind her back as she sat. She lifted it high. "Skyberry sauce from the Vinelands of Welcia for everyone's skilletbread."

Perrie clapped and squealed, "Another gift!"

"Do you have to be so shrieky over gifts?" Tebber grumbled.

"Better the sound of joy than grumping." Kevenor's patience seemed to be slipping. "I expect to hear thanks if you plan to taste any of Mama-Lynn's gift."

Fairlynn pried the lid, and it released with a satisfying pop. She set it by Crilla's plate, then began cutting the puffy skilletbread into wedges.

Perrie, seated on Devron's left, pointed to the hard-boiled egg he took from his napkin. "I painted that one for you. I made it dark like the cavern roof, and the silver dots are for the crystals because Papa-Lee says you're the one who makes them sparkle."

"Ah, yes, they look just like the crystal shafts, my little artist. Now let's see if I'm strong enough to peel stone."

He tapped it on the table as Perrie giggled. "It's not *real* stone, Uncle Dev."

"Stop chattering and eat," Crilla ordered.

She meant Perrie, of course, but Devron felt equally silenced. Not that he would be able to say much with the children so excited. Who could blame them? Gifting Day might be tomorrow but travel always extended the holiday into two days of gifts. He accepted thin slices of cave duck from his nephew and enjoyed them before moving on to skilletbread and Fairlynn's gift.

Perrie, her mouth now sticky with skyberry sauce and breadcrumbs, chirped, "May I start the questions?"

Her mother sighed aloud. "Be quick about it."

"Papa-Lee, why do we celebrate Gifting Day?"

"To thank Ellincreo, the first and always gift-giver."

"Why do we—

"It's my turn!" Tebber snapped. "Why do we give gifts to each other, Mama-Lynn?"

She answered sweetly slow. "To remind ourselves that the gifts we receive from Ellincreo let us create gifts for others."

"I'll ask Jojo's question," Tebber said, apparently more intent on getting to the next question than on considering the answers. "What gifts—"

"You asked all the questions last year," Perrie whined. "I should get to—"

Crilla splayed a hand ceilingward, and Kevenor said, "No arguing. Uncle Dev, will you tell Jojo the three substance gifts that Ellincreo gives to his children?"

Devron took his cue and recited the words with the solemn honor they deserved. "He gives formers—to fashion stone so we may build. He gives streamers—to channel the waters so all may drink and grow. He gives wind weavers—to freshen the air for all who breathe through his gift of life."

Crilla began the closing, and they joined her in unison. "We humbly accept the gifts Ellincreo bestowed upon us, and in gratitude, we use our gifts for others."

"But I had another question," Perrie murmured, her lower lip sneaking forward. She, at least, knew that this tradition shouldn't be rushed.

Her mother smiled, tight though it was. "Remember, we have long travel ahead of us and time for the rest of the questions when we have dinner with your other grandparents tonight."

"Not the regular questions," Perrie said. "A different one."

"What is it, dear?" Fairlynn asked in her gentle way.

"Well, Tebber says not everyone gets a gift, and Ellincreo probably won't make me a former, *or* a streamer, *or* even a wind weaver. So, then what?"

Under his father's narrowed gaze, Tebber squirmed and snorted an unrepentant laugh. "I was just teasing."

Kevenor pinned his erring son with a stern glare. "No one can predict what gifts Ellincreo will bestow on anyone."

Alverlee responded to Perrie. "There are far more than just the three substance gifts."

Her eyes rounded. "What are the others?"

"They are called the life gifts, and there are many." Alverlee tapped the side of his jaw as he thought. "Like the mayor, for instance. He cannot form, stream, or weave, but he was elected because he is gifted at organizing the community."

"And he has a loud voice," Tebber said.

"That, too." Alverlee rested his gaze on Fairlynn. "And then there are the really important gifts, like a smile. Like your Mama-Lynn has. Don't you just always know that she loves you, Perrie, when she smiles at you?"

"I do!"

Fairlynn's eyes squeezed almost shut as she rested them on her husband.

"Speaking of gifts..." Devron pushed his chair back.

A sigh escaped Crilla, though she managed to keep her voice soft. "Could they perhaps wait? We have two entire days for gifts."

Devron went to pull them from his travel bag as the children whined with the politest begging they could achieve. He returned with gifts, saying to Crilla, "You might consider these a gift of ease for *you* as we journey." To Perrie, he handed a highly polished, quartz tablet with a dozen colored pastels tied in a cloth. "You may practice your gift of art on this and wipe it clean whenever you want to start a new picture."

She accepted it breathlessly. "Oh, thank you, Uncle Dev!"

He turned to Tebber. "This may look like plain jet, but it hides three forms and a secret."

By his narrowed eyes, Tebber was already searching for joints in the design Devron had etched over the ebony cylinder. "A puzzle tower! Thanks, Uncle Dev."

Jojo twisted to avoid having his face wiped as Devron handed over a stuffed doll. "And you, young Joachin, I must still shop for until you can be trusted with stone or metal."

The boy clutched the offering and blabbered random sounds.

"You are most welcome," Devron replied.

Crilla produced an appreciative twist of her lips. "Your uncle blessed you with gifts for the trip. Put them in your bags, children. The sooner the dishes are cleaned, the sooner you can play with them." She got everyone moving again, which meant they left the house in the next few minutes.

Time to deal with the worry on his and Alverlee's minds.

After a short walk to the rail terminal, Devron, Alverlee, and Fairlynn settled onto padded seats in the first of the two carriages that would transport the family along the outbound rail. Kevenor's tribe climbed into the next carriage. The boost wheel gave them a push, and soon they hooked into the chain of conveyances kept moving by burros yoked alongside at intervals.

"A few hours of peace, now." Alverlee looked to his wife beside him. "You are the most forgiving woman in all of Welcia."

Fairlynn arched her brow. "Ah, well, Crilla sees us daily but only gets to visit her parents and other family a few times a year. I understand why she wants to set out as soon as may be."

He made a sound in his throat. "That doesn't excuse her rudeness while she hurries, but I suppose I'm glad that you hold back the words she deserves to hear, for they would only add fuel to the strife."

"Indeed, they would do nothing more than that in one who does not wish to hear."

Opposite them, Devron leaned deeper into the cushions of the broad seat. At least Alverlee was aware of the strain and honored Fairlynn for her patience. And though Devron wasn't the target of Crilla's ire, somehow it eased him that they spoke of it. He set his awareness to the grooved rail beneath them and the fitting that glided along it with no more friction than ice. Not that they had ice in Dirklan, but he'd discovered its properties during his training aboveground. The very thing that had convinced him to become a polisher, though he could have used his skills for much larger building projects.

Alverlee interrupted his thoughts. "Are you polishing?"

"No, the rails are in good shape."

"Oh, you two!" Fairlynn shook her head in mock scolding, and the carriage lanterns revealed gold streaks shifting in her dark hair. "Even if it weren't a holiday, this is Family Day and tomorrow is Savoring Day. Aren't the six workdays between enough for you?"

"Well, we needn't form," Alverlee said. "I just want to check the arch of the tunnel as we travel. And as for the floor..." He glanced at Devron. "If the rails are unflawed, we'll know nothing moved."

Fairlynn tsked. "Alver, you told me there was nothing to worry about."

He took her hand. "I did, my dear. And I intend to confirm that is irrefutably true." He continued teasing counter-assurances until she laughed.

None of which fooled Devron, who stretched his awareness along the rail from every stop to the next. Tedious, but Fairlynn had brought a book to share, and her fine reading voice sweetened their travels between mining settlements until, at last, they arrived at the first of Crysalan's sprawling caverns.

When his brother's eyes turned to him in silent question, Devron replied, "Smooth as ever. I checked the gear wheels, too, when we crossed the river. All aligned."

"The same overhead." Alverlee released a tight breath. "I'll find the chief former from LourEstelle and see what he has to say."

His chipper voice didn't fool Devron. Even with their tunnel proven flawless, Alverlee still worried.

The two men stepped from the carriage onto the platform first, then supported Fairlynn as she climbed out. Her hip was usually stiff after sitting for a long time. Devron handed her cane to her as Alverlee shouldered his and her travel bags, only letting Fairlynn carry their half-empty food basket. They waved goodbye to Kevenor's family, who were continuing to a chamber on the opposite side of Crysalan. Crilla's kin always took rooms on that side, since it was nearer to LourEstelle, where most of them lived.

The trio strolled the crowded avenue into an adjoining chamber, wholly occupied by an inn and its hot springs. One wall sparkled with crystalized deposits under cascading streams. They yielded a continuous supply of mineral waters, which the proprietors included in their signature soaps, lotions, and salves. Fairlynn loved this place, but Devron caught her sudden frown at Alverlee, who had paused outside the inn's double doors, his gaze distant.

She tugged his arm. "What is it, dear?"

"Why don't you and Devron get settled into our rooms. Take a dip if you like." He passed the bags he carried to Devron. "I see a former I want to talk with."

Struggling with three bags, Devron had no time to question before Alverlee was striding along the avenue again. How was he supposed to hide his concern when—

"Well!" Fairlynn stared at her husband's departing back. "Nothing to worry about, he says!"

"Mm. Maybe we should keep it...uh...wait to talk about it until he comes back."

"We can try." She entered the inn's reception area. "But I'm pretty certain I've already overheard scraps of it from people we passed on this short walk."

They took a suite with two bedrooms and a small sitting room that provided access directly to the spa pools. The moment they entered it, Fairlynn began digging through her bag. "I'm all for taking a soak now." She pulled out her pale blue bathing dress, which wasn't much of a dress at all. "The spa doesn't look too busy, and it likely will be after tomorrow's Gifting Day ceremony. And who knows whether the gifted will be summoned into some nonsense meeting."

"Just give me a minute to change."

"You don't have to if you'd rather not, you know. I can take my cane, and that will prompt some kind soul to help me up from a pool."

Devron paused in the doorway of his bedroom and grinned at her, shaking his head. "I'll be right out." As though he'd desert her when Alverlee wasn't on hand. He doffed his travel clothes, tied on bathing shorts, and got back to the sitting room quicker than Fairlynn so he could offer her his arm.

"Thanks, Dev." She slipped her hand into the crook. "I really hate to take the cane Alverlee made for me out there. The mineral waters stain, and such a nuisance it is to get the shine back." They descended a curving path, and she pointed. "Let's use this pool with the streamer couple in it."

Likely, she felt their gift, for it matched hers. The moving water was Devron's only clue. They stilled the motion as Devron helped Fairlynn step in.

"Streamers, in truth," the young woman said, "but we're not a couple. At least not the married sort. I'm Olanni, and this kid is Talmarq."

The young man smirked, forming creases in his short golden-brown beard. "You'll still be calling me a kid if we live to be eighty." He allowed her no time to reply. "We're from Mount Maundette, here for our training. I just arrived a couple weeks ago, but aged Olanni there is almost done."

That explained his brown skin and faded hair. Sun-baked. Devron eased himself lower into the water, inhaling the exotic mineral scent of moisture-laden air.

Fairlynn offered them a kind welcome and ended her introduction with "...and this is my brother-in-law, Devron."

"Do I sense a former?" Talmarq asked.

Ah, this one had high sensitivity. "As you say. So if we're going to get a massage with this glorious heat, it's up to you three."

They all joined in and set the water to frothing while they relaxed with their shoulders cradled in the grooved edges of the pool.

Olanni stretched her legs to the center, letting her toes float. "I'm going to miss these hot springs when I go back home." Her hair spread around her, with the brown to blond ombre look of one who'd lived years aboveground before spending several months below. "What's this hush-hush that has all the formers nearly bumping their heads together?"

Ugh. Devron hoped Fairlynn would answer. She was married to the chief former, after all, and could speak on his behalf. But she just looked at Devron. Well, he *was* a former. No getting out of it, despite having nothing to say. "You might know more than we do. We've just arrived from Jourendia. Whatever occurred was so distant that only two of our formers sensed it."

Talmarq's brows shot up. "Wow. Jourendia? It was even felt that far away?"

"Only the faintest hint. No movement occurred between here and there. My brother, Alverlee, is the chief former of our city, and we checked the tunnel on our way here. All is well." He hoped that was the right approach. Alverlee would want to keep alarm down.

"In any event, we're well met," Olanni said. "Talmarq has a commission from the king and queen. I'm coming along to Jourendia to make sure he does it right."

Talmarq groaned and rolled his eyes to the cavern ceiling. "Must you?" She chuckled but left him to explain. "It came up in a joint assembly of the three substance guilds. I was lucky enough to arrive in Regissa Province in time to attend. Yes, King Tandorad and Queen Dizelle were in attendance, and I got to meet them, but it's not like they gave me a direct commission."

"Was the crown prince there?" Devron asked.

"No, but Prince Queltin was. I thought he was titled Judge Queltin now, so I managed to stumble over that."

Fairlynn shrugged dismissively. "He only uses the title of Judge in matters of law. What is the commission you spoke of?"

"It just came up because some formers were talking about new light shafts on the high ground above the harbor."

Devron exchanged a grin with Fairlynn. She extended her hand toward him. "Here is the polisher who lets the sunlight through those shafts."

Talmarq's blond brows rose again. "It's like our meeting is providence or something. The chief streamers at that guild assembly assigned me a training task. I'm to update the level map for the environs of Jourendia. Mostly underground rivers, of course, but I'm also to confirm with the formers where the cavern boundaries lie and any deposits you are mining."

"Don't be modest, Talmarq," Olanni prodded. "Tell them the hard part."

He glanced down, and the corners of his mouth pinched. "I'm supposed to try to feel for the harbor water from within Jourendia."

Devron remembered challenges of his own early days. "It wouldn't be training if they didn't assign a goal to stretch for. That's where you'll find the most exciting discoveries." He considered for only a second. "You should stay with me instead of at the overcrowded boarding house. I have two empty bedrooms, and I live near the lake cavern, which is the part of Jourendia that extends under the harbor."

Olanni blew out a slow breath. "I've heard as much but…few believe it. How would you dare live there if it's really under the harbor?"

"The same reason that the cliffs stand firm against the ocean—ipenrock. You know what that name derives from, don't you?"

"Impenetrable rock," Talmarq answered slowly.

"Exactly. The very fact that the peninsula and harbor have resisted the ocean current for eons proves that we are safe in Jourendia."

They both looked skeptical, and Fairlynn offered a soothing explanation. "The lake chamber isn't under the entire harbor. It's near the cliffs. I saw the area from above when I went up for my training. That area isn't as deep as the port or the rest of the harbor."

"It's still an awful lot of water!" Olanni sent a spurt up between their feet and let it plop. "If it did break through, wouldn't it flood all of Jourendia?"

"No," Devron answered. "You'll understand when you see it. The original settlement sits higher than the lake's surface, and the new expansion is higher yet. Beyond the settlement, a labyrinth of crevices descends into the depths of the planet crust. The wind weavers call them endless."

Talmarq rolled onto his chest and then to his back again. "None of the gifted can reach farther than a wind weaver. If they call a channel endless, so will I. But could channels drain off even the top foot of an ocean?"

Typical. "That's not in question. Streamers think in terms of continuous motion. Formers understand the immovable. The very weight of the water compresses the chamber's roof. Even if a crack formed, which is hard to imagine, we would get nothing more than slow seepage. The lake's natural drainage could easily handle it. The chamber is shaped rather like an egg, and yes, I can feel the distribution of pressure through every inch of the structure. It is *not* moving. *Ever.* If people do not fear living under the pressure of Mount Estelle, it seems absurd to fear the harbor's pressure."

CHAPTER 3

Sated with luxurious warmth, Fairlynn rose from the pool, needing little aid from Devron. Ah, there was Alverlee coming down the path—finally. She squeezed water from her hair, while he grabbed a towel for her from a nearby stack. "What a shame that you're too late for a soak, but at least I can introduce Olanni and Talmarq. They are streamers here for training and on their way to Jourendia next." She wrapped the towel around her head. "This is my husband, Alverlee, who as Devron mentioned, is our chief former."

He said all that was proper, for he was ever smooth, but Fairlynn noticed what they would not. There was something subdued about him. She almost abandoned her next intention, but that wouldn't do. With the greetings exchanged, she turned to the young streamers. "Since you have no family in Crysalan, we would be delighted to welcome you to our table in the dining room. There are just the three of us tonight, since we must share our children with extended family."

They accepted, of course, as they dried off.

Now to find out what was going on. Fairlynn turned for their suite and soon faced Alverlee in the sitting room as Devron closed the glazed door. "What's wrong, dear? What did you learn?"

"Nothing of importance."

She slid her hand into his and gave it a squeeze. "Don't try to hide things from me."

His mouth made a rueful twist. "But I really don't know anything useful. Local formers felt it here, but all place it nearer to LourEstelle. The same with visiting formers. Some have called it a heave, but the term *thickening* is preferred, for no one has actually detected where this so-called *heave* was." He shifted his gaze between her and Devron. "The Crysalan formers tried to downplay it, but with visitors converging for the holiday, that isn't working. Too many non-formers know. If they cannot get answers, they speculate."

"What do the formers from LourEstelle say?" Devron asked.

"That's the problem. They're not here. Hardly anyone came from LourEstelle. What we're told is that they are checking every mine—active or abandoned—for signs of any movement."

"That is a lot of mines," Devron murmured. "A lot of tunnels."

Why were they frowning over this? "But that is wise, is it not?" Fairlynn asked.

"It is, my love, but that also means they don't have a single location where they can identify exactly what happened. I doubt we'll get to see Charodee on this trip."

Sad. Fairlynn felt a little more like a true stepmother with Charodee, since the girl hadn't been quite grown up when she'd married Alverlee. They shared a closeness unknown with Kevenor, or especially with Crilla. "Well, that's too bad, but I see why. If her husband is checking mines all through the holiday, she's bound to stay home so he can have at least a little time with their children on Gifting Day. But I'm sorry you don't get to see your daughter."

"I will soon, I'm sure. It's already decided that we formers are not assembling the full guild tomorrow. Instead, we'll convene a special meeting on sixth workday. By then, we should have complete information from LourEstelle. Hopefully, just an all's-well. In the meantime, we can enjoy our celebration as planned." His smile looked forced.

"Hm. Here I am, married to a former, and you still all mystify me. You spend your gift coaxing rock to move. Then, when a little of it moves without your command, you act like something horrible has happened."

Devron laughed. "Spoken like a streamer." He turned to Alverlee. "She has a point. The immobile bedrock, which we have charge of, has now been still for a full day after its little twitch. There is really nothing we can do. I, for one, am not going to stare at its stillness and command it to be still."

Finally, Alverlee relaxed enough to chuckle. "I admit, that particular madness would give everyone else good reason to be nervous. Ah, my dear, you are shivering. Let's don our festive clothes. I suppose we should get to the dining room before our guests."

In their room, Fairlynn scrunched her hair, asked the water to leave it in haste, then let it fall into long waves. She checked the back with a hand mirror. Perfect. Nothing like the mineral water here for holding a soft curl. She slipped her best gown over her head. Azure, for streamers wore blue to this celebration. She fluffed her double-layered skirt before the full-length mirror, long and full in the back and tapering to just below the knee in front.

Alverlee stepped behind her to fasten the clasp of her gold necklace. "No matter how many gems I add, it barely hints at how precious you are."

She leaned back against him, answering his compliment with a caress. Multicolored jewels glittered from the gold, resting cool against her chest and following the scoop of her bodice. He'd added a new gemstone to the broad necklace, as he did each Gifting Day, rearranging them to give it a fresh look.

She touched the new center stone. "Ah, a hint of violet in that sapphire. Lovely contrast between the tinted diamonds."

He bent his head to kiss her hair, then side-stepped enough to view them both in the mirror. So handsome in his crisp slate-gray shirt. Ebony buttons closed it to the waist in the front, where it split to form long tails in the back. He had worn this color for celebrations ever since they'd married. Because it set off her blue, he had once told her.

So many memories surfaced here where they'd first met. He'd worn brown on that Gifting Day. A widower bringing his teenage daughter to Crysalan for the holiday, while his grown son was aboveground for training. A waiter had seated them together, since Fairlynn, being unwed, was often asked to fill social gaps. Her nearest friend—who always included her in family events—had huffed, but Fairlynn didn't mind. She'd met people from different settlements that way, which was fun. And when Charodee had gone off with her late mother's relations, Alverlee had not joined them. Instead, he'd spent the evening and next day wandering the gem hills and lakes of Crysalan with Fairlynn.

She turned and reached up to rest her hands on his shoulders. "The memories of meeting here seem sweeter every year."

"Ah, that year when we were Ellincreo's special gift to each other." He kissed her lips gently, then whispered, "I think we'd better wait to get any more sentimental until after dinner."

"Quite right."

They found Devron waiting for them in the sitting room, proper in dusky brown, styled much like his brother's formalwear. Their blacks and browns blended with that of the many formers as they gathered in the dining room, which wrapped two sides of the inn. Most celebrants wore shades of green today, representing the life gifts. As for substance gifts, formers prevailed in Dirklan, the kingdom's primary source of mined wealth. Fewer were dressed in streamer's blue, and fewer yet in the white that represented wind weavers.

A waiter seated them at a round table off to the side, the center being taken up by long tables for larger family gatherings. The homogenous drone of background chatter was already growing. As within most buildings of Crysalan, magnery lamps mounted on the walls glowed with steady light, courtesy of the spinning magnet discovery. Magnery was Fairlynn's personal favorite of all the inventions that came from Illia.

Olanni and Talmarq soon found them at their table. Her eyes were radiant, and she showed off an opal pendant flecked with blue crystals that her fiancé had sent her.

"Oh, lovely," Fairlynn purred. "But how was he clever enough to get a package to you today, when you are traveling through Dirklan?"

She swept her hair back. "That part was easy. He gave it to Talmarq weeks ago."

"We're from the same village," Talmarq explained, "pretty much overlooking each other's houses as well as the rice fields."

"Rice?" Devron asked. "But isn't that grown in wet flats? I thought you said you came from a mountain."

"We do." Talmarq got the look of someone who had heard the same remark many times. "Have you seen any mountains other than Estelle, with her perfect cone?"

All three of them shook their heads.

"She stands there all alone, so proudly pointing at the axis star." He propped his elbows on the table and peaked his fingertips together, modeling Estelle's shape. "Few mountains have this perfect form. Mount Maundette is more like..." He began spreading his hands, falling in irregular dips. "Oh, like the queen's wide skirts when she sits on her padded stool and they mound up around her."

Fairlynn couldn't help but laugh, for in her young training days, she'd thought the broad skirts of the aboveground ladies quite unfathomable. Particularly those of the queen, who dressed more elaborately than all the rest. By their droll looks, her guests understood her mirth, but Talmarq still spoke.

"No matter which side you view Mount Maundette from, it looks different. As though the sides of it cannot decide if they should descend or spread out. So, yes, we live among rice flats that step down the mountainside. Which provides plenty of work for the Streamers' Guild, to keep flats from overfilling after rainfall, and to drain them for the harvests."

"And for the Wind Weavers' Guild too," Olanni added, "in case the rains don't come on their own."

Two servers set a laden tray in the middle of their table and hurried on. Talmarq pointed to rice pilaf nestled beside vegetables and the steaming feast meats. "It's just possible that rice came from our mountain, for we export a great deal. Sharing rice here seems like a fitting way to honor the varied gifts, which we should be doing at this of all meals."

"True, indeed." Alverlee began the traditional blessings for the Gifting Eve meal. They joined in and then started passing food to one another.

Something caught Talmarq's eye, for he faced the dining room's main entry. "If it isn't the queen of the wind, making a dramatic late entrance."

No doubt of who he meant. Fairlynn refused to turn and look. "Oh, please don't call her that."

Devron, sitting next to Talmarq, blinked and shook his head.

"More white dove feathers in her hair than last year?" Fairlynn asked. Ugh, she needed to try harder to keep that critical tone from her voice.

"None at all in her hair," Alverlee murmured, "and those are *not* dove's feathers!"

Under cover of passing a dish to Olanni, Fairlynn turned enough to see this year's spectacle. White feathers—immensely long—rose from Wandermae's back and formed a fan wider than her shoulders and higher than the black locks coiled upon her head. She gave new meaning to the word *ostentatious* yet again. "She'll be stabbing people with those feathers. Wherever could she have found any so long?"

They'd all focused their eyes back to their own table, and Talmarq suggested, "They could be ocean eagle feathers."

"What is an ocean eagle?" Devron asked.

"Huge birds that feed at sea. It's believed they stay aloft most of their lives, except when they nest on sea cliffs to raise their young. We never see them in our province, but I've heard they sometimes get a preference for young livestock, rather than fish. Those birds must be hunted, of course." Talmarq served himself from a bowl and passed it on. "Wandermae was at the joint guild assembly I told you about, so she's been aboveground lately. She must have found someone selling those feathers in the market." His eyes followed her again.

"Any mishaps yet?" Fairlynn asked.

He grinned. "Sorry, no. She was just seated at the head of a table, so she's not even tickling anyone."

"Oh, dear." Fairlynn sighed. "I suppose I sound like a stinging bat." Most idiosyncrasies didn't bother her, even the oddest. But Wandermae...such a challenge.

Alverlee patted her hand.

"I seem to find her everywhere," Olanni said. "In which part of Dirklan is she the chief wind weaver?"

"All of it, for there are few wind weavers below." Alverlee gestured around the room with his empty fork. "As you can see by the rarity of white festive wear. It's not as though Dirklan has weather in need of a wind weaver's guidance, so one guild chief is enough."

"She has such an unusual name," Olanni murmured.

Devron finished a sip and set his glass down. "Our father knew her parents. He told us that her mother saw a young wind weaver in the vision wall while she was pregnant. The name of Wandermae came to her in that instant. She believed it was prophetic, so when she had a girl, she gave her that name."

Alverlee wrinkled his nose. "Visions! Could be that hearing that tale has given Wandermae such a proud tongue. I'd guess half of those so-called visions are false anyway."

"Hers proved true," Olanni pointed out. "Gifts cannot be known at birth, but there is no doubt that she is a wind weaver, and one with great range, as well."

Alverlee acknowledged that with a tilt of his head, but no hint of agreement. "The Keepers of the Writ think poorly of the visions and advise that they shouldn't be spoken of. Too many times, they've stirred up unneeded trouble."

Fairlynn rhythmically stirred her tea. There was truth in her husband's words, but Olanni was right too. Wind weavers were rare in Dirklan. Most were women, but still, was there even one chance in a thousand that a baby girl would become a wind weaver? As for trouble...that was never hard to stir if tongues set to wagging. Witness the subdued gathering tonight. Even with her back to many, Fairlynn could hear the difference. She'd celebrated Gifting Eve in this inn for many years, but tonight held one distinct difference. The noisy good cheer was missing. In no way could that be blamed on the vision wall!

CHAPTER 4

Luminous gold—the vision wall captured Devron as it always did. He stared at it, awestruck by the outer layer. So pure that it was translucent—a mystical depth over the more ordinary golden underlayer. Even that could only be called ordinary if one could envision an entire wall of naturally occurring, purified gold. To this day, no one could explain the possibility of its existence.

Fairlynn's voice penetrated his abstraction. "This way, Devron." By the way she plucked at his sleeve and spoke distinctly, he must have missed earlier words.

The chamber, with its buzz of conversation and shuffling feet, came back into focus. He followed her between chairs on a terrace midway up the natural floor. Terracing the slope was one of few changes that had been allowed—at least, on this side of the vision wall.

The back side was dull and ordinary rock. He knew, for he'd climbed it in his teen years. Not an approved expedition, but what young former could resist? Toeholds had made scaling the cliff easy, and he'd belly-crawled across the top to peer into the sacred chamber. Empty. He'd scooted forward and looked down on the pool—about a twenty-foot drop—and then dared to rest his hand on the smooth, inexplicable surface. Unskilled though he'd been, he had still sensed that this was unlike any other gold.

The original explorers must have felt the same—not that they'd crawled in, like he had. A tunnel, hewn out by a long-gone river, had led them here. Their first find in the sprawling caverns, now called Crysalan. A network of intersecting crystal veins etched the ceiling. Naturally occurring. What had the discoverers thought when they first glimpsed the veins' dim glow reflected from the golden wall? Well, he knew—after a fashion anyway. They believed they saw a vision in the gold. Later interpretations explained it as a reflection of the glowing veins, for they had not yet been polished to scatter the light. Nonetheless, the explorers' declaration remained—the chamber was sacred, and mining its gold was forbidden.

Devron sidestepped along a wrought-iron railing that edged the straight drop to the next level. Only four chairs fit in the front row of this small tier. If age wasn't enough to give him precedence today, his gifting was. He, Alverlee, and Fairlynn took the front seats. Kevenor could have had the other, but he entered the second row to sit beside his wife. Possibly with an additional motive to keep an eye on Tebber. The second and third rows began filling with Crilla's extended family, engaged in debate as to whether there were enough chairs and which children were young enough to sit on laps.

Fairlynn said, "Come and sit beside me, Perrie." The girl beamed as she climbed into the chair, then snuggled closer when Fairlynn wrapped an arm around her.

The vast space was filling as family groups found places. The floor stepped gradually up and away from the vision wall and the pool before it. On the broad, flat rock that edged this side of the pool, musicians readied instruments at one end, while Keepers of the Writ, in deep green robes and iridescent sashes, lined up shoulder-to-shoulder. Their backs to the pool and wall, they faced the gathering with hands folded at their waists and expressions of peaceful waiting. Did they practice that look? Patience was indeed necessary, for quite some time was needed to fill the chamber with the multitude that gathered for the Gifting Day ceremony.

Devron leaned back and let the echoing chatter subside to a distant corner of his awareness. It was fitting that Gifting Day fell on Savoring Day, but the annual celebration tended to overwhelm the restful enjoyment that should end the week. This might be his only chance to savor. To gaze upon the beauty of the world, to enjoy the results of past work, and to treasure all that was good.

He turned his attention to the golden wall before him, which rose from the pool. A natural arch above it supported the domed ceiling, so distant that it dwarfed the mystical wall. But only in size, not in beauty. Rarely did he get a moment to savor it. He delved his forming senses into the outer layer. A truly stunning degree of perfection. A treasure of infinite value set aside in gratitude to Ellincreo. Pure. Radiant. Sublime. Awe grew into a physical ache within his chest. He didn't mind that some doubted the visions, but if they ever gained enough sway to desecrate this jewel, his heart would bleed tears.

They were seated high enough that he could also make out the nearest of the gem hills beyond the vision wall. The discoverers had not seen those hills, for they rose in a chamber hewn to vast proportions by mining. Indeed, they were mostly quartz, the waste stone surrounding raw gold. The finest colored stones were always carried to the top, and the light shafts above them sent sparkles dancing across the hills. A splendid backdrop to the golden vision wall.

The surface of that wall puzzled Devron in so many ways. Never had he seen any image within it. Why? Because he understood its substance too well? Did that dilute its mystical properties and render him blind to a message? Or perhaps it had no message for him. Visions were rare, after all.

A string of chimes rang as a musician drew her striker over hanging tubes. The notes descended, rose, and fell again. A hush settled within the chamber. The keepers waited, their heads bowed. The stillness was so complete that Devron could hear the lapping of water in the spring-fed pool. A single chime sounded. The keepers lifted their heads and began the melodious chant of gratitude. Next, the chief keeper read the shortened version of the creation story, followed by the full gifting story, when Creo's name was changed to Ellincreo—the giving creator. On that ancient day, he'd bestowed the three substance gifts upon his beloved children, that they would have powers once under his control alone. Now, they would command air, water, and land.

With the reading complete, the newly gifted adolescents were invited to stand, while an admonition and blessing were pronounced over them. Cherished moments for each youth, but all very predictable for Devron. Useful for teaching children, but tedious after forty years. The keepers began a lengthy chant, backed by somber notes. At its end, the musicians smiled and picked up a lively tempo. Time for the songs that all knew and could join in. Jubilant melodies to complete the ceremony.

How odd. The singing sounded different. Devron cast glances from side to side. The outermost terraces held empty chairs. When had that last occurred? Usually, crowds extended into the tunnels, for the chamber could no longer hold all who came. How many had feared to attend? Was that why the singing—the whole celebration—felt subdued? Or did worry leach the joy from hearts?

Halfway through the first song, gasps and cries stalled the melody. Devron glanced around as people shouted, "Look!" and "The vision wall!" They pointed, eyes round.

He snapped his gaze back to the wall. Shapes took form within its depth—while shrieks and wails echoed. Why? What did they see? For Devron saw swirling waters and a structure begging to be sculpted. A dome made of embedded sliding panels. Breathtaking!

Around him, people clutched one another or stared about, perplexed. The Keepers of the Writ had turned to see what others viewed, and now they traded puzzled frowns and shrugs. The chief keeper motioned his colleagues to draw near. Whatever he asked caused them to shake their heads. Then he seemed to question those in the nearest tiers of seating, moving quickly across the groups.

Devron caught snatches of exclamations around him. Words like *collapse, trapped, crushed, no escape, choking,* and *all dead.* They were mixed with place names—cities of LourEstelle and the access avenue. Horrific portents. Hair rose on the back of his head, at odds with the exhilaration coursing down his arms. For he saw only a magnificent creation awaiting his skill.

The chief keeper called out, trying to be heard over the din. Impossible. He turned to the chimer, and she executed the sweep of notes again, but even this did not still the chaos. It wasn't until all the musicians joined in to play the rising and falling notes in harsh staccato that the crowd finally attended to the chief keeper.

No point in watching keepers who saw nothing. Devron scanned those behind him. One face said it all. A girl in her teens, her teary cheeks half buried against her father's chest. Her grip on his shirt, white-knuckled. Strained eyes that didn't want to look but couldn't stop. Then her face sagged with mournful relief.

Devron checked again for his own vision. The translucent gold shone pure—as empty as in the moment he'd arrived.

The chief keeper raised his voice in accents of intentional calm. "Good people of Dirklan, children of Ellincreo, do not allow dismay to ensnare you on this blessed Gifting Day. It is apparent that some have glimpsed visions, but I call to your remembrance that many past visions have not proven true. From those seated nearest, I have already heard reports that vary greatly. Some saw fearful images, but others glimpsed hopeful visions. This tells me that discernment is needed, and the Writ explains how to judge visions. They must never contradict the truth of Ellincreo. We know that he creates all for our good and never for our harm. We will study the hope-filled visions to determine what new gifts he wishes to bestow upon us. As for the fear-filled visions, do not let them alarm you. Perhaps some saw…" He cleared his throat. "…saw shapes meant for other eyes. The misaligned viewing angles coupled with worries over the recent thickening could have distorted perception."

He paused and smiled benignly upon them. "Now, let us sing our final anthem. Musicians." He nodded to the leader, who struck a count. The notes rang out from instruments, and the keepers lifted their voices, but it took several measures before the crowd joined in. A joyless rendition at best.

Someone knocked on the suite's hallway door, and Devron picked his way past travel bags and scattered clothes. The sitting room seemed much smaller since Kevenor's family had rejoined them. They'd taken the boys out to play in the children's pool, but Perrie clung to her grandparents. Devron reached the door and opened it. Ah, Talmarq and Olanni. "Come in. Watch your step—the hazards of children."

Talmarq dodged a shirt and three shoes, then swung his travel bag to a bare spot along the wall. He looked back and forth between Alverlee and Devron. "We saw you among the keepers and formers after the ceremony. What's going on?"

"I really don't know what to say." Alverlee spread an empty hand. "Very few of us had visions. Like the chief keeper said, they are varied."

Olanni's eyebrows drew higher. "What do you mean *few* and *varied*? Must be more than a hundred who saw visions of collapse. What difference if the areas are varied?"

Alverlee put warning into his expression and tilted his head toward Perrie, who sat on the short couch between him and Fairlynn.

The corners of Olanni's mouth twitched down. "Sorry, but I need to know what formers make of all this."

"That group you saw wasn't all the formers," Alverlee told her. "It was mostly people who saw nothing or hopeful visions. I cannot explain what I did not see."

"I saw it, Papa-Lee." Perrie's childish voice caused a breathless silence.

"What did you see, dear?" Fairlynn asked.

She clutched her hands. "Tebber said it was stupid."

"Pay no attention to him. Please tell me what you saw."

"Everything got dark and dusty. I was crying, but then Uncle Dev made the light come back. Kind of like when he opens up a crystal shaft, but, um, different. A huge light."

What did that mean? Granted, she wasn't quite five yet. Maybe children had simpler visions, but there was absolutely nothing that anyone could do with that knowledge. If it could even be called knowledge. Not that his vision was any more useful. He didn't know what the dome was for, or even where it belonged. For, the one place where it seemed to belong could not *possibly* be true.

Alverlee patted Perrie's shoulder and addressed Olanni. "Does that match any other vision you've heard?"

"If anything falls, there will be dust and plenty of it. Darkness too. I saw the exit avenue collapse in my vision. And yet...somehow, it seemed distant. In the future. But still, people were trapped!" Her voice grew squeaky and hoarse. "Can't you admit that would be really *bad*?"

"Of course, it would be bad. But what should we do? Round up thousands of people and stampede them out of Dirklan?"

Olanni huffed and looked away. "I don't know. Real stampedes shake the ground, so maybe people should leave slowly. But *surely* everyone should be warned."

Was fear why she clutched the strap of her travel bag, still slung over her shoulder? "Maybe they already are warned," Devron suggested. "You certainly are. It's no small matter that you have a fiancé and your life's work waiting for you aboveground. You do have reason to leave. But I saw a vision too, and it doesn't make me want to leave. It makes me want to return to Jourendia and build something."

She exhaled a rumbling grunt. "Talmarq keeps insisting he's going to Jourendia, too, on account of his contrary vision. And I can't just leave him behind when we've been friends forever. Besides, my sister would never forgive me."

Her sister? Ah, by the glint in Talmarq's eye, Devron didn't need to ask about the woman. "What did you see in the vision wall?"

Talmarq cleared his throat. "Underground rivers—some not on the level maps." He looked apologetically at Fairlynn. "I hope I don't sound like some arrogant fool...like I'd know more than the streamers who live here. It's just...I feel like there is something that needs to be discovered. In Jourendia. And if formers think it's safe there..." He looked from Devron to Alverlee. "Olanni and I agreed that we will still journey with you, and I promised to see her back to the exit within a week."

"Easily done." Alverlee's gaze caught on something beyond the glass door, and he stood. "I'll be traveling that way later in the week, and you may join me."

The outer door opened to admit the rest of the family. Introductions were squeezed into the returning chaos, and Crilla summoned Fairlynn to help get the children changed.

Alverlee intervened. "No, Fairlynn is going with Devron and our guests to claim two carriages for the return journey."

Devron took the hint and quickly got the four of them out of the inn. When they reached the avenue, he slowed down. "No hurry. A stroll will do."

Olanni's expressive face was one big question. "What was that all about?"

Fairlynn only smiled, so Devron answered. "Crilla often acts as though Fairlynn is an unpaid nanny, and my brother insists that she is not."

"Oh, that sort!" She looked beyond him to Fairlynn. "Aren't you good at saying *no?*"

"Sometimes it's easier to help her. Their family lives with Alverlee and me."

They claimed two carriages along the busy platform and climbed in to wait. Olanni settled herself next to Fairlynn, across from the men. "I keep wondering about what the Chief Keeper of the Writ said. About what he called the fear-filled visions."

Devron scoffed, "Even a streamer couldn't get water to stay in that leaky argument."

She snickered. "That bad?"

"Absurd. Of course, Ellincreo is good, but that doesn't mean that we never face challenges. Why would we even need gifts—or visions—if everything was perfect on its own? And as for people seeing—what, the *edges* of other people's visions? Nonsense. Alverlee sat right next to me, Fairlynn next, and they saw nothing. Perrie was next, and she saw something very different than I did." He paused. "People can be wrong. Sometimes we see what we wish to see, or even fear to see. But the chief keeper's explanation is *not* the answer to this strange abundance of visions."

"Then what could be?" Talmarq asked.

"I don't know. But a false explanation cannot lead people to truth."

Apparently, his voice carried to a woman with black hair cascading down her back. She turned around and locked her piercing blue eyes with his. Wandermae. It seemed she considered for a moment, then crossed the platform to them in her signature style of effortless movement. "A pleasure to hear sense from a former, which has become dreadful rare these past few days."

Fairlynn's shoulders straightened. "I would say it is a pleasure to hear a compliment from you—if you didn't feel the need to bury it in *criticism.*"

"Oh, Fairlynn, don't be so sensitive. I haven't spoken with your husband, so I didn't mean him. You ought to know by now that I say what I think. And what I have discovered in the past few hours is that precious few formers saw anything in the vision wall." She swung her gaze back to Devron. "Did you?"

He nodded. What should he tell this wind weaver known for her troublemaking tongue?

"I'd wager all my feathers that it wasn't a collapse, was it?"

"No—a device that I could build. Nothing ominous."

She nodded sagely. "None of the formers saw disaster. But then, they already knew of this heave—a thickening, supposedly—and they tried to hide *that* warning."

How he hated these tight-rope conversations. "Not entirely. They are searching for what danger it may portend. Better to speak of what one knows than of infinite possibilities without certainty."

"Agreed. For which reason I am trying to discover the visions, that I may piece together the message before the—*Keepers of the Writ*—hide the truth." Both the curl of her lip and the contradiction of her words showed her disdain all too clearly. With one of her swift changes, she spoke pleasantly to Fairlynn. "Did you see anything?"

"Nothing."

"What of our visiting streamers?"

Talmarq replied, "I saw underground rivers that need to be mapped."

"Curious." Wandermae turned a questioning look to Olanni.

"I saw the access avenue collapse. I daresay, that scene will haunt me until I'm aboveground, if not longer, so I'm glad someone is taking this seriously."

"If that's what you saw, why are you at the rail that will take you into the farthest reaches of Dirklan instead of out?"

"I don't much like it, but I have one thing to finish, and I think there is still time." The way Olanni's eyebrows knotted up...how sure was she of that?

No chance for Devron to consider, for Wandermae pinned him again with her birdlike gaze and asked, "What was the device you mentioned?"

"I can give it no name, for though its parts and movements were clear, its purpose was not."

She snorted. "What you really mean is that you don't want to tell me."

"Untrue. Blame none but yourself when people refuse to share their thoughts with you. As the saying goes, a dove has more friends than a falcon."

Hard to tell whether the toss of her head indicated acknowledgment or dismissal. "I need facts more than friends. No matter how I sweeten my words, a wind weaver finds little companionship belowground. I wish I were not called here, but that was not my choice. Nor is it the purview of any but Ellincreo. I'll fulfill my destiny, whether it earns me thanks or not." She turned to leave. "I wish you all safety in the days ahead." Pleasant voice again, with ominous words.

When Alverlee came with the rest of his family, Fairlynn slid to the center of the seat, and he squeezed in beside her. Before they were even moving, he steered the conversation to glean news from their guests regarding aboveground Welcia. As though they never read the printed circulars. And when that subject grew thin, he inquired about every detail of Olanni's and Talmarq's village...mountain...anything but the subject he apparently dreaded.

CHAPTER 5

Devron stretched and rolled his shoulders, enjoying a whiff of the ocean. What a relief to climb out onto the platform in Jourendia. To end the hours of his brother skirting the subject on everyone's mind.

They hurried to unload belongings so that the empty carriages could be pulled away from the platform, allowing room for other arrivals. Like the newcomers they were, Olanni and Talmarq stared all around.

Devron shouldered his travel bag, then gestured beyond the people milling around the platform and off to the right where tall narrow houses were set back from the busy rail terminal. "This is the original settlement." He pointed left, up the slope. "We are building the new city up there, where we've been mining out a bigger cavern over the years."

Joining the steady stream of returning travelers, his family and guests descended the steps that edged the platform and strolled down the thoroughfare toward home. At the farthest end, the dark tunnel to the lake cavern yawned. It was only a matter of time...

"Is that it?" Talmarq pointed. "Is that the lake under the harbor?"

"It is, indeed." Devron caught Fairlynn's smile in profile.

"Can we—if it's not bothersome—can we go there at once?"

By the turning of Alverlee's head, he must be about to object, but Devron had his own reasons for going to the lake. "We'll have to. I don't have enough in my larder for guests, so we'll need to gather some oysters for dinner." That should be enough to separate the parties and hint that no invitation to dinner was necessary from Alverlee's household. Crilla was already pushing open the door to their home, so Devron said, "That is Alverlee's house, and mine is a little farther down on the left. We'll just drop our bags there and get what we need."

"I'll come along and help you with the water," Fairlynn offered. "You two, bring your training logs, and you can add a line on oystering." That coaxed smiles from Olanni and Talmarq, as Fairlynn turned back to her husband. "I'll likely be back in time for dinner, but don't wait for me if I'm not."

Alverlee nodded and followed his son into the house, while Devron led the way to his own door. He tapped it. "Remember this metallic teal in case you get lost. You'll not find another like it." He stepped within.

Olanni swept her fingers over the door. "Ooh, what a lovely sheen!"

Fairlynn basked in the praise on his behalf, her chin high. "Isn't it! Devron always makes light of his work, but he is an accomplished artist."

He hid his grin and pointed out rooms on the first floor. "Bedrooms are upstairs, but I'll show you later. We should hurry before the light completely fades, so let's keep this to a quick break." He crossed to the storage closet under the staircase and pulled out waders, gloves, and oyster baskets, then rummaged deeper to find his old waders. He took the armload out the rear side door, tossed everything into his hand cart, and pulled it out.

Talmarq had followed him and stepped into the alley to study the structure on the back of the house. "What's this for?"

"It's a lift and water pipes. Our gardens are all on the roofs. Let's go." Devron pushed the cart between houses to the thoroughfare, where Fairlynn had just brought Olanni out to meet them. It was all he could do to hold his pace down to a speed Fairlynn could manage. Hopefully, no one else would join them.

Soon, they left the light of the settlement to pass down the tunnel. Devron was used to it, but newcomers always hesitated at the darkness. Approaching dusk didn't help. "The tunnel floor is a gentle slope," he said. "About a dozen yards. Just follow me." They came through into the evening glow.

"Wow!" Olanni took in the sight. "I thought it might be pond-sized, but this really is a lake."

"A dark one," Talmarq muttered, like the abovegrounder he was. "Only one light shaft."

"There are two," Devron said as he pushed his cart down the slope to the water's edge, then set the brake. "The eastern one falls into shadow first."

Talmarq angled his head toward the spreader high up the wall. "How long will this one light us?"

"Long enough."

Olanni chewed her lip. "I suppose we should be glad there is even one. I don't understand how that is possible if we are under the harbor."

"The shafts angle a long way back and up to the top of the cliff." Devron went to the alcove where the lanterns were kept. Fairlynn had already lit the first one and hooked it to the diagonal chain. He turned the crank to draw the chain over the high pulley, as Fairlynn lit more lanterns and hooked them to the links. With mirrored backs, they etched golden ripples across the lake's surface.

Talmarq watched Fairlynn's use of the striker over the oil-soaked wicks. "I have to admit, these make me feel a lot better." He looked over the raised platform that flanked the tunnel. "How much of this is natural?"

"The walls are," Devron replied. "The tunnel used to be a crevice, and it was always above the lake surface. When my father widened it into a tunnel, he also formed the ramp to the water's edge and built up this verge we're standing on. Those are the only changes to the lake basin."

Talmarq nodded, passing his gaze over the water. "It's almost a perfect circle. Probably would be if this platform weren't here."

"That brings us to training," Fairlynn said. "Where is the inlet stream?"

In seconds, both Talmarq and Olanni pointed to it. Clearly by their gift, for it was hidden in shadow and echoes made it hard to place the trickling fall.

Fairlynn beamed. "Exactly. Is it briny or fresh?"

"A little briny," Olanni answered.

"Not as much as seawater, though." By his intent look, Talmarq must still be sensing along the flow of the stream. "Where does it get its salt from?"

Fairlynn waved vaguely. "From farther away than I can sense water content. It has multiple sources, and at least one must pick up seawater, perhaps at high tides. How many outlets are there, and where?"

Devron enjoyed a few minutes of listening as they searched the waters. Always a pleasure to watch the gifted—to hear how they perceived the liquid substance that his solid treasure held. When Fairlynn's questions grew more technical, he opened a storage closet and lifted down a couple oyster rakes from the tool rack inside.

He propped the rakes against the cart and spread his forming senses through the walls. Higher and higher, ipenrock rose in majestic symmetry. Unmoved, as always. The vast structure tapered inward and domed over at the top. This was his real reason for coming as soon as possible. To compare the lake cavern to his vision within the golden wall of the sacred chamber. And it matched. Exactly.

His heart quickened as shivers coursed down his back. The reaches of the cavern were lost in darkness—yet he could perceive the curved panels of his vision superimposed within the very rock itself. The vision demanded of him, but *no!* The mere thought of it was utter madness. Never could he build such a structure here. Yet he analyzed so long and intently that the strain grew tangible in the sensory base above his ears. Barely realizing it, he ran his fingers through his hair to soothe the pressure.

Fairlynn touched his arm and whispered, "What is it?"

He hadn't noticed her draw near. The other two were at the water's edge, which now swirled past their feet.

"The vision I had this morning." His hushed voice strained. "It fits this chamber." Even if he wanted to, he couldn't have said more. He cleared his throat and began pulling on a pair of waders.

Talmarq turned to Fairlynn to give his report of the lake basin. "As regular as the inside of a bowl. Based on friction, I'm guessing the surface is a little rough, with a fair amount of rubble in the center." He cocked an eyebrow toward Devron. "What's out there?"

"The roughness you sense is probably oysters." He tossed the extra waders to the young man. "Which you will soon help harvest. The stones in the middle are ipenrock grindstones, rounded smooth."

"Can you even tell what they are made of?"

"Yes." Devron hooked the suspenders of his waders.

Olanni released the circle her lips had formed. "You must be a really powerful former!"

"There's no such thing. Alverlee can sense much farther than I can, but he's not as good at determining content." Devron handed a pair of heavy gloves to Talmarq and held up his own. "I'm good at polishing, but the wire mesh of these gloves was formed by a polisher who works in a different sort of detail than I do. There isn't more or less power. There are just different nuances in our gifts."

Olanni looked thoughtful. "I suppose we see it differently because the amount of water a streamer can move really matters to us. Movement isn't your concern."

Oh, how little they knew. But Devron's stomach knotted so tight that he didn't enlighten them.

Talmarq had gotten himself awkwardly into the waders. "Why do we need these crazy gloves?"

"Because oyster shells are slippery and sharp as blades. When you and Olanni drain off a bit of the lake, we'll harvest them."

"Drain the lake?" Olanni squeaked. "Through that little crevice?"

Fairlynn took over again. "So far, you've only found the lowest outlet—the one that keeps the lake at a steady level. There's a bigger one a foot higher, and another even bigger, higher still." She waved to indicate about a quarter of the chamber wall. "You'll be looking for them over there. When you find them by water flow, you can each describe the position and angle of one. We'll spin the water to send it up the walls, and I'll hold it off the platform. Once you've found the outlets, you can alternate between keeping the platform clear and draining off water through the high outlets."

"Oh, wow!" Olanni beamed. "No one else belowground has done anything like this."

"Only Jourendia," Devron said, "has the base remains of an ancient whirlpool. Let's get to work." He leaned against the cart and watched them take charge of the water. Even though their commands were internal, streamers couldn't seem to help moving their hands in sync. It added a little drama to the show as the roaring echoes built. Amazing in its own way, but not unusual to him. He focused on the grindstones. They always moved a little, though streamers kept most of the motion away from frictional surfaces. The stones were smooth and mostly spherical. The oddity of the one that always settled at the top struck him anew. Lighter than the rest—that, he'd known for years. But wait, it was egg-shaped, almost a small copy of the cavern! Intriguing. Could he...? Hm.

"That should do it," Fairlynn said. "Let the water fall back to the basin and still it."

After much sloshing, the lake surface smoothed. Only tiny ripples spread from the inlet stream's descent along the slope they had exposed.

Olanni rubbed her ears. "That was fun, but...the echoing!"

Talmarq tilted his head side-to-side, perhaps for his ears' sake or to settle the streaming sensory area behind them. "This is a welcome hush. What next?"

"My turn now." Devron scanned the pool with his forming sense. "The biggest oysters are..." He added dramatic, double-arm pointing. "...over there." Only Fairlynn understood him enough to laugh. Devron handed a rake and wire baskets to Talmarq, picked up his own, and led the way down the exposed lakebed into shallow water. The young streamer copied his actions with the rake. Double hands halved the effort, and Devron's polisher skills made quick work of skimming off the seed oysters that stuck to the larger shells. They'd grow to be harvested in some future year.

He and Talmarq filled the baskets enough to satisfy three rumbling stomachs and send some home with Fairlynn. The men trudged back up the slope with their haul. Fairlynn used one corner of the cart to prop the logbook she wrote in as the last of the sunlight faded from the crystal shaft.

Getting late, but Devron might not have another chance. He cleared his throat. "Can I ask you to add another task to that?" Even in the dim lantern light, he caught the surprise in Fairlynn's eyes as they met his. "There is an unusual grindstone that always settles at the top of the pile, and I'd like to, uh, to have it. Maybe we could shift it toward shore enough so that I can roll it in. I'm sure it's lighter than all the rest." He hoped he didn't sound as uncomfortable as he felt.

She blinked at him. "Well, we can try."

He managed a nod and smile that probably looked weird.

"All right. Let's see..." She pursed her lips. "Olanni and Talmarq, you stand on either side of me. You'll each control half the lake. We'll stream two oblong swirls, away on the outside, and straight toward me down the center. Devron, you line up between me and this stone you want. Point at it with both hands together so I can get a fix on where to guide the center stream."

Devron squatted in front of her to give her a line of sight over his head while he pointed. He sent his forming awareness into the grindstones of the pile, especially his prize at the top. He felt the pressure affect them as water beat harder and harder. His prize rolled a little, but a slight incline stopped its motion.

"Is it moving?" Fairlynn asked over the swishing roar.

"Some. It keeps jamming against other stones. Keep it up, as stable as you can." All this movement. Rocks shifted as though gravity was weakening. The lightest one more so, making it harder to control as he held others back. He had never commanded an object that was moving under another power. Finally, he got the knack of it, and his prize bounded past another rock and careened forward. It picked up speed from the current as he summoned it nearer. Stone and water working together. "Yes!"

Fairlynn laughed. "Dev, I've never seen you so excited with forming."

"Well, I've never done this. Ugh. It's slowing down. Out of the rubble now, but it has to climb the solid slope." He strode over the exposed lakebed and splashed into the current that fought him. Stupid oysters underfoot. "Come on. Keep rolling!" he muttered as he commanded. Slower and slower. He had to grab it before it stopped and rolled away. Water crested the lip of his waders and headed to his toes. Might as well go all in. He groped in the churning current, trying to reach the stone.

Behind him, Talmarq shouted, "Take control of my side, so I can help him." He approached in a splashing run.

Devron's glove scraped over a curved surface. Was it as he believed? He jerked one glove off with his teeth—yuck—and pressed his bare hand against the surface, sensing deeper. Yes, ipenrock, hollow within. "I've got it!" he called out as best he could through closed teeth. Now, if he could just get behind it and push. At least it wouldn't move away with his hand upon it reinforcing command.

As he shifted aside, Talmarq reached him—with an oyster rake, of all things. The streamers were doing something different with the water now. Between the current, Devron's command to the stone, and ultimately even the rake, he finally got his prize far enough up the slope where he and Talmarq could roll it using ordinary muscle. They paused beside the cart, and he took the oyster glove from between his teeth and spat out salty water.

"I can't believe that worked," Olanni said, as Fairlynn exclaimed, "You are soaked!"

He coughed out a laugh. "You should feel my waders." He fiddled with the cart to drop its back end, then put his glove back on. "The stone's hollow," he told Talmarq. "Let's try to lift it on the count of three."

They positioned themselves, counted, and heaved together.

"Not as heavy as it looks," Talmarq said as they steadied it against the edge of the cart, then rolled it in. "Whew."

With many hands, it didn't take long to load the oysters and stow the cavern supplies in the storage closet embedded in the wall. Devron was still struggling out of his drenched waders as Fairlynn lit the lantern mounted on the front of his cart. Its pool of light was all they had once they'd extinguished the cavern lamps, but enough for Devron to guide them through the tunnel.

He should explain to his guests how the settlement's few lights marked the dark thoroughfare and how to find houses by their reflective markings. Fortunately, Fairlynn told them before she set off toward her own door with a bucket of oysters. A good thing, because struggling in the midst of that raging current had left Devron spent. Pushing the cart up the slope didn't help. Besides, he needed time to think. Partway home, Talmarq took over pushing. Devron liked these two—nice manners and full commitment once they took on a task.

They helped in the kitchen too, and Devron changed into dry clothes as the oysters steamed. Quiet settled while they gathered around the kitchen table and dipped the hot meat in some sauces he kept on hand.

Talmarq eyed the last few oysters in the bowl. "Who wants more?" Devron and Olanni shook their heads, and he finished them off. He sopped up the last of his preferred sauce with a scrap of bread, then slouched back in his chair. "Long day."

"Indeed." Devron sighed. Was it only this morning that he'd seen that vision? In some ways, he felt like he was still seeing it, so heavy it sat in his mind.

"And eventful too." Olanni picked up her training log and spread the last page to show her friend. "Look. Full to the last line with the work we did tonight. I won't even be skipping out early from my final training when we leave."

Talmarq inclined his head. "Congratulations, Olanni. You're going to be a fine streamer for our village. I was even thinking that when we worked together in the cavern."

Did Devron imagine it, or was Talmarq's smile forced? Olanni's initial glow faded as her brow bunched up. Talmarq fiddled with a thin oyster fork before he turned to Devron. "I overheard you say something to Fairlynn in the cavern. If I wasn't meant to hear it...sorry, but I did."

"I know it's not a private place with the curve of the walls. What troubles you?"

"You told her something about your vision...that it fits the chamber." Devron compressed his lips, but that didn't stop Talmarq's questions. "You said before that it was something to build. What sort of thing?"

"That's the problem. Building it...there..." Devron shook his head. "It's pure fantasy. An absurdity to think it would have any purpose or even be safe to construct."

"Does that mean you..." Olanni didn't seem to like her question. "That you think the visions are false?"

"I didn't say *that*." The problem was, he knew the demand of his vision. That would never let him call it false. But did he dare tell them? This wasn't something he could risk spreading. Devron stood and picked up their dishes. "This day has been long enough. We can wash up tomorrow. You two should head up to bed."

That worked. He listened for their climbing footsteps, then waited a little longer before heading into his workshop. The ipenrock grindstone lay on its side where he'd left it when they'd unloaded the cart. He felt an urge to curse the thing, for it didn't belong here. Instead, he took a support rack from his orderly tools. With a little rolling and propping he got the support adjusted around the stone, so that it stood upright, with the tapered end of the egg shape pointing to the ceiling. It stood about four feet tall.

He pulled a stool over and sat down, spreading his knees enough to rest against the stone. He laid his hands atop it and sensed. Composition. Density. Shape, both outside and the inner hollow. He'd been right. It was a close match to the lake chamber. What were the chances that he'd find a small copy of the chamber, lying for years among the grindstones? Nigh impossible.

It wasn't perfect, of course, but likely he could make the inner surface an exact model of the chamber's interior. Already, he found himself commanding the changes, proving that he could. Yes, remove a ridge there, indent that spot, smooth the walls. Just a little more, he told himself again and again. Until it was perfect. Right down to the pile of shavings that he'd let fall to the basin. For an instant, he thought of rounding them. No. A ridiculous degree of perfection. The night must be half gone. At least he felt a sort of release. As though the vision had a voice and said, "Enough for one day."

Even as he closed the door of his workroom, he knew it would demand more tomorrow.

CHAPTER 6

Maybe some ordinary task would get Devron's mind off that insistent vision. Fairlynn had stopped by right after breakfast and taken the two streamers with her. No sooner did the door close, than he wanted to dart into his workroom.

No! Today was first workday. He had shafts to polish. A former aboveground might even be waiting. If not, one would come soon. He grabbed his folding chair, strode up to the town square, and got to work. And then struggled to stay awake as he leaned back in motionless labor. Getting only four hours of sleep had been a mistake. One snore and he'd be fighting the snide slur of *lazy polishers* for months. Better to stand. He formed a spreader, trying to concoct a reason to slip away early.

A few hours later, Alverlee came to his side. "What's with all this neck craning? Has someone been criticizing you again?"

Devron huffed with a sideways grin. "To tell the truth, I can barely keep my eyes open. I didn't get much sleep last night."

"You're not alone in that! What with all the worry about a collapse, it seems no one did."

Devron's thoughts stuttered. Worry was the farthest thing from his mind, but he couldn't say that. "A lot of short tempers?" he asked.

"Some. Mayor Borchel is angry that I didn't tell him about the thickening—as though it would have changed anything. The stuff people are saying is simply unbelievable. You might as well go home and grab a few winks. There's no hurry with the light shafts."

"No hurry?"

Alverlee's lip lifted in disgust. "After weeks of pushing, Borchel has canceled the construction meetings for today and tomorrow. That'll stop practical work in a matter of days. And he'll probably blame the Formers' Guild for that." A rueful smirk contradicted his kind grip on Devron's shoulder. "Go home and rest."

Perfect. Now he could escape. A nap did sound tempting, but as he headed home, only stonework filled his mind. Not sleep and certainly not worry. Was something wrong with him that the one thing troubling his city was a complete non-issue to him? Still, if Alverlee couldn't get people calmed down, there was nothing Devron could do about it. Maybe he'd see if it was possible to form a panel.

Envisioning how to form the design allowed no pause between his front door and back workshop. He wouldn't cut it out and shape it...but somehow form it *within* the stone. He didn't want to ruin the dome, though. Maybe he'd practice nearer the base where it wouldn't matter.

He was still shifting the elements—separating and realigning, grain by grain, to isolate a little slab encased within rock—when he heard the street door open and Fairlynn call out, "Devron, are you home?"

What brought her here in mid-afternoon? "In my workshop," he answered as he aligned the particle he'd just loosened.

Footsteps and voices from her and his guests approached, then she entered the workshop. "What are you working on? Oh, the stone egg you found yesterday. It looks...exactly the same."

"Stone egg?" he chuckled. "I assure you, ipenrock does not reproduce, but like an egg, the changes are all within."

Olanni joined them. "What's in there?"

"Nothing, really. It's hollow."

"Is it a geode? It doesn't look like one."

"Something like that, but no crystals inside. I'm altering the, uh, shell. I just want to finish this one part I'm holding steady." Hopefully, they would take the hint.

Fairlynn uttered a high-pitched snort. "I'll show these two how to work your magnery stove before I leave, so they can start dinner. They bought a couple days' worth of food at the market. But fair warning—when dinner is ready, I insist that they drag you away from your art, even if that means physical force."

He grinned. Hours must have passed. The little slab's double plane and hairpin edge was a few inches long, after all. When they left him in peace, he smoothed the division he'd sliced by command alone. Its invisible beauty became clearer as he worked, and it answered core questions. Ipenrock was stubborn compared to the materials he preferred, so he'd never reshaped it. A different sort of separation and realignment were necessary, but he had found its preferred structure. Most importantly, he'd proved he could isolate shapes within the stone.

Talmarq stuck his head into the workroom. "Dinner's ready, and I have clear instructions. Is brute force really necessary to get you to eat?"

Devron stood. "Not when I'm satisfied with my work." He strode to the door, for Talmarq was eyeing the stone and Devron didn't want to answer questions. "I completely forgot yesterday that you wanted to search out the harbor waters while we were in the lake cavern. Did you get a chance today?"

The three of them sat down at the table as Talmarq answered— disappointed, by the sound of his voice. "I tried a little today, but we didn't stay long. Fairlynn suggested I spend a full day there. Perhaps if I experience the full cycle of a tide change, I'll be able to sense it. The half year may help too, for they told me at the joint guild assembly that the strongest tides occur at the beginning of each half. Something about the moon alignment."

The half year—Devron had forgotten. He ought to have gone to check the small moon shaft. If misaligned, it might light early, which would be important to know if they needed to adjust it. Had Alverlee remembered, or had all the upset distracted him too?

Olanni was rattling out plans for the coming days, although it sounded more like a full-scale assault on Talmarq's plans. "Of course, you should try tomorrow," she conceded, "and absolutely stay through an entire cycle. Then, if you can't sense the currents, you'll know for certain it's not possible. No one else has ever done it, so it was crazy nervy of them to ask it of you. Then, on third workday we can head back."

Talmarq's mouth held to a straight line. "You said you'd wait until Alverlee sets out."

"I know, but if you've already given your best effort to your assigned task, you needn't stay longer." She kept making little forward motions in her chair, as though she was about to jump up and dash out the door this very moment. "I do try not to worry. It's just hard to get that vision out of my mind. Please understand."

"I do understand. I can't shake my vision either. Those rivers must be located."

"Well, maybe you could tell Fairlynn—or Jourendia's chief streamer—where to search for them. You could leave the level maps you brought here. If things really are safe, someone could bring them out later. And if the visions are true..." Her glossy eyes widened more than ever. "Well, the people down here will need the maps, not those of us aboveground."

"I'll think about it, but you know, Olanni, the carriages run every day. You can get into one tomorrow morning."

"I'm not leaving without you!"

Time to divert the circular debate. "Then you may as well eat your dinner," Devron said. "What else did you buy at market?" That topic got them through the meal, and Alverlee stopped in while they were cleaning up. He seemed to want privacy, so Devron took him into the workshop.

"I thought sure you'd come to the small moon's shaft." Alverlee raised his eyebrows. "Did you sleep too long?"

"Not at all, actually. I forgot about it until I sat down to eat. Did it light early?"

"Not directly, but it showed a faint glow." His smile stretched. "Which promises well for full light tomorrow evening. I've told the mayor and musicians. We could use the celebration."

"Has something else gone wrong?"

"For one thing, Mayor Borchel was thinking of canceling the usual event for half year because of the general anxiety."

"How would that help?"

"How indeed? Give people more time to worry maybe. They'll have plenty of that anyway, because stone cutting is on hold."

"What?"

"Supposedly, people will *feel* better if no stone is disturbed until I come back from LourEstelle with a report that all is well." By the bitterness of his tone, Alverlee didn't need to be told that made no sense.

"Building will stop even faster than you predicted." Devron considered his own work in the new city. "When they restart, I suspect someone will demand I do *real* work." Alverlee began to shake his head, but Devron continued. "I'll alter my one-at-a-time approach. If I set up the initial planes of many shafts, the aboveground polishers can continue even if we have delays below."

"That wouldn't hurt," Alverlee murmured. His gaze settled on the upright grindstone. "Ah, there is the *egg* Fairlynn told me about. Have you found some use for it?"

"A most interesting object. Do you notice anything about it?"

"Mm." Alverlee extended his forming sense into the stone. "Hollow, but we always knew it was lightweight." His brows drew close. "Have you formed the interior?"

"A little. It reminded me so much of something, that I couldn't resist the finishing touches."

"The shape of the lake cavern?"

"Exactly. I cannot imagine how a model of the chamber is duplicated within a grindstone."

Alverlee shrugged it off. "Perhaps by the same process."

He hadn't thought *that* through. "A whirlpool within a grindstone?"

"Fine. Perhaps a bubble of air got trapped in the lava as it cooled. That would make more sense. This would have been part of a big boulder before it ground down, just as the cavern is really a space in a landmass of ipenrock. Nature does tend toward a certain symmetry, as seen in the cavern also."

"Nature didn't create the egg-shaped symmetry of the cavern. The whirlpool drilled a uniform hole, but formers closed it."

"What are you talking about?"

"Don't you remember what Father learned from the formers at the port? Oh, wait, you had stayed home because there was so much to do here. It was our first trip aboveground to report our find and the new settlement of Jourendia to the king and queen."

"Oh, yeah! I was peeved that I couldn't go with you."

"You didn't miss much. We waited hours, then Father got a ten-minute audience and a fancy piece of paper with the royal seal. But the important part was what he learned from the Formers' Guild archives and the port lore. The harbor used to have a persistent whirlpool that got really wild during certain tides. It made the harbor too unstable to establish a port. So, the formers—lots of them, over a long time—created a vertical fault in the high cliffs. At the lowest tide, they joined forces to sheer it off and drop it flat over the seabed."

Alverlee's eyebrows arched high. "Are you telling me that worked?"

"It broke up, of course, but it was enough to disrupt the whirlpool. Father took me up to the clifftop over the harbor, and we tried to place where the lake cavern would be. I wasn't skilled enough yet, but I could sense a lot of broken, flat rock sitting at odd angles and filled in with sediment. Father thought he found the lake cavern's roof, but mostly because he had studied it from the inside. Don't you remember that it was irregular, and that water dripped into the lake? After we came home, he set about reshaping it, bit by bit. You must remember *that*."

"Not as well as you do. I found a wife. You're the one who followed Father to the cavern every evening instead of doing a little strategic socializing with the newcomers."

"Sure, Alver—with so many of them my own age."

Harking back to their sarcastic banter from years ago brought a grin to Alverlee's face. "What does any of this have to do with your..." He extended a hand toward the grindstone. "...egg?"

Devron looked at it. How much should he tell his brother when he couldn't believe it himself? "It's, um... It's like my vision."

Alverlee groaned, tilting his head back. "The last thing I want to hear about is a vision. So far, the only thing stopping an outright panic is unity among the formers. You, of all people, I must have on my side, Dev."

The look in his eyes—half frantic, half pleading. "Alver..." He gripped his brother's arm. "I will always be on your side."

Alverlee drew a deep breath and blew it out. "What about your egg? I hear these visions are compelling."

"When has my latest art project *not* compelled me? I haven't quite decided what this one will be. Perhaps a decorative container with a curious or hidden opening."

Alverlee shook his head, but at least he managed a quip. "I won't lie. Your art always looks crazy to me at first and brilliant when finished." He grinned. "Most of it, anyway."

Devron laughed, and they left the workshop. His guests were lounging in the welcome room, though he suspected Olanni was lying in wait.

Alverlee paused. "I must congratulate you, Olanni. Fairlynn tells me that you completed your training."

She hurried to her feet as he spoke. "Yes. And thank you!"

"We usually recognize such on Savoring Day, but since you're leaving soon, we'd like to announce it at tomorrow's half year celebration."

"Ah, speaking of that…" She entwined her fingers. "Do you know yet when you plan to set out?"

"On fourth workday." Alverlee looked to both streamers, for Talmarq had stood too. "It's a long journey for me, because the guild will assemble at Government House, which is well within LourEstelle. Quite a distance beyond the access avenue. We'll reach one of the small caverns near the access arches around nightfall and sleep there. You'll be aboveground by morning of fifth day." He reached for the door latch. "For now, pleasant night."

"Pleasant night." Olanni clutched her hands tighter as the door closed behind Alverlee.

"That's a day sooner than you expected," Talmarq said. "Can you stay that long?"

Her gaze seemed to turn inward. "I…I suppose so."

Devron pitied her, but it was hard to know if his advice would be welcome. An uncomfortable feeling wormed through his mind. What was happening to him? He'd been afraid to tell Alverlee the truth and now was afraid to utter a little encouragement? He couldn't keep silencing words that ought to be spoken. "May I make a suggestion as someone who has lived longer than you?"

She blinked those anxious eyes at him. "Sure."

"You're letting fear overwhelm every minute. You're suffering as much agony as though something terrible has already occurred. But it *hasn't*. Don't waste today experiencing pain that may or may not occur tomorrow."

"But what if it does?"

"Do you think worry will prevent disaster?"

"Well, no, but…"

"One way or another, we all feel pain on the day that tragedy hits. But there is no need to feel it on the pleasant days that come before. Yield no place to fear." Enough said. "Pleasant night, my friends."

Devron climbed the stairs to his bedroom, pondering his…what? Cowardice? Had he ever hidden anything from his brother? Not that he could remember. Why this time? Because of Alverlee's rant? Because of his own uncertainty? In truth, the device of that vision made no sense to him. None at all. But how dreadful if he were hiding something critical. Maybe even something that could save lives.

CHAPTER 7

Devron subtly checked his guests' expressions when they came down to breakfast. Olanni greeted the morning with a smile and plans. He felt secretly proud of her. Talmarq went off to spend the day in the lake cavern, where Fairlynn had agreed to join him. Devron walked to the city cavern with his brother and nephew, then watched for a while as they worked together to isolate rough quartz in a vein and shift it to form a rudimentary light shaft. They'd made so many of them that they were fairly quick at it now.

He set about his own work and completed the upper planes of a few shafts. Raised voices reached him as he considered which one to start next. A cluster of people—all non-formers—surrounded Alverlee and Kevenor. What needed such a frantic argument?

Heat began to rise within him as he grasped the gist of it. Insistence that making light shafts might compromise the integrity of the cavern roof. As though they comprehended rock. Ridiculous! Utterly absurd! Non-gifted instructing the formers now? And beyond stupid, they were also defying the royal decree that guaranteed autonomy to each of the three substance guilds. How could they think they had a better understanding than those gifted by Ellincreo himself?

Devron shook with the outrage spreading through his chest. He wasn't staying for this insanity. Even his inexplicable vision made more sense than these crazies. He fumed all the way home over the stupidity sprouting from a vague fear that most claimed they didn't believe.

Within the quiet peace of his workshop, Devron battled the urge to rehash his anger. That would solve nothing. He must calm himself. Unconsciously, his hands had come to rest on the stone egg. As the minutes passed, the intricacies of its structure flooded him, choking out chaos.

If this mattered as much as it felt like... It terrified him. Strange. Everyone else was anxious over collapse, and he...*he* was afraid to make a model of the vision he'd seen. Just a model. No, he was afraid of what it meant.

An almost panicky gratitude swept from him to Ellincreo, that he had been granted the opportunity to start with this small copy. "Guide me, for I did not choose this creative gift. *You* made me a former." Did that sound like...like he was blaming? Shirking responsibility? "It's not that. Not entirely, anyway. This is just too big for me." Ellincreo ought to understand that.

A weight seemed to lift as Devron stared at the stone egg. A calm sort of clarity. He should etch the plan. He imagined a perfect circle around the egg, roughly where the straight internal wall curved over into the dome. He commanded with the power of his gift, and the foundation line formed within the stone, forever hidden from sight or touch, though not from former's sense. A little higher, he marked the outer crest of the ring—a faint indentation that his fingers could barely detect—and then its counterpart on the inner surface of the shell. These three marked the circular groove he would form to support the panels.

He envisioned them—concave and overlapping. The internal image was so clear, he could count them. Three sets of nine. The largest reached from groove to dome's peak. Nine more hid within. They would only show if the tallest spread. The shortest nine—never to be seen—were fully embedded in their taller neighbors, giving critical guidance and support. Inspiration rose, and he knew he could send an etched outline shooting up from the ring all at once.

The tallest first. Those would be visible. He commanded. Before his eyes, nine lines spiraled upward at identical speed. They paused and turned where he ordered, then hurried on to the top, where they converged into a tiny circle—as though to kiss the center of the dome—then down again to mark the internal edge, where only a former could perceive them. He laughed in exultation. What could be sweeter than a true and precise forming?

The two shorter sets now. He stretched them up in complementary spirals. No kiss for these, but just as perfect. Oh, how he loved his gift!

Devron paused to consider...and yes, to admire. The panels would need space to move as they opened, yet must fit as snug as they now stood when closed. Stability? A shaft at the bottom center of each, ending in a ball joint embedded below the groove.

He began forming the base groove, the decision to start merely the natural flow of design, rather than conscious choice. Always slow at first, but yesterday's experiment proved useful. Once he figured out a pattern for the work, it went quicker, inching around the egg. Again and again, he advanced the groove. At the center of each etched panel, he sank a hole, allowing a shaft to extend from the panel. Below that, he separated a ball in its joint. Then on to the next. At last, the end of the ring groove met the beginning.

Was the dome free to move? He must know. With shaking hands, he gripped the dome and gently nudged it. Nothing. Was he being too careful? He attempted a vibrating pressure. It moved! Not easily, but there was slight give around each shaft and a subtle shift along the groove. His pulse thumped so strong he detected its pressure with former sense. He could hardly catch his breath. "By your gifting," he whispered in acknowledgment. An odd sensation pulsed through him. Excitement that this strange, untested design might actually work? Or terror at what it confirmed?

In a way, the egg was now two inseparable pieces, locked together by the embedded ball joints. The dome could shift a smidge but could not be lifted. He rubbed sweaty hands against his thighs and strove to calm himself. He walked to a window facing the back alley and checked the angle of the light from the nearest hour shaft. Still time for more. Further details of the panels' design coalesced in his mind.

Talmarq's incessant pacing reached the end of the raised verge along the lake, and he cycled back toward Fairlynn. Each time she saw his intent upturned face, it held all the frustration of her last view. She wished she could guide him in finding the harbor waters, but she had never felt them. Probably a futile task, even though he had impressive skills. Perhaps the streamer chiefs aboveground wanted to test how far was *too far* for him. She hoped the failure so early in his training wouldn't discourage him too greatly. One thing was certain. He had unshakable tenacity. And she wouldn't give up this effort until he did.

The long wait was alleviated when a family came to gather oysters mid-morning. She and Talmarq lowered the lake level for them, but then he settled against the wall to stare at the ceiling again. Apparently, that made the adults of the family nervous.

"What is he doing?" the eldest whispered to Fairlynn.

"Searching out the waterways. He is a streamer in training, you understand."

Soon after, Mayor Borchel came and asked the same question. She tilted her head sideways and gave the same answer.

"He isn't moving anything, is he?"

She stared at the mayor and hoped he squirmed inside. "No, it so happens that he isn't moving anything at the moment, but it would make no difference if he was. Please listen again. He is a *streamer*. Not a former. A streamer. Water moves all the time, and if it stopped, I would set it in motion again. Because moving water is healthy, and stagnant water will eventually kill you."

"Yes, yes of course. Please don't take offense. I have enough of that from the formers."

"Perhaps they will take less offense if those *without* substance gifts would stop behaving as though they possess more structural knowledge than the formers."

"Really, Fairlynn—"

"Yes, really!" She swallowed and subdued her tone back to her natural calm. "And of you, mayor, with your gift of leadership, I have a request. Please permit and encourage our fine citizens to occupy themselves with something other than fear. For, though I am convinced that our caverns will stand strong..." She blended irony into her voice. "...the needless panic has shortened even *my* fuse."

He seemed to accept her implied apology. "Short fuses are common enough. Maybe the dancing this evening will help. Our first half year celebration in the new town square."

She chose to ignore how forced his good cheer sounded. "I'm looking forward to it."

As the mayor's footsteps grew faint in the tunnel, Talmarq came to her side. "Hm. After reprimanding him, you acknowledged his position and gift. I'll remember that for any fires I may start in the future."

She twisted a corner of her mouth down. "It probably only worked because I'm reputed to be even-tempered. Better not to start fires."

His attention wandered ceilingward again. "I don't know if I agree with that. At least not every time. No victory can be won unless the challenge is engaged."

Was he right? She hated battles. Her way had always been peace. But Alverlee thought she took it too far. "How do you choose which challen—" Talmarq gasped so loud that she jumped. "What? What is it?"

"It's there!" He hopped, stabbing his forefinger upward, then spreading his arms to encompass the dome. "The current! I can feel it!" He panted and then shook his head oddly. "A lot closer than I expected." Fleeting puzzlement soon left his voice as he took his bearing from the tunnel and pointed this way and that. "The light shafts of the city cavern are above the high cliff—there. So, the port must be about there, and the harbor mouth is over that way." He faced that unseen feature above rock and water. "The tide must have reached its lowest point, and the flow reversed. That change is what I finally noticed, and now, I feel the current." He swung around to her.

Midday light in the shafts glinted from his glossy eyes, as though his joy would overflow in tears. Thrilled as he was, she squeaked, "I'm so happy for you!" She wrapped her outstretched arms around his lean chest, for they must hug—must celebrate.

They both needed several minutes to calm down after his great success. Had anyone *ever* felt the harbor waters? Fairlynn waved a cooling hand before her heated cheeks. "We'll share a dance over this tonight, but for now, we should try to record what's happening. Can you judge depth?"

"That's hard. The deepest reaches vary, and the surface is rising. I think force and direction will be the correct measurements. Within the heaving mass, I believe I sense a curve, like so." He motioned with his lifted hand. "This is going to take a couple full cycles to understand."

Devron's feet hurt. How long had he been on them? What time was it? Another glance out the window relieved him. After noon, but light enough. Too early for the moon shafts to glow. Nor had his guests returned. Were they still in the lake cavern? He would look for them there, which provided a good excuse to hide his own desire. He'd isolated one panel, which meant that the edges of adjoining panels were also defined. And that revealed so much more. He must study the cavern dome again.

On his way through the kitchen, he grabbed a hunk of bread—having forgotten lunch—and consumed it as he strode down the thoroughfare. He swallowed the last of it as he entered the tunnel. No voices echoed from beyond. Had they left? No, they were just intent. Fairlynn, Talmarq, and Olanni stood with their backs to him, all looking to the cavern's ceiling lost in the shadows.

"What do you see up there?" he teased.

Talmarq answered with a breathless sort of shout. "The tide!"

"You can sense the harbor water?"

"I can! I first recognized it as the tide turned. It was at its lowest before midday, and I think it might be cresting about now, or near it anyway."

The young streamer's joy reminded him of his own early successes. The harder they were to achieve, the sweeter they tasted. He gripped Talmarq's shoulder from behind. "Well done." Of the ladies, he asked, "Have either of you found what he describes?"

Olanni's mobile expressions shifted to rueful. "Not I, but he always did have ridiculous sensitivity. Through rock, for pity's sake!"

"Not yet." Fairlynn stretched her answer.

He knew that look. When it came to her gift, she wasn't one to surrender easily. "What do you sense of the seabed, Talmarq?"

"Well, it's closer than I expected." He glanced sideways and lifted an eyebrow. "Does that surprise you?"

"I suppose not." It had been a long time since Devron had inspected the full external height of the cavern roof. He stretched his awareness while Talmarq continued his answer.

"There is no whirlpool, but I do sense a curve in the current."

Devron nodded as he studied the high rock. A faint worry passed, for the mass was unaltered. But there was a change at the farthest reaches. Using his gift to discern it felt like moving his fingers over a textured surface in the dark. The dome remained as when his father had reshaped the slabs and sediment, aligning its inner structure to bear the enormous weight more evenly. The area surrounding it was not as Devron recalled. More sand—greater uniformity. Had the larger rocks shifted outward? "Tell me about the current," he said, "specifically around the dome."

"I can't lay claim to feeling the dome itself." Talmarq spread his arms, encompassing the cavern. "But the current does circle around us. Eddies form and dissipate at times, which I suspect may correlate to when the edges of the harbor get submerged again."

What did that mean, and why would it cause eddies? But no matter, for Devron never fully understood water. "That curve you mentioned—which direction does it turn?"

Footsteps echoed in the tunnel as Talmarq swirled a hand overhead. "Around like so."

Devron nodded. "The sand around the dome is shifting in the same direction."

Talmarq fisted his hands at shoulder height. "Yes! My first outside confirmation."

"What is this?" Alverlee joined them.

Devron waited as Talmarq shared his success, accepted congratulations, then asked whether Alverlee could also confirm the sand movement.

The chief former didn't bother to lift his eyes. "Let me check."

Devron sensed his brother's awareness, starting low through the immense structure that encased the cavern and rising to the sea floor.

Alverlee's eyebrows darted together. What had he noticed? Heat surged through Devron. He must distract. "It seems to me that the seabed has smoothed out like a broad, shallow basin. Perhaps filling in more with sediment, though not as much as Father predicted."

"You haven't moved anything up there, have you?"

"No, of course not."

"I see what you mean by smoothing out." Alverlee turned to Talmarq. "I can tell that loose matter lies on the surface, but I cannot sense as much detail as my brother, so I can't confirm movement. His skill is well known, though, so his confirmation in your training log will be as solid as a chief former's." He smiled, almost like he'd suddenly remembered he ought to. "Your discovery of a harbor current is intriguing. We must celebrate it tonight. In fact..." He swept his gaze over them. "...that is the reason I came looking for my gifted friends and family, lest you forget that we should all be in the town square *before* the moon shafts light."

Talmarq groaned. "I wanted to wait for the highest tide and follow its turning all the way back to low tide."

"That," Olanni said, "will take half the night. You'll miss the lighting of the moon shafts and dinner as well. Besides, the most extreme tides are *after* the two moons rise together. I'm sure you'll be down here at first light tomorrow, lantern in hand, so you can find your way home in full dark."

Fairlynn uttered her gentle laugh. "She is right, you know. Best join in celebration tonight, get some sleep, and hold your long vigil tomorrow."

"Come along." Devron started for the tunnel. "We must pack up some food to share and dress for the dance." Not a bad excuse for getting out of the cavern before Alverlee could ask about whatever had made him frown so sharply.

The scarce sunlight faded in the city cavern. Though lanterns were hung, only three had been lit to provide bearing points, their oil wicks turned low. All eyes faced the moon markers, none more expectantly than Devron's.

Two ebony plates waited high on the cavern wall, their carvings filled with the purest, most reflective white quartz available. One bore all the month markers, and with each rising of the largest moon in full phase, the current month's symbol would catch its white rays. Offset, was the smaller plate with only the two half year symbols, waiting for the small moon to rise full, in symmetry with its big sister. This unproven moon shaft and marker—this was the one Devron watched. Perhaps tonight it, too, would shine.

The glow of the large moon began to creep over its symbol. The cavern hushed, no echo louder than a whisper. Perhaps others breathed as they waited, but not Devron. Then, a glow reached the half year marker, intensified, and flashed a bright, crisp reflection on the lower half-circle. A warm rush flowed through every cell of Devron's being. Oh, yes, he loved his gift.

A cheer rose from the crowd and now took on the chant of *Alverlee*. Devron had lost track of his brother in the darkness—probably standing with the mayor.

Then, the gong sounded, and Alverlee shouted from beside it. "My thanks, but Devron deserves more credit than I. Devron. Devron. Devron..."

The crowd picked up the cheer, and Devron had to admit—the recognition lifted his spirits even higher. The other lanterns were hastily lit, and hands clapped his shoulders as light revealed people's faces.

A pleasant evening began. They nibbled varied finger foods, some warm and some cool. Several beverages were available, but one in particular, everyone tasted. Chief Streamer Fezlie dispensed water from the new shaft in the center of the square. A precious find, that deep river of pure water.

To each congratulation offered her, she responded, "We streamers heartily thank you!"

In due course, the mayor sounded the gong and stepped onto a temporary platform to announce commendations, Olanni and Talmarq among them. That done, he spread his hands. "And now, we shall dance. Musicians!"

The drummer beat out a rhythm, and the instruments joined in. The first was a ring dance for all, with larger circles encompassing the inner ones. With this tune, singers joined in to welcome the half year. The traditional Welcian verse came first, followed by the Dirklan verse, then the local additions. Hundreds of different versions were sung all through the provinces tonight. A new one closed Jourendia's dance, commemorating Alverlee's and Devron's names. His gift tasted all the sweeter.

The musicians began alternating between music suited for couples or groups. Fairlynn danced first with Alverlee, switching places with Olanni halfway through, so she could share several measures with Talmarq.

During a ring dance, Devron joined Fairlynn where she sat beside Kevenor's children. The next couples' dance accommodated steps in slow or fast tempo. Devron stood and offered his hand to Fairlynn. "Will you join me? We can stay in view of the children." She took his hand, as warm as their friendship. He kept their steps to a slow tempo for her, attentive enough to notice when a faint hitch began to trouble her. "Perhaps I should give Perrie a quick turn."

Fairlynn's smile stretched. "She will love that!"

He switched partners, and Perrie glowed at the treat of standing on his feet as he finished off the dance. Fairlynn, watching from her place with the boys, seemed to enjoy it as much as Perrie did.

Soon after, Devron gave Olanni a turn, and for the next couples' dance, he bowed to the chief streamer. "Good evening, Fezlie. Will you favor me with a dance?"

"Oh, sweet of you, Devron, but I'm too old for that now. But sit and have a chat with me."

Did his jaw drop too obviously? "As you wish." Old? He could think of nothing to say after that, but she filled in during his first dumbfounded minute. Old? Even when he recovered enough to converse, that word echoed in the back of his mind. She had come to Jourendia when he was twenty-something, and he'd always considered her roughly the same age as himself. A little older, true, but...ugh!

He made a point of dancing with Bekta and then joining another group dance before he was forced to sit the next one out, breathing much heavier than he liked. Fairlynn, of course, could never dance for long, so he joined her on a bench. Sleepy Jojo leaned against her chest, but the older children must be with their parents.

She raised a brow at Devron. "You're dancing a lot tonight."

He almost tried to act like that was normal, but he was breathing too heavily, and this was Fairlynn. He nodded toward the chief streamer, not far off. "Fezlie told me that she's too old to dance."

Fairlynn stared at him for a minute before a peal of laughter burst from her. Maybe his heaving chest gave him away. "Oh, Devron! She must have twenty years on you." Fairlynn tucked a hand around his arm. "You are not old."

He grunted.

"Don't you dare. I'm two years older than you, and I will *not* be called old, even if I could only manage two dances."

That was hardly the same thing. In fact, that made it worse, for he didn't have a weak hip. None of which could be spoken. Grumping about being out of shape—just like the stereotype of a sedentary polisher—it was not worthy of his breath. Better start running instead of walking when he took a break. He'd look ridiculous. He shook his head and searched for a topic. "It's good to see the normal turnout tonight. I was afraid people might stay away."

"Mm."

"What?"

"There should have been more because Jourendia is growing. Alver told me two families—that he knows of—have left. Bekta says that all of the non-formers at the boarding house suddenly decided to celebrate the half year aboveground."

That quick, the gaiety around them appeared fake. Had people already started leaving the celebration? Of course, he never stayed the full length. A moment later, Talmarq tapped his shoulder and said, "I'm turning in early. Will you see Olanni home?"

"Of course." A courtesy far more than a necessity. Devron couldn't remember the last time he'd heard of a crime, even with all the newcomers. The accused were sent up to be tried by Judge Queltin in Regissa's provincial court. If they were found guilty, they were forbidden to return to Dirklan, even after their debt was paid. Who would want to be banished from home and family for life? A strong deterrent, but necessary. A partially isolated environment was not one that could tolerate crime.

Still, Olanni wasn't used to the dark streets. In due course, he walked her home. Just inside his door, Olanni grinned and pointed at the small pile of supplies on the welcome room's round table. Talmarq's logbook, a food pouch, and a lantern. "I bet he's gone before we wake for breakfast."

She headed upstairs. Devron waited until the tap of her feet ascended the second flight of steps to the third floor before he turned off the magnery lamp. The second floor was dark and silent when he reached it, Talmarq likely asleep beyond the folding partitions that gave him some privacy. Devron had not bothered to form interior walls on the second floor except to enclose his own front bedroom.

Dark being no problem, he walked straight through his door and closed it. Without thought or groping, his fingers found the knob of the lamp. Fed by the same copper stem as those below and above, the lamp brightened as he turned the knob.

The familiar room seemed more boring than ever. He had changed nothing at all since he'd built the house twenty years ago. Was this what an old man's bedroom looked like?

Devron gritted his teeth. He was changing something tomorrow. Anything!

CHAPTER 8

An obnoxious jangle pierced the night, and Devron jolted upright in bed. What could possibly make such a sound? Metallic beating...that much he could tell as he hastened to light his lamp. The racket stopped, but he still jerked his door open.

Light glowed from beyond the partitions. Doubtless, the din had woken Talmarq as well.

The streamer folded the partition open beside the wall, wearing only a pair of trousers. "Sorry that my alarm woke you."

"Do you always beat metal when you're alarmed?"

Talmarq stared, slack-jawed, at Devron for a moment, then flopped against the wall, trying to muffle laughter with both hands over his mouth. The blond hair on his chest vibrated with the muscles beneath.

Apparently, whatever had occurred was not a threat. By now, Devron would have expected Olanni to be running down from the third floor, but she made no appearance.

After Talmarq's first burst of laughter abated, he staggered toward his bed, then returned with a shirt and one of the circular timepieces that the abovegrounders used. Two brass bells extended above it on short posts, with a striker between. Its hour pointer hovered at the *4*. Was this little device the cause?

Still trying to subdue his mirth, Talmarq put it in Devron's hand.

He used his forming sense to discern its hidden workings. Gears, springs, and a release tab associated with the hour pointer. "You set this thing up to make that racket on purpose?"

Talmarq pulled his shirt on. "Shh. I'm so sorry. It's called an alarm clock. I want to be in the lake cavern before moonset and sunrise."

Ridiculous though it was, Devron hushed his voice. "You really think *that* didn't awaken Olanni?"

"She'll know what it is and go back to sleep. You can too." He took the beastly, ticking device. "I really am sorry I disturbed you."

Devron managed a grin. "Never mind. Get off to your duties." He retreated to his bedroom, rubbing a hand through the mess of his hair. Go back to sleep? Not with the way his heart was racing. He opened a window an inch, then sat in the single chair and waited until he heard his front door open and close below him. The world outside was still hidden in darkness. Talmarq's lantern cast a faint glow and made swinging shadows of his legs.

Despite the rude awakening, Devron fully understood his drive...was even grateful for it. He never bothered much about water, but Talmarq's underground detection of the harbor currents was a discovery of great import. Yes, it boded well for the streamer's future career, but there was much, much more to it than that. Devron couldn't explain why, but he knew it as deeply as he knew his own need to create. *Compulsion* was a better word for it lately. As his heart calmed its pace, the call to his stone egg thrummed all the stronger.

Devron dressed and went downstairs to his workshop. He'd realized something in the lake cavern yesterday that was not evident when looking at the egg free of any surrounding stone—or sand. He pondered it long. Sand would be an insurmountable problem. Which implied—much to his relief—that this device was not intended to be implemented in such an environment. A sour sort of relief, that.

He shook off the irritation and focused on what he knew. Over the next hour, he separated another panel. The window was still dark, and he began the next. Somewhere in the midst of it, the rising sun touched the many light shafts, and the settlement burst into dawn's golden glow. It spilled through the back windows, and Devron extinguished the magnery lamp on the wall. He'd best make some breakfast before Olanni came looking for him and started asking questions.

Why was he so nervous about questions on this? She wasn't even a former, so she wouldn't see anything except an egg-shaped rock with a geometric design etched around the top.

But he avoided the subject anyway, and as soon as she left to enjoy her final day in Jourendia, he was back at it. Still slow, but gradually faster as he got used to the pattern of work needed for the identical joints. He even forced himself to pause and eat at intervals, so he could endure the hours better. No matter what the non-gifted thought of his stillness, forming took effort.

No one returned to join him for dinner. Good. He snacked and kept working until the final panel was free. At the peaks of three of them, he fashioned overlapping extensions to close the tiny hole.

He gripped the dome and jiggled. Something he had done many times now, but for the first time...all twenty-seven pieces...moved independently. Barely, but they moved. The recesses were big enough to allow more, but the shafts at the bases had little room. The final tweak. Extend each hole to a slot, so the shafts could angle as the panels rocked outward. He lit the lamp again, for light was fading, then accomplished the simplest task of the whole project.

Devron stepped back and stared at it. Still a rough grindstone on the outside. The etched top hinted that it might be a puzzle structure like the toy he'd made for Tebber. Now to test it.

He spread his fingers wide, pressed his hands to the dome, and twisted with a vibrating motion. The entire dome jiggled, but the weight of the stone resisted. He hooked his thumbs in his belt and considered it.

Dark handprints on the gray stone showed where his sweaty palms had pressed. Even the pressure of his hands helped keep it closed. A good thing, really, for the very shape of a dome made it stand firm against downward pressure. But what was the point of an opening that could not be opened? Another force was needed to counteract gravity's pull, either pushing up from within or lifting from above.

Well, there was one obvious force at his disposal. He was a former, after all. It felt a little like cheating, but he just had to see this thing move. He commanded the motion he had designed for. The panels obeyed, sliding apart as they lifted. He slipped his index fingers into the exposed hole and gently pulled it wider. Though they grated, the panels rocked outward in the ring groove until they rested against its outer lip. Their shapes kept the panels nested, for they could not spread wide enough to escape the deep recesses that encased them. Now they formed a wall that arched inward.

He stared at it for a long moment, then his shoulders began to shake with silent laughter. It worked. *It really worked!*

He released the panel he held, and with a rough scrape, the entire dome slid back together under its own weight. He laughed aloud now. A self-closing structure with the strength of a dome. Exactly what he had seen in the vision wall.

He opened it again and, this time, stuck his arm down through the gap. Wide enough to accept his upper arm. He couldn't reach the bottom, of course, but he could slide his fingers over the inner surface of the panels he'd formed. Partly rough, where they had no need to slide, partly smooth where he had separated and aligned within the heart of intact stone. Wonder swept him again. "By your gifting," he whispered.

Tingles spread through him as he held a single panel and moved it in and out, thereby controlling all of them. He sensed the tiny catches, for no surface could be wholly perfect on the first try. He smoothed each imperfection. The stone was so fully known to him, now, that little urging was needed. The grating of its movement faded to a swishing whisper.

Finally, he let out a long *phew*! He loved his gift, but oh, he was tired! His body asserted a dozen needs, starting with a stretch of hunched shoulders. Time to leave this for tonight.

He closed the workshop door behind him, not sure that he wanted the egg seen, and turned on the lamp in the kitchen. Where was everyone? He crossed to the priv. Washing his hands a moment later, he jumped at Alverlee's shout from the welcome room.

"Dev, where are you?"

"I'll be out in a minute." His face in the mirror looked tired, and he splashed cold water over it to bring a little color to his pale skin. He took a couple steps from the small room. The door of his workshop stood open. Light shone from within.

Well, maybe it was time to let at least his brother in on his latest device. His empty stomach churned as he entered the workshop. Alverlee stood by the stone egg, and Devron moved around to the other side so he could see his brother's face. Frowning...lips compressed.

Voice low, he asked, "What is it, Dev?"

Considering, he drew a slow breath. "At the moment, it's a hollow stone egg with a curious opening at the top." He needed to get to the part about the vision but wasn't sure how.

Alverlee directed a stern look at him. "Before I came to the lake cavern yesterday, I stopped in here looking for you. I saw the ring groove you'd formed, and when I studied the cavern roof, I also saw how closely it matches where the cavern dome emerges from the seabed. Did you think I wouldn't notice?"

Devron shrugged and touched the feature. "I formed the ring here in my workshop before I inspected the sea floor. That's when I noticed the correlation, so I'm not surprised you would too."

"You're telling me it's pure coincidence?"

"Oh, I doubt that! Try to open it."

"I have no patience for puzzles today! What—"

"Try, Alver. It's no puzzle." Devron swung a finger around the top. "Twist it this way."

Alverlee huffed but pressed his hands against it and pushed futilely. He glared at Devron from beneath his brows.

"I can't budge it that way either," Devron said. "It's still a solid dome, held shut by its own weight. Some other force must start the movement." He commanded the stone as he spoke, just long enough to make a small gap at the top. With a single finger, he pulled it the rest of the way open. "Both the ring's lip and the ball joints stop the panels from opening wider. Their shape keeps each one recessed within its neighbor. And when external force is released..." He withdrew his finger, and the panels swished together. "...the dome closes itself." Their eyes met over the top of the egg. "I know you don't want to hear it, but this is the design I saw in the vision wall. So, no, I do not believe there is any coincidence in the ring's position matching the sea floor so closely." Devron frowned. "Although I am worried about all that sand out there."

"Sand! You're worried about *sand*?" Alverlee grew redder by the second. "Have you forgotten the *ocean* in the harbor?"

"Of course not."

"Why...*why*...would you even consider the possibility of flooding Jourendia?"

"Please calm down, Alver. You must know I would never do such a thing. I couldn't if I wanted to. Even if this design was implemented in the cavern dome—"

"I forbid it!"

"Even if it was, I could not shift such immense panels to open it. I doubt any former could, and with the weight of the water above—impossible."

"Yes. Impossible. An opening which cannot be opened. No such design is ever to be attempted beneath the harbor."

"I didn't say that it cannot be opened." Devron commanded the dome again and held it with his fingertip. "An outside force can open it. In the vision, I saw a great swirling above the cavern—"

"The vision!" Alverlee thundered. "Now, you want to open the cavern to the whirlpool, do you? Let's also destroy the port and sink ships, while we flood Jourendia."

"No! I wish you would—"

Alverlee stomped over to the tool bench, shouting over Devron. "I forbid it and will always forbid it!" He grabbed the sledgehammer and swung it overhead with the momentum of two strides. Devron jumped away from the egg. The dome closed as the hammer descended with a loud crack. The hammer's handle snapped, and the head sprang away from the dome, crashing into a stand of brass tubes. They bounced and rolled across the stone floor, coming to rest in brittle silence.

Devron didn't move—only explored the dome with his forming sense. He'd thought to see it destroyed, but it was unharmed. Ah! "The weakest part always breaks. The hammer shaft was not made of ipenrock."

Alverlee cast aside the broken handle he held. "I suppose you think that proves something, but it doesn't." His voice, still harsh, rose with every word. "No matter how strong the dome is while closed, it is weak while open. The water will always be countless yards above it, even at lowest tide. As soon as the panels move, sand will grind into every groove and recess, so that it never seals again. Even if you fused the sand, it would all be back with the next wave." He shouted again. "This will never work, and it is never to be attempted. I speak as Chief Former, Devron. Do you understand me?"

A stranger stood before him. Warped by fear-driven rage. "Yes, Chief Former. I understand you clearly."

Silence.

A relief. Devron dared to step around the egg. "That topic being finalized, I would like my brother back now."

Alverlee closed his eyes, and every portion of him seemed to shift in some way. "Dev, you don't understand."

"Maybe not everything." He took his brother's arm and turned him toward the door so the mess, and especially the egg, lay behind them. "But I do know of the anxiety pressing down on everyone since that thickening occurred. Waiting several days with no explanation is bound to cause strain. But take heed to yourself, Alver. We've had our differences, but never have you spoken to me like this."

"It's not the thickening. It's the visions. People have gone crazy over all those conflicting messages. And yours is the craziest of all."

"Forget mine. I never would have acted without consulting you, and that decision has now been made. But what are others doing beyond stopping work? I thought I was the only one with a vision about Jourendia, and I have told no one what it was."

"Thank Ellincreo for that much good sense!" Alverlee shook his head. "No one else has mentioned visions specific to this end of Dirklan. They just twist and twine more upon what they've heard, no matter how distorted it all is. We must not harvest ore, gems, or rock. We mustn't move a single stone. Yet, we must build great columns up to all the cavern ceilings to reinforce them, and that without any material to build them from. Yes, you stare, but I listen to this and more absurdities every minute of every day."

His brother's red face paled in blotches, stark against his black hair. So worn, he looked, that Devron sought soothing words. "Upsets always fade with time." Inadequate. "You possess another gift as important as your forming. You have the gift of calm guidance. Let it flourish again and watch how it restores sense and order."

The corner of Alverlee's mouth lifted. Acknowledging, perhaps, but unconvinced. Whatever he might have said was lost, for the front door slammed.

"Devron, are you here?" Talmarq shouted.

An odd entry. Was something else wrong? Devron strode through the kitchen. "Yes, right here." Both Olanni and Talmarq had arrived, but neither seemed to have anything to say.

Alverlee followed Devron and asked, "Were you able to sense more turnings of the tide?"

Talmarq's smile flashed, for his discovery surpassed any concern. "Indeed. I think I've learned as much in the last two days as...as since the instant my gift manifested."

Alverlee nodded. "Perhaps you can tell me on the journey tomorrow. We'll leave after breakfast, though you needn't hurry on my account."

By the tension in Olanni's stiff movements, she would be packed before she slept, but she just stood there after Alverlee left. Talmarq too.

"Did something go wrong today?" Devron asked.

They spoke over each other. "No." "Nothing."

Devron looked back and forth between them. "Good." He paused. "I just need to put away a few things. If you decide you want to talk about...whatever it is, I'll be done in a few minutes." Maybe that would loosen their tongues.

He returned to his workshop and righted the overturned stand. That egg...perhaps he should cover it. Never had bothered to with any of his art, but maybe a bed sheet would spare him some trouble. He gathered handfuls of the brass tubes from the floor and replaced them in their stand, then caught movement in the corner of his eye. His guests hovered in the doorway.

Talmarq rubbed the side of his neck. "We, uh, decided that we should tell you that we overheard Alverlee shouting."

"Oh." Oh, no! "You heard him from outside?"

"No." Talmarq kept fidgeting. "We had already come in, but I'm sure neither of you knew. And then it got quiet, and I could just imagine him walking out and seeing us all wide-eyed. So, well, maybe I should have faced up to it, but...I just opened and slammed the door and called out, so it seemed like we had just arrived."

"Ah!" Devron considered. "You may count *that* as an act of discretion. I hope you will maintain it with Alverlee tomorrow and with all others." They both nodded as he spoke. "Besides, no one will believe you if you claim Alverlee ranted. He is known for his steadiness. Please don't think ill of him. It's just that all the anxiety and a great overload of stupidity have exhausted him at the moment."

"*That,* I can understand." Olanni's fingers moved continuously.

Talmarq's gaze lingered on the stone egg. "He shouted of a whirlpool and sinking ships and flooding. But I don't understand. What did he forbid?"

Devron tried to figure out when that part had been said—and what had come after. Pointless, really. He must either refuse to tell anything or explain all. He should refuse. Rumors would be disastrous. Alverlee had forbidden the project, so it could never be constructed. But the vision glowed in his mind's eye. He could not hold silent. "I must have your solemn, considered word that you will not speak of this. Such rumors in Dirklan would wreak untold havoc."

"I will not repeat what you share," Talmarq promised, low and deliberate.

Olanni also uttered earnest assurance.

Devron licked his lips. "I told you I saw something in the vision wall. A device without a purpose."

"Is this it?" Olanni asked.

"Not exactly. The interior of this stone *egg*, as Fairlynn dubbed it, is shaped like the lake cavern."

Talmarq narrowed his eyes, considering. "It seems like the cavern walls are straighter."

"The *inside* is shaped like the cavern. The outside is a fair representation of how the stress spreads from the domed roof, but in reality, most of the cavern is embedded in compressed ipenrock." Devron held his hands horizontally near the ring groove. "Understanding that this models the cavern—then the sea floor is about here. Everything below is encased in rock. But it is the dome that matters."

"You asked about the dome," Talmarq murmured, "when I first found the harbor current."

"Yes. It's not entirely natural. There are records aboveground of how an ancient whirlpool caused problems and the cavern was sealed off."

Olanni wrinkled her nose. "How would that help with the whirlpool?"

Devron blinked. "Are you asking *me*?"

The streamers laughed, and Olanni flicked her hand. "Never mind. You were saying?"

"Uh, the dome. When the settlement was begun here, my father, who was the chief former, realigned the irregular roof to make it into an actual dome."

"Why?" she asked.

Devron smiled. "*That* is a fair question for me. A dome distributes weight to the walls—a very stable configuration to cover a large space bearing much weight." He spread a hand over the dome before him. "I separated the pieces of this intact. Thus, when it is closed, it still has the strength of the original dome. Only when an outside force draws it..." He commanded as he spoke and slipped a finger into the opening. "Only then can it open. When that force is removed..." He let go. "...the entire dome closes under its own weight."

They stared at it in silence until Olanni asked, "Are you thinking of duplicating this in the cavern's dome?"

"Frankly, it is quite *un*thinkable. Yet, that is what I saw in the vision wall."

Her eyes narrowed. "But it would always be underwater, right? Even at lowest tide?"

Devron raised questioning brows at Talmarq. "You understand tides better than I do."

"Don't forget that I was raised inland, but I did observe the lowest winter tides today. Seawater continued to flow above the entire lake cavern throughout. I believe the summer tides are lowest of all, but not by much. I can't see how the dome could ever be exposed."

"I don't believe so either," Devron said. "I would have noticed the pressure change if ever the cavern roof supported no seawater."

Olanni spread a hand toward the egg. "Then, what use is this?"

"Exactly. That is why it seems that the device has no purpose."

She heaved a sigh, and her shoulders relaxed. "So you did not see a flood or whirlpool or sinking ships in your vision?"

"No." He gave her a faint smile. "That was Alverlee's imagination of what would happen if a dome like this were opened in the cavern. But that's not even possible, for the water pressure will always force it to remain closed."

Talmarq snorted. "That's what happens when a former predicts water events. As bad as when the rest of us predict land events."

His words left Devron momentarily speechless. Steadfast Alverlee fell into error when he stepped out of his own expertise—just as badly as others had erred when they stepped out of theirs. "Those without substance gifts never understand formers. Nor do the few wind weavers, it seems. Streamers do in part, for waters rest upon earth and may shape it, to a degree." He laid his hand on the dome, its rock cool beneath his palm. "I wonder... How would this device respond to a streamer's touch?"

Talmarq squinted and quirked his mouth. Olanni looked equally puzzled. Devron didn't blame them. He didn't understand, either. Talmarq circled his hand above the dome. "The primary current flows this direction."

"That, too, will always keep it closed," Devron said.

Olanni tilted her head. "What do you mean—primary current?"

Talmarq shrugged. "It gets odd around the lowest tides. Really, though, I can't speak with any certainty. I've watched low tide once from above and twice from below. Without at least a full month to study it, I don't even know what a normal cycle is. Much less, how they compare to the lowest tides of the half years. Then there is that ancient whirlpool. I have no idea if some remnant of it remains, or how it may behave."

"We can check into that when we go aboveground," Olanni suggested. "The harbor's chief streamer must know all about it."

Talmarq nodded, his lips tight. "I'm watching the morning tide before we leave."

"I hope you will return someday." Devron rested his hands on their shoulders as they moved toward the door. "I would love to understand more about the harbor currents. But remember, Alverlee has forbidden any change to the dome, and you have promised to spread no word of this. Imagine the panic if any believed that the ocean could flood into the caverns."

CHAPTER 9

Fairlynn clung to Alverlee's arm as a passenger carriage was pulled to the rail platform for the travelers. If only she could grip him tight enough—long enough—to keep him from climbing into it. All her pleading had been futile. His own determination drove him even more than the mayor's insistence.

Despite Alverlee's reassurances—his calm explanation that all was well—she could feel the tension in his body. Olanni's fidgets and Talmarq's silent frown didn't help matters either. She kept her voice cheerful as she bade them goodbye and hoped her eyes didn't reveal how falsely she spoke.

She released Alverlee's arm when he turned toward Devron, who also looked subdued. Hopefully, not with hard feelings. Troubled by remorse, Alverlee had told her of his harshness yesterday. Perhaps now they would make amends. Their soft words and a grip of shoulders hinted at peace between them. Then Alverlee returned and kissed her goodbye. Which he never did in public and had already done in the privacy of their home.

"Safe travels," she murmured, forcing a smile as her husband and the two streamers stepped into the carriage. She watched them borne away along the rail until the dark tunnel swallowed them. Olanni and Talmarq would be out of danger by tomorrow morning. And Alverlee would be in more.

The breath that escaped her must have been audible, for Devron pressed a hand to her back. "Are you all right?"

"Oh, Dev, I try not to worry, but it's dreadfully hard."

She began to wonder if he would answer, but finally he said, "A difficult time. How are things at home?"

She shrugged. "A little sharper than usual, I suppose. At least I can go and check the local waters. There's not much to do, really, but more than the formers are allowed."

He offered his hand to help her step down from the platform. A secretive smile twitched his mouth. "No one can stop my small creations. You are welcome to take refuge in my house if you need a break from, shall we say, excessive family."

She took up his offer for an hour that day, and more hours the next, even making him dinner.

Devron set plates on the table as she flipped the steamed vegetables into a bowl. "What has Crilla so bothered?" he asked.

"I cannot imagine. If anything, she has more help than usual, for Kevenor is home most of the day now. Can you believe she snapped at me for being gone this morning? Fifth day is always my turn to refresh the duck pond, but she acted like I was dallying to shirk some task."

"There was a ruckus in the market today too. It seems like everyone's nerves are rubbing against each other's."

"Well, I promised to help her with laundry tomorrow, so perhaps she will feel less aggrieved." Fairlynn hoped so anyway. Really, her heart was so torn with worry, that she had no patience for Crilla's demands.

On sixth workday, Devron accompanied Kevenor to the town square for a meeting with the mayor and city council. Kevenor was filling in for Alverlee, but with the chief former absent and all the guild members disgruntled over the needless hold on work, Devron figured his nephew could use support.

The same refrain began. Formers insisting that their work endangered no one, and non-gifted arguing on the side of *reasonable caution*. At least that was what they called it.

Devron kept only half an ear to the repetitions, instead checking for progress on the light shafts. The polishers above had clearly been working them, and he would need to begin more soon if—

"What are you doing?" one of the council members demanded.

Oh no. He'd made the mistake of staring upward. "Just sensing structure."

"You see," another said. "The formers are worried too."

"Not so," Kevenor insisted. "We only check to calm groundless fears. Nothing has changed in Jourendia's caverns. Let's return to the suggestion of building at a slow pace."

The same battle that had flared for days raged again. Devron strolled around the edge of the group, for he saw no value in joining such a pointless discussion. The non-gifted would be none the wiser if he worked the light shafts. Formers would know if they checked. Would they all have the good sense to keep their mouths shut?

Bekta was trying a new angle of persuasion and—

A shock wave struck Devron's forming senses. He staggered and turned toward distant LourEstelle. The pressure! Unbearable. He couldn't even hear!

The non-gifted gesticulated, their mouths moving. Formers gaped, many pressing hands to the sides of their heads as though they could shut out the assault. Bekta dropped to her knees.

Distant, silent crashing thundered through Devron's senses. Wave after wave of pressure. He gasped through a brief pause and then doubled over as another collapse made his stomach heave. Another pause. Another collapse, even nearer, sent pounding agony through him. Would it not end? Was each collapse triggering another?

A longer pause enabled him to hear, then he wished he couldn't. Frantic demands from the non-gifted—to explain—to protect the caverns. What did they think the formers could do? Hold up the entire crust?

A former was begging for silence, unheeded.

Devron swung around to the mayor and growled through clenched teeth, "Make them stop shrieking!"

Mayor Borchel waved his hands and demanded quiet as another quake shuddered through Devron's senses. A lesser disturbance this time—perhaps a secondary fall where the first had occurred. He sniffed and wiped his watery eyes. At least he could hear properly now. He looked around at the faces of other formers. Even those with shorter range looked haggard. Vomit soiled the cavern floor, and the most sensitive formers were on their knees.

Devron went to Bekta, who rocked, clutching herself. If only he could do more for her than grip her shoulders.

"Please..." The mayor's voice quavered. "Can none of you tell us what has happened?"

"LourEstelle," Bekta wailed. "It has collapsed!"

Stunned seconds passed. Then dismayed voices rose. The crowd loosened as though some would run. To where?

"Wait!" Devron rasped, but no one seemed to hear him.

Kevenor wiped his mouth on his sleeve and struggled to his feet. "Listen! Don't spread panic through Jourendia."

The mayor seemed to remember his duty and demanded order.

Devron swept his lacerated forming senses through the caverns of Jourendia, searching for damage. He felt other formers doing the same. A few minutes later, it occurred to Kevenor to instruct them to do so.

Before long, the formers conferred, and all agreed that their home caverns were unharmed.

That seemed impossible after the battering Devron's senses had taken, but now that he had time to think it through, he had not felt any movement even as near as Crysalan. A pity that offered no relief. For him to sense what happened beyond Crysalan—there was only one explanation. The death toll in LourEstelle would be staggering.

And Alverlee was there.

Devron struggled to keep his mind from his own grief, for people *here* needed all the assurance that he could offer them.

At least the mayor showed sense over the frantic suggestions that all should flee Dirklan immediately. "No. Absolutely not. No carriage will move for either people or freight until the rails have been checked."

When challenges rose again, Kevenor shouted, "Jourendia is still the safest place in Dirklan. We may even have people fleeing to us. If the rails need repair, they must be kept clear so we can get material to wherever it is needed."

"Exactly," Mayor Borchel declared. "Now listen to me. We will face this tragedy together and with order, not with panic. First..." He slowed his heavy breaths and quieted his voice. "First, we must go share the sad news with our families and neighbors. And we must take a couple hours to shed our tears, to comfort where we may, and to consider. The town will meet here again at noon, and we will *calmly* discuss what we will do next."

An uncomfortable pause ensued, but none argued.

"Council members..." The mayor stepped toward the group, for they'd withdrawn from the formers. "When you have told your families, you must each take a street and ensure that all hear the sad news and the meeting time." He lowered his voice further, as though his words fell like tears to the cavern floor. "Let us go now."

Devron and a young former helped Bekta to her feet.

Kevenor gripped Devron's arm. "Please come with me. I don't know how to tell Fairlynn."

Devron nodded, unable to force words through his constricted throat. They followed everyone else to the settlement cavern, their steps as determined as they were reluctant. What were they going to say?

Through the door...into the kitchen, where the washtubs stood. Fairlynn was churning the soapy water while Crilla lifted a wet garment. The women's eyes widened at the sight of them.

"Put the wash down," Kevenor said flatly.

Crilla dropped the garment, and the water stilled in one instant. Through the silence, she whispered, "What has happened?"

Kevenor rested his gaze on Fairlynn at the near end of the tub. "I'm so sorry—LourEstelle—it has collapsed."

A strangled cry squeezed from Fairlynn. "Alver!" They took a step toward each other, but Crilla dashed around the tub and threw herself on her husband's chest, wailing.

Fairlynn startled like she'd been slapped. She wobbled, and Devron hastened to gather her into his arms. She hid her face against his shoulder and hardly breathed until silent sobs began to shake her. Tears streamed down Devron's cheeks for his lost brother...the grief made even worse by the deluge of Fairlynn's pain.

Around them, his nephew's family cried, even little Jojo, who knew only that others wept. Alverlee...Charodee and her family...Crilla's family...friends...perhaps the chief formers from every city in Dirklan...countless others. The death toll would be in the thousands. Devron could only hope that some had heeded the warning in the vision wall and left before it was too late. That warning—dismissed by so many. An unholy fury burned in his chest against the Chief Keeper of the Writ. Was his grief not burden enough!

When sorrow exhausted them, he led Fairlynn to a couch in the welcome room and sat with her. Perrie soon crawled into Fairlynn's lap. In a way, it seemed to help her to have a little one in need of her comfort.

Or perhaps she received as much comfort as she gave. Kevenor, Crilla, and their two boys ended up sitting opposite them in mournful silence.

Eventually, someone knocked on the door, and Kevenor opened it to the mayor and Bekta.

Heavy though his face was, Borchel moved smoothly from condolences to community matters. "The town will meet soon," he said, "but I feel it wise to consult first."

"Yes, of course." Kevenor brought two chairs from the kitchen for them. "Please sit down. Bekta, you have the best range in Jourendia. What more have you sensed?"

Her voice lacked its natural force, but she answered calmly. "There have been some aftershocks, but nothing severe like those initial collapses."

"Do you agree with that assessment?" the mayor asked Kevenor.

"I only felt one, but I trust Bekta's judgment."

The mayor nodded. "Believe me, I truly hate to bring this up, but people search for someone to blame, and they will blame the formers. I would rather know ahead of time how I should answer them."

"That is so unjust," Bekta snapped. "No former can support a mountain."

Borchel raised shocked eyebrows. "Do you suggest that Mount Estelle fell through into LourEstelle?"

"No, of course not, but it must have suffered a severe quake." Bekta already sounded exhausted by an argument that had yet to occur. "Part of my training took place at Mount Estelle. It only looks like a serene cone from a distance. Up close, the base is scored by cliffs. Huge boulders and vast mounds of scree flank it. The edges have fallen before, and no one has ever stopped it. We must acknowledge that earth moves, no matter how much we hate that fact."

Kevenor nodded, addressing the mayor. "Inevitable, but remember that it is *very* infrequent. A shift releases pressure. Once the aftershocks subside, we'll not suffer another for generations. So, there is *less* to fear—not more."

Borchel murmured, "I see," but he didn't look convinced.

Devron had best add his support as well. "People may blame formers aboveground too, even claiming they may have caused the tragedy. But such a collapse as this *could not possibly* be caused by any former. We simply do not have that ability."

"I'll not protect the reputation of aboveground formers," the mayor snapped. "I'll have enough trouble protecting all of you."

Bekta fired up. "For what cause? Because we told you Jourendia was safe? It has proven true! Even Alverlee, who was an excellent chief former, never claimed safety beyond Crysalan."

The mayor leaned toward her. "Speak with that heat to the whole town, and they will shout accusations all the more." He straightened and included Kevenor and Devron in his next words. "I will do all that I can for you, but be wise in how you plead your own case."

Fairlynn finally spoke. "They should not have to plead any case at all. Ellincreo warned many with visions. Some departed—even from Jourendia. Others stayed, all by our own choice. But Ellincreo warned no formers of the collapse. I now see why. They simply could not prevent it. You, Mayor, will be heeded more than any other, so you must make this very clear."

"Ah, Fairlynn, I know you must blame me for sending Alverlee to LourEstelle. I am so very sorry, and I beg your forgiveness."

Her head twitched. "Alverlee knew the danger but chose to go anyway. He, like the rest of us, made his own decision. I uttered not a single word of blame. Did you hear me at all?"

He inclined his head respectfully. "Yes, I heard you. I will do all that I can to protect Alverlee's honor."

She exhaled a rough breath. "Give heed to the living, not the dead."

"You are right, of course." Borchel shifted his gaze to the formers again. "And to that end, we will need to know the extent of the damage."

Devron patted Fairlynn's shoulder. Borchel seemed deaf to her point, but he would not hear it right now, no matter what anyone said.

Kevenor answered the mayor. "It was beyond Crysalan, for certain."

Though Bekta and Devron stated agreement, Borchel's tone remained firm. "I understand you, but I feel it wisest to confirm that."

"Are you suggesting," Fairlynn demanded, "sending another former into danger?"

How could a squeaky voice sound so lethal? Devron pressed her shoulder. "I don't think it need be into danger. I must travel to Crysalan anyway, so I can check the rails for damage. Every city will do the same, for Crysalan is the hub of Dirklan's rail system. By the time I reach it, they will have word of the damage toward LourEstelle and, also, of the *un*damaged caverns elsewhere."

The mayor nodded his approval, but Fairlynn clung to Devron's hand and hissed, "I cannot lose another."

"I will go," Bekta said.

"You may join me, but we both know you cannot check or polish the rails as I can."

Bekta grimaced. "True enough, but I'm going, just the same. I have family nigh the access arches, and I must know what has become of them."

"The access is my greatest worry." Borchel inclined his head to her. "I thank you for risking the journey to bring us word, Bekta." He turned to Fairlynn. "And then you may be spared concern over Devron's safety." He stood. "I must get to the square. Will you join me now or come in a few more minutes?" His tone held a summons.

Kevenor stood to open the door for him. "We'll be along soon." He closed the door behind the departing mayor and practically moaned, rubbing his forehead. "Um, I suppose we must take the children..."

"No, I cannot bear to hear it." Fairlynn sniffed. "Leave them here with me." She stood and shook out the damp apron she wore.

Kevenor gripped her shoulders. "I am so sorry, Mother Fairlynn, for your loss and for what is still to come."

She nodded, swallowing convulsively.

Devron patted her shoulder yet again, then followed Kevenor, Crilla, and Bekta to the meeting that they all dreaded.

It played out much as he'd expected. Lamenting the could-have-been. Blame-casting. Prophecies of doom. Extreme safeguards to prevent future collapses—none of which would work. Two hours of fear-ranting that strained every nerve to the breaking point and accomplished *nothing*.

CHAPTER 10

Early the next morning, Devron checked the upper light shafts before anyone could tell him not to. No one had worked them yesterday, nor was any former present now. No surprise, for aboveground Welcia would have suffered from the quake too.

He returned home to find Fairlynn in his welcome room. She gestured to a food basket on the table beside his packed bag. "I baked travel cakes for your journey."

"Thank you." What else to say? "Um, feel free to come here while I'm gone if you want some time alone."

"I imagine I'll need it!"

His brows darted together. "Is it...bad there?"

Her lips made a few failed attempts before she answered. "At dinner last night, Kevenor left Alverlee's place vacant. It was dreadful looking at his empty chair, never to be filled. But this morning, Crilla took my place before I had a chance to sit down. And that was worse yet."

Couldn't that woman wait even a full day? "Did Kevenor say nothing?"

"He just looked confused until she bade him sit at the head of the table. Don't mistake me. I do realize that the house belongs to Kevenor now, which means Crilla is the mistress of it. In fairness, her words were gentle, but she speaks of moving on with life." Fairlynn drew a strained breath and cleared her throat roughly. "Maybe she is right. I try to remind myself that she has also lost family."

"Not her husband. Nor a stepdaughter and grandchildren."

"No, but maybe more than we have. Parents, siblings, nieces, and nephews." Fairlynn tried a weak smile. "It's almost a relief that I was an only child, and that my parents died some time ago. But anyway...I will use your offer when I need it."

Devron had left the door standing open, and now Bekta tapped it with her knuckles. "Come in," he said. By the travel bag slung over her shoulder, she was ready to set out.

"How long do you expect to be gone?" Fairlynn asked him.

"Two days at the very least. Probably three or four—depending on how much news has come in and how long we need to wait for more. If any guild meetings are called, I will need to attend those." He rolled his lip between his teeth. "If it gets longer than four days, I'll send a letter on the first carriage to head this way."

She nodded and took a breath as if she was about to offer some normal parting. The typical *safe travels* would close her throat for sure. She looked away. "I, uh, hope all goes well."

He hefted his own travel bag and picked up the food basket, then wrapped his free arm around her shoulders. "I will return."

Bekta stepped back outside, and he followed her, closing the door...and tried not to think of Fairlynn, likely sobbing behind that shield.

The mayor had a carriage waiting on the platform when they reached it, and he sent them off with fine words.

They kept their silence as they entered the tunnel. Only a single lantern on their carriage pierced its darkness, for the other had not been lit. Restricting oil use already. A yoked burro plodded along beside them, for this was no train like the one in which they'd traveled a week ago. Was that burro a rare commodity now? They were grazed aboveground and cycled below for a couple days at a time. How many remained? Would they die if the access was blocked?

Once they passed out of hearing distance from the settlement, Bekta grumbled, "I don't much like the mayor these days."

Devron grunted, remembering all the placating words of yesterday's town meeting—and the folly. Formers were forbidden to work, but no good would come of complaints. "We'll get no suspicious looks in the tunnel. While I check the rail, you check the tunnel's arch. If you find any veins of quartz or any suitable crystals, we'll stop and form rudimentary light shafts."

"They'll have our hides if they find out."

"They won't know, for I won't complete anything except the top. There's no oil source in Jourendia, and not enough belowground to light all of Dirklan. If the access avenue is blocked, they'll eventually beg me to clarify every light shaft that can be found."

The easily formed veins in the tunnel had already been cleared long ago. Some of the deposits they found ended too soon, but they managed to trace a couple twisted veins to the surface so Devron could push an obelisk up to gather light. He could only hope that the polishers above would eventually find them.

"Two measly shafts in miles of tunnel," Bekta griped when they neared the first cavern of Crysalan.

"Hush."

A distant voice shouted, "There's a carriage coming from Jourendia!"

Running feet thumped, and by the time they halted at the platform, a small crowd pelted them with questions.

Devron and Bekta stood in the carriage. "Quiet, please." He waited for them to still. "I can tell you that Jourendia's caverns are unscathed. The tunnel is also solid, and the river turbines between us still function. The local streamer came up when we stopped there and reported that no change has been detected in the river's course."

Murmurs of relief greeted his words, despite the people's careworn faces.

"How fared Crysalan?" Devron asked.

A deep-voiced former seemed to be the spokesman. "Well enough. This side is untouched. All the caverns are stable. The formers on the far side report some distortions, but they have not compromised stability."

Even minor disruption this far from Mount Estelle was ominous. Devron steeled himself. "How bad is the news from LourEstelle?"

"Well…" the man shifted his stance. "We've all decided we'll only state confirmed facts. The nearest fringe settlements survived. Inhabitants have abandoned them for now, seeking refuge in Crysalan until the caverns can be reassessed. We're hoping, of course, to get more refugees as there is time for them to make the trip, on foot if not by rail. Weslin, Illia, and Alluthin have also reported that they are undamaged. There are likely more reporting in by now. The news is all being gathered at Crysalan's government hall. We were told to send any arrivals from Jourendia on to them immediately."

Bekta practically vibrated with impatience. "Do you have news from the access avenue?"

"Not yet." Sorrow etched his face. "The rail goes partway, but it's broken. The tunnel extends some way beyond, but I don't know how far."

Her lips tight, Bekta turned and dropped onto the seat.

"We had best continue on at once." Devron sat down beside her and slapped the burro's reins. Bekta's hands gripped her knees. He covered one of them with his own for a moment, but she seemed to want no comfort. They spoke not a word until they were met at the central station.

Again, a crowd gathered. They shared a repetition of news and heard of more areas declared safe—until Bekta demanded, "Tell me of the access avenue."

A somber look weighted the face of newly-appointed Chief Former Pondarro, a middle-aged man with a protruding chin overdue for a shave. "The tunnel collapsed several miles out. I'm still waiting for word on the far terminal arches."

Bekta didn't budge from her seat. "I'm a former with long range. I'm continuing as far as the rail will carry me."

"We have need of you there." His heavy words carried no hope.

Best to set her on her way at once. Devron gathered his things and stepped from the carriage. "Return when you can."

Two people hefted trunks of food and canteens onto the carriage's empty front seat, and one of them sat beside Bekta. Someone must be managing operations and permitting no transportation to be wasted. In seconds, the carriage glided from the platform.

Pondarro escorted Devron into Crysalan's government hall. The first floor was a vast open room for city-wide meetings. Given the abundance of waste quartz from the local gold mines, the walls were frosted white. Dingier than he remembered, but still pale enough to reflect light from the magnery lamps. The familiar map on the far wall caught his eye. Dirklan—all of its cities, settlements, tunnels, and waterways—rendered on the highly-polished quartz. Metals or gemstones represented the primary resources of each. Artistically executed, but reasonably accurate, too. Now marked with the waxy lines of colored pastels.

He'd seen markings on it before to indicate a proposed settlement or mine. Jourendia itself had once been shown as a small hand-drawn circle. But even with his view obstructed by busy, milling people, he knew these markings meant something entirely different.

Pondarro guided him to a stranger and introduced Mayor Sairtoka. Devron blinked. "What has become of Mayor Varch?"

Sairtoka tightened her lips in the grimace that replaced smiles now. "The late Mayor Varch went to the guild assembly in LourEstelle. Many mayors and chiefs did so."

Devron closed his eyes. The utter stupidity! Frustration forced a breath between his teeth. "Why?"

He hadn't meant to utter it aloud, but the mayor took it as a literal question and answered with brittle irony. "To demonstrate to everyone that LourEstelle was safe."

He wanted to be sick—an unwelcome phantom of yesterday. "Please remember I'm from Jourendia. We must have felt the collapse with less precision than you did here. All I know is that the area of LourEstelle was affected. Not specific locations within it. Can you tell me where...whether there is any chance that..." His throat locked up.

Pondarro rubbed tired eyes, his words falling harshly flat. "I won't stretch this out. They were all to meet in Government House. The primary cavern was hit in the first collapse and again in the fourth. We don't believe survival was possible." He cleared his throat. "Chief Former Alverlee was your brother, wasn't he?"

Devron could only nod, barely hearing the condolences they both murmured.

Pondarro gripped Devron's arm, perhaps as brief comfort, but also to nudge him toward the map wall. He named the other caverns that had collapsed, and when they neared the wall, pointed to them. All circled in dark red—the color of shed blood.

Devron's niece, Charodee, and her family had lived in one of them. Another was home to most of Crilla's family. Gone forever.

"The red areas are all unstable rubble now." Pondarro still spoke in a monotone. "The orange were damaged but may hold survivors. We are trying to determine how we can safely reach them. Brown indicates abandoned areas, but the survivors have already escaped—may even return someday. Unmarked means we don't know yet."

Someone knelt on one knee, coloring green around Jourendia. Mayor Sairtoka gestured toward it. "We are using green—the color of life—to show the many areas that are confirmed safe. Also, the Keepers of the Writ, being excellent scribes, have offered to record every known survivor as they arrive and to produce updated copies of the official record. A full copy will be given to you when you return to Jourendia. We hope it will ease at least some troubled hearts."

Devron swallowed. "It's a relief to see the…the order here and the efforts to give aid." He spread his hand toward the map. "The majority of green is a comforting reminder that all is not lost. But that orange leading toward the access avenue…and the bare area beyond it. Do you…" He turned toward the new chief former and lowered his voice at the sight of the man's burdened frown. "How likely do you think it is that a passage remains?" Pondarro was already shaking his head, and Devron added, "Or that it can be re-opened?"

"We haven't colored it yet because, well, a couple reasons. The two primary portal caverns and the avenue between collapsed. We don't know about the tunnel portion beyond, but the aftershocks may have caused rockslides down Mount Estelle. The string of small caverns carved along the inner avenue…" Pondarro shrugged. "We suspect some are lost but don't know how many."

"But it *must* be opened," Devron whispered.

"Yes." Certainty infused the mayor's voice. "And it will be—when the time is right. That is why it is not colored as though it were fully blocked. But tell me, was it hard on the formers in Jourendia when the rock shifted?"

His mind darted back from her subject change. Had she just implied that the access avenue was labeled amiss—the way they wanted it to be instead of the way it was? But her brow was still lifted over her last question. "Uh, yes, though I imagine trivial compared to here. But is it possible—"

"It might seem trivial to you, but the leading doctors wish to understand this phenomenon better. What symptoms did you experience at that distance?"

An irritating distraction. Perhaps best to answer so he could return to important matters. "Some couldn't stand, nausea, shaking, we couldn't hear for several minutes. The pressure was…was awful!" Devron couldn't help a commiserating look toward Pondarro.

He shuddered. "No word will ever describe that force! I sure hope the memory loses its edge. We dropped under it, too, and didn't recover hearing for hours. At least, that's how it was for the few I was with."

"The formers of Jourendia were all together, meeting with the city council."

"I didn't realize you had a government hall yet," Sairtoka said.

"We don't. We just gather in the open cavern where we've leveled the town square and set foundations."

Her voice sharpened. "You haven't been cutting rock, have you?"

Here too? "Not since that thickening event," he assured her. "But—"

She pressed a hand to her heart. "A relief that you have good sense."

He nearly snapped hasty words that it was *not* good sense, but she kept talking.

"I didn't mean to imply otherwise, of course, but Alluthin keeps insisting on continuing everything as usual. The dissension they create is just unthinkable—and at this of all times. One would suspect they don't know people have died. Or that more will die if they cause a shift."

Someone hastened to the mayor with news of another arrival, and both she and Pondarro left Devron alone with gaping unanswered questions. He studied the map, spatially correlating to his memory of the collapses. Second nature to a former, but it was hard to concentrate. Was *he* the one who was messed up? The one who was seeing this all wrong? Maybe he could find someone else to talk with. Get another perspective.

He did find a status center, housing information, a donation repository, a huge message board for people who were searching for family, and sundry attempts to address needs. But most people hurried this way and that, too distracted to converse. Those who stood wringing their hands would not be able to help him—or he, them. At least he was able to find a room to spend the night in, post a note so Bekta could find him, and figure out when and where the local Formers' Guild met each morning.

Though his hope dragged on the ground, Devron joined the crowd around the lists of survivors from LourEstelle. Few words twined through the incessant coughing and throat-clearing. He inadvertently jostled a shoulder, which released a cloud of dust, and when he begged pardon, the man neither uttered a sound nor glanced his way. As though a dead man had crawled from dusty burial to search for the living. Worse, Devron found no name he recognized. No comfort to take home.

He must get out of this hall. The crowd choked him with an uncanny feeling of isolation. Why had he deemed this an orderly response to tragedy? He looked back from the broad doorway. Action was all on the surface. People hurrying about to do things, but what? Perhaps the market would give him clearer insight.

That, it did. Bare food stalls stood layered with dust. Others were scantily stocked with aboveground products at exorbitant prices. The only former that he saw doing actual work was fashioning a lock on someone's door—paid in advance with food, rather than money.

Mayor Sairtoka's confidence was not shared. Would tomorrow's guild meeting provide any answers or direction?

CHAPTER II

Devron arrived early for the meeting of Crysalan's Formers' Guild. He meandered through the cavern that had been designated solely for their use. A small one, but still! Ample space for training, material storage, and a broad assembly area with an odd assortment of chairs and stools. The previous chief former must have had no taste for beauty. The only adornment was practical—white quartz reached about ten feet up the walls. The heights lay in shadow, dotted with light shafts. Considering how many there were, the cavern should be brighter.

Devron mingled among the other early arrivers. Conversation revolved around personal experiences during the collapse. Not useful for the future, but he couldn't blame them. Maybe they still needed to talk it through. He wouldn't have minded the repetition if the blocked access avenue wasn't so critical. Dozens of other needs must also be pressing. Wasn't that why they'd assembled? Perhaps once the meeting officially began.

He moved on, found himself in deeper shadow, and stepped back to determine what caused it. Ah. The nearest light shaft was riddled with hair-line cracks, absorbing rather than reflecting. This cavern lay closer to LourEstelle and must have been affected by the pressure. A quick sweep to sense the other shafts revealed the same problem. Devron began polishing, ridding the luminary of its imperfections. This was his comfort, far more than words. A small solution to a small problem, but at least it was a solution.

"What are you doing?"

The demand made Devron jump and turn to the man glowering at him. Such ire from the non-gifted would have been no surprise, but this fellow was a former. "I'm just repairing one of the light shafts. I'm a polisher—"

"Well, stop! No forming has been approved yet."

"But..." Devron paused as several pairs of eyes skewered him. "Surely everyone here knows that polishing a shaft does not shift *anything* adjacent."

"Makes no difference," the man snapped. "If people start rationalizing their own decisions, we'll have everyone doing whatever they please. Pure chaos! Either stop or I'll report you!"

Devron stared, speechless.

"Calm down," another said. "Can't you tell that he already has stopped? Courtesy is still in order, even in trying times."

The accuser turned his back, sparing Devron from deciphering whatever nasty words he grumbled. Just as well, for Devron longed to defend common sense. By the looks others gave him, they all would have ganged up against him.

A young man quietly stepped near. "Don't take it personally. They're just scared. Can't blame 'em. Give it a couple weeks from the last aftershock, and everything will go back to normal."

Would it? "I suppose so," Devron muttered. Then, Mayor Sairtoka entered with Chief Former Pondarro, and they stepped onto a platform to lead the discussion. Devron's hopes rose and ebbed time and again. Much talk, planning, and assignments pertaining to the LourEstelle settlements where survivors were still possible. Clearly, they intended to recruit everyone present.

Pondarro soon called Devron's name and asked, "Do you have a specialty?"

"I'm a polisher."

"Ah, no need of that. When you report back to Jourendia, tell them we need all the formers they can spare." He didn't even wait for acknowledgment before moving on to another.

Idiots! Let them all sit in the dark and walk beside bent rails. They probably couldn't even repair the magnery copper lines. He fumed through the proceedings, for he couldn't leave until they discussed the access avenue. At least for that work, he could understand their preference for heavy moving and melding skills.

The room grew ever more crowded, with many more standing than sitting. Devron edged along the wall toward one of the exits so he could leave without fuss when he learned what he came for. The late arrivers were clearer to him now. Non-formers—probably here to glean news or plead for help. Hopefully not to rant, but he knew well that a single word could set them off.

When the mayor and chief former could no longer talk of LourEstelle's environs, the mayor tried to adjourn the meeting. Big mistake.

Voices rose with the words *access avenue* predominating.

Pondarro raised both hands. "Hear me." He waited a moment for relative silence. "We would like nothing better than to give you certain news of that important tunnel. We have a special team working diligently there. As soon as we determine facts, we post them in Government Hall. If any formers with long range particularly wish to be assigned to the access avenue, come and talk to me after we adjourn."

Clamor arose. The non-gifted shouted of all the products from aboveground that the people of Dirklan could not do without.

The mayor acknowledged each need for several minutes, then called for quiet. "You are all correct that we have need of trade with the rest of Welcia. That is why we are working diligently on the access avenue."

A new voice—silken yet commanding—rode a sudden breeze across the cavern. Wandermae. "What was the most important commodity to come through the access avenue from aboveground?"

The mayor's eyes half closed. "Stop stirring the dust, please. Food, of course. We all know that."

"No." Wandermae parted the crowd somehow and stepped onto the platform. "Not food. Not at all."

An earnest woman called out from the side. "Our families. Our friends. The rest of *us*."

Wandermae nodded in the woman's direction. "I'm glad some of you still have hearts with your minds, but even our loved ones are not the most critical need." She took a broad stance and lifted empty hands as though she held something. "It was...*air!*" A rushing current whooshed around the rugged angles of the cavern roof.

A former near the platform sneered. "If only you had a *mind* to go with your *heart*. We still have plenty of air. That is the one thing that we are *not* short of."

"I expected such nonsense," Wandermae said, "because no one but a wind weaver can tell the difference in the air. It must flow. It must be fresh. Overused air will weaken your muscles." She angled a snide look to the man who had taunted her. "Even your illustrious mind will not function without rich air."

"Oddly enough, it continues to function despite the collapse."

She smirked. "Yes, functioning as much as it ever does. But only for a while yet." She paced slowly across the platform before her audience. "You won't notice the change. It will take many days and come so gradually that you will think all is the same. You'll just feel drowsy and rest more often. Your head will ache, and you won't remember what you were thinking of a moment past. Until you lie down in a stupor for the last time."

Murmurs swarmed through the crowd. The former at the front must have been about to speak, for the mayor pointed at him. "You've had your turn. Be silent." She addressed Wandermae with a tight smile. "You say it will take time for the air to, uh, thin or whatever. That is good news. We shall keep the need in mind as we work on the access avenue."

"I have been there." Wandermae faced the mayor. "I understand the need to search for survivors. I even commend your efforts." The sweep of her hand included the formers, though she still faced Mayor Sairtoka. "But I have tried to pull air from aboveground through the rubble."

The mayor clenched her front teeth. "You spread more dust through our tunnels?"

"No. I could not pull the air through. Do not think that your work on the avenue will answer this need in time."

"I will not permit you to spread panic."

"No panic is needed, Mayor." Wandermae kept respect in her tone, likely an extreme challenge for her. "Small channels can meet the need if I can find enough of them. I ask that you assign a former to assist me." She raised her voice to surmount the rising din from the crowd. "With my skill to find air channels and a former's skill to widen or angle them as needed, we can restore the flow of fresh air to Dirklan."

The mayor began calling for quiet, but only those nearest seemed to hear—until Wandermae used her gifting to amplify the mayor's words. In the sudden silence, the mayor stared at Wandermae, who inclined her head. "At your service, Mayor."

Would the mayor complain about dust again or make use of the opportunity? She took her time, then cleared her throat. "No former is permitted to move any rock without a thorough assessment. Until we are certain that the restriction may be...eased...we cannot assign a former to do the work you suggest. When we have had a couple weeks without aftershocks, we will reconsider your concern."

"This is no assurance at all that you will ever heed me," Wandermae said. "I do not yet know where I will find channels or how new pathways may affect the flow of air through Dirklan. I need to get started now, for the weakening I described *will* occur."

"By your own words, it is not imminent. We have greater needs at this moment. Should we find that your rather odd prediction is coming true, we will provide as many formers as required."

"When we are all too weak to act?" Wandermae's black locks swayed as she shook her head. "By the time you have proof of the disaster you inflict upon yourselves, I'll be suffocating along with the rest of you. All because you refuse to honor a gift you don't understand."

"Oh, it's about your honor, after all!"

"No! Honor the *gift*." Wandermae shifted her focus to the chief former as the mayor continued to sneer. "Let me use my wind weaving on your behalf. *With* you!"

"All in due time," Pondarro responded coldly. "We heard your request."

Wandermae's restraint fled. She swung toward the exit, but the crowd had filled in, blocking her upon the platform. "Let me pass!" Before any could move, she extended a hand like a knife. A hiss of wind spiked forth. The crowd split where she drove the gust. Dust swirled up the walls as people stumbled out of her way.

Wandermae's flying steps carried her to the archway as the mayor snapped an order. "Wandermae! Settle the dust!"

She spun to face the mayor. "What is this demand? I am a wind weaver. Dust is of solid matter. It only follows the wind because the formers do not restrain it. Bid *them* to settle it. Surely formers can solve all problems." Then, she flitted through the exit.

Devron ignored the uproar, quickly hushed when the mayor again adjourned the meeting with great finality. The non-gifted left, and formers with immediate assignments soon followed. A few remained, unknown to him. He stood alone again with his own thoughts. Troubling—every one of them.

Wandermae's parting jab piqued his curiosity, and he commanded the dust around him to the floor. Naturally, it obeyed. Pointless, for every movement stirred it again. What a pity Wandermae ended her efforts with anger. Only that would be remembered. Even the formers seemed not to notice the devastating news she'd conveyed. Did they not hear that the access avenue was blocked? Or did they choose not to hear it?

"Ahem."

Devron lifted his head. The young former who'd approached him earlier had returned. Devron quirked a corner of his mouth. "It's oddly pleasing to hear a throat clearing that is not prompted by dust."

The man grinned. "Like you, I bade the dust settle. My name is Greehan." Gold flecked his brown eyes, giving them a liveliness at odds with his calm demeanor.

"I'm Devron of Jourendia. Are you a polisher too?"

"Yes, the lowly sort of former." The twist of his lips showed wry humor rather than inferiority. "For the time being."

"You may find it gets rather tiresome as the years pass."

He rubbed his fair jawline. "So does eternal youth. Yes, I really do shave. I'm thirty-one."

"Ah!" Devron looked closer. Greehan had the sort of lips that shifted color easily, rather pink at the moment. "Perhaps you should cultivate a few wrinkles."

Greehan chuckled more than the quip deserved. "Thank you! I guess I was desperate for a laugh."

"Aren't we all!"

"What thought you of Wandermae's...revelation?"

Devron's voice dipped. "Most disturbing."

"You think she is correct, then?"

"She's often criticized, but never for lying. If Wandermae cannot draw air through the access tunnel, then it is solidly blocked."

A ripple formed between Greehan's eyebrows. "I meant about the air going bad."

Devron grunted. "If a wind weaver knows the tunnel is solidly blocked, so too, should every former who has been anywhere near it. Yet the chief former and mayor do not acknowledge that fact. Or the fact that we cannot get aboveground without full-scale tunneling. Which is not an option for quite some time. No trade. No contact."

"Then...you don't think air is the most significant problem?"

"Air is a bigger problem than food, but not as bad as leaders who lie. As long as they hide the true problem, we cannot explore other solutions. Today, they even forbade searching for *air*." Devron frowned deeper. "In fact...if they give credence to her claim, they must admit that the access avenue cannot be opened."

Greehan blew through pursed lips, now a shade darker. "I hope you don't mind if I search for holes in your reasoning."

"I hope you prove me wrong!"

"I suppose I must first check the access avenue myself. They won't assign me there, so I'll have to make up some excuse."

"Don't bother. A friend of mine, Bekta, is there now. I expect her back, hopefully, today. She has excellent range and will not lie to me."

"Hm. That will confirm the avenue's true condition. Once she reports to Pondarro, we'll know whether he is...revealing what he learns. That doesn't necessarily prove intent to lie. He could be having trouble accepting it."

Devron shrugged away that excuse. "In a leader, lying to oneself is as bad as lying to others. In either case, sensible action cannot be taken because the true problem is obscured. I gather that most formers here deem obedience to authority—even usurped authority—more important than truth. Am I correct?"

"I...imagine so. Not that I've asked. Authority and truth don't normally conflict."

"Would it damage your future if you did ask?"

It took Greehan too long to answer. "Probably."

"Then, I would say that truth is going to need a strong champion indeed."

Greehan stared at Devron. "All I wanted was to hear your thoughts on air. If only Wandermae wasn't so unbelievably arrogant!"

The normal criticism, but— "Is she?" Devron murmured.

Greehan widened his eyes. "Even if you've never heard her poison tongue before, you heard her today. Didn't she ruin her own chance?"

"What I heard is this," Devron said. "The chief wind weaver of all Dirklan made a request of the local chief former. She outranks him and could have demanded a former to work with her. But she *requested*. As for the mayor, eh, a different chain of authority, but she ought to help the gifted chiefs work together. They both disdained Wandermae's rank. So, who is really arrogant? Wouldn't we criticize her more if she had demanded? Would the outcome have been any different?"

"Never in my life have I heard a former stand up for Wandermae."

"Nor have I ever done so." Devron squirmed at an odd sensation of fault. "Outside of formal presentation, I don't think I've ever heard her addressed by her title."

Greehan blew out another breath. "Point taken, but you still haven't told me whether you believe our air is at risk."

"Only a wind weaver knows. Why are you asking me?"

"I heard that you are wise."

"Really? A minority opinion, I assure you."

"Why do you say that?"

"*Very* few listen to me." Devron straightened from leaning against the wall. "If we can meet up when Bekta returns, you are welcome to join us."

"I would like nothing more!"

Devron told Greehan where he was lodging, then left the guild's cavern. He needed to walk—to think. Why were the locals so dismissive of an obvious and crucial fact? Was he the one who saw it all wrong? An assessment did require agreement from two gifted, after all. He should wait for Bekta's report, but he was nearly certain she would declare the avenue impassable. He'd better have an idea of what he should do next. Where could one find sound counsel when everyone was grieving, lying, or contentious? Or all three?

His route took him past the sacred chamber, and he entered. If ever he needed a vision, now was the time. He passed through the broad arched tunnels into the chamber that had been crowded only a week ago. Wait—wasn't it Savoring Day? Of course. If they had held the normal service, it was over now. Some lingered, either alone or in small groups scattered around the chamber. Mourners, perhaps. Keepers of the Writ attended them. It was their duty, after all, to offer comfort or to advise the troubled from the words of the Holy Writ. What did they say now? Pay no attention to the vision wall?

Devron crimped his lips. Not much point in coming here if he indulged bitterness. Besides, he just wanted to sit alone in a peaceful place so he could reason through this puzzle. Air really was the biggest practical concern. If Wandermae was right...

Why bother with the *if?* The other wind weavers in Dirklan considered her gift and skill extraordinary. If the local formers wouldn't help her...another *if* that was not in doubt. They wouldn't. What should he do about it? No one here would listen to him. He didn't answer to them, but he had no right to alter anything outside of Jourendia and its tunnel. Could the work she requested be done without revealing it? His skin crawled.

Significant unapproved alterations could get a former sent to the king's court for judgment. Not that anyone could be sent up to Regissa with the access avenue blocked. Whatever might happen instead—yi! Worse, using your gift to harm others was the one sure way of losing it. If he made a mistake with an unassessed alteration... Devron shuddered. Hard to tell what would crush his heart worse—killing people or living without his gift. Better to die from his own mistake.

This was not helping. He looked up from his hands hanging limp between his knees to the golden wall. Lovely as ever, but no vision. Oddly, he found his mind filled with the image he'd seen while crafting the music disc. Useless for music, but now he recognized it as an early version of the design he'd seen in the vision wall.

It seemed that a voice whispered within. *You don't need this wall to see.*

He almost hmphed aloud. *What good is it to see when the device would flood Jourendia?*

In his mind's eye, he saw again. Two curved panels emerged from stone. They met, locking in place. Gears...chains... This, at least, he understood. A gate or perhaps an entrance to a grand hall. What about a groove in the floor and ceiling to guide and support? Multiple variations were possible. The curve wasn't necessary, but it might be aesthetically pleasing in some applications. He loved this stage of inventing almost as much as creating and polishing!

Footsteps approached, damping his sudden excitement. Where had it sprung from when he'd been so troubled? His spirits plummeted again, leaving a sharp pain that made him wish they hadn't lifted at all.

A man angled a chair from the row and sat down facing Devron. A Keeper of the Writ, according to the thin strip of green fabric looped around his neck. The ends were anchored with a golden pin atop his right shoulder. Gold to represent Ellincreo's words, which they were sworn to protect and copy with faithful precision. Many of them had great portions of it memorized, able to offer its counsel at a moment's notice. "May I be of any assistance to you in this trying time?"

"Not likely." The words came out harsher than Devron intended.

The corners of the keeper's mouth dipped. He inclined his head. "I don't blame you. I recall that you were here on Gifting Day—with Chief Former Alverlee, I believe."

"Yes. My brother. Who is now dead."

"So, too, is the Chief Keeper of the Writ, who gave such poor advice that day. His judgment now rests in the hands of Ellincreo."

Devron hoped his judgment would be harsh...until he remembered that Alverlee agreed with the misguided Chief Keeper. And he could not wish ill upon his brother. It took supreme effort, but he pronounced the traditional words. "May they both rest in Ellincreo's abundant mercy."

"Indeed." The man shifted in his chair. "Did you know the Chief Keeper very well?"

"No."

"He was like all the rest of us. Partly admirable, partly flawed."

Devron got the message, but forgiving the dead was more than he could deal with right now. Especially with the way the living behaved these days. A nod would have to suffice.

The keeper let a moment pass in silence, then said, "You are the first former to come here today."

Odd remark. "The formers meet daily at this time...in the morning."

"Yes, I know. Understandable. The couple I just spoke with were at the end of the formers' meeting, so I have heard that Wandermae is stirring up fear and dissension."

"Is that how they phrased it?"

"Not exactly, but her words did produce fear. What else could be expected when she predicts that everyone will suffocate?"

"What would happen," Devron asked, "if I repeated her with the honor due to the chief gifted of Dirklan?" The keeper's brow rose at the rhetorical question. "The Chief Wind Weaver of Dirklan explained a risk and a solution. She offered to solve the problem with the help of Crysalan's Chief Former. She made a respectful request and was disregarded."

The keeper grunted. "Since she coupled it with the threat of suffocation, it caused fear at a time when people need reassurance."

"Threat?" Devron huffed. "She neither caused it nor threatens to cause it. She explained the current state and the ramifications, based on the knowledge inherent in her gift. Just because she is not well-received, does not mean that she is incorrect. She wants to solve the problem, which cannot be done unless the true situation is first acknowledged."

"You don't understand what fear does to people."

"Oh, I think I do. But you cannot overcome fear by hiding facts. Sooner or later, it will become known that the access avenue is irreparably blocked."

The keeper's eyebrows dipped along with his voice. "Are you sure of that?"

"Not yet, but—"

"Then do not say it."

Devron slowed his firm words. "If you placate fear with false promises, the problem will only get worse. True solutions need to be pursued, not fake ones that do more harm than good."

"Doubtless, but should we listen to those in authority, or to a known troublemaker? Or even to a lone former who may have good intentions but does not know the local environs?"

Why was he wasting his time? Devron stood. "Doesn't the Writ tell you to pursue truth? You needn't worry about the lone former from distant Jourendia. I will leave Crysalan as soon as I hear from the one person who will not tell me pleasing lies."

CHAPTER 12

Devron strode from the chamber...fuming again, worse than ever. *Please let Bekta be on her way back.* Maybe he could work off some steam with a walk to the central station.

It took little time to reach at his pace. He paused only to listen at the rail leading toward the access. No sound of an approaching carriage nor vibration in the rail. He had to get away and clear his head before anger led him into unwise deeds.

He headed into the residential caverns, vaguely familiar to him. Fairlynn occasionally visited old friends in Crysalan, and he'd accompanied her now and then. Traversing many streets, he found them all but empty.

A sudden voice near a fenced pond interrupted his churning thoughts. "Well met. Formers are hard to find these days."

Devron swiveled around to find the source. A woman shooed cave ducks away from the fence's gate and passed through it. They must have met at some point. He struggled to recall a name while she enquired about Fairlynn, then asked, "Would you be able to make a lock for this gate?"

For a gate meant to keep ducks from escaping? The flock must be their livelihood—and now a prime target for theft. "Do you have any scrap iron on hand?" he asked.

Her husband, listening nearby, began rummaging through a chest. A couple drakes showed off their flying ability with short flights on stubby wings—dramatic hops, really. A good thing that their antics required a tall fence. The man hurried over with an iron fire hook, a relic of the days before magnery heat replaced the need for cooking fires.

Devron took the offered iron and delved its structure. "This will work. How about an exchange for payment? A mated hen for a lock."

"A hen?" the woman squawked. "That's a steep price. Do you even know how to take care of it? I'll not have it butchered for one meal."

"No, I'll give it to Fairlynn."

"Well...she knows ducks." The woman fidgeted with her pocket-covered apron. "But it's still too steep. How about eggs, instead?" She drew one from a pocket and displayed it.

Devron released bonds in the iron and coaxed the first bend. "Is one hen really too much for the protection of your entire flock?"

The husband hemmed uncertainly. "One of the older hens could be bred. I suppose we can part with it for Fairlynn."

"As long as the duck can produce a brood, an old one is acceptable." Devron formed a lock and two keys while they asked too many questions about the state of LourEstelle and the access avenue. "I haven't been there." An inadequate response to stop questions—he'd better try something else. "You should check for updates in Government Hall." Now he felt like a liar. It was a relief to hand the lock over and arrange to collect the duck when he was ready to depart.

He strolled toward his temporary abode. Forming the lock had been a certainty whether they'd paid him or not, but a duck? An undercurrent of food worries must be driving him, too, for never in his life had he bartered for livestock. Would it be a nuisance on the trip home?

When he reached his door, Bekta and Greehan approached. She looked terrible—like she hadn't slept since he'd seen her last.

"I've been keeping an eye on the rail station," Greehan explained, "so Bekta wouldn't have to go searching inside Government Hall for how to find you."

Good thinking. Devron inclined his head. "Come inside. I have a private room." Once the three of them were behind a closed door, he asked her, "Have you reported to any formers or the mayor yet?"

She plopped into a chair by the small table. "No."

Devron sat in the other chair across from her and motioned Greehan toward the bed. "Sit if you like." Bekta's bloodshot eyes held back the most pressing questions. Instead, he asked, "Are you well?"

"Worn thin, but I'll live. Sorry it took me so long to return." She swallowed. "I found my youngest brother in one of the makeshift infirmaries. They think he'll make it, but he's still coughing up muddy phlegm. He's an adult, I guess, but not by much, and...it seems certain that our parents and middle siblings are lost. I couldn't leave him for a while."

"Understandable."

She propped her elbows on the table and pressed her eyes against the heels of her hands. Devron didn't have the heart to ask yet. After a moment, she leaned back in her chair. "I suppose you want to hear about the access avenue."

"Yes. The worst of it, please, even if you've been warned not to tell."

"Well, I have been." She threw a look toward Greehan. "I could get in loads of trouble for saying anything except to Chief Former Pondarro."

"I've already heard the truth from someone else," Greehan said. "I just want it confirmed."

"Who told you?"

"I will not reveal my sources." He added a soothing smile. "Not the first one, nor you."

Devron had best provide her grounds for defense. "Since Jourendia doesn't yet have a new chief former, consider me a proxy chief. We have as much right to know the truth as Crysalan." Would that be enough? "If you ever need to, you may say that I ordered you to tell me."

Bekta huffed a tense breath. "The short truth is that damage stretches halfway from the external arches to Crysalan. It's a cursed unstable mess. It's not safe to tunnel, and the worst of it is…" A bitter edge seeped into her voice. "They will never let us make it safe."

"What do you mean?" Devron asked.

"Some of us have ideas for stabilizing it in a way that—eventually—might let us tunnel. But they won't even consider it. The only work they will allow is to slowly shape, um, kind of random collections of honeycomb cells. As long as we can do it without shifting matter beyond each cell. And get this! They want us to reinforce the safe tunnels with arches. The very ones that withstood the shock and didn't budge. They're crazier here than they are in Jourendia. And I'm talking about *formers* here!"

"So…they're not looking for survivors, then?"

Her lips spasmed. "They tried. I did too. There is no soft matter— alive—within a reachable distance. They got a shaft into one cavern and got fifty-two people out, but there won't be more along the access avenue." She drew heavy breaths, trembling despite the tight clutch of her hands.

After a moment, Greehan asked, "The honeycomb cells you spoke of—would they let air pass through?"

"No. Wandermae was there yesterday and asked if we could do that. But they'll be sealed bubbles. Even if we could snake them long and narrow, we can't reach far enough to reshape like that all the way to the surface. And by the way, the old access arches are no longer *at* the surface. There's a vast stretch of rubble beyond. I'd bet the abovegrounders in Regissa don't even know where to start digging to find the arches. And it must be less stable out there than it is belowground."

Devron propped his elbows on the table, resting his mouth against his entwined fingers. This was every bit as bad as he'd expected. Maybe worse. The sort of support they planned to form would become unstable if disturbed. How long would it take before Pondarro or Sairtoka admitted to the locals that the avenue would never reopen? What would happen then? He suppressed a shudder. "I need to get this information home. How soon can you get your brother here?"

Bekta looked down, then met his gaze. "I'm not returning to Jourendia. I'm really sorry if you, um, if you feel you need me there, but they need me here even more."

Hard to argue, though he wanted to. "We do need your range, but I understand your decision. You will always be welcome if your situation changes."

She managed a bittersweet smile. "You'll make a good chief former, even with the range you have."

His stomach turned. Not a position he wanted, but some duties could not be avoided. Still, he could think of no answer.

Bekta stood and went to rummage in her pack. "I need to freshen up and then I'd better report to Crysalan's chief former."

"Down the hallway, second door on the left."

Greehan stood as she was leaving. "When you're ready, I'll escort you to Government Hall and help you find Pondarro if necessary." He closed the door behind her and joined Devron at the table. "That is worse news than we expected."

"Yes, it is."

"Are you really about to become the chief former of Jourendia?"

"Either me or Alverlee's son, Kevenor. He's rather young for the job. Er, twenty-seven, if I remember right, which is old enough, but he's...used to relying on his father's judgment instead of his own."

"Mm. I was going to ask you—that is, I went to see Wandermae."

Devron straightened. "How did that go?"

"It took a little while to convince her I was in earnest, but I got her to explain what she needs to find and what might be required to create good airflow. And, by the way, once she believed I was listening, she really isn't so unpleasant."

"Might be enjoyable to her—being heard for a change."

"Probably. Have you ever seen her home?" When Devron shook his head, Greehan continued. "If you ever go there, be ready for stairs. It was excavated into the cavern wall above the level of the rooftops. The doves fly right into her hands, and she's trained them not to foul her balcony. Who knew that was possible? She doesn't even have a garden, beyond some vine fruit. Did you know that the king paid her salary?"

"I suppose. Her rank is equal to Dirklan's Chief Former and Chief Streamer." Worrisome. Even though Dirklan was a domain rather than a province, the throne provided for the three substance guild chiefs. That would be impossible now. Yet another problem that was beyond Devron. He shook his head and returned to the moment. "What did you want to ask me?"

"Whether you might help her form wind tunnels."

"Me?"

"Certainly. It's polisher work, not heavy movement. You don't answer to Pondarro, and he already expects you to leave. No one in Jourendia can forbid it, either, because they haven't heard her request."

Tempting, for a few seconds, but there were too many other things he couldn't neglect. Duty...a vision...Fairlynn. "I cannot forsake Jourendia."

"Will you let Wandermae work there?"

"If she needs to, but we have an ocean breeze, so other areas will need her more than we do. Is your range adequate for the task?"

"It's considerable, despite everyone assuming a polisher has little sense for distance."

"Why don't *you* help her?"

"I'm way down the pile in Crysalan. No authority, even if forming was allowed."

"You need to get past the authority snag. No one will grant permission. If you are convinced that most of Dirklan will suffocate, then you will have to act without approvals."

Greehan licked his darkening lips. "No validating assessments? You realize what would happen if I'm wrong? I could lose my gift. Have you ever thought of that?"

Devron shuddered. "Hard to imagine, but devastating, I'm sure. But what is a gift for, after all? If we do not use it, maybe it is already lost by our own choice."

Greehan lowered his forehead to rest on stiff fingers.

Devron wanted to insist. Unfair, considering the burden. "Please don't think I'm pressuring you one way or the other. Only you can make this decision within your own heart."

D evron—and his duck—were the only occupants of his carriage. That allowed him to stop and buy Fairlynn's favorite products at the inn where they had stayed, now filled with refugees from the collapse. The owner asked for payment in food, but he did accept coins when that was all Devron could offer. Had it been safe to leave his belongings unattended at the station? He hurried back to the carriage where, thankfully, the duck still waited, asleep in its crate beneath a cloth.

With a nudge from the boost wheel, he started out again, and the burro kept the carriage moving along the slick rail. He let it slow near the crystal veins so he could do a little work as they passed. No point in making the creature stop and restart, for Devron was anxious to reach home. Today, he was the official messenger, but in days to come, more word would flow from Crysalan. He needed to get the truth heard and wise decisions made before conflicting voices bred confusion.

Someone must have been listening at the rail, for Mayor Borchel and Kevenor awaited him. A crowd was gathering so fast that they jostled the terminal worker who tried to take charge of the burro and carriage.

This was not the time, place, or the right people. Devron kept his remarks to the hearing of those nearest. "I have a mail pouch and some packages that can be distributed as usual. As for the rest of my news, please assemble the substance and craft guild chiefs. I realize everyone will want to hear, but..." He made firm eye contact with Borchel and stressed his final words. "There is a lot to cover, so this will need to be an organized meeting. Shall we say in half an hour?"

"Understood." Mayor Borchel turned and began bellowing instructions.

The rail's platform gave Devron enough height to see that Fairlynn was approaching along the avenue behind those who could move faster. He nodded to her, then grabbed his things out of the carriage.

At Kevenor's offer of help, he handed over his travel bag, and they pushed through the crowd. "I realize why you want to wait," Kevenor whispered, "but allow me one question. What happened to the chief formers?"

"A son has every right to ask, Kevenor. The Formers' Guild assembly—which Alverlee attended, along with many other chiefs and mayors—was held in Government House. A foolish choice of location, deep within LourEstelle. They are all lost." Devron paused, for Kevenor had turned aside, rubbing his brow. "I'm sorry to be so blunt."

Fairlynn strode near and flicked her gaze between Devron and Kevenor. "Is all hope lost for Alverlee?" she asked. "Quickly, please, without condolence."

"He is gone, Fairlynn."

The mayor drew Kevenor away, leaving Devron and Fairlynn alone. He absorbed the calm of her deep slate eyes.

She simply nodded. "Let me take the food basket. It looks like mine, anyway."

He handed it to her and shouldered the travel bag Kevenor had left at his feet. "It is. So are the soaps and lotions inside. I stopped at your favorite spa."

She lifted the lid as she fell into step beside him. "Oh, how sweet of you."

"I bought a brooding duck, too." He raised the crate.

"A duck?" She peeked under the cloth and half laughed. "What possessed you?"

"There will be food shortages," he whispered. "Has that occurred to anyone here yet?"

"No." The way she drew that out...she must be thinking beyond it, but she closed her lips.

To avoid questions in the street, he told her how he came by the duck and offered it to her.

"If I take it home, it will become Crilla's duck." Fairlynn glanced at him. "Don't worry. I'll help you make a brooding pen in your roof garden."

"All those stairs?" He opened his door, and she entered with him.

"As though you won't give me your arm. For now, put her crate on the roof, so she can start getting used to her new home." Fairlynn uncovered the crate and looked through the slats at the white-speckled gray duck. "Refill her water dish but leave her inside the crate."

Devron followed her instructions, then came back down from the roof. He found Fairlynn in his kitchen, wrapping some cold meat and lettuce in a circle of flatbread. "Is that bird going to destroy my garden?" he asked.

"Only if you let her. I'll help you with feed, and you can make a fence." She handed the rolled snack to him. "What did you mean about food shortages?"

"The access avenue is blocked and cannot be reopened. All trade with Welcia has ended. They're hiding that fact in Crysalan, which is foolish."

Tiny wrinkles beside her eyes deepened. "At least, the harvest has been delivered."

He finished chewing a bite. "Yes. That will let us survive for some months while we learn to grow adequate food. Alluthin might be close to self-sufficiency. That means Jourendia should be able to feed itself too."

"They already have a lot of soil," Fairlynn murmured. "We don't. Nor as much light beyond the settlement either."

"True. What do you do with the guano in the duck ponds?"

"Most, we flush away. Geon takes some of it. I suppose he mixes it with used soil, but it's harsh. I would think we still need a base of good soil—a lot more than we have."

"I don't know, but Geon probably does. If not, he could try different mixtures. He once advised me to add ground oyster shells when I used too much dung in my garden. We can't over-harvest, though. The rail tunnel is due for cleaning, so there is burro dung."

Fairlynn wedged a fingernail against her teeth, while Devron consumed the snack she'd made. "This will change everything."

"It certainly will. I'm not going into all of it during this first meeting, but our economy is devastated, and the top half of our government has been sliced off. If panic sets in, we are going to fall into terrible chaos." Devron took the final bite and reached for a glass of water.

"What of Bekta?"

"She's not returning. Only her youngest brother survived, and he's not in great shape. Besides, her skills are needed there more than here."

Fairlynn nodded. "Somewhat expected. You and Kevenor are the other two candidates for chief former. He's twisting himself through contortions to please everyone. If he is chosen, I will scream."

Devron smiled despite everything. "Don't let Crilla hear your scream. We'd better get going."

Now, to see if he was a good enough leader to keep chaos from erupting.

CHAPTER 13

Devron joined Mayor Borchel on the platform in the town square. Bare foundations surrounding the square showed how grandiose their plans had been. Only one foundation supported walls a few feet high—a government hall bigger than Crysalan's. Now desolate, with all work stopped. A ghost town of aborted dreams.

People still hurried up the avenue from the settlement, but the council members and most of the formers and streamers already clustered near. Fairlynn stood next to Chief Streamer Fezlie, and Kevenor was so close to the platform that his knee must be touching a front corner. The small audience that Devron would have preferred was not to be.

The mayor called for silence, then addressed the crowd. "First of all, Devron will tell us what he learned at Crysalan. Then we will choose a new chief former."

Odd. The new chief was the purview of the Formers' Guild. They held their meetings in the settlement's little hall. What did the mayor—

Borchel turned to him. "Please share your news."

Devron looked over the hushed crowd. The strain in their faces seemed to thicken the air. A good thing he had prepared opening remarks. "Many of my words will be hard to hear. But take heart, because I will also share hope and solutions. Decide right now that you will give no place to fear." It was impossible to read any reaction from their rigid faces. "The first part is not news, but confirmation that much of LourEstelle has collapsed. Government House of Dirklan is lost, along with much of the leadership of the Formers' Guild. Many chiefs and mayors from other cities and settlements had also chosen to attend the guild's assembly."

A long groan emanated from the crowd, as though it possessed a single voice.

He must keep going—speak louder than despair. "However, some fringe caverns withstood the quake. Detailed records are being compiled, and I have brought copies of everything known so far." He held up the tubes of rolled lists that Crysalan's Keepers of the Writ had provided. "These contain the names of people whose survival is confirmed. Some are known to have left Dirklan before the collapse. Some escaped damaged areas and have now made their way to Crysalan. There is another list of every cavern of Dirklan. It states whether the cavern is entirely destroyed, damaged, or confirmed safe." He slowed to emphasize his next words. "I encourage you to remember that the majority of Dirklan is *unharmed* and *safe*. It is the hope of the keepers who labor to compile these lists, that we may find some relief amidst sorrow."

A bit of a clamor began, so Devron turned to Mayor Borchel. "I ask you to see these safely posted behind glass, where everyone will have a chance to read them." Devron passed the tubes to the mayor and murmured, "Quiet them, please. I must speak more."

The mayor's voice boomed with a promise of quick posting and a demand for silence.

Devron steadied himself. "Before we speak of solutions, I must now share the worst of the news." Oh, he didn't want to say this! "The access avenue is completely blocked and cannot be reopened."

The crowd gasped as one. Eyes widened, and mouths gaped. He'd expected more hubbub. Instead, ominous silence whispered through the cavern like a breathy beast. It seemed harder to speak over the hush than the noise.

"This has been confirmed by Bekta, who went all the way to the blockage of the tunnel and returned to report the truth to me. Half the tunnel, the access arches, and indeed, far beyond is now unstable rubble that cannot be tunneled through. I emphasize this because the cavern list, which you will soon read, contains one lie. It purports that the access avenue's status is unknown."

"But why?" a council member asked, his tone a desperate plea.

"Crysalan has a new mayor, Sairtoka, and new chief former, Pondarro. They fear panic and are still hiding the truth. I believe this is a mistake because our lives depend on immediate action." Mumbles from the crowd grew, so he spoke louder. "Remember that Alluthin grows a great deal of food. It behooves us to do the same since we will no longer be trading aboveground. Some of us will resume our work, although perhaps in different ways, and some of us will learn new trades, but we *will* survive this calamity."

The din had grown too loud. He could no longer surmount it. Best, perhaps, to let them vent for a while. Many seemed to be grasping at the false hope inherent in the lie, insisting that a mayor and chief former would not speak falsely. Or claiming there had to be a way through but maybe in a different place. Or wailing that they would all starve.

Devron turned to the mayor. Borchel's lips opened and closed as he watched the crowd. "Please quiet them when you can," Devron asked him, "so I can get the rest of this out."

The mayor threw him a skeptical look, but he raised his hands to motion for quiet. After stressing the need for calm order, he nodded to Devron.

Holding his head high, Devron tried to imbue his words with the confidence that Alverlee's voice once carried. "Remember who we are!" He stepped forward, spreading his hands. "We are descended from miners who transformed dark caves into beautiful cities. We are renowned for our innovations. Never has a challenge stopped us. We mined far more wealth than anyone thought we could. Such abundance that animals couldn't transport it all, so we built rails and harnessed the rivers to drive trains. Then, we employed the river's power for other purposes and discovered magnery—a power still unknown aboveground. When our cities grew to thousands, fire was choking us. We solved that problem by designing a way to draw heat from magnery. Why should we wring our hands when we can put them to work? For each new problem, we find an answer. Why waste our minds in fear when we can devise solutions? Food, for instance. We have a harvest in storage. If we eat only that, it will last around four months, but if we begin growing more food immediately, it will last much longer. Those who once earned a living from trade will have time to learn cultivation—a worthy craft in its own right. Alluthin has proven that true."

Devron gestured to the vacant space. "Look at all the bare land in this cavern. We could dedicate much to gardens. We could still build slowly, and then move gardens from the cavern floor to the new rooftops."

Grumbles from the crowd exposed his mistake. He shouldn't have mentioned building, but he pressed on before they could drown him out. "Burro dung from the tunnel system is usually taken to Alluthin, but we could gather what lies between us and Crysalan. I believe oyster shells may help with soil, but there are those who know such matters better than I. Geon has always advised me, and perhaps others are also knowledgeable. I propose that we select a Chief Cultivator and start a guild with those who are skilled enough to teach others."

Disgruntled voices were rising again, but someone shouted, "This can work!"

A few joined that chorus, but before they got too loud, Devron forced out the last necessity. "While cultivators start working on soil, I will bring sunlight to the cavern."

That sparked dissent like his mention of building. The mayor stepped near and hissed, "Forming is not approved. Stop speaking of it."

"I've said everything I need to." Devron took a step back.

"Good!" Borchel managed to get the roar down to a hum and addressed the crowd. "Please calm yourselves. Forming is still forbidden. It will not recommence until it has been duly approved. Now, we—"

Geon shouted from the crowd. "We *must have* additional light. The more sunlight we have, the more food we can grow. The formers have sworn countless times that opening the light shafts is safe. Approve it now!"

That drew a hearty cheer from the formers, but Borchel spoke in his most authoritative voice. "The council will consider this request at our next meeting."

Only formers possessed the knowledge to make this decision. Devron wanted to declare that fact, but the mayor smoothed his voice into placating sentences.

"We have no issue with approving requests that enhance the safety of our caverns. Are we not considering such measures even now? We were only waiting to appoint a new chief former, which we could not do until Devron returned." The mayor summoned Kevenor with a flick of his hand. "Formers' Guild, I asked you for nominees, and Bekta was among those. Since she did not return, have you any other names to replace hers as a candidate?"

Kevenor mounted the platform and reached Devron's side in time for Devron to whisper, "What is going on? The *formers* must meet to choose."

"The mayor and council decided that the mayor has the final choice among nominees approved by the formers."

"Was I sent out of the way so he could force this folly through?"

"Please, Uncle Dev. This cannot be undone now."

"What safety measures are they considering?"

Kevenor's deep inhale and pause boded ill. "They want to wall off the lake cavern."

"Insanity!" Devron abandoned quiet. "The lake cavern is a source of food and soil products."

Enough of the crowd heard him to create another uproar. The mayor turned and glared at him. "Must you create chaos?"

Devron's jaw dropped. "I? Common sense is not chaos."

The mayor had already turned away, and it was Kevenor who whispered, "Timing and audience are crucial considerations."

Debate surged like molten iron. Fear blazed from one contingent that a quake would shatter the sea floor. Fear of hunger stoked the countering side. The mayor was hard-pressed to control this contention. He must have wanted to avoid, or at least delay, this question. Should Devron suggest that now? He clamped his lips, for he could not even hint at condoning such stupidity. He had thought to take on the leadership of Jourendia's Formers' Guild—what did a leader do with this situation?

The design he'd envisioned in the sacred chamber—sliding doors. Their curve made sense for the lake cavern. His fingers twitched to draw the plan, but chaos must be driven back first. He must speak. "Ah, I see the need now. Doors that are shaped correctly can be as strong as a wall. Two sets of doors would allow harvest *and* provide safety."

This time, the mayor's narrowed eyes fairly stabbed as they turned his way, though his face maintained mask-like calm.

Devron hurried. "Forgive me, Mayor, for bringing this up at such an inconvenient moment. The formers need time to assess the design, so perhaps we should set this matter aside for now."

"Yes. We will consider it at a future date." Maybe the mayor would forgive him. Eventually. Borchel kept a shoulder turned to Devron as he addressed the crowd. "And now, we will return to appointing the new chief former."

Many more silken words flowed from Borchel's tongue as he extolled Alverlee's past accomplishments and commended his foresight in raising a son so well-fitted to the post of chief former. A son, moreover, who would know how to make use of Devron's unique brilliance.

Eccentric was what he meant. Disparaging while calling him brilliant. Devron hated these word games.

"And thus…" The mayor left a dramatic pause. "It gives me great pleasure to announce the appointment of Alverlee's son, Kevenor, as our new chief former."

At least the overload of eloquence had given Devron advance notice of the mayor's intent. He turned to his nephew. "May I be the first to congratulate you, Chief Former Kevenor. I am sure you will fulfill your duties with skill and integrity."

Kevenor's throat convulsed with a swallow, but his voice held steady. "Thank you, Uncle Devron." His lips parted again, then closed. He stepped forward to address the crowd. Alverlee's son, in truth, using all the right words.

Devron stepped back. What would he have said? A promise to be honest with them? Likely interpreted as an accusation that others lied, which would offend. This had all happened so fast that he didn't even know if he should be disappointed or overjoyed. He just needed to get off this platform and become invisible.

The first was easy, the second much harder. Some people at the fringes looked sadly at him or tried to commiserate. A calm smile served, along with words like, "Kevenor will do well. Please give him your support, as I do."

Away from the crowd, he maintained a steady pace through the quiet settlement cavern. Finally alone in his own house, Devron collapsed onto the couch in his welcome room. He flopped his head against the depleted cushion atop the stone back and pressed his hands against his eyes. He should feel something. What? Humiliation? Anger? Relief? Yet exhaustion left him dry. Squelched emotion. That fear-driven chaos—how long had he endured it? A half-hour? More tiring than a full day of forming. His mind refused to think beyond simply existing.

Eventually, a soft tap struck the door. Should he answer?

The door opened an inch, and Fairlynn's hushed voice called, "Devron?"

The one person in Jourendia he was willing to talk with. "Come in." He achieved a smile. "And shut the door."

Devron looked as spent as he sounded. The steady ache in Fairlynn's chest intensified. She joined him on the couch, angling sideways to watch his face. "Well, I didn't scream out loud, but I'm still screaming inside. What a horrible, dreadful mistake. If it had been left to the guild, where the decision belonged, I'm sure they would have chosen you."

"Mm."

That told her nothing. "Are you disappointed, Dev?"

His frown looked more thoughtful than anything. "I don't know. I think I'm more disturbed about *how* the decision was made than by the outcome. Do you know how that came to be? Did the formers agree to let the mayor decide, or did the council somehow force it upon them?"

"I'm not sure. I wasn't there, but I know the mayor attended the last two Formers' Guild meetings. They had specified a private meeting to discuss the selection of the next chief former, but he still attended. I think I could have forgiven the mayor and council for interfering if they had made you chief former."

"That is not forgivable, no matter who he chose." Force was returning to Devron's voice. "There is a reason that the kings of Welcia keep the three substance guilds autonomous. Our duty is to steward matter for the good of all. Not to influence civil factions, and certainly not to become pawns. Is Mayor Borchel moving to take control of the streamers also?"

Only a week ago, she would have sworn that could never happen. Now? "I'll have to talk with Fezlie. Make sure that she—all of us—are prepared to resist." She knit her brow. "There doesn't seem to be grounds for him to do so. No one is heaping blame on us."

"Am I somehow blinded by being a former?" Devron asked. "Do people actually believe that we— especially Jourendian formers—caused the collapse in LourEstelle? It's just so far beyond reason."

She swayed her shoulders. "The mayor still insists that the formers are not at fault, but as soon as formers seek to shift the tiniest rock, the uproar begins. The mayor forbids work to quiet the chaos."

"Then, the root cause is fear, which is overriding reason. That means the Streamers' Guild could also lose autonomy. Fear makes people grasp control to gain a sense of safety. But control doesn't protect them, so fear remains. Tightens its grip all the more, making people clutch for ever greater control." He shook his head through a long sigh. "All I can think of is to offer rational explanations." He grimaced. "And hope people listen better than they have for the past week."

Not likely. She pressed her fingers flat against her thighs to halt their fidgeting. "A theory is bouncing between tongues that Jourendia was spared from collapse because all work was stopped after the thickening."

Had she ever seen such worry on Devron's face? He rubbed his brow. "It's like they are grabbing any random fact to support the lie they believe."

"I've tried to figure how this all got so out of control." Still, it mystified her. "Little decisions that seemed right have clumped together all wrong. Even Alverlee fed it. He knew there was no cause to stop work, but he went along with it to placate people. When they said that proved the danger was real, he claimed he was complying with the mayor's authority. That was the first nudge toward surrendering the guild to the mayor's control. It's no surprise that Kevenor was chosen. He bends to the mayor even more than Alverlee did." She hadn't meant it to, but her tone had soured.

"Oh, Fairlynn." Devron gripped her hand. "You don't need to lay the blame on Alverlee. Grief is painful enough without that too."

Her lungs demanded great draughts of air. It was so hard to keep the breaths silent. To hide the true anguish. Her temples throbbed.

Devron gently gripped her arms. "I am so sorry I couldn't bring you better news...relieve your pain."

"Oh, Dev, I feel like I'm going to explode." Her voice rasped, but she couldn't help it. "Everyone talks of my loss—they think only of mourning." Her fingernails bit into her palms. "But I am so, *so* angry!"

Devron's mouth gaped.

At least he didn't say anything, because she couldn't bear to hear the condemnation she felt. "I begged him not to go, Dev. All those visions..." She shook her head. "He claimed duty required his presence. So I decided to go with him, but he refused that too. Insisted he wouldn't put me at risk. You see? He knew, even though he pretended the visions were false. I pleaded all the more that he not leave me. Amidst all his talk of duty, do you know what he said? 'How would it look if I stay here?' How would it *look*! Can you believe that? When he kissed me on the platform..." A breath squeaked through her throat. "...he was saying goodbye forever. He abandoned me. For the sake of appearances!"

She covered her face with her hands and folded over onto Devron's lap. "I feel so betrayed!"

Devron smoothed his hand down her back, time and again, as sobs ripped through her chest. They grated, tearing inside until her raw lungs demanded she stop.

At last, she pushed herself upright, then brushed at the dampness on Devron's trousers. "Oh, I'm sorry to have cried all over you." She gulped and sniffed. What did he think of her? If he disapproved, she'd never be able to tell another soul. Who would understand if Devron didn't?

"It's no burden to bear your tears, Fairlynn." He rubbed her shoulder, so much feeling in his eyes that she almost cried again.

"I shouldn't have spoken badly of him, I suppose. He is your brother, after all, and I..." She looked away.

"If it's any consolation..." He drew a strained breath. "I mourn him, but I am angry with him too. Even more so now, for he hurt you."

The pressure around her chest eased. "Thank you for understanding." She wiped at her cheeks, which only smeared the wetness. She sniffed again. "I'd better go clean myself up."

As she made her way back to the welcome room a couple minutes later, Kevenor's voice filled the space. He stood just inside the door with his feet spread. Why must he sound so disgruntled when he'd just attained an honorable position?

"Now that I'm Chief Former," he asserted, "you must pass your ideas by me. Never announce them in a public meeting. You've got everyone expecting some massively strong doors, and never have I seen a door as strong as a wall."

"Only because they weren't designed to be." Devron also stood, though his posture remained casual.

"Do you know a strong design?" Kevenor demanded.

"I do. Floor-to-ceiling with no gaps. Recessed within solid rock when open. Sliding within ceiling and floor grooves to close. The set nearest the lake will curve to match the cavern. The other should curve in the opposite direction. You may claim the strength of an arch to hold back the ocean if you like, though seawater will never touch it. Perhaps we should call them gates to give that all-important *feeling* of strength."

Fairlynn marveled. Devron had a complete solution within minutes of hearing the problem. Kevenor had none. How, *how* could the mayor be so blind?

Kevenor's scowl faded. He must have been worried that he couldn't deliver on the promise. "They'll need to be impressively thick. That's a lot of weight to move."

"True. Perhaps geared mechanisms, one for each of the four panels. Manual cranking could work, but I'd rather try magnery motors. You may want to talk to the technicians. We can put several formers to work to make those parts. I've devised a way to separate the gate panels from solid rock without any visible stone cutting. It's polisher work, so I will do that."

Kevenor's shoulders relaxed. "Do you have a drawing?"

"I'll make one. Provided it can be reviewed at a *closed* guild meeting. Formers only. Not even the mayor present."

That look on Kevenor's face—sorrowful eyes with a mulish cast to his mouth. "I hope you're not upset about...about me becoming the chief former."

"No. But I am upset about the mayor usurping authority over the guild. How did that come about?"

"People have lost faith in us. Every time a former says we should cut stone, build, or even polish shafts, they fear the cavern will come crashing down. It's sort of like the mayor is an extra layer in the decision processes—to make sure that safety concerns are met."

Devron snorted. "So they can *feel* safer—false, though it is. Did you try to retain the guild's autonomy?"

"That was already a lost cause. We have to listen to other viewpoints and accommodate them."

"Listen, yes. Implement the dictates of the misinformed? No. We do *not* have to do that, and we *should* not. That path will destroy our gifting."

"The mayor has promised to accept our assessments. We'll just need some patience while he gets agreement for implementation."

Devron shook his head. "Surrendering autonomy was a huge mistake. The misguided of Crysalan have rejected a proposal for healthy airflow. The misguided of Jourendia reject sunlight to grow food. The ramifications of this are going to make our situation worse, not better. I am stunned that so many are blind to such obvious facts."

The mulish look returned to Kevenor's face, and Fairlynn dreaded what he might say.

"'Misguided. Blind.' The things you blurt out! You would never be able to work with the mayor. You should be glad I was made chief former."

"I am. Extremely glad." Kevenor looked suspicious, but Devron spoke calmly. "You will do well in the position. Please don't think I hold any ill will. My gift is still at your disposal."

That seemed to diffuse Kevenor's rising heat. He finally managed to acknowledge Fairlynn's presence, then left with reasonable courtesy.

Fairlynn stepped close enough to touch Devron's hand. "Are you glad—that he is chief former and you are not?"

He looked down at her. "No fate could be worse than to bear heavy responsibility without the authority to fulfill it."

CHAPTER 14

Carrying no lantern to alert anyone to movement, Devron slipped into the empty city cavern. Dawn's rays were beginning to find the obelisks aboveground and flash through the shafts. Pools of light glowed as morning reached Jourendia. He began searching.

The completed light shafts were as clear as the day he'd finished them. It was the partially completed shafts that he studied—seeking intentional changes, not catastrophe. First one, then the next, on and on. Someone's footsteps echoed. Devron began to stroll, lest he appear to be hiding in the shadows.

"What are you doing?"

Devron looked toward the voice. Council Member Cadmore strode toward him, importance sparking from every footfall. Devron recited the answer he'd practiced. "Confirming, once again, that no harm threatens our cavern roof. There are no cracks, no faults, no shifting. I will be here every morning performing exactly the same check, so I hope you can get past the rather insulting suspicion in your tone."

The man hooked a thumb into his pocket. "I didn't mean it that way. Glad to know you're being careful."

"I have always been attentive and precise in my work." Devron continued his stroll. The council member took the hint and went about his business. Or perhaps to interfere in someone else's business. This was a man who would not get Devron's next vote. If that mattered.

Another shaft checked. Unchanged. No sign of any polishers aboveground, even though it was second workday and the morning progressed. Was the damage severe above? Were formers searching for trapped people? Or rebuilding their own city, rather than bothering about little Jourendia's planned expansion?

Devron swept his senses up the next—There! A polisher reached down. A familiar presence. They held stillness within each other's awareness as though they silently, blindly, gripped hands. Did the polisher above feel Devron's relief? Perhaps, for he sensed something similar, along with worry. They remained thus for a moment, then the polisher turned his attention to the upper planes of the shaft and began clarifying. Yes! Devron mixed gratitude with relief. The best he could do to communicate.

More footsteps approached, so Devron withdrew his forming sense. It was Kevenor. What did he dare tell his nephew?

"You look pleased," Kevenor said with a hint of question.

"Of course. I can report that the cavern is still free of cracks, faults, and shifts."

"We all know that. What else?"

"I sensed a polisher I've worked with before, and we were...mutually relieved to find one another. I got the impression that he'd been looking for me. After feeling so cut off, it's nice to know they are thinking about us."

"Is that all?"

"Is that not enough to look pleased over?"

"Enough, indeed. Don't tell anyone, though." Kevenor ran fingers along the nape of his neck. "I'll figure out some way to phrase this to the mayor. To tell him someone up there cares, without hinting that they are doing anything...dangerous."

"True, I sensed nothing dangerous."

Kevenor let the barbed comment pass. "I've convinced the mayor that the guild's design sessions must be private. We're keeping the gate plan secret until the, uh, interior work is finished. If no one sees you working, they can't rage over it."

"I do have to be there. One of the council members even challenged me in here this morning."

Kevenor rolled his eyes. "Cadmore?" When Devron nodded, Kevenor griped, "He even asked me if you had approval to check the cavern! *That,* while assuring me that he appreciates our concern for everyone's safety." Devron snorted as Kevenor continued. "I've made it clear that all formers can check anything. In the extremely unlikely event of a problem, they are to report it to me, or if I'm not available, to you. No one else. I will inform the mayor."

Devron stilled for an instant. Was Kevenor implying something beyond the words? Making a way for Devron to polish shafts on the sly? Was that intentional?

Kevenor glanced around, then whispered, "It's the best I can do to retain some autonomy for the guild."

Hm. If he thought that would work, he wasn't smart enough to give Devron a loophole. "I'll do a regular morning check in here. I'm the one most likely to recognize aboveground formers, after all."

Kevenor opened and closed his mouth.

What was he not saying? Devron prompted. "Would you like to assign me to monitor the lake cavern and tunnel as well?"

His lips twitched. "Not a bad excuse for being onsite. Thanks, Uncle Dev. It means everything that you're working with me."

It wasn't hard to give him a sincere smile and murmur assurance. He did feel for Kevenor, even if his current tight spot was his own fault. Devron had watched his nephew grow from a lad to a man, and affection would always remain. Besides, every new chief or mayor was probably feeling overwhelmed and doubting they could pull off their role.

Devron formed the top planes of one unworked shaft, then went home to make sure his duck had not escaped her makeshift pen to invade his garden. He moved some plants and extended the pen with permanent fencing. The rattle of his lift chain caught his ear, and he went to peer over the edge of his roof.

Fairlynn had put something into the lift bucket and swung the chain to get his attention. A smile lit her upturned face. "Raise this. I'll be up in a moment to explain."

He cranked fast, then hurried halfway down the stairs to help her ascend. "What is that mess you put in my lift?"

"Ungrateful man! A little more nesting material to help your duck feel comfy enough to lay her eggs, plus some weed from the duck pond and fresh-water oysters." When he made a sound of revulsion she nodded. "Awful to us, but ducks like them." She approved Devron's construction and filled him in on the care of brooding hens.

Listening to her instructions soothed him. An unexpected balm. Such a simple day-to-day matter, that required no sneaking or careful wording. Her calm hinted that she found it equally relaxing.

She accepted his offered arm as they descended, resting her weight upon it to ease her bad hip. "I do wish I could get up and down easier. I'd love to tend her for you. At least, if you're home, I can do so."

"You're always welcome, but please wait to climb until I can help you. I suppose I can manage her myself, but—do ducks get sick? What does that look like?"

Fairlynn chuckled. "Not often, but I'll check on her. I can handle the stairs once a day with support. What else are you doing today?"

"I get to inspect the tunnel and cavern for quite some time to come. Have you heard about the gate plans from Kevenor?"

"No, he doesn't speak of such. Children hear everything that you least want to have spread around, and then they chatter." She gave him an arch look. "I, of course, would know better than to repeat anything you were to say."

Devron explained the double gates he envisioned and the story to keep prying questions at bay.

Her eyes widened as she grasped the complexity. "You're nothing short of brilliant, Devron."

His chest warmed, though he didn't know how to answer. Maybe he wasn't as alone as he felt. Maybe he could even tolerate the backlash if his true purpose for the gates was ever discovered.

The days settled into a routine of so-called inspections and daily tasks. The relief of having work to do eased Devron's irritation over the fearmongering that slithered or stampeded through Jourendia. Suspicion, griping in the market, accusations of food hoarding, arguments over whose turn it was to harvest oysters, and countless debates. At least it all kept the mayor too busy to interfere with the formers—much.

On the hopeful side, his duck laid ten eggs, and someone came from Alluthin to explain experiments for creating soil. Apparently, it could be made by mixing dust or ground-up rock with every last scrap of plant and animal matter that could possibly be gathered. Some formers were even allowed to fashion screens to filter wastewater before the streamers sent it downriver. Gathering the rust-proof metals for those screens had been another chore for Mayor Borchel to figure out since mining was still forbidden.

Best of all, Fairlynn often streamed the lake waters for oyster harvesting. And that meant she was both away from Crilla's demands and near Devron. Every time she passed him in the tunnel, they shared a moment of calm friendship that carried none of the angst infiltrating once-hopeful Jourendia. She must be taking more shifts at the lake than anywhere else. That would not have happened unless she requested it.

Not only did her gentle voice lift his spirits, he often joined her in the lake cavern after finishing the day's work. Alverlee would have expected Devron to watch out for her. Of course, that was Kevenor's duty, but Devron had begun to wonder if he was doing it. Or *could* do it.

One day, when Kevenor came to softly discuss the gate project with Devron, Fairlynn stomped past them. The staccato beat of her heels echoed after her.

Kevenor's sentence trailed off as he stared at her back. He rubbed his forehead when the tunnel fell silent.

"What's wrong," Devron whispered.

"Oh, Uncle Dev, I just never had any idea how hard it would be to live between them after my father died." The air must weigh a pound per lungful the way he heaved it out. "Sorry. I don't mean to complain or criticize. Where were we?"

"You asked about progress. This gate panel is going faster than the first."

"Good."

Devron sensed Kevenor exploring the uniform curve he had been carving to separate the gate from the surrounding mass. A cursory effort at best. Odd. "Are you tired?"

Kevenor's eyes darted away. "Sort of. It's too soon for a full inspection anyway." He nudged the extra bucket with his foot. "What's with the rocks?"

It sat beside the dust bucket, which Devron filled by capturing the grains that he drew through a fine crack in the tunnel wall. He checked that no one was in hearing distance. "When people pass by, I hold a rock and shave some dust off into the bucket. Useful for soil and all. That way, dust from the tunnel wall won't arouse suspicion."

"Good forethought. I told the mayor that formers aboveground are still polishing the shafts. He's worried but relies on your morning assessments confirming they have caused no harm. He doesn't seem to look up enough to notice the gradual brightening of raw quartz, but he'll have an explanation if anyone points it out."

Footsteps approached, and they both turned their heads toward the sound. Still too far off to have heard their soft voices, a bored young former neared to collect the dust and drop off an empty bucket.

Kevenor left with only a nod and went off to whatever so-called work he did these days.

Devron formed in silence, commanding the gate to separate as though an invisible razor cut narrow slices from top to bottom. Similar to creating the dome panels of his hidden stone egg—it gave him relief from the vision's demand. At least he was allowed to use his gift. A pity that secrecy tainted the joy of creating. These days of irrational fear had better be short!

On his roof, Devron stood up from tending a vegetable patch and stretched his back. It was Savoring Day, but every hidden accomplishment he called to mind was immediately tarnished by the frustration heaped around it. Nearly a month had passed since the collapse, but all miners and most formers were still without work.

The mayor's refrain was getting old. *Just one more week—you can do that for the safety of Jourendia, can't you?* As bad as the oft-repeated and totally inaccurate excuse of *reasonable caution.* All more aggravating than frugal rations. As for the market, it had become a place to trade insults more than wares.

Devron sought again for something to be thankful for. The only good that persisted was that Geon had become the first Chief Grower of Jourendia. The two of them met surreptitiously whenever Geon had soil enough to build another box garden in the city cavern. Geon never asked how Devron knew where sunlight would shine brighter in the coming days. He just built where Devron pointed, then slipped him a jar of compost water.

Money still had worth, but the means to grow food was of far greater value. In fact, Devron had to pledge two ducklings to the communal flock in order to get enough feed to raise his little brood.

He emptied the evening ration of duckweed and freshwater oysters into the shallow feed pan. The ducklings swarmed it. That would keep them busy for a few minutes. Measuring carefully, he added a spoonful of compost water to the quart jar of his mister, then crossed to the front of his roof to spray the roots of the experimental aerial plants. Their rickety trellis chose that moment for a slow twisting collapse.

No! He caught it inches above the dirt. Too late? After careful investigation, his heartbeat eased. Only one stem had broken on the rubbery vines. He never used to panic over a plant.

Devron wedged a stool against the short roof wall to prop up the trellis, then used the severed vine to tie it in place. He should have the strongest trellis in Jourendia, but with metals in such short supply—no chance of that. Not after the flack he'd caught for using scrap wire to fence his duck pen. Instead, he'd constructed the trellis from dead plant stalks. Pathetic. Maybe he could make a stone version.

As always, he kept an eye to the street below, watching for Fairlynn. Instead, he spotted two strangers approaching the door of her home. Hard to get a good look at this height and distance, but they weren't family. A tall man with blondish-brown hair and travel bags knocked on the door. A short woman next to him—or perhaps an adolescent—clutched a ragged sack. The man carried himself much like Talmarq. Impossible, since he and Olanni left Dirklan before the collapse. Unless... Had some access route been found? Devron's pulse surged even though there had to be another explanation. The door opened, and the man stepped through. The hunch-shouldered girl straggled after him. Who was she?

Devron sprayed roots as fast as the mister allowed, then hurried down the staircases within his home. It may be rude to show up when guests had just arrived, but desperate hope drove him. He strode along the thoroughfare, halting when Talmarq emerged from the door and took two long strides toward him.

Talmarq checked for an instant of recognition, then his heavy frown lifted in question and a tentative smile.

They met in the street, and Devron gripped his arm. "Talmarq! I don't know if I should be delighted or appalled."

"A little delight would be a nice change. Those without a home city are welcomed nowhere." Hardly the words of one bearing fabulous news. "When we arrived just now, we had to wait for a council member to come to the rail terminal, and then explain how long we plan to stay and how much food we brought. Which he recorded while oozing disapproval. So cruel to the poor waif who arrived with me."

"Come." Devron kept a light grip on Talmarq's arm as he started for his own home. "I saw you from my roof. Who was that with you?"

"An orphan—Santear—whom I discovered sitting in the rail tunnel from Crysalan. No money or food, and too famished to walk that far. She told me she was trying to reach her Aunt Crilla in Jourendia, so of course, I took her into the carriage."

"That must be a joy to Crilla. They welcomed her, I take it?"

"More than me. Crilla promptly asked where I was staying, with the strong hint that it wasn't in their house. Trust me, I had no desire to linger."

"No matter. I'm glad you headed toward my house next, but why are you here?"

"Can't you guess? Tides. I want to watch the harbor waters for a couple days. And I am very much hoping that I can count on your hospitality at the beginning of every month."

Not the point of his question. "Of course, you can count on it."

"Thank you." Talmarq sighed. "I did bring what food I could get, though I gave a little of it to that poor child."

"Naturally. I'm glad you've been able to find some." Devron opened his teal door, and they went in. "How does a wandering streamer find work to be paid for?"

"Not easily. Twice, I discovered a river and traced them both to aboveground. The source for one and the mouth for the other. I was able, barely, to convince the local streamers that the rivers might be significant. They paid me to map them."

"*Are* they significant?"

"Not yet. Too contorted with ferocious currents." Talmarq dropped one bag on the floor and opened the other on the table. "A former named Greehan and I tried putting a message in a canister and sending it downriver. He told me it didn't get very far before it wedged between rocks." Talmarq took food from pouches in his bag—a square of hard bread and plant matter dried beyond recognition. "Can we heat some water to soak these in?"

"Sure." They went into the kitchen. "Where did you meet Greehan?"

"Weslin. I told him I was coming here, and he asked me to convey a precise message. I'm to tell you that he is doing what the two of you discussed. Which is incredibly vague for being precise, but he said you would know what it meant."

Devron filled a pan with water and set it on the magnery heat ring, trying to avoid Talmarq's scrutiny.

"Well, do you?"

"Yes."

"Are you going to be as tightlipped as he was?"

"I am pleased to hear his words. Let that be enough. Formers are treated with great suspicion, for fear that we might do something useful. Don't try to learn what. Above all, do not hint that any of us might be active."

Talmarq put his food into the pot. "Even I get questioned. The crap that's going on...it's insane! Crysalan's mayor is trying to collect a food toll from anyone who travels through their hub, so now the other cities are threatening counter tolls. To make matters worse, some of the Crysalan caverns are splitting off to create a sub-city called Free Crysalan. The mayor forbids it—or tries to. Plus, the market cavern, which has a bigger population than I realized, wants to create an autonomous guild. So now they have three factions fighting and hoarding. Something's got the Keepers of the Writ tense, but they're tightlipped." He shook a little salt into the pot and stirred. "Mayor Sairtoka has put together a group she calls *security guards* with the sort of captain that no one will square up against. A fiery-haired guy big enough to make even me feel short."

Devron let a groan pass his teeth. He broke a small portion from a piece of leftover meat and tossed it into the pot. "Only a month, and already what little government we still had is falling apart."

"Thanks." Talmarq stared wistfully into the pot. "But you don't have to feed me. You must be short of food too."

"That wasn't much beyond flavoring. Consider it payment for news." When Talmarq shook his head, Devron altered his tactics. "Fine. You may clean my duck pen in the morning."

"You have ducks?"

Devron chuckled at his tone. "A brood on the roof. And they are *filthy* creatures. Did you meet anyone else in your travels whom I might know?"

"Wandermae. She looked thinner than I remember. Apparently, she had been in Weslin before I came, but I ran across her in Alluthin. Wind weavers actually get paid there—something to do with pollinating plants, which we never think about aboveground."

"Did you talk with her?"

"A little. She was interested in the rivers I found and wondered if their tunnels carried air."

"Do they?"

"Not much, if any. I could sense friction all around the water flow, so the rivers must fill the tunnels."

"Beyond that one question, did she—or anyone else—speak of air channels?"

"No. Why?"

"Something else you probably shouldn't ask about or mention again." Devron could only hope that Wandermae and Greehan were succeeding. Why weren't they together?

Talmarq stirred the unappealing concoction until it boiled, then turned the lever to break the magnery connection and lifted the pot. The heat ring's glow began to fade.

Devron reached for a large soup bowl and set it on the counter for Talmarq to pour the, uh, mush into. "What in all of Welcia above and below made you stay in Dirklan?"

Talmarq twisted his mouth into a rueful contortion and carried the bowl to the kitchen table. "Hardest decision I've ever had to make."

Devron brought a glass of water and a spoon for him and sat down opposite. "So why did you?"

"The vision. I must find those rivers."

"What of Olanni?"

"She went aboveground—after a lengthy argument."

"I seem to recall that Olanni has a sister. Apparently of some interest to you."

Talmarq lowered the spoonful on the way to his mouth. "Adelle." He rolled his lips, then ate. To avoid speech?

"What of her?"

"In our land, we aren't allowed to engage to marry until the man, at least, has begun a profession. So we are not formally committed yet. I...I hope that..." He seemed to need extra air to get through these sentences. "She is studying music—enrolled in a year-long program while I was away for streamer training." The strain on his face melted for an instant. "She has the most lovely voice!" His smile faded as quick as it began.

"Anyway, I hope that she waits...at least for a while. I hope that *somehow* we get a passage opened. Not just for my benefit, of course, but...I do long to return to her. Even though I have a task to do here, I never felt I was destined to live in Dirklan my whole life." He crimped his lips. "If I am wrong...Adelle is young and free to find someone else."

"Your vision drives you to that extent?"

"I thought you would understand that part."

Devron tilted his head in contemplation. "I do, but my vision meant staying with those I care about, not leaving them."

"I still have hope it's not a permanent separation. Am I crazy? I see why no one wants to tunnel right now, but someday? Isn't there anywhere else to tunnel out? What about here? You've told me how stable ipenrock is."

"If it was easy—or simply hard—we would already have another access route. Jourendia, especially. You need to understand that every existing tunnel follows natural formations. Even the access arches were built to support a gaping hole in the mountainside. We widen, we level, we mine. But we have never cored out a channel through an unknown structure to an unknown destination. Proposals for such a tunnel have always ended the same. The immense challenges and effort could never be justified."

"The *need* for it has drastically increased!" Talmarq stared into Devron's eyes. "Or are you really telling me that it's...impossible?"

"I don't much believe in that word, but these facts are certain. The undertaking would have to be started from above. The bulk of the stone must be hauled out, not in. There must be a way to coordinate between the above- and belowground terminal points. We would need at least two formers with *astonishingly* good range, both for distance and for content determination."

Talmarq found the scrap of meat and chewed it. "I suppose that would take years to complete."

"Many years. And with our current approach, we aren't going to survive beyond one."

CHAPTER 15

Fairlynn lay awake most of the night. Santear huddled in the place where Alverlee used to sleep. Crilla had offered her the spot without so much as a by-your-leave. Of course, there was no other bed in the house for her to sleep in, and Fairlynn would have agreed had she been asked. They might even have rested well if the poor girl didn't shake the bed all night, either from coughing or her silent sobbing. A particularly wracking cough drove Santear from the room sometime before dawn.

Torn between pity and relief for several seconds, Fairlynn knew nothing more until banging pans startled her awake. Intentional, no doubt, for the room was filled with daylight, and Crilla did not admire those who slept late.

Sure enough, her loud voice forbade someone from entering the priv through the kitchen access. "No, go upstairs. Mama-Lynn will be in there soon." What a subtle hint.

Groggy though she was, Fairlynn dressed, then entered the priv through its door to her bedroom. She grabbed her comb from the top shelf, halted by the grimy feel of it. She stared at the residue of oily dust. Pushing down irrational annoyance, she scrubbed it clean. Santear had been destitute for a month. Probably didn't possess a comb. Nor a home to bathe in. She needed kindness, not a reprimand. Fairlynn twisted her messy hair into a knot and anchored it with a pick, then reached over the tub to fill the water heater, which nested in the wall.

How was she going to fix all this? Oh, for Alver to take her side, for she never did confrontation well. Time to stop cowering. Fairlynn opened the door into the kitchen. The children were making noise upstairs, and Kevenor was gone. Santear scraped the last crumbs from her plate onto her spoon and ate them with a guilty look. A single slice of bread remained on the table.

Her bed. Her comb. Her breakfast. Santear was even sitting in her place at the table. What else would they take? Fairlynn drew deep, silent breaths. She mustn't lose her temper. Not with Santear present. It wasn't her fault.

Almost hoping that Crilla would object, Fairlynn sat in her old place at the table's end. Crilla paused in her listing of the day's activities. "It's unfortunate you came late to breakfast. I fear we ran a little short."

Fairlynn rubbed at the throb in her temple and took the last piece of bread. She wanted to say, *How could you have guessed that I would wake up and need to eat?* Instead, she murmured, "Never mind."

Crilla resumed explaining her weekly routine to Santear, who nodded a great deal and interjected that she could help with this or that task.

"Well then, I'm sure you'll fit right in," Crilla said, "and be like a big sister to the children soon. Let's get these dishes washed."

The girl jumped up to help, perhaps anxious to be accepted and unaware of how many demands would be made of her.

"Really, Crilla!" Fairlynn dusted her fingers and stood. "Has your routine blinded you that badly? Neither Santear nor I got decent sleep last night, and she has been living in those dust-filled caverns, probably with no hope of a bath in weeks." Crilla's jaw dropped, and Fairlynn took Santear to the door of the priv to make sure she knew how to work the water heater so she wouldn't get scalded. She pointed to the shelf beyond the children's reach. "Everything on that shelf belongs to me, and the rest is for the family's use."

"Oh, I'm so sorry to have dug in your things. Aunt Crilla told me I could use whatever I found."

"No harm done, my dear. Just have a nice soak and relax for a change. Your aunt can take you to the market afterward to buy what you need. In, you go now." Fairlynn closed the door on the girl and turned on Crilla before she could give vent to the outrage on her face. "And as soon as she is finished with the hot water, my bedding must be washed and we—no, *you*—must see to getting her a bed."

Crilla lifted her nose. "Well, as to that, Kevenor and I already discussed the matter."

"Good."

"It's high time we move downstairs to the master bedroom anyway. You're all alone in that big bed, and the child's double that we sleep in is too small for the man of the house."

It would have been easier to breathe if Crilla had kicked her in the stomach. Fairlynn's ears buzzed through whatever the woman was saying with a haughtily bland look. Fairlynn drew a deep breath and clutched a chair back. "How, exactly, will we sleep better if we move upstairs to a—slightly—smaller bed? Since when do the elders of a family sleep with the children?"

"I never expected you to be so selfish toward an orphaned niece." Crilla shook her head with a fine show of astonishment. "But you needn't share a bed if you'd rather not. Perrie may sleep with Santear in the double, and you may use Perrie's bed."

"There is nothing but a folding screen between the beds in the children's room. You just complained a couple days ago that Jojo still awakens in the night."

"I daresay that Santear will soon learn to quiet him. You need not stay on the second floor—just until things are arranged so we can set up a bed for you on the third floor."

Fairlynn gasped. How could they? Beyond the insult, the mere thought of climbing and descending many times a day spiked an ache in her hip. "Will I be sleeping in the playroom or your sewing room?"

"You needn't use that tone with me. We'll get things decently set up, and I daresay Kevenor can put up another wall. Please don't be so sour over this. Changes are hard for all of us, you know."

"Are they? You've gotten the nanny you always wanted and pushed me as far out of your way as possible. The change looks pretty sweet for you. And as for all your rationalizing, I know perfectly well that Kevenor's parents slept in the same bed that you and he share. They didn't move downstairs until Alverlee's father and mother had both passed on."

"I'll take your word for that, but you are not Kevenor's mother, are you?"

Fairlynn couldn't even gasp this time. She just stood there, dimly aware that the street door had opened while Crilla spoke.

"Oh, by the caverns!" Kevenor snarled. "Now, what is going on?"

Other footsteps joined Kevenor's. Fairlynn couldn't bear to turn around and face whoever entered.

Crilla angled her head to look past Fairlynn. "Nothing of any matter. What is that you're bringing in?"

"The head piece of a bed frame, obviously. I told you I would look for one."

"Ah, and rather fine. I do hope it wasn't too expensive."

"It is needed," Kevenor snapped. Feet shuffled. "You go up the stairs first, I'll take the lower end."

Crilla went to superintend, and Fairlynn fled into her bedroom. Hers? No more. Her head ached worse than her hip. Little sleep and less food. All trivial now compared to the stunning realization. She had no family.

Never again would she believe Crilla's rarely stated affection. Her faint hope that Kevenor might spare her the third floor was born dead. Whatever respect or fondness she imagined when he called her *Mother*

Fairlynn didn't flow from any depth in his heart. He knew full well that her hip couldn't stand that much climbing.

Tears flowed as she sat on the edge of her bed. They must stop, for she had to get out of this house, and she could not do so red-faced. This room—her sanctuary—felt cold and foreign now. Somehow emptier than when she'd lost her husband. Her gaze moved over furniture...belongings...some of them Alverlee's. She gulped and swallowed, fighting the pressure of more tears. How to get past this? She stripped the bed, knowing that she would not sleep on these sheets again. Perhaps she should stuff her pillow into the closet to keep at least that for herself. As though Crilla would be above pulling it out again.

How was she ever going to get away from these thoughts? Fairlynn pulled the pick from her hair, redid the twist, and anchored it with a fine clip, which she kept in her jewelry box. A gift from Alverlee.

A gentle knock struck the door.

She didn't answer.

"Mother Fairlynn?" Kevenor's voice. "May I come in?"

If she kept silent, would he leave? No sound of his footsteps moving away. She sighed and opened to him. "I'm running late and need to get on with my duties."

He looked down at her and drew a deep breath. "At least let me say that I heard Crilla when I came in. Those were her words, not mine, and they are not how I feel."

What to say? Nothing came to her.

"You didn't raise me, of course, but you are still my father's wife, the second mother of our family, and you are Mama-Lynn to my children. None of that will ever change. And even though I'm *awful* at dealing with the problems between you and my wife..." He floundered and tried again. "The traditions are different in Crilla's family, so she doesn't...You're not all that much older than her—not much above a dozen years—so she feels like she'll never have her own home, just your home." He blinked and seemed to realize he was chiseling out a deeper hole. "Anyway, I honor my responsibility as a son, and you will always have a home here."

"On the third floor." She didn't beg, didn't sneer, just stated it matter-of-factly.

"I will make it nice. The bed is used but of fine quality, and I will put railings on both sides of the stairs to make it easier for you to climb them. You'll have a space for your things in the welcome room, so you needn't run up and down too often." A hint of pleading had entered his voice. "I want you to feel comfortable here."

What was she supposed to say? She couldn't forgive when he acknowledged no fault. Nor thank him—not when the scraps he offered were pitiful beside her loss. He just wanted her to quietly accept it. As though she had a choice. "Well, that's all settled then, but I do need to be getting along."

He stepped aside, and she left the house. Now where would the chief streamer be? That search might give her time to drag her thoughts away from home. The home that was not. Another streamer had likely taken Fairlynn's task, and she must find out if she should do something else or relieve whoever filled in for her. And apologize. Which seemed rather unfair.

She found Fezlie in the city cavern, where she often met with the streamers near the central fountain. At least that had a use, though not as the majestic centerpiece of a thriving new city. Watering gardens instead. A noble purpose in its own way, but the fountain still seemed...diminished. Just like her. Another stone added to the weight in her heart.

"Don't worry about being late." Fezlie waved it off. "Talmarq told us that Crilla's niece arrived yesterday, so it wasn't all that surprising when you didn't come. He took your shift in the lake cavern, so no one else was even inconvenienced. You may help me here if you like, and we'll be done that much sooner."

Fairlynn drew water up from the gushing stream below to fill stone barrels. They had been formed from the rock once intended to build walls. Troughs carried the life-giving flow to the raised gardens, which were still far from adequate.

Complaints flowed faster than water. Formers grumbled that they couldn't quarry and were now reduced to reworking the stone blocks they had dressed for building. At least they created something from it. The formers assigned to the shattering duty looked too forlorn to gripe. Diminished, too, perhaps worse than she was. The architect worked among them, assigned that duty as punishment when he'd refused to break up the dressed stone blocks and dared to shout that it was fools' work. How tragic.

Rock, dead plant matter, and waste were piled before them. All these must be fragmented to fine particles for soil production. As always, a few council members hovered nearby to *preserve safety*—or so they termed their work. Shoving their noses everywhere that they didn't belong. Monitoring the formers, questioning the streamers, and demanding that the Growers' Guild stop any experimental practices that didn't instantly grow plants faster.

When Fairlynn topped off the last barrel, Kevenor's voice reached her ears. Only a word here and there, but the subject became clear when a council member snapped, "The light is too focused in small patches."

"We would be happy to address the problem." Kevenor drew nearer. "As soon as the mayor approves our frequent requests, Devron will finish polishing the lower ends of the light shafts."

"He is here every morning," another council member complained. "I believe he is polishing light shafts himself, not merely inspecting what is done aboveground. The dispatch that Talmarq brought from Crysalan reported an aftershock just last week. We cannot allow him to alter the light shafts, and the abovegrounders shouldn't be doing it either."

"Tell the mayor your concerns."

"I'm telling you. Reverse what the abovegrounders are doing, so they will stop interfering."

Kevenor raised his brows. "One of you wants more light. One of you wants no work, immediately followed by a demand that I do a different type of work. And I must add, work that would damage our ability to grow food. Never ask formers to do harm with their gift, for they will lose their abilities. I should not need to tell you this."

"What good is food if we are all crushed? Stop those crazy, interfering abovegrounders before they shatter the cavern roof."

"They are quite sane," Kevenor replied, "and they are helping us. Once again, I remind you, the majority of Dirklan survived collapse and needs food."

Fairlynn whispered to the chief streamer, "How do you stand it, working in the city every day and listening to all these contradictions?"

"I don't much listen, actually, and I leave as soon as I can. They are free to talk, and I am free to ignore them."

"But what if their talk and decisions lead us to starvation?"

She laughed. "They are already doing *that*!"

"How is this funny?"

"We are still alive, so there is still time for the pendulum to swing. They are so far on the foolish side, they can only get wiser. Come along, dear. Let's get out of here before you fall prey to madness."

Fairlynn walked at her side. She hoped the chief streamer was right, but it didn't seem so. More like these pompous fools would gouge out the cavern walls if it gave them space to force the pendulum further into stupidity.

CHAPTER 16

Devron left the formers' secret assessment meeting they'd held in Earlman's workshop. The dusk of shortening days had emptied the side street, allowing Devron a moment to enjoy success without guarding his expression.

Earlman had done fine work forming the gears and shafts that would soon draw gates along their grooves. All the parts that could fit in his workroom had tested perfectly. Now they must be joined to the two largest gear wheels that waited in the mechanical room beside the tunnel. An accomplishment that ought to be celebrated—instead it would be hidden forever behind locked doors.

Devron still marveled over the amount of stone that formers had silently moved during night shifts to carve out the mechanical room and hollow the shaft conduits. The mayor knew—in theory. He claimed the council members knew, too, though not the quantity. They weren't allowed to attend that work, lest they attract attention. No one was to fully grasp how much cutting, channeling, and forming had gone on behind those nearly invisible doors that were tucked into alcoves flanking the tunnel.

Devron, Kevenor, and Earlman had inspected every inch of it. They had asked the architect to join them, but he refused to leave his house these days. Worrisome, but they couldn't delay assessing the outer gates that Devron had isolated.

Most people knew only of the twin narrow gaps that ran up each side wall of the tunnel and of shallow grooves in the floor. None of which looked too worrisome. After all, the mayor had promised gates that would save them from flooding, so some work had to be done. What would they all think when they saw the completed gates closed for the first time? Devron *liked* to hope they would perceive that the excavation had harmed nothing. Perhaps their trust in the formers would even return. He tried not to think about the more probable reaction. No point in getting irritated before the cause.

Devron left the side street and angled across the thoroughfare toward his house. Off to his right, the lake cavern murmured as always. Wave upon wave echoing into a hushed roar. A sound he took for granted, soon to be lost. Would he miss it? The first set of gates would let it through whenever they parted, but once the second set was complete, only one pair would be allowed open at a time. Never again would the cavern's echo whisper through the settlement.

For the first time, he wondered how the gates would affect the atmosphere within the lake cavern. Occasional visitors wouldn't notice—he assumed, anyway—but what about the streamers who took shifts there? Why hadn't he thought to ask Fairlynn? She'd spent the last few days by the lake. Her morning trek through the tunnel was slower than usual, which worried him. Not limping, but it seemed she leaned more weight on her cane. She hadn't come to help with the ducks, either, so clearly, the climb was too much for her, no matter what she said.

He couldn't wait to show her his latest idea...and to see the smile it would bring to her face. He would work on it again this evening, and if she didn't stop by on her way home tonight, he'd invite her tomorrow. His pace quickened toward his door, its teal sheen barely visible in the reddish glow from the last few light shafts exposed to the setting sun above.

Running footsteps brought his head around. A threesome raced past him with the vigor of adolescence. A shiny rod flickered for an instant between them, and one hissed, "Split up," probably louder than he intended. They darted into three side streets.

Devron's hand froze on its way to his door latch. What did this mean? Nothing good, he feared. Most homeowners had removed decorative metals from their houses after the first theft. What little remained was embedded. Devron looked down the thoroughfare where the youths had run from. Hard to see much. He'd best check before the light faded completely. He took to the middle of the thoroughfare, scanning the houses on either side as he walked. The glow from windows gave faint illumination, but the adjoining side streets hid in shadows. Something moved on the ground.

Oh no—a person! He sprinted. *Please don't let it be Fairlynn.* But he knew it was, even before he saw her face. He dropped to one knee beside her as she pushed her torso up from the street. "Are you all right?"

"I...I think so...I don't know." Her wavery voice squeaked. "Oh, Dev!"

He wanted to beat someone. And to instantly heal her. Both impossible, and here he sat staring helplessly. At least she could prop herself up. Her arms couldn't be broken. She finished turning to sit on the ground with her knees drawn up.

He wrapped an arm around her shoulders. "What happened?"

"Someone grabbed my cane. I didn't hear them till they were right behind me."

"Did they hit you? Push you down?"

"Not exactly. I was just putting my weight on the cane when they snatched it and ran."

Oh, to take a rod to the culprits' backs. "Did you damage your weak hip?"

"I don't think so." She panted between words. "I fell toward the other side." Her breath shuddered. "Take me home, Dev."

"Of course, but I want to be sure nothing is broken before—"

"I'll stand up myself if you won't help me. Now."

He hurried into position to lift her full weight. "Please let me do the work." If she was that adamant, she was either uninjured or in shock. He supported her upright for a moment, trying to see her face in the dusk. Her lips trembled. "Do you think you can walk?"

"Yes! Just get me out of the street."

She sounded like she was going to burst into tears. He almost asked if she wanted to go to her house or his. No—his was nearest. With one arm snug around her waist and his other hand beneath her elbow, he got her to his door and then into his welcome room. She favored her weak hip but managed the walk steadier than he'd expected. He eased her onto his couch, where she put her hands over her face and sobbed.

Best not to ask questions now. He turned on the lamp, which told him more than she did. The heel of one hand was scraped and bloody. Devron went to get his bandage kit and some extra pillows. She was wiping her tears away when he returned and pulled a chair closer to the couch.

She let him wrap her hand, then pulled up a sleeve and tried to see the back of her elbow.

"That's bleeding, too." He inspected it. "Scraped, not cut. How does the bone feel?"

"I don't think I broke anything. Just bruised. I suppose I'll ache everywhere tomorrow."

A relief, but Devron was still so furious that his quick pulse wouldn't settle. He propped pillows against the arm of his couch. "Lie back here and rest while I bandage your elbow."

She leaned against them with a sigh. "You're so good to me, but I'm really not that badly hurt."

"So it seems, but there's always shock with a fall, so you should take it easy." The little smile she gave him seemed to imply agreement. He set about tying a pad over her elbow.

"Dev! There's a hole in your ceiling!"

He glanced at the opening beside the staircase. "Yes, I've been wanting to show it to you."

She started to laugh. "You sound awfully proud of it—but why?"

He gave in to her infectious laughter. Somehow, things seemed a little less terrible. He finished tying the bandage. "Do you think I haven't noticed that your hip has been worse lately? I know you like helping with the ducks, but I won't let the climb harm you. So I'm putting in a lift. The mechanism will work with a simple crank." Why did that twist her smile and strain her eyes? "I thought you would like it."

"I do." She looked like she was about to cry again. "But the problem's not *your* stairs, Dev. You always help me."

"Then, what?"

"It's the stairs at my—at Kevenor and Crilla's house. They've moved my bedroom up to the third floor."

He would have reeled if he hadn't been sitting. "Their house? Third floor!"

"Sort of a bedroom, anyway. I've just got a folding screen right now, though they talk of a wall. They put a bed and most of my things up there. Kevenor says he'll put railings on both sides of the stairs so I can climb easier."

"When did they do this?"

"A few days ago."

"Why didn't you tell me?"

"Well..." She pulled her lip between her teeth. "Lots of mixed-up reasons, I guess. I was so angry and trying not to be. And hurt, too, but trying not to complain. Trying to get over it, which was bound to be harder if you knew, because I figured you'd be every bit as furious as you look right now. And I don't want to make things bad between you and Kevenor on top of how crazy everything else is these days."

"Of all the—" He snapped off the words, realizing they might harm more than help. "Do you mean that you don't want to hear me verbally shred both of their characters?"

The corners of her lips twitched. "As long as I know you're on my side, I don't need to hear it."

"Of course, I'm on your side!"

"Well, yes, but you did sound mad at me when you realized I'd hidden it from you."

He leaned near her. "That is for an entirely different reason." Then he realized his fingertips had touched her cheek and quickly sat back again.

"Maybe you needn't be so angry with Kevenor. I'm sure it was Crilla who put it all in motion. She made it seem related to arranging a place for her niece to sleep. Really, it puts a night-nanny on the children's floor and gives Crilla her preferred...*position*. And I'm not just talking about space." Fairlynn's expression skewed. "I tried to stand up for myself, but it didn't do any good. Probably made it worse. And then Kevenor returned...but it wasn't as though he would help me when he'd only left to get me a bed, which he promptly hauled upstairs." She shrugged. "He tried to make it right with me afterward—as best he could, under the circumstances."

"The only way to make it right would have been to stop it. But he won't, and that makes him party to it."

"I suppose, but I know he wants to keep family peace." She angled her head. "I do too, even though that means giving in to Crilla, who has now been all kind words amidst her bustling about. I don't believe any of them, but fighting her now will only hurt Santear and help no one. That poor girl is so terribly fragile. After all that she's been through, I just can't expose her to a battlefield of harsh tempers."

Devron imagined stomping into his ancestral home and demanding that Fairlynn be given her old room back. He could make it happen on the grounds of injury and no cane, but it would only be a matter of days before she was evicted again. Even if he could make it last longer, Crilla would harbor resentment. Fairlynn would bear the brunt of that.

The door opened. Talmarq walked in and stopped short. Oh, yes, Devron had a houseguest, and it was dinnertime.

Talmarq fixed his gaze on Fairlynn. "What happened?"

"Someone attacked Fairlynn, stole her cane, and left her lying in the street."

"What?" He slammed the door. "Who did it? How badly are you hurt? Do you need me to fetch a medic former? Doesn't anyone keep watch in the streets here?"

Fairlynn grinned. "I'll be fine. I'm sure they wanted the silver and copper from my cane far more than they intended to hurt me."

"That is no excuse!"

"Of course not." Devron stood. "There were three of them. I saw them run, but not their faces. I will inform the mayor, but Fairlynn is my immediate concern. I need to go talk with my nephew, but I'll be back soon. Will you put together a little dinner for us to share?"

Talmarq looked like that mundane request was utterly bizarre. "Uh, sure."

Fairlynn began sitting up. "What are you going to say? I'd better come—"

"You rest here. What I say will depend on them, but I won't cause trouble to come upon you." He strode for the door.

Her voice reached him as he passed through it. "The streets aren't safe."

"I'll watch from the doorway," Talmarq offered.

It wasn't all that far to the door of his childhood home. Within easy range of help if needed. Could he be at risk? It seemed unfathomable, but Devron was glad he carried nothing, particularly no metals or food. Just as he reached the door, it opened. And there stood the mayor about to leave.

"Ah, Mayor Borchel. How convenient, for I must report a crime." Devron entered as he spoke, which set the mayor into awkward backing. Kevenor sidestepped, and Crilla gaped from beside the couch. The children must have been sent upstairs. Just as well.

"A...a crime?" the mayor bumbled.

"Fairlynn was attacked, and her cane was stolen."

The reaction was all he could have hoped for. Spluttering words all around, and Kevenor paled. He seemed about to run out the door, but Devron gripped his arm. "She is safe in my home."

To the mayor's demand, Devron gave a quick statement of the few facts known.

Shoulders back, the mayor declared, "This outrage will not go unpunished. Her cane was distinctive. I'll get the word around the market the moment it opens tomorrow. Anyone who tries to barter—"

"Pointless. It will be melted down, for certain."

The mayor left a heartbeat of silence. "You think it was miners, then? Or their children, perhaps?"

"Others have learned to melt metals now that they are in short supply. But I'm sure miners will be blamed since they have no work and no money to buy the food that rationing allows them to purchase." The mayor snorted, but Devron pulled the door open before he could launch into his typical rebuttal. "I won't detain you, Mayor. I advise you to keep a sharp watch around the streets on your way home."

Kevenor's rounded eyes darted between the departing mayor and Devron. "Uh...Mother Fairlynn...how badly..."

"Scrapes and bruises. She tells me nothing is broken, but she will no doubt ache for some days to come. Her hip was strained before she was attacked in the street." Devron eyed the stairs, sliding his gaze from the base to the top. "I suspect that the attack itself disturbs her more than the injuries. Coming so soon after her well-being was disregarded in her own home, I can only guess how unsafe she must feel."

Both Kevenor and Crilla drew breath to speak, but Devron continued before they could. "I assume the upper flight is without handrails, as is this one. I cannot fathom any reason to move her to the third floor. Even less why you would do so *before* you prepared the room and stairs. It was hard for her to climb with only a cane, and now her strongest hip is also bruised. I should not have to point this out, but obviously I must.

Climbing without railings will damage her weak joint even more than it did before."

"Of course," Kevenor said. "We'll take care of everything for her. She can sleep down here."

"Where?" Devron asked.

"Um…" Crilla seemed to need involvement. "We'll figure something out. We won't let her climb a single step until she has completely healed."

Devron looked long at her. "Fairlynn's hip was injured two years ago. It has never *completely* healed, and it never will."

She lifted her chin. "Oh, I see what this is. She—"

"No, you do not. Fairlynn made no request of any sort. She will not resist you, nor argue for her own rights. If Kevenor carried her up to the third floor tonight, she would raise no objection."

"I won't do that." He sounded like a young version of himself—scolded for a fault.

"True, I suppose. You will wait until she can struggle up on her own."

Crilla jumped back in. "You don't understand. My family's custom—"

"It is you who does not understand." Devron attempted to quiet his words. "You won't grasp what this means until young Tebber takes a wife and makes her mistress here in your place. But I did not come to argue customs. I only wanted to know whether you would give Fairlynn her rightful bedroom tonight. I already have my answer, so she will stay with me. Please pack up her personal things and a change of clothes immediately, so I may take them to her."

In the stunned silence, Crilla bridled, her compressed lips seeming to fight one another before she managed to speak. "Well, I shall, then, if that's what you want." She bustled away.

Kevenor squeezed his eyes shut, rubbed his hand up the side of his neck, and made a mess of the hair on the back of his head. "She's going to think I'm failing her worse than ever." His voice dropped almost to a whisper. "I just can't figure out how to please both of them."

Devron considered that for a moment. "That might be impossible if Crilla wants to be the only one who is pleased."

"She's not like *that*. You don't understand women."

"Do you?"

Kevenor hmphed, then grumbled, "I suppose not."

"I just assumed they...they are people. Which means they're all different. I think I understand Fairlynn pretty well." Devron quirked his mouth. "Except that she didn't tell me you'd...er, tell me about moving upstairs."

"She didn't?" Kevenor asked. "You sure sounded like you knew."

"I mean before. She told me tonight." It dawned on Devron that hiding it revealed how much it hurt. Maybe he wouldn't say that to Kevenor. "I forgot to mention that I'll need her ration of food, too."

Kevenor grunted, walked into the kitchen, and returned with a small loaf of bread and Fairlynn's apron. "Dinner isn't cooked yet, and I've no idea how to divide her part. I'm not asking Crilla."

"Reasonable. We'll count this loaf as a day's ration."

Kevenor began wrapping it in the apron. "Probably not a good idea to walk the dark street with food in hand."

"I..." Devron shook his head. The previous incidents he'd heard of seemed isolated...distant. "I suppose it is that bad." Even if thieves were caught, there was no judge to try them. The full import of that nudged a creeping dread. Relying on the king's court had always seemed reasonable. Judge Queltin understood Dirklan's situation and special laws so well that they'd had no need of any other. Now, it seemed short-sighted, even negligent.

Santear came downstairs with a partly filled basket, looking confused, and went into the priv. She soon returned and said, "That's everything from the high shelf. Aunt Crilla told me to pack it up, but not why."

Kevenor put the wrapped bread into the basket. "Fairlynn was attacked, and her cane stolen. She's staying with Devron tonight."

Santear moaned, "Oh, the poor thing. I can't understand why you all go out in the dark."

Devron got a sick feeling. "Didn't you go out at night in LourEstelle?"

"Sure, but not since the collapse. You hold anything in the dark, and someone's bound to tear it out of your hands. Least, that's the way of it in Crysalan. And they even have some magnery lamps on poles, but the streets still aren't safe." She twitched a shoulder. "Probably worse now, 'cause someone stole one of those lamps a few nights before I left. They figure it was a former, what with the way it was sliced off at ground level, and besides, the Crysalan formers have even less work than here."

Ideas blossomed in Devron's mind. Magnery lights facing the streets...behind clear crystal embedded in house walls. Would they be bright enough? Would they overtax the magnery system? Could he get the materials?

Crilla returned with another basket, interrupting his creative moment. "I packed several things for her to wear so she will have a good choice. Please tell her I will stop by tomorrow to see if I forgot anything important. And also that I am terribly sorry that she was attacked...and hurt...and...oh, just everything."

"I will." Devron accepted the baskets from her and Santear, then turned to Kevenor. "Will you watch the street for me while I head home?"

"What? Oh...yes." Kevenor opened the door, muttering, "Things are worse every day, and no hope in sight."

"Plenty of hope if we dare take it. I'll share a lighting idea at the next formers' meeting."

"Stop pretending, Uncle Dev. We're running out of resources."

CHAPTER 17

As Devron started across the thoroughfare, he caught movement in his window. A few seconds later, Talmarq stepped out of his door and gave the street a good look-over while he waited for Devron to enter. A guard in front and behind. Even still, it felt risky to carry baskets a few hundred feet.

Talmarq locked the door behind him, and Devron's shoulders eased. Fairlynn was sitting up on the couch and looked more herself. Well, perhaps a worried, messy-haired version of herself, but not so shaken.

"How did it go?" she asked.

"Well enough—in my opinion, anyway—meaning that you will stay here." He set the baskets next to her, and she peeked into the first as he spoke. "I prompted to see if they would give you your own room back on the first floor and got nothing better from Crilla than, 'We'll figure something out.'" He eased his snarly tone. "I can provide you a bed—without stairs—and no *figuring* is required. So I asked for some of your things." He took the bread bundle out and unwrapped enough to reveal the loaf to Talmarq. "You can add some bread to our dinner if needed. After we've eaten, will you help me carry some furniture?"

"Sure. There's enough in the larder to eat without cooking if neither of you mind it cold."

They soon gathered around the kitchen table, and Devron told of his talk with the mayor and of Santear's comments. He raised a brow toward Talmarq. "Is her view exaggerated because she was homeless, or is it really that bad in Crysalan?"

"It's that bad. Crysalan might be the worst, but not by much. Whatever a city lacks, is being stolen. Even in Alluthin. I guess they haven't mined in many years, so metal theft is a problem. Everywhere else, food is the preferred loot, with other short resources next."

Devron frowned at the table. Even though he'd crafted locks for his doors, and anchored his lift works so they could not be stolen, it just hadn't hit home. Until he'd found Fairlynn in the street—and feared to carry a basket in the dark.

"If we could mine ores again," Fairlynn asked, "would Alluthin trade food for them?"

"I don't know." Talmarq shrugged. "They may not starve as soon as the other cities, but they don't have a surplus. You'd have to guard the trains too—and not one rail cart has a cover. In Weslin, I saw a few carts of dung stopped on the rails. All gone in a matter of minutes. People hurried up to it in complete silence and grabbed what they could get. Some were even carrying away chunks of dung with their bare hands."

"Ugh!" Fairlynn set a bite of meat back on her plate and looked away.

"Oh, sorry." Talmarq ducked his head. "Maybe we should talk of rivers."

"I don't see why." Fairlynn swirled the glass she had picked up. "Water, we have in abundance."

Talmarq licked his lips and took a second to answer. "Aboveground, we use rivers for transport."

"I've seen them," she said. "Broad and slow. Barges floating on their flat surfaces."

"I know Dirklan's rivers are mostly tunnel-bound torrents, but nonetheless, some flow into and out of Dirklan." His mouth hardened like he expected an argument. "Some of us think it's possible. We just have to figure out how."

How to do what? Devron wondered. "What is it you think is possible?"

"River transport. The problem isn't just that we need food. We need trade. Abovegrounders would feed us out of kindness if they could. At least for a while, I'm sure. But sooner or later, we should be sending payment."

"Ah, yes." At least this unpopular subject was addressed somewhere. "That would give us work. An economy."

Talmarq's gestures spread broader as he spilled ideas that he must have held close. "Someone in Illia mentioned moving ore as a slurry. It would be easy to send—comparatively, anyway—but abovegrounders must know that it's coming, and *where*. Also *how*, because they need a way to capture it." He leaned back. "Getting food down to us is the hard part. We're talking about moving food *within* a rough river, not on top of it. Bins, glass jars, or pouches are no longer an option. What could they pack it in? It must endure careening off boulders and still arrive as edible food. And if they tried sending it downriver, how would they know whether it worked? Maybe they have tried and failed so badly that we didn't even find one scrap."

Much to consider. The opportunities would require varied skills and testing. Impossible—unless one refused to accept that word. "You told us before that the rivers you found weren't useful."

"True thus far, but I'm sure there are more to be found. That's why I'm traveling through all the tunnels and caverns."

"Oh." Devron cocked his head. "You said you were here to study the harbor tides."

"That, too, but I did find a river in Jourendia just today."

Fairlynn sat bolt upright. "Where?"

"North side of the city cavern. It's stone-encased, so a tunnel would be needed to reach it."

"Wait," Devron interrupted. "I don't follow this at all."

Talmarq gave him a wry smile. "I'm almost as surprised as the rest of you. Most streamers can trace a water course for a mile or more, provided that some portion is near enough to see or feel—or at least hear. But I can find them through rock. It's hard because I don't know where to look. But it's possible."

"If we assume that transport rivers can be found..." Devron stared at the opposite wall. "We need the means to package food...or whatever. It needs to be durable and lightweight. Probably an alloy we have yet to design. Shape might be significant. We need a way to test options. Aboveground, they will soon be metal-poor, so we need to get the alloy to them. But just like with the slurry idea, they must know it's coming. Or, if we send the components, they must know how to combine them."

"Are they up to that if they had the natural ores?" Fairlynn asked. "They've always been so averse to new ways of doing things."

Devron quirked the corner of his mouth. "I'd rather send it intact anyway. Let's say we tried several designs and put, um, something inside. Maybe a test substance...a message...a gemstone as payment. Whichever containers survived the trip could be repacked with food and returned. We'd duplicate the most successful materials and design." They smiled at him now, which he doubtfully returned. "Might be a long round trip before they got loaded with food and hauled to a different inbound river, but...if the cycle could be started, eventually it might prove adequate."

Fairlynn pressed a hand to her chest. "Oh, Devron, in the worst moments, you make hope seem like a possibility."

A quiver rushed through him too. This was creating. And whenever he created, he felt the wild raging chaos falter before every idea. Before every command.

The chaos shouted back at him. *Mining is not allowed! Tunneling is not allowed! Those sending the payment would never get the food. If it were even sent.*

No, he would not speak those words. Yet reality could not be ignored, for the fear that people *believed* rejected possibilities. Hope could not produce unless it was acted upon.

Finally, he said, "There are a host of difficulties, of course."

Talmarq still fixed an unwavering stare on his face, but Fairlynn braced her hands on the table and stood, then picked up her plate. "True. And there were a host of difficulties with creating gates and their works. But I happen to know someone who has accomplished it." She set the plate beside the sink. "And I know that this amazing person can accomplish much more."

Oh, it felt good to be believed in again. Even if only one person saw him, she made him feel like he could leap through cavern roofs.

Devron wrapped the remaining bread in a linen cloth. Nothing else remained of their small portions. "Don't mind the dishes. We've more important work to do." He led the way into the workshop and pulled a stool over near the door. "Sit here, Fairlynn. The most I'll let you do is superintend." Parts of the lift filled in the central work area. He addressed Talmarq and pointed. "Let's carry this over there."

"What am I supposedly superintending, anyway?" Fairlynn asked from her perch on the stool.

"Making room for your bed."

"What? No. This is your workshop, Dev. You can't tell me this isn't your...your sanctuary."

"I can move that anywhere. You know the houses of Jourendia—this would have been the primary bedroom if I hadn't lived alone. Besides, I'd rather not have my materials in view from street-level windows anymore, so the second floor is better for the workshop." The two men hefted the lift's framework and carried it aside. "We'll bring the spare bed down as soon as we push the bench over to the side wall. Anything we cannot finish tonight, we'll move tomorrow."

Fairlynn looked around, frowning. "What happened to all the metals you used to keep in here? You had brass, copper, silver, and I don't know what all besides."

"I stowed them in the closets to keep them out of view. I've a mind to hook up the lift support and use that for moving. It's not safe for you yet, but we can tie things to it. Save us carrying so much up and down the stairs."

The men put their muscle into moving the bench. Finished, Talmarq stretched his back and groaned. "That bed frame upstairs is carved stone. Please tell me it comes apart."

Devron chuckled. "Of course, it does. Just because I'm a former, doesn't mean I'm an idiot."

On the second floor, they disassembled the bed, stood the pieces on end, then lowered them with the lift's pulley. Seldom used muscles enjoyed the strain. How good to work together without concern of who might disapprove. When they carried the last section into the old workroom, Fairlynn had crossed to the dimmest corner.

She rested her hand on a stack of stone slabs. "What are all these, Dev?"

"That's my share of the rock cut out to make equipment rooms for the gate mechanisms. There are stacks like this in every former's house now."

"It's not being ground down for soil?"

"Not yet. We didn't want anyone to see how much we excavated, so we hid it all away on each night that it was cut."

"Have you been working all night as well as all day?"

"No, other formers did that part, but I stored a share. That way, no one can see a huge pile of it all in one place."

Something seemed to catch her eye, and she leaned over to pull on a cloth. It fell away, revealing the stone egg. "You saved it."

Devron swallowed, remembering the last time Alverlee stood in this workshop. It seemed very long ago. All he could do was murmur, "Yes."

"Have you…done anything with it since…the collapse?"

"No." The word seemed too bald. Almost condemning. "It was a useful project, though. The gate design borrows from it." And that sounded stupid. "Not the dome, of course, but the concept of nested, curved panels."

Talmarq looked from the egg to Devron, a line between his brows. "It seemed to be really driving you at the time."

"Yes, it was. But I still…don't know how to make use of it. Implementing a bit of the design in the gates…" He stretched the muscles he'd been using. "Well, it relieves the compulsion." *Sort of.* He wished Fairlynn hadn't exposed it.

"Does it?" She sounded doubtful.

She must know. He shrugged. "A little with the outer gate panels. More so with the inner gate, because the curve is a truer fit."

"How do you know?"

It seemed obvious for a second. She seemed to understand so much, but she couldn't see his latest work. "I haven't told anyone this. It must not be repeated." They both promised secrecy, so he told them, "I've already started the inner gates."

"You still sit by the outer set?" A question lilted in her voice.

He smiled. "I have good range, you know."

"Oh, I see." She knit her brow. "Why are you keeping it secret? Doesn't Kevenor know?"

"He doesn't mention it. He never checks very far. I'm not sure if he's trying to stay a little ignorant of my work or what."

"Why would he do that?" Talmarq asked.

"I can only guess. Maybe he wants me to move ahead with whatever needs to be done. He can't forbid it if I don't ask permission. I think both gates should be cut before anyone catches on to how extensive the work was. Assuming he agrees, he'll just want it quietly accomplished without mention."

Talmarq grunted. "What a way to lead."

For all his smooth talking, Kevenor was not a great leader. That much was already clear. But another explanation worried Devron far more. And that, he could never state—nor even ask about. Not unless he had proof. "Regardless, keeping Kevenor's smooth tongue between me and Borchel suits me just fine!"

Fairlynn grinned. "I don't doubt that. But what about your vision? Has it really stopped calling?"

He wanted to say *yes*. So very badly. "I know I need to make the inner gate. I suppose I won't know until that is complete."

"But didn't you say the gates are not necessary?" she asked. "You assured us the cavern roof will not collapse."

"It won't. But if we don't finish the inner set, fear might stop people from opening the outer set. We could lose the oysters."

Her creased brow cleared. "Ah, that would be an awful mistake."

It was true. He'd explained that reason to himself many times. It just felt like a half-lie, for he knew another purpose. One he could not speak. "Let's get this bed put together, and then I'll start making you a new cane out of that excess ipenrock."

"Out of rock?" She sounded as disappointed as she looked.

"I'm sorry, but it cannot be metal. A plain surface will be best, so it is no temptation to thieves."

"Won't it be awfully heavy?"

"Not at all. More air than stone. I'll fashion the interior with the union of beauty and strength."

A faint wistful smile touched her lips. "But I'll never get to see it."

"I'll show you before I seal up the heart of it."

The more Devron thought about lighting the night streets, the more he worried that the magnery system couldn't handle it. He wasn't sharing this until he knew. Which took him to the technician's house while her family was still eating breakfast. Embarrassing.

He dipped his head. "I apologize for arriving too early, but I...I cannot let an idea be heard around town until I'm sure."

The technician was young enough that her children's ears and tongues would reveal nothing. She cradled an infant on her arm, swaying to keep the little one content while her husband took their toddler elsewhere. "What's the concern?"

"The possibility of overtaxing the magnery system."

"Ah. Have you turned on the gate mechanism then?"

"What? No. Why..." His stomach did weird things with his hastily swallowed breakfast. "Have we overlooked a problem with powering it?"

"I'm not sure yet. Motors are a really new development. I don't know what those gates weigh or how you're dealing with the friction. Slick as a rail, I'm sure, but I won't know how it draws magnery until we try it."

"Why didn't you mention your concern?"

She hmphed. "It's all so hushed, but mostly because of the hand crank. The gates can move either way, true?"

"Yes." A relief to be able to say that.

"Don't worry too much. I'm pretty sure the system can handle the draw as long as you only move one set of gates at a time. That's the plan anyway, right?"

"It is, but that's not what I was going to ask about." She raised her eyebrows as Devron paused. "I have an idea about lighting the settlement streets at night. That would add a lot of lamps, and I don't know if the magnery system can power so many."

She angled her head. "We're getting close to the limit. Not that we have a certain way to know what that is. Accidental discoveries may be thrilling, but they leave a lot of questions." She swayed faster as the baby kicked. "The Magnery Guild was planning new conduits to feed the city expansion, but of course, that's been stopped. We even had the material mined. Pity. No one will let us tunnel halfway to Crysalan to reach the river turbines now."

His spirits sank...until the last few words registered. "River?"

She blinked and shook her head, giving him a perplexed look.

"The rare earth and copper—is it still in Jourendia?" Devron asked. "Any river would do, right?"

"Well..." She shifted the baby, who was starting to fuss. "Yes, it's here, but Jourendia doesn't have a river. Or do you mean the fountain river? I'm not sure if that one has current enough, and it powers the—" Her baby let out a wail. "Could we discuss this later?"

"Certainly. Forgive me for disrupting your morning." He hastened from her welcome room and drew a deep breath beyond her door. Problems. Always problems, but likely a solution as well. Hopefully, Kevenor was still home.

No luck there. After a false lead, Devron found him in the city cavern with the mayor and several council members. The way they kept turning shoulders to the people drawing near, they were getting more involvement in their conversation than any of them wanted.

Devron drew closer in time to hear a disgruntled voice say, "It's those damn miners thieving again."

Idiot. Devron could make no sense of the griping, nor did he try. He drew Kevenor away from the crowd and whispered to him, "We need to talk. I have an idea for lighting the streets at night, but we might have a magnery issue."

Kevenor's forehead was more crumpled than usual. He'd be looking like an old man soon. "Later. I don't have time for that now." He pulled away.

Fine. Devron would just check the light shafts and get out of this fray. A streamer he barely knew touched his arm and murmured, "Can you spare us a minute?"

Devron followed him to Chief Streamer Fezlie, who waited with Talmarq near the north wall. She clutched Devron's arm. "Talmarq believes he's discovered a river, but none of us can find it. By any chance, can you discern a river channel? Er, the absence of rock?"

"There are some channels and voids. I've noticed them before, but gaps in the rock are usually empty. I cannot tell which one holds water."

"Oh, dear." She darted a look past his shoulder. "We cannot afford to lose track of his discovery, and Talmarq must still travel. I need you to mark the wall."

What did she mean? His face must have shown his confusion.

"Assuming," she said, "that we are someday allowed to sink a tunnel, we need a marker that shows what direction and how far to the river."

"Ah. I still don't know which channel contains the river."

Talmarq launched into a rapid description—which wasn't much help—then dropped to his knees and pointed like Devron had done to direct Fairlynn a month ago.

Devron studied the rock for a moment. "I think I might have it." He etched a circle in the rough wall and some lines converging on a center point. Without direction, it was useless. He focused again, then separated a thin rod and drew it from the wall. "The hole is only a foot long, but I've etched a couple yards farther. It points in the general direction. What would you need to confirm—"

"Stop!" The councilman's shout was so loud, it echoed and silenced every person in the cavern. He was pointing at Devron and running. "Did you excavate?"

Great. Here he stood, holding a rod of stone, with markings behind him on the wall. The rest of the crowd was now converging.

Fezlie snatched the rod from his fingers. "You all stop right there," she snapped. They were close enough that they would have smashed into the wall soon, so it was doubtful that her words caused their halt. She held the rod high. "This is mine. I needed it, so Devron gave it to me. Are you going to call this tiny little rod an excavation? Because if you are—and if you're going to claim it's dangerous—then you have a lot of explaining to do about those gates down in the lake tunnel."

Devron half closed his eyes. *Please don't bring the gates into this.*

"Size is not the point," Mayor Borchel declared. "No cutting can be done without the council's approval."

"Council approval!" She spat the words. "Pretending you are formers!"

"No, we're not. We get their assessments before deciding."

"Yet you reject what they confirm safe. As though you are little gods. Ellincreo alone can grant the forming gift. He alone can judge when a former would use it to harm. He alone can withdraw what he has given. You have neither the wisdom nor the right to forbid the use of substance gifts. King Tandorad would *never* have allowed this, and if we could reach Judge Queltin, you'd be standing trial."

The mayor used the full depth of his voice. "This council is the only government we have now. It must be obeyed, or we will have chaos."

"Oh." She drew the word out with a dangerous smile. "So, you harass the people who are doing useful work all day, and let thieves run in the night. One of our best streamers was injured after completing her work, and you have the *nerve* to tell me you are preventing chaos?"

"We will implement a curfew so that—"

"A curfew? Oh, brilliant! Those who obey will be locked up inside their houses, while thieves run unchallenged. You would surrender the night and the streets to thieves? What sort of government are you?"

The mayor's tight lips paled. He snapped, "The council and I were elected by the people and—"

"A people controlled by fear elected a government of fear, and gain nothing from it but the amplification of fear." Fezlie pointed her stone rod at him. "You constrain those who can help us. Your mindless restrictions only feed chaos. If you want to turn this around, get your council members out of this cavern and put them to work guarding the streets. It will be the first useful thing they've done in a month."

"In the dark?" one of them demanded. "We wouldn't stand a chance."

"Well, make some lights," she snapped. "We've got them inside, don't we?"

Was Devron's idea that obvious? How deflating. Clearly not obvious to most, for several were already scoffing. Devron mouthed the words *we can* to his nephew.

Kevenor looked puzzled but made a vague offer. "There might be a way if you just give us time to check into it."

The mayor snatched the delay tactic and used it to disperse the crowd, shifting them all away from the small group in front of the river marking. Devron watched him. He seemed to want to return, but he must know that the council members, perhaps the whole crowd, would follow him back.

As soon as they were clear, Kevenor spoke under his breath. "What were you trying to tell me? What are you doing back here?"

"I just hoped you would offer the lights and get rid of the mob."

Kevenor glowered at him. "That has nothing to do with a rod of stone or streamers." He turned his glare toward the circle and narrow hole.

Talmarq's lips closed, and his eyes rounded with a pleading message to Devron.

Fezlie intervened, offhand and quiet now. "I merely needed a river location marked. Just so we can remember it easier."

"A river? Where? For what?"

Talmarq gave Devron a tiny shake of his head. Too small for Kevenor to see while he focused on Fezlie.

She shrugged. "I never throw away information. No one else needs to know, since it bothers you."

Devron grabbed his chance. "But as Chief Former, you, of course, need to know. The magnery system will reach a limit. At some point, we'll need another turbine and spinning magnet. We should be prepared with knowledge of rivers and an access plan."

Fezlie gave Kevenor a tight smile. "As gifted chiefs, we should be working together. I will never yoke the Streamers' Guild under the mayor, but I will work with you, Chief Former."

Kevenor swallowed. "I appreciate your cooperation. If you'll excuse me." He got himself away with dignity.

Did the others see through his fake assurance as easily as Devron did?

CHAPTER 18

Family Day. It was bound to come. Fairlynn took a firm grip on her shaky heart, accepted the support of Devron's arm, and attended family dinner—in the house that had once been her own.

By Crilla's demeanor, absolutely nothing was wrong or even faintly unusual. Kevenor played along, though his rendition was stilted. Tebber pouted through the meal, while Santear kept an eye on her aunt, anxious to please. Only little Jojo and Perrie were free of restraint. Only they gave Fairlynn a sense of family.

Perrie delightedly sat between her Uncle Dev and Mama-Lynn at the table, and afterward, she squeezed into a space on the couch between them, resting a hand on each. "I miss you, Mama-Lynn."

"I miss you too, dear."

"I'm not allowed to ask anymore when you're coming back. Mama says I'll know when it happens."

"Oh. Well..." What could she say? There was no change here. No railings on the stairs. No place of ease for her on the first floor. No acknowledgment of any issue, much less resolution. It hit Fairlynn like a blow to the chest. How dreadful it would be to return to this place. A house that was not home and a family that did not value her. Except for

Perrie. Fairlynn had been silent too long now and still didn't know what to offer the child beyond a sideways hug.

Devron filled the gap. "Some things in the future are harder to know than others."

That probably went over her head, but Perrie turned serious eyes to her uncle and asked, "Like when you're going to bring the light back? Papa says we must obey the mayor, and he won't let you. Can he stop you, Uncle Dev?"

Perhaps she understood far more than Fairlynn thought. More than any of them realized.

Devron regarded her solemnly. "Not forever."

"When will you do it?"

"I don't know yet. Time rests in Ellincreo's hands. We will be patient."

"I hope he doesn't wait too long. I don't like being hungry so much."

Perrie's matter-of-fact words made tears sting Fairlynn's eyes. She blinked hard, losing track of the conversation. Crilla's brisk footsteps brought her back. She hardened her resolve against whatever the demand would be—probably for help with dishes. But Crilla had shed her apron and sat down in the welcome room for conversation. By the sound of splashing in the sink, cleanup must be entirely Santear's job now. Poor girl.

Crilla soon grabbed an opening to speak. "Chief Streamer Fezlie did not stop by this morning."

An odd subject change. "I suppose not," Fairlynn said. "Had you asked her to?"

"No, I just mean that it seemed strange, for she has come every week as long as I've lived here. Always had a little talk with Alverlee and Kevenor—guild chiefs, of course—and she delivered your wages."

Kevenor stiffened, and Crilla's intent dawned on Fairlynn. Wages. Best guard her tone. "She knew I was staying with Devron and brought my wages there."

"Oh, good. I assumed she had, but I just wanted to be sure all was well. I—"

Kevenor cleared his throat. "I told you not to worry over this."

"I'm not worried, but I need to buy at market, and I must know if I'm buying for Fairlynn. And even though your pay increased when you became chief former..." She shifted her eyes back toward the couch, not quite meeting Fairlynn's. "The household still lost a wage-earner on that dreadful day of collapse, and I—"

"Leave it, Crilla." Kevenor's ill-concealed tension revealed that they'd had words over this already. "We are better off than most."

Devron stood. "I will take Fairlynn to the market while she is with me, so that needn't concern you." He offered his hand to Fairlynn to help her rise. "You wanted to get a few of your things, did you not? May I help you upstairs?"

She put her shaking hand into his. They knew each other's movements well enough to smoothly climb to the third floor despite her churning mind. Crilla's true concern was obvious—one less wage in the household funds. Fairlynn had planned to just pack up some clothes, but she placed her jewelry box into the basket first. She even took a quick check of the contents, for there was no telling what that woman would do.

Devron escorted Fairlynn to his home in silence. His thoughts could not be spoken in public. Despite all the tension, Perrie's words stung the worst. They were all at risk of starvation, but to watch innocent Perrie starve... That would be unbearable. And worse, he had blamed Ellincreo for the delay, while their stunted plants needed light. Devron's own words shamed him, for Ellincreo had gifted him to deliver that light.

No sooner did the door close, than Fairlynn huffed. "Maybe I'm being over-sensitive, but…I'm nearly certain that Crilla wants some of my income."

Devron stared at her for a moment. "I suppose that's the only way to make sense of her strange remarks. You wouldn't agree to that, would you?"

She closed her eyes. "She'll make me feel selfish first. A family of six, now—her income from making clothes will cease when her fabric is used up—and any other burden she can lay upon me."

"Then, point out that you lost your husband's entire wage, while her husband's wage increased. You are the one most harmed by his death, for it looks to me like you have lost your home too."

Fairlynn sank onto the couch. "It doesn't feel like a home, but I suppose I can still live there. She may push for my return, because I contributed more to the household funds than I ate."

Should he tell her? He didn't want to be disloyal to Kevenor, yet this would affect her too. Memory stirred—how he'd felt when she hid something from him. He could not hurt Fairlynn to spare Kevenor. Devron cleared his throat. "You can stay here. I doubt that Kevenor will ever install railings or a wall to make a proper bedroom for you."

She fixed her dark gray eyes on him. "Why do you say that?"

"Because he… This mustn't go any further. It's only a guess, not a fact." She gave him a little nod, and now he must finish. "When I was alone with him before we ate, he asked me in a sideways fashion to make the railings—if I had some spare time. But I'm quite certain that he has more spare time than I do. Unless he truly doesn't know all that I'm doing, but that points to the same conclusion."

She tilted her head. "What do you mean?" Her eyes rounded. "Are you saying that he's lost his former's gift?"

"Not lost. At least, not yet. But I have suspected for a while that it is weakening."

"I didn't even realize that could happen. Gradually, I mean. Do you think he has used it for harm?"

"I doubt it. Unless one considers that he leads the guild but prevents forming. Some of us have tasks, but highly restricted ones. In this, he harms all formers and everyone who needs our gift. Or, I suppose, it could be simple lack of use. If that is the case, all formers with heavy movement skills will also lose their gift."

Fairlynn let out a mournful sigh. "That would be his fault too."

"Not entirely. Some of them agree with him, at least in word. Any loss they suffer will be on their own heads."

She was silent for a time. "You're not going to say anything, I take it?"

"No. If I'm wrong, the kickback would be horrible. If I'm right..." A little smile tugged at the corners of his mouth. "Considering the mayor's determined inaction, a chief former who doesn't know what I'm doing is not all bad."

She sort of chuckled, but her arched brows looked doubtful. "Oh, dear."

"Don't worry. I'm careful, but we've strayed from the point. You are welcome to stay here as long as you like. Even permanently. There's plenty of room, and no need for you to pay any rent. And I hope that you would find comfort in being appreciated again. For indeed, Fairlynn, your presence is a joy to me."

Her eyes grew a little wider. Maybe his did too. His unplanned words were true—but what else did they mean?

Savoring Day included the anxiously awaited *Closing of the Gate* ceremony. A big event to most, but not to Devron, for he was among the formers who had tested the closing and opening of the outer gate while Jourendia slept. He waited between Fairlynn and

Kevenor, while Mayor Borchel expounded on the great care taken during construction. Finally, he ordered the gate to be closed, smiled as the crowd uttered a long *ahh*, and then thanked Chief Former Kevenor for the gate's flawless design and construction.

Kevenor acknowledged politely—and in the moment when Alverlee would have given credit to the other formers—Kevenor held silent.

For all the world as though he had designed them! Separated them from solid rock, dug out the equipment rooms, and crafted the mechanisms! Kevenor's blatant omission disrespected every other former.

Devron realized his jaw had dropped and closed it. Fairlynn's hand resting on his arm went rigid. She must have risen two inches taller. Oh, no. Her rigid stance revealed every ounce of outraged shock that was about to spill from her stiff, opening lips. He patted her hand and whispered urgently, "It's all right. It's fine."

He absorbed the fire of her gaze, meant to burn Kevenor. Tiny lines radiated up from her tight mouth. At least she kept her voice to a nearly silent hiss. "It isn't fine!"

"Later," he whispered, hoping to calm her. Doubtful that it worked, but she held a brittle silence until the gathering dispersed and he led her toward home. Best not to chat among friends, or their tension would be noticed. The walk gave him time for a realization to worm through him. *Could* Kevenor give him credit?

In the privacy of his welcome room, Fairlynn spat her words. "The self-important pretender! As though he was the only former who worked on it. Did he actually *do* any of it?"

Devron looked down at Fairlynn's agitated face. "If Kevenor comes here, are you going to give him your...unmitigated opinion?"

She made a guttural sound in her throat and rolled her eyes, then muttered, "I used to be such a kind person."

He laughed and took her hands. "You're still kind, just sorely pressed."

"Do you think he will come here?"

"If he saw your face, not immediately."

"Devron!"

He laughed again. "Seriously, though, it's possible that he believes he *cannot* pass the credit on to others. I don't know what he has been telling Borchel, or what that dictatorial mayor has been demanding. I do know that Kevenor feels insecure in his position."

"That doesn't make it any better."

"No, but…I have more freedom to act if the mayor doesn't know what I'm doing. Not much, but a little, and I will take all the freedom I can get."

She sighed. "So, you want me to hold this tongue that longs to lash him?"

"That is your choice, not mine. Just remember that words are creative gifts too. Create whatever you choose to."

She leaned back. "Whoa. Devron, that was profound."

"Was it? I hope I can remember it in the heat of so many infuriating moments. What do you say, should we go up to the roof and play with those crazy ducklings?"

CHAPTER 19

Devron strolled with Fairlynn up from the lake with a bucket of precisely counted oysters—three rations of five—for Talmarq had returned to watch another cycle of lowest tide. He'd lingered in the lake cavern while the last of the oyster harvesters finished gathering.

Fairlynn glanced around, probably making sure they were alone enough for her soft words. "When are you going to reveal that the inner gates are finished?"

"When I complete the changes to the equipment room wall."

She shook her head. "You showed me the finished interior a week ago. I study the exterior every time I'm in the lake chamber, but it never changes."

He laughed. "I love this part of my gift."

"What are you doing? Please don't make me wait until everyone else sees it."

"You're as inquisitive as Perrie."

"How dare you liken me to a five-year-old!" She snorted a laugh. "Tell me!"

This time, *he* checked all directions before whispering, "I'm making a clear crystal window. Anyone in the equipment room will be able to see into the cavern."

"Ooh! Nice touch. Does Kevenor know?"

Good question. "He never tells me of anything he has sensed. Just remember that *you* don't know."

They had reached his door by this time, but the people hurrying up the far end of the thoroughfare distracted him. He angled his head toward them. "There must be an arrival on the rails." A rarity now. A mail pouch had come with Talmarq a few days ago. It was too soon for another unless there was reason for a carriage to move. "I think I'll go see. Do you want to come?"

"You can tell me if it's anything interesting. I'll start dinner." She took the bucket of oysters he carried and went inside, while he continued on.

When Devron came into view of the platform, Mayor Borchel stood upon it, confronting Wandermae. A courier had taken a position at the far end of the platform with a stack of packages, for which he called out names. Just as many people gathered around the chief wind weaver, for she was known to travel through all parts of Dirklan and would likely have news.

Devron saw no sign of Kevenor, which gave him the excuse he wanted to mount the platform in his nephew's place. None too soon, by the mayor's strident tone.

"I have enough food for tonight," Wandermae replied to the mayor. "Each day that I work here, I will use my wage to buy whatever ration you allow the residents of Jourendia."

"We don't need your services, which you ought to know, for we have a good ocean breeze. You can depart with the courier as soon as he finishes."

That got the fellow's ear. "Well, I'm not leaving till morning," he snarled, "and don't forget that I'm entitled to a meal for bringing your mail."

"Just as well..." Devron spoke soft enough to reach only Borchel and Wandermae. "...for we need an assessment in the lake cavern." To her, he added, "You are welcome to stay with me this evening, for Chief Former Kevenor's house is somewhat crowded."

"Thank you, Devron. I will join you. At once, please, for I must walk after all that tedious sitting."

She turned toward her travel bag, which Devron swung over his shoulder before escorting her down from the platform. He hoped to outdistance the mayor. No luck.

Borchel jogged to his side, out of range of the crowd. "Why should the lake cavern need a wind assessment?"

"The gates close it off."

"What gates?" Wandermae asked. "Is that why it's so quiet?"

"Yes." Devron pointed down the slope. "There is one set now, but there will be two very soon."

"You allow forming here? Well done, Mayor!"

"No! Only if it's strictly necessary. The gates will protect us if the dome of the lake cavern fails."

Her black brows darted high. "Is it at risk?"

"No. Not at all," Devron declared.

The brief approval left her face. "Oh, I see. Forming is allowed when one fear surmounts another."

The mayor lifted his chin. "We employ rational caution."

Devron spoke before she could mock that nonsense. "We still harvest oysters from the lake, and a streamer is always on duty there. I just want to know if the air is going stale—and if it is—how often and how long we must open the gates."

"Ah. It's possible that the gates could disrupt airflow to all your caverns. Don't worry about it, though, Mayor Borchel. I will check it tomorrow and let you know whether there really is a problem."

"Don't spread that around. Report to me directly."

She flashed a smile at him. "A commission from you, after all. I shall see to it. Pleasant night, Mayor."

That probably made Borchel sour, but at least he stopped shadowing them.

Devron ushered her into his home, where she greeted Fairlynn and then Talmarq, who arrived as they spoke. Convenient.

"Sorry to send you right back out, Talmarq," Devron said, "but will you take a message to the chief streamer and then to the chief former? Tell them that the chief wind weaver is here, and they are welcome to join us after dinner."

Talmarq gave him a wry smile. "Well, I can't refuse to deliver a message to my own chief, so I may as well tell them both. Save me some oysters."

Devron turned to Wandermae. "I'll take you up to your room. I hope the third floor is acceptable."

"The higher the better." She ran lightly up the stairs ahead of him, barely looked at her room, then climbed the last flight to the roof.

He should have guessed. As long as they were quiet, the roof would be as private as within. "Have you been working with Greehan?"

She looked up from the duck pen, which had caught her eye, and her brows lifted. After a moment, she answered, "I often see him. By strange coincidence, I depart each city a day or two after he arrives."

"How bad is the air? Are you able to find channels?"

"Some caverns are worse than others, but yes, we believe there will be enough. I analyze before he comes, then we decide together which channels to use. He lingers behind to do the work. Once we've gotten through them all, we will cycle back around to ensure that the overall airflow can maintain itself. In case you're worried, Greehan told me that when he widens a channel, he uses the excess rock to strengthen the walls."

"Makes sense."

"Good." She loosened her hair from its constraint and shook out the long black curls. A gentle breeze stirred them, summoned by her gift, no doubt. "Who have you told?"

"No one. Greehan sent me a vague message through Talmarq, which made him curious, but I didn't explain. I believe you could trust him and Fairlynn if you need to, but don't trust Kevenor or Mayor Borchel."

"We haven't told anyone." A musing tone softened her words. "There are times when a messenger would be a great help. Talmarq also has his own reasons to travel." She began sweeping her gaze over the cavern ceiling.

Devron inspected his lettuce varieties, tearing off a leaf here and there. None were fully mature, but the vegetables in his larder would not be enough to feed four at dinner. "I'll get a bed ready for Greehan. You and he may work from my roof and escape notice. When should I expect him?"

"Probably not at all, unless I find something tomorrow. I doubt that, for I already sense that you have the freshest air in Dirklan. I told him to go to Crysalan and see if he can sneak some work in without detection."

She caressed a young vine, which Devron desperately hoped would produce fruit when the days lengthened. She shook her head mournfully. "For a few seconds, I thought Jourendia might be sane, but no. There isn't a single city that doesn't forbid forming. Alluthin says they would allow it if a double assessment confirmed the need and safety, but they haven't mined in ages, so it's really a moot point."

"We hear strange things of Crysalan," Devron prompted.

"It's so dreadful there," she said. "The most chaotic of all. The meeting place of Ellincreo, too, so you'd think it would be the most peaceful."

"That only works when all parties want peace."

"Sairtoka wants peace through control. She tried to influence the choice of the new Chief Keeper of the Writ, but the keepers refused to comply. Now, they are at odds with her too. The entire city..." Wandermae blew a mournful exhalation. "They spend all their energy fighting and make little progress with food production. Their air is the worst, too, and I wonder if it affects their capacity for logic."

"Have you tried reasoning with them any further?"

"I don't dare. Greehan agrees that if we are to help them, we must do it in utmost secrecy. Even most of the formers of Crysalan rant about the dangers of altering rock. Worse yet, Mayor Sairtoka becomes more despotic every day, and the formers encourage her worst tendencies. She conscripted all the unemployed miners to create a security force and put that giant bully in charge of them. There's plenty of gold stored in Crysalan to press their own coinage. So now, her government employs an awfully big percentage of the population. Won't that be handy when an election comes?"

Another chilling worry that he hadn't thought of. Jourendia's mayor and council had authorized minting of silver coins, though they conceived some way of restricting the quantity to reflect the value of assets. An untested method.

Wandermae eyed him. "What of the formers and mayor here? And the unemployed?"

"A lot of miners work with our new Growers' Guild. Others are now called safety guards and patrol the streets at night. It's a small force assembled over the past few weeks. The guards answer to the mayor. He took control of the formers, particularly the chief, immediately after the collapse. Most formers believe the restrictions are excessive, but we can say nothing. I don't even tell my peers what I am doing. The only work I acknowledge is making the gates and monitoring what the aboveground polishers are doing. They seem quite determined to send ample light into the city cavern."

Her eyes lit. "They are working on that?"

"Indeed." He smiled broadly. Those touches from above were precious.

Wandermae closed her eyes rapturously. Most would clasp their hands to their chest, but she spread her arms wide. "They haven't forgotten us!"

"Nothing gives me more hope than my morning surveys." Devron opened the stair access. "Come, let's go down and see if Fairlynn needs help with the oysters."

Talmarq returned as they sat down around the table, with the vegetables and steamed oysters already divided onto each plate. No bread tonight, grain being strictly rationed.

Wandermae glanced around the table. An easy count—four oysters on each plate except Fairlynn's, which held three. "Wait a minute. Fifteen. This was the ration for the three of you. No, no." She began pushing her chair back. "I have food for tonight. I cannot eat your ration."

"Sit still." Fairlynn deftly extracted an oyster from its shell. "We had enough vegetables to fill the ration, so save your food for your next journey."

Wandermae stared at her, then picked up one of her oysters and held it out to Fairlynn. "You shouldn't give me the fourth one too. I'm small and—"

"But I chose to, Wandermae." She spoke with quiet determination. "You are thin. Worse than most of us. Are you allowed to buy food where you travel?"

Wandermae pulled her lower lip between her teeth. Slowly, she picked up the oyster fork and inexpertly tried to remove the meat. "Not everywhere. How do you get these things out in one piece?"

Devron demonstrated with a shell on his plate. Her hands were shaking. No point in commenting when he could do nothing about it. Talmarq took up the conversation, asking a great many questions about experiments in Illia. Fortunately, Wandermae followed them, too, and was able to report some progress.

Devron absorbed the hope—as rare as grain. He found even more from Wandermae's questions of Talmarq—how far he was reaching up the hidden rivers and his knowledge of the water's reaction to rock friction or the lack thereof. Ah, if the water did not contact rock at the top of its flow, then there was space for air movement. Fairlynn's eyes glowed too.

The air began to vibrate with Wandermae's excitement. "Have you, by any chance, made contact with a streamer aboveground?"

Talmarq's mouth quirked as though he felt foolish. "It's silly, I know, but I try. The chances of anyone reaching through the waters at the same moment that I do...pretty much impossible!"

"Perhaps," she murmured in her silken voice. "But try anyway. I have found wind weavers aboveground. Twice. Trust me, it's worth every failed attempt." The last syllable snagged. Her blue eyes closed, and when they opened, tears drenched them.

Devron froze. What should he do?

Fairlynn touched Wandermae's arm. "What is it?"

"Sorry. I try not to think about it, but sometimes it sneaks up on me."

"What?" Devron asked. "Are you being abused for using your gift?"

"No," she gently scoffed. "That would make me rage, not weep." She spoke as one trying to make light of something...get past it. Much to Devron's relief.

Not to Fairlynn's, apparently. She kept her gaze on Wandermae. "What makes you weep?"

A tear escaped and crept down her cheek. "I...I'm afraid I'll never get aboveground again." Another tear. "Most people down here...they just need things. But I need the sky." She snatched up her napkin to catch more tears before they fell. "So constricted belowground. Our wind weavers usually have...a different kind of range. Mine is vast. I could stand it before because...I could go above for relief. To beckon the wind and caress the storms." She drew in controlled breaths and sniffed, then tried to joke. "This is what comes of someone being kind to me. I'm not used to it."

Talmarq frowned at her in concern—that made sense—but why did Fairlynn look so appalled?

Fairlynn licked her lips. "Wandermae—you believed the visions. *Why* are you still *here*?"

"Oh, I longed to flee! But I couldn't."

"Why not?" Fairlynn asked.

"My gifting. I had a vision too."

Devron's voice sank low. "What was it?"

"People gradually suffocating. Falling to their knees...to the ground. It had a dream-like feeling that it all happened in slow motion. Behind the people, there was an image of the big moon cycling thrice through its phases. It illuminated thin passages in the rock—like a broken spiderweb. I realized what needed to be done."

Their own breathing seemed loud in the silence.

Wandermae leaned back and shifted air through the house. "So, you see, I couldn't leave. And believe me, I *wanted* to. Yet Ellincreo gifted me, and he called me here. For this very event, perhaps. I'm even called to those who doubt his existence, for the king commissioned me too. The health of Dirklan's air is my inescapable duty. No matter what anyone thinks, I *must* open the air channels."

Such loyalty—even to the undeserving! Such unshakeable commitment. Devron's admiration swelled. And his shame, along with it. So many light shafts polished, so many spreaders as well. Yet most remained blocked with an opaque layer, lest the fearful see light and tremble more. Or be forced to admit their error.

He almost snorted out loud. As though they would admit it. No, they would rant and stop him from ever forming again. And that revealed *his* fear.

Talmarq interrupted his thoughts. "You mentioned that the moon cycled thrice. Is three months significant?"

"It seemed so—like that was all the time I had—though every cavern is different, and many are already safe."

"We must be safe here with the ocean breeze," Fairlynn said.

Wandermae flicked her hand. "It's all about movement. When the air enters warm, it lingers above the cooler air. During winter, the winds rarely reach the inlet and may even draw your air out. You are better off than most, but that inlet you rely on is not enough."

"But the rail tunnel allows movement, so—" Fairlynn's face fell.

Wandermae nodded. "Ah, yes, and at the far end of the tunnel is Crysalan, which still has poor air. The hub of Dirklan—where I am least welcome. I've been hoping that they'd recognize the effect of stagnation, but I cannot wait, for their caverns need much work. We must begin if we're to finish in a month."

"We?" Talmarq asked.

"I have a helper. He and his work must never be suspected, so we rely on your discretion." Wandermae waited for Fairlynn and Talmarq to agree, then said to him, "You travel much as you search out our waters. Would you be willing to carry messages between my helper and me if your duties allowed?"

"Most certainly."

They finished their scant meal and, soon after, gathered in the welcome room with Jourendia's chief streamer and former. Wandermae began to summarize conditions in the other cities, but Kevenor interrupted. "Shouldn't we wait for the mayor?"

"I didn't invite him," Devron replied.

"You should have." Kevenor stood as though he would go to get him.

"Not at all," Fezlie said. "You may bow to him if you like, but I do not. And neither does Dirklan's Chief Wind Weaver."

"If he comes here," Wandermae added, "I shall go up to bed. He's already given me a commission—most unwillingly—and I will meet with him tomorrow. I've had quite enough disdain from mayors, as it is, so if you want to hear from me, you will have to do so without him."

Kevenor sat down again, and they managed to get through a mild discussion. When it was over, Devron stopped Kevenor with a touch on his arm while the others left.

The moment they were alone, Kevenor griped, "You should have invited the mayor."

"I couldn't. He was rude to the chief wind weaver when she arrived, and I wanted her to speak freely to us."

"Why do you keep belaboring her title?"

"Because too many forget it. But this is far from the point. Earlier this evening, I had to make reference to the inner gates in the mayor's presence, and I used the word *soon*. I thought you would want to know."

"Oh. Yes. Are they ready to be tested?"

He didn't know. "They are. Also, it occurred to me that sooner or later, someone will refuse to open the inner gate for fear that the cavern has already flooded."

Kevenor's eyes widened. "We would surely know if that happened!"

"Obviously, but they won't believe us. I have clarified a crystal glass window between the equipment room and the cavern. Even the ungifted could confirm that the cavern is not flooded."

Kevenor stared at him. "You planned this all along. That's why you wanted so much space where we should have left solid rock. You've got to stop unnecessary forming!"

"All that I have done is necessary. Are you angry that I plan for contingencies? I am trying to help you in every way that I can. You may explain as much or as little as you like to the mayor. If you want, I will even wait to clarify the final layer and do it before his eyes. Then he could see what a simple matter it would be for me to finish the light shafts."

"What? No!" Kevenor's fists clenched. "Polishing the shafts has not been approved, and you know it."

This time, Devron stared long at him. "Kevenor—the light shafts are already complete. Only a thin opaque layer blocks the light from the spreaders. Which are also complete. Do you not know this?"

His rigid lips grew white. "Did you form them?"

Rage? Probably fear-driven. Kevenor could not be trusted with the full truth. Instead, Devron said, "I told you that polishers above were working them, but you do not answer me. Kevenor, is your gift weakening?"

"You ask because of *this*? Why should I inspect what is not being worked? *You* were responsible for assessing the city cavern roof."

"A task I have fulfilled. I report every day that it remains strong. Which has nothing to do with the light shafts, for we all know that polishing them cannot weaken the cavern roof. I assumed that you knew, so it's a good thing I mentioned them tonight. Now you may share that information—or not—as you deem best. You are good at dealing with the mayor and council—far better than I."

Some heat left Kevenor's face, though his jaw was still clenched. "Have you anything else to spring on me?"

Devron assumed a puzzled look. "Not at all. I'm sorry if it seemed that way. I am on your side, you know."

"Thank you," Kevenor snapped and stomped out the door.

More deception, and whether Devron shared full truth or partial, none of it went over well. A good thing he hadn't told Kevenor how that shaft to the new-found river came to be. He'd enlisted Earlman's help, and they'd made it look like a natural formation beyond a thin layer of rock. Kevenor had simply nodded when Devron spoke of it. Which could have meant that he knew what was going on all along—or that he had no idea but dared not reveal ignorance. Then all it took was a word to the magnery techs and a promise to the mayor of lit streets in the night. For a few weeks, several formers were employed, and a faint glow now illuminated the settlement from dusk to dawn. The satisfaction still warmed Devron.

Yet the design and resulting shaft had never been assessed by anyone but its creators. Ironic that fear of forming was causing that very act to be performed with fewer safeguards. Which should have been obvious to any former who bothered to check. Did they not know? Or did they not tell what they knew? A critical question that he could never ask.

CHAPTER 20

"You missed quite the meeting." Fezlie's dry pitch conveyed far more than the words as she settled into one of the chairs in Devron's welcome room.

He and Fairlynn had missed it on purpose. Not that they could avoid hearing about it, but the chief streamer was a friend, which would make unpleasant news easier to endure. Maybe.

"Did any of it pertain to us streamers?" Fairlynn asked.

"Not directly, although one of the council members suggested Talmarq's status should be revoked." Devron halted for a split second in the motion of sitting down beside Fairlynn on the couch, but Fezlie continued. "It's a good thing I got him declared a resident of Jourendia the first time he came back here. Took a battle to maintain it today. Can you believe it? The strongest streamer in Dirklan, and they suggested he should not be allowed rations when he returns to us."

Disturbing, though Fezlie must have prevailed. "Why did they even bring it up, if they weren't discussing streamers?" Devron asked.

"They've cut off allowing any newcomers to reside here. Did you hear that Parrel returned yesterday? The Keepers of the Writ have sent all their students away. Crysalan is refusing them rations. Naturally, he returned to his family, but since he's been away two years, the council was actually debating whether he should be allowed to stay! That's why the matter of Talmarq was brought up again. But not to worry about those two—they can stay. That wasn't the bad part."

Devron steadied himself, and Fairlynn slid her hand within his.

"Theft is now punishable by death."

He exhaled. After the worsening fights and food thefts, he wasn't surprised. Tragic, but probably unavoidable.

"It's retroactive."

"What?" Fairlynn's voice cracked.

"That's right. Those young men they have in custody for thieving—they'll be dead by tomorrow."

Devron's empty stomach nearly ejected bile. Fairlynn was sputtering that they couldn't do that...the injustice of it all. Though Fezlie joined her in outrage, he knew. They could do it. The decision was made. He interrupted the ladies. "Who is carrying out the executions?"

Fezlie snorted. "The council hopes to escape that deed. The condemned will each be given a blade to take his own life tonight. If they are alive in the morning, they will be hanged. The mayor granted them the right to be visited by the Keeper of the Writ if they desired. Poor Parrel. He just stared with his mouth agape through the whole thing."

"What a foul task to dump on him within his first day here," Devron muttered.

"Mm." Fezlie gave Devron an appraising look. "There's one other thing. You aren't going to like it."

He set his jaw.

"The mayor announced that the chief architect died. By his own hand."

Devron stopped breathing. Fairlynn's grip tightened within his. She turned her face to him, but he couldn't meet her eyes.

Fezlie spoke again. "Borchel gave him a nice little eulogy about his contribution to Jourendia, then expounded on his honorable death."

"What?"

"According to our fine mayor, he shortened the days of his old age so that others could live."

That was a lie! Devron ground his teeth. The poor man had been hiding away, refusing to see friends or even speak to his family. His gift, his wisdom...disregarded. No, punished. Shamed. His purpose stolen. "It is the senseless fear and chaos that have killed him!"

"I don't doubt you," Fezlie said. "He wasn't much older than me and could've had several more years to finish his dream. Anyone who ever talked to him knows that he lived to see the city built." She shook her head, stretching a mournful moment. "To be brutally frank, I believe that the decision about executing those young men, and the mayor claiming that elderly suicide is honorable...it's all about food. The fewer mouths there are to feed, the longer rations can be eked out."

There was nothing to say to that, and silence pressed down upon them.

Finally, the chief streamer slid forward in her chair. "Should I not have come and burdened you with today's folly?"

"We must know, regardless." Devron tried to lighten his tone. "It is not your fault that the news is grim, and I thank you for telling us."

"I'd best be getting home before dark—even though the new lights do help." She shoved herself upright with the aid of the armrests in the manner of one whose knees hated the burden. "Whether news be grim or hopeful, it is up to us to make our own joys in the days remaining. Do not waste them, children."

Devron blinked at her remark, but she marched out the door before he could think how to question her. "Children?" he murmured.

"I suppose she means that we are younger than she is." Fairlynn's brow furrowed as she stared at the door, then turned her eyes to his. "I keep thinking that we will find a way out of this mess. Ellincreo wouldn't have given the visions that he did if there wasn't some solution. But it seems like we are ruining all our chances. Running out of time."

Running out of time... The phrase seemed to repeat in his mind. A fading murmur echoing with Fezlie's remark. *Up to us to make our own joys in the days remaining...*

The corners of Fairlynn's mouth wavered. "How long do you think we really have?"

He swallowed hard. "I...I don't know...and I don't know how to say this. I keep waiting for a hopeful moment...or at least a touch of happiness in the dark, but it doesn't seem to come, and I dare not wait any longer."

Her brow puckered. "Do you know of some way...?"

"Not for anyone else. Only what will bring me...and, I hope, you...joy of our own." He shifted awkwardly. "I know one is supposed to wait for a decent mourning period, but...we may not have time for that." Her lips parted, and he couldn't tell if she was surprised or appalled. "Do you want more time to..."

"If my days are shortened, I will not waste them on some arbitrary rules of sorrow."

"Then..." He swallowed again. "Dearest Fairlynn, will you share the rest of your days with me? In marriage, I mean."

Her breath whooshed out over his chin, then she flung herself against him, pressing her cheek to his chest. Did this mean...*yes*? Or...tender-hearted as she was...maybe she couldn't look at him to say *no*. His arm had naturally come around her, but should he hug her? He barely touched her shoulder.

S hock swept through Fairlynn. Could this be? A tumultuous current beat against the protective walls around her heart. Of course, she knew better than to build walls against love. But the loss of Alverlee had convinced her she would never be happy again. Betrayed on all sides. Her family's love proven so shallow. Her community failed her too.

Thieving sprang from hunger, yet the attack showed that her own people would harm her. With their tongues and raised eyebrows too. The unsmiling questions of whether she had recovered. Whether she still lingered in Devron's house.

She never explained what they wouldn't understand. That there was peace here. A place of comfort. And yes, she had noticed the quiet pleasure that came with Devron's presence, but she'd held firm against hoping for more. One existed these days. One carried on—endured. One did not hope for happiness. That was foolish. Especially the giddy sort of happiness that vibrated the foundations of her walls. The streamer buried deep within her heart would not help at all to turn the current of hope away from those protective barriers. And then Fairlynn realized why. Her walls were built from stones of fear. Held in place with the mortar of—choice. So she made a new choice, and hope swept the fear away.

She needed to answer him. She took a few breaths, not wanting her voice to rasp.

"I'm sorry, Fairlynn." He sounded sad. "I suppose I have made everything awkward now."

"It's not that," she mumbled into his chest, her voice husky. "I just didn't think I had a chance to be happy again." She turned enough to look up at him without leaving his light embrace. "No matter how many days remain to us, I will share all of them with you."

He seemed to have gone as rigid as the metals he worked. Only his lips and eyes showed an awed sort of expression, like he wasn't entirely sure yet whether a too-good-to-be-true thing had just happened.

She smiled. "I believe we are engaged now, so your hugs can be much tighter than a proper, brotherly hug."

His chest shook as he pulled her in snug with both arms. "Is this better?"

"Ah...much!" She let out a long, audible sigh. "I didn't realize how desperately I have needed a loving embrace." She nestled deeper into his arms and wove one of hers around his back.

"That, my dear, sweet Fairlynn, is one thing we will never need to eke out on short rations."

She gave him a tighter squeeze. "Can we wed quickly, Dev?" She sat up but stayed within the arm that rested around her shoulders. "I like the normal traditions, but...a ceremony in Ellincreo's sacred chamber would mean traveling to Crysalan. And guests. Besides, a wedding lunch made of rations would be such a travesty. I cannot bear to think on any of it."

"Ellincreo is everywhere, so he can bless our union right here in this house. The hidden benefit of Crysalan sending away the younger Keepers of the Writ is that we have one on hand for the ceremony. We just need two witnesses. I would ask Kevenor to stand for me anyway, so that will bring immediate family, and that provides guests enough."

"Mm." Nope, Fairlynn couldn't ask Crilla to stand for her. "One more, for I will ask Fezlie to be my witness. Perrie may bear the sash and ring, which she will love to do." She began tugging the ring from her finger, for she still wore her wedding band. "Alverlee told me this belonged to his and your mother. It's rather worn. Perhaps that's why the gold is oddly colored, and I could never even make out what the carving was supposed to be."

"The traditional entwined spiral was carved into it." Devron accepted it from her and held it up between his finger and thumb, giving it a weird look. "It's off-balance."

"It was too big on me, so Alver thickened the band."

Devron pursed his lips. "Should have let me do it. The gold is an alloy including copper and silver." He held it horizontally over his cupped palm, and soon, a coppery dust began to collect below it. The grains rolled around, adhering until they formed a blunt pin. The ring soon lost its pinkish hue, now a pale gold. Devron stretched the copper pin into wire and wrapped it around his little finger, then repeated the process, drawing silver from the band.

"I love watching you polish. It's a true golden color now." She teased with her smile. "Awfully rough, though."

He shook his head in mock reproof and slipped the ring onto her finger. "Slide this on and off a few times to make sure the fit is right."

"A little tighter, please." Amazing! She could feel it snugging closer around her finger. She moved it again. Already, the inside was much smoother. "I do believe that's perfect."

"A beginning, anyway." He held his hand out, and she placed the ring in his palm. He slid it partway down his little finger until it settled, then began shaping the outer surface. Uniform at first, then details began to emerge.

What would he create? Fairlynn suppressed her impatient inner child. She must think of something else. Of life and plans. "Did it just occur to you to propose? Because of what Fezlie said?"

"No, I've thought of it a lot. This whole courtship thing... I've never understood how it's supposed to be done. Much less how one is to court a recent widow!" He gave his head a tiny shake. "And even though I knew my love for you had changed—drastically—I still wasn't sure what was best for *you*."

"What do you mean?"

"Associating with me could become—difficult. With or without marriage. Either way, I wanted to make sure you inherit my house. Legal matters have become questionable, with the courts now unreachable. So marriage would be the surest way to provide for you." He drew a deep breath. "But—marrying me could also bring other troubles much closer to you." He darted a glance to her eyes, then back to the ring. "I've been trying to figure out how to explain that *before* proposing. Which didn't work. I won't hold you to your...uninformed answer."

"What in all the caverns below are you talking about?"

"I do what is forbidden. I form without permission or assessment."

"Sure, but...not really. The mayor and council don't know the extent of it, but the formers must. If your work concerned them, they would say so. Silence is their implied approval."

He turned the ring, studying the design he'd made, then took the silver and copper wires and anchored their crossed ends into the gold. "The trouble is, their silence may also mean they *don't* know. Every light shaft in the city cavern is clarified. I've created and polished every faceted spreader. Only a thin opaque layer hides the fact that we can have full daylight whenever we want it."

Excitement thrummed through her. "Devron, that's wonderful!"

"*I* think so. Kevenor was appalled when I told him, which means that he didn't know. He has not passed that information on to the mayor. Nor has anyone else uttered a single word about it. They either don't know, or they're afraid to reveal it."

"Afraid? To tell good news?"

"It will prove that forbidden forming has been done. Maybe they don't want to get me into trouble. Or they might fear suspicion falling upon themselves. Our architect was vocal—and then treated with such shameful disdain that...well, you know. It sickens me that the mayor pretends his death is a matter of honor. More deaths are coming within hours. Thieves are responsible for their choices, but changing the law retroactively is *not* justice."

Fairlynn hung her head. She had tasted happiness...while mothers in other homes must be crying.

"Now, I can't help but wonder..." Devron turned the ring slowly, twining and embedding silver and copper. "Would the mayor and council have been so hasty to condemn others to death if they knew we have light enough to increase food production?"

"Don't blame yourself. We still need more soil."

"I know there are many aspects to growing food, but I am responsible for providing from the gift I've been granted. If—no, *when*—I do reveal the light shafts..." He joined the wire ends, then looked up into her eyes.

"The mayor and council will realize what I've really been doing every morning. They will accuse me of breaking their new laws. And I suspect my punishment may be far more severe than the architect's was."

His meaning swept through her, and she tossed it out as quickly as she understood. "No. Impossible." Her hands splayed and jerked. "He argued for stone cutting, and that wasn't crucial. But you will give light, and everyone will know it is a precious gift that we are in dire need of. It's not the same thing at all."

He gripped her hands. "I completely agree with you." His determined eyes kept their somber expression. "I just don't trust them. Not the mayor, or the council, or the frightened masses."

She tried to think of something to say, but there was nothing. Because she didn't trust them either.

Devron lightened his tone and resumed sweeping his thumb over the ring. "Mind you, I really don't think they will kill me, but things could get nasty. Are you sure you want to be married to a lawbreaker?"

"Hm." She tapped a finger against her chin, pretending deep consideration. "Not just any lawbreaker, but I'd like to be married to this one." She pressed her fingertip to his chest. Oh, she just loved seeing that kind of smile spread across his face. Better yet, *she* had triggered it.

"I think I can wait a few more days to reveal my crime." He seemed to look into a distance within the ring he held. "How about this? Tomorrow is sixth workday. After the vile deed is done to those poor souls in the morning, I'll find the Keeper of the Writ and ask him to perform our ceremony in the evening. I'll talk to Kevenor, and you can get Fezlie alone to ask her. Then, once we are married, our few guests can head to their own houses, and we shall keep Family Day and Savoring Day for just us." His smile warmed her. "We deserve at least two full days to ourselves as much as any other bride and groom."

She leaned nearer. "Indeed, we do, and your plan will be quick enough, even for me."

He was looking over the ring now with an appraising—and satisfied—expression. When he turned his gaze to her, she knew perfectly well that his satisfaction was not all about a ring, pretty as it was. He'd made the traditional entwined spirals from the copper and silver.

"How did you embed the spirals into a flattened band *and* make them look three-dimensional?" she asked.

"Correct alignment takes advantage of a trick of the light."

"You're an amazing artist. May I try it on?" She extended her finger for him to slide it on, but he drew it farther away.

"Uh-uh. Expectancy is half the pleasure of receiving."

Devron skipped his morning check of the city cavern roof. He had no idea when they would start the executions—if there were any left to be done—but he refused to be present. Better to wait until he was sure it was over. A vantage point on his roof allowed that, for the comings and goings of people through the settlement were as familiar as the stone of his house. Someone passed, sobbing, and turned down a side street. Returning to an emptier home. Pity welled—such discordant emotions on his wedding day. He waited longer, his eye on a certain house. Fortunately, he was spared more audible sorrow by the time Parrel entered his family home. Devron put his cultivator in the toolbox, went down to wash his hands, then traversed the thoroughfare to the keeper's house.

He asked for a private talk with Parrel, which made the young man look more careworn than ever, but as they conversed, his expression passed to surprise, relief, and even a touch of pleasure.

"You may be sure that I will," Parrel replied to his request. "Nothing could please me more than a wedding ceremony, for I expected nothing but misery from this day."

"Thank you," Devron said. "I must go, for it suddenly seems that I have much to do today. I'll see you right after dinner then."

His errand to Kevenor was less auspicious, for he was difficult to find, harder to get alone, and greeted the news with a blank stare. After an awkward pause, Kevenor asked, "Are you sure that's wise?"

What could that mean? No, he wasn't even going to try to figure it out, much less ask. "Yes," Devron replied with firm simplicity.

"Well—I'm happy for you and all that—but you might not have heard because you were single. Do you know that no one is allowed to get pregnant?"

"Council members watch your bedroom now too?"

He sneered. "Of course not. But extra rations will not be supplied to a newly pregnant woman nor to any child she may birth."

What? As though an unplanned pregnancy never occurred! Devron suppressed the words he longed to say. "You may have noticed that we are past most of our childbearing years, and I'm sure Fairlynn knows how to count the days of her cycle."

"No doubt. I just wanted to be sure you knew. And Fairlynn is perfect for you. I do wish you joy. We'll be over right after dinner."

Devron hoped his nephew could find some joy for his face before that time came.

Fezlie was the first to arrive, the bearer of as much good cheer as any bride and groom could have asked for. She took charge of the sash and ring, sliding the center fold carefully through the band and forming a floret, then folding the long strands back and forth. When Perrie came in with her family, Fezlie instructed her on how to carry and present the folded bundle of fabric, with the ring on top and the ends dangling.

A smile beamed from Perrie's face. "It's so sparkly and beautiful!"

"Yes, dear child," Fezlie said. "You're doing a fine job holding it just right."

Fairlynn had donned her festive gown. She glowed like she was trying to subdue a fountain of bliss. Her hair was swept up in an elegant style, and she wore her carefully guarded perfume. Was that how she managed to seem so radiantly fresh—even young, though tiny smile wrinkles spread beside her eyes? Devron straightened his formal shirt and hoped he was worthy of her.

Parrel took a central position, holding a small book of the Writ against his white tunic and broad green sash. He cleared his throat and, in deeply solemn accents, began the greeting. Which took all eyes away from little Jojo.

The glistening sash ends that dangled from Perrie's hands had tickled his babyish curiosity for too long. And now his sister was standing in the middle of this group, staring at the stranger. He toddled forward and snatched one end.

Perrie gasped. Tebber crowed with laughter. Crilla swept Jojo into her arms, but he kept a tight-fisted hold on the sash, which he shoved into his mouth. Kevenor moved in to free it as Jojo squirmed. Perrie let out more squeaks, each one higher than the last.

Devron stiffened. Chaos for his wedding too!

"It's all right, dear," Fairlynn murmured, her hand on Perrie's shoulder. Though she spoke to the child, her gentle voice acted the same on Devron. Really—nothing was terribly wrong.

Fezlie recovered the strip of fabric and swiftly refolded it, one dangling end now wet with drool. Her chest shook with glee that she suppressed behind pinched lips.

Devron let a bass chuckle vibrate his throat. "There now, Parrel. I believe you may continue."

The Keeper of the Writ closed his sagging mouth and proceeded. Better yet, he forgot his solemn tone and spoke the blessing like it was, in fact, a blessing instead of a dirge. At the proper moment, Perrie lifted the sash.

Devron and Fairlynn gripped one another's forearms, capturing the ring floret between them. Together, they wound the strips, crisscrossing to symbolically join their arms. Devron had heard the poem of *Weaving*

Hearts and Days from the Writ many times, but slowly weaving the sash with its cadence gave a whole new meaning to the poem's words. They really were creating something new. And somehow, when the spitty end of the sash slipped between his fingers, he didn't mind.

Neither did Fairlynn, apparently, for her lips twitched when that end slid through her hand in the last round, and she let it drape toward the floor. Laughter, joy, and everything true and good in the world flowed from her eyes, as he took the ring from its floret, and they exchanged their vows. There really was hope.

CHAPTER 21

E very day seemed to be a procession of strange new things. Waking up on their first workday was no different. Devron had a wife asleep beside him. Lightly, it seemed, for within a moment of him watching her sleep, her eyes opened, and she gave him a dreamy smile.

They snuggled for a moment. "I thought you always got up early," she murmured. "Went to check the city cavern."

"No more."

The corners of her eyes crinkled. "Well, I still have work."

"So do I—at least today." He rolled over and stood, then offered her a hand to help her up. It still seemed strange to sleep in the room that had once housed his workshop. More convenient than his second-floor bedroom though.

Devron went to the kitchen to fry the single egg—courtesy of their duck. May her offspring soon begin laying. He mixed in some vegetables from his roof garden. Cooking for two was normal enough that his thoughts went to the task he dreaded. How should he do it?

He still hadn't figured it out when they finished a cozy meal, washed the few dishes, then walked up the thoroughfare to the big cavern, with Fairlynn's hand in the crook of his arm. The news of their marriage was clearly out, and they received many wishes of joy.

When they reached the fountain, Devron left Fairlynn with Fezlie and the other streamers, then tried to catch Geon's eye. That wasn't hard, but getting him alone was. Devron went to sit in a place removed from the crowd and waited. Doubtless, they all thought he was checking the roof, but really he considered the opaque layers within the light shafts. He could clear them one at a time. Too obvious. There'd be an immediate uproar, and he would be stopped. Gradual lightening of the chamber wouldn't work, either—unless he had months to do it. Too many people noticed small changes now, and he'd been reprimanded before. Not that he had accepted any fault in the matter.

Geon slipped to his side and sat down. "Do you have any news for me?"

The phrasing—both funny and sad. Geon never used the word *light*, though that was the information he wanted. "No one dares speak the news," Devron said, "nor is it new. The shafts are all complete except for a minimal tweak to each."

Geon's lips parted, then he closed them and reverted to a mundane expression. "When will we see it?"

"I cannot imagine it being approved. How is soil production? How soon can you make use of more light, and how much area can you plant?"

Geon shook his head. "We need all of it. Now. The days are lengthening, but the plants remain in winter stagnation. We won't get flowers or fruit until we have..." He glanced around, then whispered, "...daylight. I've tried seeds that germinate in the dark, but the sprouts are pale and anemic. Those that need sun to germinate just lie atop the dirt. And grain takes months to mature. We must start it now!"

"Shh." Devron allowed no change in his expression. "Don't let on that you know anything about the shaft progress."

Geon huffed. "Fine. Do you mind if I stress our desperate need for light?"

"That, you may do."

Geon returned to his duties, and Devron found Kevenor, unfortunately with a couple of council members. An unavoidable irritant. He joined them anyway.

And of course, Cadmore, the one he liked least, spoke first. "I heard you married Fairlynn, and I quite understand you taking a few days off, but we haven't had a report on the cavern stability in a few days now."

Devron was tempted to thank him for his kind wishes. No, he would either miss the irony or take offense. He would do that anyway, but better that it not be personal. "Almost three months have passed. Jourendia's caverns have not moved—*at all*. Not from the collapse at Mount Estelle. Not from the aftershocks. Not from the aboveground polishers working so diligently on our light shafts. As I have repeated many times, Jourendia is safe. Endlessly checking stability serves no purpose."

"Then what are you doing here?" the other council member asked. "Checking is your only approved task."

Cadmore bunched his fists. "We have to figure out a way to stop those aboveground workers." He scowled at Kevenor. "Can't you do something?"

Though Kevenor opened his mouth to answer, Devron said, "You needn't worry anymore. They have finished their work."

Tension lines twitched in Kevenor's lips. "I'm tired of this debate." He addressed that to the council members but took Devron's arm and turned him away. "Come, I need to talk to you." They walked a short distance, while he tracked the council members with sideways scrutiny. "Why must you prod them? Look at that. Off they go to the mayor."

Not worth answering. Devron stopped and followed his gaze. Geon was with the mayor too. "Have you told him yet that the shafts are finished?"

"Hinted that they were close. Don't press it, Uncle Dev. He's not happy with you."

"Really? And here I personally crafted his street-facing magnery light."

Kevenor slowly shook his head. "I just don't understand you. If an apprentice spoke like that, you'd bring him right back to his place in an instant. Yet you speak disrespect for the mayor."

"Hm. Interesting point," Devron murmured, furrowing his brow. "It is the uneducated who need to show respect to greater knowledge and wisdom." He paused thoughtfully. "Yes, that should explain my low respect for the mayor."

Kevenor stared at him. "That was worse!"

"Granting respect to folly does not produce wisdom, Kevenor. We are running out of time."

"Keep your voice down. He's coming this way."

"If we do not let the daylight through—*very soon*—we will be starving when we should be harvesting."

"Say nothing," Kevenor hissed between his teeth.

The mayor reached them and inclined his head to Devron. "I hear you and Fairlynn have wed. My wife and I wish you joy."

Not a hint of a smile with that. "Thank you, Mayor Borchel," Devron replied.

"Yes, all the joy that can be had in this difficult time. I do wish you had talked to me about it."

What in the caverns? "Ah, if the matter of children concerns you, that is not in our current plans."

"I suppose not, but...challenging times are worse when loved ones suffer. I would have spared you if I could."

This still made no sense. "I love her whether I married her or not."

"Ah, yes." He infused some heartiness into his voice. "And of course, no disaster is imminent. Enjoy!"

Enough of *that* awkward subject! "I saw Geon with you a few minutes ago. How is food production?"

The mayor's expression soured, though he had never truly smiled. "Longer days approach, and we are doing all that we can." He turned pointedly toward Kevenor.

Devron listened to their standard discourse. Always the same. Kevenor even reported on cavern stability.

Devron held his tongue—hoping—but when the mayor turned to depart, he said, "We now know, Mayor, that the cavern is safe and light shafts are nearly finished. When do you expect to approve their completion?"

He turned back to Devron and quietly enunciated his words. "We have run out of stone to grind, and we do not have enough plant matter to make soil. More light will have no gardens to shine upon, and changes to the ceiling will raise doubts of stability and cause more panic. I know you disagree with my decision, but I have the authority to make it—and you do not." He strode off.

Devron watched the mayor leave, while Kevenor hissed a few angry words at him, none worthy to be answered. "This is why the mayor should not have authority over the Formers' Guild."

"Do you listen to anything I say to you?"

"Yes. All the time, constantly hoping that you have begun to see reason. Only formers can bring light to this cavern, and we must have light to grow food. It is up to us to prevent mass starvation."

"I know you want to believe that, Uncle Dev, but it won't work." Kevenor couldn't seem to maintain eye contact. "Don't skip this afternoon's meeting."

Why did a reference to a meeting intrude so ominously? Devron fought it while repairing the damage caused by an attempted theft of metal from a neighbor's lift mechanism. When the meeting time approached, he went in search of Fairlynn among the city gardens, where she had been irrigating this morning.

Not there. One of the streamers on duty told him, "She's taking a turn down in the lake cavern."

"Oh. Thank you." Devron looked toward the settlement. Was there time to go get her and return? Not if she was in the middle of diverting water for oyster harvesting. She might even be avoiding the meeting. Much as he wanted her at his side, he headed toward the half-walled enclosure of their make-believe government hall.

A haphazard collection of old chairs provided inadequate seating, and a permanent platform allowed speakers to be seen. Devron stood near the outer fringe as he always did. The meeting began with some trivial matters, then spiraled in on the issue of food.

Mayor Borchel cleared his throat and adopted his somber tone. "It grieves me to say this, but we must face facts. We have calculated the likely production of food, plus the quantity remaining from the imports we received before the collapse. I also receive reports from around all of Dirklan. The news is not good."

Murmurs increased. Devron couldn't hear much, but the mayor was looking at someone who must be asking a question.

The mayor answered, "At our current levels of rationing—which are already meager—we will run out of food in about six months."

Someone spoke of food growth rates increasing in the longer days of summer, and the mayor replied, "Yes, and we will take full advantage of that, but we must acknowledge that there was a reason that we imported most of our food. We simply cannot grow enough within caves to feed the population belowground. That is why I feel such deep gratitude toward those few who have made the difficult decision to shorten their lives so that others may live."

Devron's brow knotted. There had been other suicides? Who?

But the mayor wasn't giving names. He slowed, leaving weighty pauses. "I know that such discussions bring anguish. Perhaps in your own homes, those who are elderly...weak...unable to still provide service in the family or community—in brief, those who feel they can best provide for others by shortening their own lives—perhaps they have raised the subject. Perhaps you have even begged them not to do it. And I do understand that." Oh, how sincerely empathetic he looked. "But consider the nobility of their sacrifice. Consider giving them a supportive, loving goodbye instead of resisting the great gift they seek to bestow on the children of Dirklan. That the young might survive as long as possible, and a remnant of us may continue on."

All grew utterly quiet—except for the buzzing within Devron's ears. As the mayor cast his fear-spawned web, seductively wrapped in compassion and honor, the truth dawned on Devron. This was not the worst that the mayor would propose. It was another step in a heinous direction.

He knew he would be reviled, but Devron could not let his own fears stop his tongue. "Mayor, are you now recommending that we should encourage the death of others to prolong our own lives? Isn't that murder?"

"I did not say that. Do not twist my words, Devron."

"Mm. People of Jourendia, do not be deceived. There will not be enough suicides to save a remnant, and Mayor Borchel has stated the criteria of death. Those who are elderly, those weak—or the conveniently vague, 'those unable to offer a service.' Soon, these people will be pressured into suicide. When that has not worked, they will be executed. For we have already seen what a simple matter it is to change laws and penalties."

Devron turned and strode away. The mayor would now discredit him. No point in listening to it. The most he could hope was that the hearers would take his words to heart and see the deception twisting through their isolated world.

He didn't break his stride until his door was within reach. He'd hoped Fairlynn would be home, but she wasn't. He dropped onto the couch and leaned his head against the cushion she had replenished with carefully gathered duckling down. His beloved wife. Not elderly yet, but weak, by one standard. Few knew how strong she really was.

Perhaps it was good she hadn't arrived yet. He needed time to find words to tell her of the mayor's latest atrocity. Maybe he could start with—

The door opened, and there she stood, her smile blooming when she saw him...then fading. "Dev...what's wrong?"

He spread an arm along the couch back. "Come and sit with me, my love."

She nestled against him, propping her cane against the arm of the couch. "There's more bad news, isn't there?"

"Yes. I've been trying to figure out a gentle way to explain it."

"Don't bother. Just relate it the way it came to you."

He sighed, all the energy of his bold statement long gone. He did as she asked, pausing after he related the mayor's words.

She stared straight ahead, her eyebrows puckered. He tightened his arm around her, for she began to shiver.

"Strange," she murmured, "how a person can get so cold when the temperature hasn't changed."

Clearly, she'd reached the same conclusion as he. "I couldn't help but see where this was headed, so I spoke up." She nodded, and he related what he'd said. "After that, I stomped away because I knew he would discredit my words." She nodded again. "Do you think I am wrong?"

"No. Anyone who fits his definition of *unnecessary* will understand where this is going."

"You provide a regular service. I won't let them call you weak, for you are stronger than the naturally strong. I will not let anyone hurt you."

She turned and laid her cheek against his shoulder. "Maybe people will wake up now."

She didn't sound like she believed that any more than he did. The silence stretched long.

Finally, she straightened. "This is one of the moments where we need to remember that we have chosen to reject fear of the future. Right in this moment, we have each other, and we have our love. Let's rest our minds in that blessing."

"Wise words." He kissed her. A pleasure he'd waited so long for. He hoped familiarity would never rob him of its sweetness. Would they even have enough time for familiarity? After a moment, their stomachs rumbled in unison. They both chuckled, and—

A fist hammered on the door.

CHAPTER 22

The harsh beat triggered dread. Oh, how Devron hated the thrumming pressure in his chest and the sheer fact that he couldn't stop it. The daylight was nearly gone, and he hadn't yet locked the door. His mind leapt to the possibilities. Robbery? Some show of force to punish his words? But he had to either lock that door or open it. He stood, crossed the room—and opened the door.

"Talmarq!"

The streamer stepped forward so quickly that Devron almost stumbled in getting out of the way. He looked awful.

"Welcome." Devron gave him a reassuring touch on his shoulder, then locked the door. "Has a carriage arrived this late?"

"No. I traveled on one that went as far as the river settlement with a delivery. I walked the rest of the way."

Small wonder he was shaking. Only seeing him once a month increased the shock of his sunken cheeks. "Come and sit at the kitchen table. We were just about to start dinner."

Talmarq sank into a chair and propped his elbows on the table. Head in his hands, he mumbled, "I couldn't bring food."

Fairlynn set a full glass of water before him. "Because of rationing? Or can you no longer earn a wage?"

"I can't get ration tokens in Crysalan. Even if I could, my coin pouch was stolen two days ago."

"That's a long walk on an empty stomach," Devron said. "I'm glad you got at least half of the ride."

"I figured it was better to walk in anyway. No challenge at the terminal station, and I...just can't bear to be sent back to Crysalan."

"No, indeed." Fairlynn cut a thin slice of bread. "Enduring a robbery is awful." She held the slice out to him. "Don't argue with me about food. Just eat it."

The look on his face! Then he bit off at least half of the bread. How dreadful these portents of what was to come.

Talmarq swallowed and whispered, "You sound like my mom." His eyes still looked so haunted. "Theft, I can at least understand. Some are starving while others eat. That isn't why I never want to see Crysalan again."

The strain in his voice...this was something far worse than hunger. Devron put plates on the table and sat down across from Talmarq. "What happened?"

"Wandermae saved them. Maybe all of us. They killed her for it. Greehan too."

The bowl of greens slipped from Fairlynn's fingers and clunked hard on the table.

Devron drew her into the chair next to him. She plopped down, her jaw slack. His empty stomach turned to an immense void, as Talmarq rubbed his shaggy hair and shoved more bread into his mouth. *Oh, Ellincreo*...the words raised a silent cry within. Devron stood to get the drake thigh they'd been able to buy, then sliced three portions of meat from the bone and brought it to the table. "Are you...able to tell me about it?"

"Well...you know that big open space near the central rail hub?" Talmarq waited for a nod. "That's where they distribute ration tokens. I was near Government Hall, talking with Greehan. In public, the two of them are never close together. Wandermae went to Mayor Sairtoka—she and Chief Former Pondarro, and that big, red-headed guy who leads security were on a platform thing. That's where the mayor stands when she plays goddess, granting the right to eat unto those who please her. The ration masters had refused tokens to Wandermae, so she had to petition the mayor to get them."

Talmarq sipped water like he was trying to avoid gobbling food. "Sairtoka started in on Wandermae, mocking her for having warned about bad air and claiming that she only pretended to provide a service. The air has gotten a lot better there lately, and—according to Sairtoka—that proves they don't need a wind weaver. Wandermae had to take some credit for the improvement if she wanted to eat. No explanation, though, of what she and Greehan had really done. She didn't mention him at all. Sairtoka kept badgering her. Gave mocking thanks for the tasty doves Wandermae kept, which are all gone now. Threatening to take her fruit vines, which everyone steals from anyway."

He squeezed his eyes tight for a moment. "Wandermae was so thin, she could probably whisk herself up to her home with a strong draft. She kept trying to get a few tokens and the wages they owed her. Pondarro joined in, probing for details of how she had helped. After a while, Greehan whispered, 'He knows about the changes—about the wind shafts.'"

Talmarq rolled dark lettuce between his fingers. "The way he said it...I realized how much danger she was in. She must have caught on too, because all of a sudden, she snapped, 'Fine! Steal from me then!' and tried to leave the platform. They wouldn't let her down the steps, and before she could jump off the side, that security guard seized both of her arms. Pondarro accused her outright of convincing a former to alter shafts. She tried to explain why she had to—that it helped them—but then, they warped every word she spoke. Twisted it into accusations. They claimed she put all of Dirklan at risk of future collapses."

He dropped the mauled leaf onto his plate and clenched his hands. "People were hollering, and I couldn't figure out what to do. And Greehan—he was breathing hard, and his lips grew dark red like he was about to explode. The mayor threatened execution, then promised they would let her live if she told which former helped her.

"Oh, she had sizzling words for them at that threat! She refused to tell. Someone yelled 'beat it out of her' and threw a rod onto the platform. One of the guards picked it up and took a swing at her, while the big guy held her arms behind her back. The mayor did that acidic smile she does and purred, 'When you're ready to tell us...'"

Fairlynn rubbed her face, a whimper escaping her.

"Do you want me to stop?" Talmarq asked.

"No," she moaned. "I must hear it."

Talmarq fiddled with his glass. "Greehan bolted around the crowd, yelling *stop*. No one seemed to notice until he reached the platform and dashed up the steps. I jumped up on a bench, trying to see what was going on in the crowd. He was screaming stuff about unlawful punishment and their crazed stupidity, but they held him off and hit her again, saying they wouldn't stop until they knew who did the illegal forming. Some people had come running in with buckets of rough quartz, and the crowd was throwing that at her too.

"Greehan shouted..." Talmarq's voice seized. He swallowed and tried again. "He shouted, 'Let her go. *I* did it! She has never hurt you.'"

Talmarq splayed his hands on the table as he rocked. "I couldn't hear the words anymore after that, but they shoved Wandermae down into the crowd. That's the last I saw of her. The mob swarmed her...swinging...throwing..." Tears etched lines down his cheeks. "Sairtoka and Pondarro just watched from the platform. Didn't say a word or try to stop it. Greehan was struggling to get away from those bullies they call guards. After a couple minutes, Sairtoka motioned to the big guy, and they threw Greehan down with Wandermae."

Devron rubbed Fairlynn's back as she cried into her napkin. Grief bled tears down his cheeks. Was Greehan's death—in part—his fault? The fires of injustice burned too hard for guilt. Wandermae's sacrifice—she gave all to help those who would murder her. Greehan knew the risk too. He faced that threat—worked three months without pay or thanks. And then he went to rescue Wandermae. He must have known that he would die for that. She would have saved him with her silence, but he'd tried anyway.

By the time Devron looked up, Talmarq was leaning back in his chair like one exhausted from hard labor. "Do you know," Devron asked, "did they suffer long? Were their deaths confirmed?"

"Probably not long. Some people fled right away. After a few minutes, the inner mob went still, and it got really quiet. The mayor ordered the area cleared. The mob high-tailed it out, and I saw the bodies on the ground. They were—" he looked at Fairlynn, her face scrunching again. His voice went flat and short. "They were dead. I'm sure of it."

He cleared his throat. "Anyway, I'm sorry about ruining your dinner. And maybe it's crass to eat after such a tragic telling, but...I'm really hungry." He consumed his portion of meat in one bite.

"We cannot let food go to waste, no matter how we grieve," Devron said. He looked at Fairlynn and her plate, then set an example. Best to force all attention onto eating, for he couldn't escape one fact. He would soon defy his own mayor.

Talmarq finished first and tried to smooth things out with talk of the rivers he had found. Bigger ones that could be useful. They would require some forming work, but a couple cities were somewhat open to necessary, well-assessed modifications. He attempted a smile. "So there really are little bits of hope here and there."

Fairlynn's expression lightened a little. "Should we tell him our news?"

"We'd better, or he will be terribly shocked when I walk into your bedroom tonight."

Fairlynn laughed, and Talmarq made a *wh* sound.

"Fairlynn and I were married just three nights ago."

"Oh! Good. That's really good!"

She laughed again. "You sound shocked anyway."

"Not in a bad way! You're perfect for each other. It just makes me truly happy and…I'm not used to that…lately." A shadow dipped over his eyes, but he hurried past it and told them he'd seen a wedding party in formal procession entering Alluthin's bantain orchard. "What else has happened here in Jourendia?"

"Hm." Devron rubbed his thumb along his jaw. "We now have street-facing magnery lights to discourage night-time thefts. Fortunately, most people don't understand about turbines, isolating copper, and such. Keeps them from asking questions. Very few know that the river you discovered is crucial to providing power for the new lights."

Talmarq's eyebrows shot up. "You excavated?"

"That's not something we talk about. Everyone *does* know about two sets of gates that were constructed within the lake cavern's tunnel. Most do *not* know how much space was needed for the mechanical aspects. Oh, and you will also like the magnery lights in the cavern and tunnel, all securely tucked behind clear crystals. We have no oil source, you understand."

"I'm just so relieved that you make progress here."

"Yes and no. It's all driven by what people fear the most—not by logic. We could have full daylight to grow food in the city cavern, but the mayor won't approve it."

"What? Why not?"

"Because it would be visible, and it is coupled with a false belief. That's the true explanation. The mayor would give you another answer."

"Is he like Sairtoka?"

"Not entirely." Devron drummed his fingertips on the table. "In some ways, it may be unfair to blame him. The council is just as bad, and many people of Jourendia agree with them. Some days, I'm not sure if he is the leader of the masses, or if he is the figurehead created by their fears."

"I suppose there is some truth in both," Fairlynn said. "These days, everyone is against someone. Every group blames some other group. Maybe that even happened in Crysalan—turned the mayor into whatever she has become."

Talmarq's entire face hardened. "You wouldn't offer her an excuse if you had seen it. The way she fanned the flames of the mob! Pondarro too. They had every intention of killing Wandermae and whoever helped her." He pressed his fist to his mouth for a moment. "In the end, we all must take responsibility for what we did or did not do."

He stared at Devron's drumming fingers. "You know this too, don't you? You hide a lot. Just like Wandermae and Greehan did. Like I do. Does your chief former hide things too, or does he side with the mayor?"

"He tries to do both, which is tearing him apart. When he is forced to choose one, I believe he will cling to the mayor." Devron curled his nervous fingers inward. "A choice he may have to make in the morning."

"Why?"

"If we don't get light for growing food immediately…" He gestured to the empty dishes. "This will look like a feast in six months. I need to reveal the light shafts now. The only way it will work is if I do them all at once." He took Fairlynn's hand. "I don't know what will come of it. I'm worried about you."

She didn't flinch or look away. "Me? You're the one in a tight spot. If you open them, the mayor will be angry. But if you *don't* open them, I will be furious. Who do you want to face?"

Chuckling, he touched his forehead against hers for a second. "That settles it then. I may be new to this husband role, but I'm not stupid." He stood. "I'll go in about an hour and try to finish before dawn." He straightened his fingers, which seemed determined to clench. "Things could be chaotic tomorrow, Talmarq, but I don't think we are as far gone as Crysalan. Either way, stay out of trouble. Better that you remain free to use your own gift than to become implicated with my supposed crimes."

"I'd better go up and check for an egg." Fairlynn crossed to her lift, stepped onto the platform, and began spinning the wheel to make it rise.

Talmarq watched with a half-smile as her feet disappeared through the ceiling, then glanced at Devron. "You're not going to help her up the last flight?"

"She likes to be self-sufficient, so I changed the railing to a stepped configuration. Looks a little odd, but it's easier for her to lift her weight with her arms."

"You're good to her."

Was that a question or a statement? Why did it sound...off? "That is my duty, and a pleasant one, it is."

Talmarq turned away to grab his worn travel bag. "Where do you want me sleeping this time?"

"My old bedroom will be the most comfortable for you. It's not like I'm using it, but I should grab the rest of my things."

They climbed the stairs to the second floor. Devron carried down an armload of clothes and went back to fetch his stack of books. Talmarq's bag was on the bed, but he wasn't in the room. Devron picked up the books from the window ledge, then stepped from his old bedroom.

Talmarq stood in the shadows at the far end of the workshop, a spare sheet hanging from one hand and the other resting on the stone egg, now free of its shroud. He stared down at it.

Hm. He'd seen it before—no matter that he looked again. But still...odd. Devron set the books on his bench and turned on the rear magnery light. "Is something troubling you?"

"Beyond...living forever belowground...among people losing their minds to fear...or else starving to death?"

It must be worse for one raised aboveground. "I suppose that's bitter fruit when you only planned on training down here for a year."

"That's not the worst of it, though. I think more and more of Adelle. That I'll...that I might never see her again. Or if I do get out, I'll be so old that..." He tried to mask the crack in his voice by clearing his throat.

"I wouldn't expect her to wait that long. Wouldn't want her to. Better that she finds happiness with someone else." He sniffed. "I know that's the right thing to want for her, but I *don't* want it. *I* want to be the one to make her happy. The one with the pleasant duty to be good to her."

Ah. Devron hadn't considered how it might affect Talmarq to see a newly married couple. He must mention this to Fairlynn and revert to friendship manners in the company of their guest. Was there anything he could say now to offer some relief?

Talmarq rubbed the stone dome. "How do you get this to open?"

He must want the subject changed. Perhaps because Fairlynn's lift was descending. "I do it by commanding the stone to slide." He hadn't touched the thing since they'd moved it up here.

Fairlynn stepped from the lift and joined them. She held up a duck egg. "Our sweet old girl is still providing." She tapped a finger against the stone. "Has this egg started calling you again, Devron?"

"Again?" Talmarq asked sharply. "Has the vision faded?"

How to answer when he didn't understand. "I used what I learned from making this model to design and form the gates. It felt like...like an outlet for the creative urge. Made me wonder if maybe that was its purpose all along."

Why did Talmarq's frown look so accusing...or shattered? "You asked what would happen to it with a streamer's touch."

"I guess I did, but what does that have to do with anything?"

"Olanni was there."

Devron glanced at Fairlynn to see if she understood what he was missing. She looked as perplexed as he.

"Don't you understand?" Talmarq stepped back, spreading his hands. "Olanni knows about this. She knows it matches the dome over the lake. It's not something she'll forget. I told her I was going to Weslin, so she'll at least guess that I'm probably alive." He looked suddenly uncertain. "The formers aboveground would be able to tell what did or didn't collapse, right?"

"Yes," Devron said. "Some of them, at least."

"Olanni was going to Regissa's guild chiefs anyway, to tell what was happening down here. And then the collapse. You must know that King Tandorad and Queen Dizelle will do all that they can. They're certain to convene joint guild assemblies. They'll put every possible resource into reaching Dirklan."

"Of course. I have no doubt of that." If only he could look like he understood.

"The rivers I told you about—at least one could transport food. But *only* if we get a message aboveground. Otherwise, they are completely useless, and we will starve with empty food conduits." The stone walls echoed his last words. Talmarq muttered, "Sorry to shout."

"It's important. I get that. But I still don't understand." Devron pointed at the stone egg. "How does this relate to the rivers?"

"It's a way to send the message."

Fairlynn straightened with a jerk, her eyes narrowed at the dome. "Open it, Dev."

That much, he could do. He commanded, and the panels began to slide.

The instant it moved, Fairlynn slipped a finger into the gap and took over. "To scale, Talmarq, how high are the waters as the tides turn?"

They might as well have forgotten Devron existed. Streamer terms—movement patterns, speed, and force—swirled like the currents and whirlpool they discussed. Hands motioning as though they commanded water, they manipulated the dome panels with a finger while they calculated pressure at various depths and speeds. With way too many unknowns.

Fairlynn suddenly turned to Devron and asked, "Didn't you say it would close under its own weight?"

"Yes, but... Am I part of this now? I don't even know half of what you're talking about. Are you honestly thinking of opening this? I mean—the real dome? *How?*"

"A vortex." She sounded so matter-of-fact.

"B-but...how could you even create such a force?"

She flipped a hand. "That part is easy. I create a vortex every time I flush the duck pond or draw water up through the city fountain. It's not like we push around blocks of water. Far easier to create a contained flow that water longs to follow."

His face must show his ignorance, for she softened her expression. "Don't ask me to explain a vortex, and I won't ask you to explain how you can *think* a slice into existence through solid rock." She arched a brow. "*And* insist that it's stronger than it was before you cut it."

Devron grinned at her description of his work. "I accept that you can create a vortex—here. But in waters you cannot sense above the dome?"

Talmarq rubbed the side of his neck. "I might be able to start it. We're going to have to hope that Olanni convinced, er, convinces the harbor streamers to help. A lot."

"Oh." Awkward silence grated Devron's nerves. "Are you telling me—no, *promising* me—that they will be able to keep this vortex from entering the cavern if the dome could, in fact, open?"

"No. It must enter or there is no point."

"What?"

"It has to lift a...container."

Container. Meaning dawned. "The message?" Devron asked.

"Yes." Talmarq seemed to find himself on firmer ground. "It must include maps, which I have from working with some formers in other cities. I can copy them. I've made duplicates already. And of course, explanations of what we want. The Inventors' Guild in Illia is already working on container designs and materials. They will provide drawings and—"

Devron gasped. "You haven't told them about this, have you?"

"No, but they are very precise about recording experiments and designs. I asked them to make me a set and..." He smiled sheepishly. "They were so excited with possibilities that they never bothered to ask why I wanted them. Or maybe they just like having people see value in their work."

"Got to admit, that is a rare and rewarding sensation!"

"Anyway, they understand that vortexes might be used in transport, though they are hard to maintain in a rough channel."

"You think you can maintain it in an ocean...and in the lake cavern?"

"In the cavern, easily," Fairlynn said. "It's uniform and without significant interference. What worries me, is the part when the vortex is withdrawn. For one thing, we don't know what surprises the ocean could deliver. A side or counter current could destroy the vortex. And at some point, it must lift above the dome panels. Sea water will enter. How *much* enters depends on how fast the dome closes."

They both stared at him. Waiting for an answer. Which he couldn't give because he didn't know the types of pressure they understood. And worse. "It also depends on whether it *fully* closes."

Talmarq's voice pitched as high as a woman's. "Is that in doubt?"

"Maybe," Devron admitted. "There's a lot of sand and debris up there. The *slices* I make can be small, but if there isn't room for give, they cannot actually move. So there must be space, and space can fill. Swirling water carries sand, you know."

Talmarq made a pathetic sound as his face sagged.

Devron patted his shoulder. "Don't lose hope yet. It's just that this needs careful consideration. That lake holds part of our limited food supply."

"I've thought of that," Fairlynn said, "but oysters stick themselves to any surface they can find. I could stabilize a sheet of water over them too, as an added protection."

"There is a pile of grindstones in the lake's basin." As Devron spoke, Fairlynn's eyes widened in understanding. "We know that the ancient whirlpool whipped them around the cavern hard enough to carve it."

She groaned. "They'll be right at the center of the vortex." Her brow knit deeply. "I can't hold them down with a sheet of water. Even if they only rolled around the bottom, they would smash our oysters."

"That's another problem we'll have to figure out," Devron said.

"We need a container too." Talmarq looked worried. "Watertight to protect the maps and anything else we may put in it."

No concern to Devron. "That's the easiest part by far. I can make that out of a grindstone. We also have a safe place to watch the cavern from." He grinned at Talmarq. "I think you'll like the equipment room I had hollowed out."

"Is that to do with those gates you mentioned?"

He grinned wider. "Indeed."

Fairlynn's open mouth formed an *O*. "Devron! You made those gates for this!"

"What?" Talmarq's eyes accused him. "Wait. You acted like you didn't understand."

"I didn't. Not fully. What you do with water mystifies me. But in my vision, I saw the lake cavern as an intact cylinder. No opening for the tunnel. When people started getting frantic over fears of the dome collapsing..." Devron shrugged. "I met two opposite needs with one project." He couldn't stop his grin from returning. "And yes, I love the paradox."

Talmarq's eyes glinted. "I can't wait to see those gates and all that you've done. That, more than anything, makes me feel that this impossible idea...was meant to be."

"You'll have to wait for a tour. Tonight, only the light shafts matter, and tomorrow, I'm sleeping late. Don't you dare set that alarming clock of yours."

"I won't." Talmarq looked thoughtful. "I'm going to slip out as early as possible to visit Chief Streamer Fezlie before she leaves home."

"Then, you'd better get out at the first glimmer of dawn. If anyone is lingering around my house, do not open the door."

CHAPTER 23

Devron changed into his darkest clothes. He wanted to linger in this room that held so much peace over the years. To keep talking with Fairlynn, so precious to him. But they'd already discussed plans, so there was really nothing left to say. "Above all," he warned, "keep the doors locked tomorrow until I'm awake."

"I think you've told me that three times." She walked with him through the kitchen to the side door.

Devron gave her a kiss and a long hug, wishing he could hold onto her forever. "I don't think they will, but if things go really bad…" He tried again. "I just don't want you to feel abandoned like when…"

"Like when Alverlee left, you mean?"

He nodded, his chin rubbing her head.

"Don't think of that. It's not the same. I begged Alverlee not to go. But you and I, we agree that you must do this." She leaned back to look into his eyes. "I'm sure it is the will of Ellincreo, so I must entrust you to him. You are brave to go, so I will be brave and *let* you go."

"You," he whispered, "are a wonderful wife." He kissed her again, then slipped out the door.

Devron waited to hear the lock slide closed before moving to the corner of the house. At the back alley, a quick glance confirmed that no one was in view. Now that the streets were lit and patrolled, he feared to be spotted by a guard more than by a thief. Neither would be good. He set out, hurrying from one shadow to the next. The back windows that he passed spilled slivers of light between closed curtains. Once, when he spotted a guard passing an intersection, Devron hid in the darkness between two houses. Nerve-wracking to linger—more so to peer down that street when he finally dared to leave the shadow. No one in sight. He eased out a tight breath and hurried on. At least that was the only delay before he entered the city cavern.

Four magnery lights mounted on poles marked the corners of the garden area. Two guards were on duty at all times with rotating shifts, but the unnatural light limited their view of the cavern's farthest reaches, where darkness lay thick over rougher ground. Devron made use of his forming gift to sense obstacles before they could trip him. He worked his way to the back foundation wall of the government hall and lay down. The rock beneath him, he quickly formed to fit the contours of his body. No guard could see him here.

In the cavern ceiling, white patches glowed dimly, reflecting the scant light from below. Or perhaps, catching a glimmer from the big moon somewhere above. If the guards looked up, they might notice a faint brightening as he worked. Unlikely, and he could do nothing about it anyway.

Time to get busy. One by one, he searched out the shafts he'd been forming throughout the months. He accessed each opaque layer and commanded the crystals to align with their neighbors above and below. He closed his eyes. No point in wearying them when they couldn't see anyway. Instead, his forming senses revealed the mass of ipenrock and the twisted shafts within it. Each one beautifully polished to bend and reflect light—to carry the sun's gift of day into the cavern.

His most threatening enemy now was sleep. Though his work was tiring, he dared take no long breaks. Between clearing each opaque layer, he paused to open his eyes and recite a passage of the Holy Writ within the silent privacy of his mind. The hours became a sacred merging of Ellincreo's gift and words. When he cleared the last shaft, Devron felt more like bellowing a triumphant shout than sneaking away. He stretched his muscles, stiff from immobility, and reminded himself that he must make no sound. Nor linger. Oh, he longed to see the first full bursting forth of the day in this cavern. But he must be gone before dawn gave a hint of its approach. Disappointing though it was, he slipped away through the darkness.

He saw no one in the settlement cavern on his return journey. Just as well, because exhaustion pursued him as he followed the alley to his house. The lock he'd made responded to his nudge. He opened the door, slipped in, and locked it again. A few more steps to his bedroom, then he nearly collapsed onto the bed.

Fairlynn stirred at the movement. Her hand found him in the darkness. "You're back." Relief murmured through the simple words.

"Yes."

"How'd it go?"

"Like singing a long, silent prayer. I didn't even know I was tired until I started for home." He rolled over and sighed a few words. "It is done."

Fairlynn kissed his forehead. "Then let the morning bring what it may."

Sleep eluded Fairlynn now. No matter how many times she turned her eyes away from the crack she'd left in the curtains, they sought it again. Had the first dim rays of morning come?

She rose the instant the blue curtains revealed a hint of their color. There was light somewhere, and she would be dressed before any knock sounded.

In the kitchen, she whispered a few words to Talmarq, who accepted a slice of the week's small loaf of bread before he hurried out the front door with his maps in hand. No hint of commotion yet. Fairlynn locked the door behind him. Now what? She must act and look normal, so she did her hair and tried to ignore that her hands were shaking.

Were they right about her staying inside? Should she be out there to hear what was happening? Perhaps have a chance to influence reactions? As though anyone listened to her. But the agony to know persisted. Oh, of course. The roof.

Soon, she looked down on the thoroughfare. It was still rather early, but a few people were out. Then someone sprinted down the slope from the city cavern. He disappeared from view, but a moment later, dashed back up it with several people following.

Heads turned. Curiosity did its work. In a matter of minutes, waves of people rushed to spread the word or view the spectacle. When a grumpy neighbor demanded, "What's all the fuss about?" another voice answered, "The city cavern is brighter than this one!"

At least one person sounded happy. Hard to judge the rest. Running and shouting certainly abounded. Was the heightened pitch from ecstatic relief or terror? Both, it seemed.

Fairlynn sat down beside a trellis to listen out of view. She caught Devron's name on a few tongues, and before long, anger infused some voices. Her heart began to thrum. She'd known this would happen, but some part of her had denied it. She was anything but ready. Harsh knocks sounded below. On her door. She clutched the stone bench. If only she could stay here and hide. For the rest of her life. "Ellincreo, guide me," she whispered.

Pretending calm, she walked to the roof edge and leaned over the half wall. "Enough noise," she called to them. "I will be down in a moment."

They tilted their heads upward, and she recognized a council member rapping on the door, four guards around him, with a growing half-circle of onlookers. At least they quieted until she reached the welcome room and cranked a window open one inch.

"Rather early to come calling, isn't it?" Fairlynn said.

"Send Devron to the door, please." Despite the word *please*, there was nothing polite in that faceless voice beside the window.

"He is still asleep."

"Wake him."

"I shall not. Return with civil manners at midday."

The voice shouted, "There is full light in the city cavern."

"Ah, I didn't realize you were bearing good news. I will tell him when he wakes."

That got some snickers from the crowd, but the spokesman snarled. "Devron will not get away with this. Get him out here now!"

"Doesn't Jourendia still follow orderly law? After what happened in Crysalan a few days ago, you may be certain that I will *not* open my door to a mob."

Several voices asked what had happened in Crysalan, but the spokesman remained silent. He couldn't ask without revealing ignorance, nor could he answer. She cranked the window shut. Let them run around seeking news. Might keep them busy for an hour or two.

If only *she* could keep busy. Feeding the ducks didn't occupy her mind. No other task really mattered, and reading amounted to moving her eyes over words that didn't reach her brain.

Kevenor stopped by, and she spoke with him through the window too. "I'm sorry I cannot open the door to you. The crowd never leaves, and they are drawing near already."

"There are guards," he whispered, "out of view at the corners of the house." He resumed a normal voice. "I need to talk with Devron."

"He's asleep. Let him rest."

"What is this that you heard about Crysalan?"

"Their mayor, Sairtoka, instigated mob murder of Wandermae and the former who helped her restore healthy airflow. Use your position to maintain order, Kevenor. If Mayor Borchel truly believes Devron harmed us, then insist upon a fair trial. If you can persuade him of the truth—that Devron harmed no one and helped all—then encourage him to publicly declare it."

The crowd was too close now for private conversation, and Kevenor stepped back, spasms tugging the muscles by his mouth.

Geon visited too—his few sentences dreadfully terse. He slipped a packet through the window crack. "Devron's a hero, and I stand by him." He hurried away as she closed the window.

Everything about Geon—voice, expression, haste—told her the worst. Fairlynn opened the packet. A day's ration of rice. He didn't want them going to market.

Devron looked down on the thoroughfare from his roof garden. People passed along the street, but no more than during a normal workday as lunch ended. The angry loiterers were gone, as Borchel had promised an hour ago. Several of the mayor's safety guards lingered to keep them away. "It looks like the mayor kept his word."

"The first part of it anyway." Fairlynn slipped her hand into his. "Do you think he will let the Formers' Guild judge you?"

"Even if he only makes a show of it, that will be enough. It will cause the trial to be held in the city cavern to allow the Formers' Guild to assess the roof. Fezlie and Geon have agreed to summon their guild members to attend there as well. And a crowd in the city cavern is exactly what I need."

Fairlynn's grip on his hand slowly tightened. Several times, she'd stretched her fingers, only to tense again. The wedge of light sliding over the hour markings on the cavern wall moved both too slowly and too fast.

She shifted and looked up at him. "What are you worrying over? The trial?"

He raised his brows to clear the frown that he now noticed. "Not really. If I get an actual trial rather than a mob attack, I'll be fine. From what Fezlie told us when she stopped by, the majority are truly appalled by the mob murders in Crysalan."

"What's troubling you then?"

"I can't guess how the mayor will go about saving face. Restrictions, probably. House arrest or set those worthless council members to hound me. I cannot do anything with the lake cavern unless I can spend plenty of unhindered time in it. And that is the last place they will let me linger."

She uttered a floundering chuckle. "You haven't even gotten through the trial for your first offense, and you're already planning your next."

He supposed it *was* funny in a way, but he couldn't laugh. The ramifications of his next undertaking—if he could bring himself to do it—would be *so* much worse.

Across the thoroughfare, the door of his childhood home opened. Kevenor and Mayor Borchel emerged. "Time to go down."

He and Fairlynn met them at his door, which he finally opened. The immediate area was clear as promised, with guards at a respectful distance. The four of them proceeded up the slope.

The only heckling they had to endure—directed more at the mayor than at him—was shouted from windows. "It's not right holding the trial where we can't safely enter..." "You're crazy going into that cavern..." "Don't you know he can bring that roof down and kill everyone who condemns him?"

They all four kept their eyes ahead and lips closed. They'd passed the worst of it when Chief Streamer Fezlie joined them, for her home was high up the thoroughfare.

The broad opening to the city cavern spread before Devron. No longer dim. Daylight shone stronger than behind him. He hadn't been aboveground in years, but surely this came close to true day. He couldn't keep the smile from his face.

"Oh, Devron!" Fairlynn's breathless voice trembled. They walked below the high natural arches, which the formers had planned to decorate as part of the city's expansion. Fairlynn shook as tears coursed down her cheeks. "It's so beautiful!"

"Yes, it is," Fezlie murmured, but Kevenor and Borchel held silent.

The mayor led their procession along a route kept clear all the way to the raised platform within the outline of Government Hall. The formers and streamers had been granted space for each guild, and many of them had donned their ceremonial color. A seat had been saved for Fairlynn on the streamers' front row, and she took her place. The new Growers' Guild—whether by designation or force of will—had taken position behind the formers and streamers. They all wore the short green scarves the growers had adopted to tie their hair back while laboring over the gardens. Some sat, but the haphazard collection of cast-off chairs was inadequate for all.

A sudden jerk and scramble among the streamers created a stir. An irritated streamer stomped from the group, carrying a broken folding chair, which he tossed onto the half-wall along with a curse.

Surrounded by abundant resources, and they couldn't even provide seating. Ridiculous! Still, an object breaking before their eyes actually improved Devron's plan. What mattered more was the heartening number of citizens who had come to witness his trial. He climbed the platform steps and turned to face them. More than half of Jourendia must be here. Some would condemn him—perhaps not even realizing that their very presence in this cavern gave the lie to their fears of collapse.

The mayor started things out in his usual fashion. He granted the Formers' Guild the right to give input, but not the right of final decision. Neither good nor surprising.

Chief Former Kevenor took over. Turning to his guild, he said, "Formers, please begin your assessment." He then addressed the full crowd. "Since most of you don't attend our meetings, I'll explain. Formers such as the medics or polishers with limited range don't participate in a distant assessment. Normally, any formers who have adequate range to sense through the cavern roof would be asked to state their analysis. That would take quite a while, and I expect they will all say the same thing. To spare you the boring repetition, I will simply ask any one of them who detects a *problem* to state it." He cleared his throat portentously. "If you'll give us a moment now." Kevenor turned aside and gazed upward.

Most of the other formers also ran their eyes around the cavern ceiling. Unnecessary, of course, but appearances helped the non-formers. Devron watched his peers, extending his own senses to join with theirs. No one need know, but this moment was the critical reason he wanted them all here. The result was chilling.

A few seemed to be trying, but he could not sense their reach more than ten or twenty feet overhead. Their gazes moved back and forth. Pretending. His skin crawled like a wind weaver had sent a draft up his sleeves. He focused on Kevenor. Either the chief former wasn't trying to sense—or he couldn't.

After a few minutes of pretense, Kevenor again addressed their guild. "Did any of you detect any changes in the stability of the cavern roof or any other cause for concern?"

Those who had once been able to sense the roof shook their heads or answered, "No." Small wonder Kevenor had asked for the negative instead of the positive determination. They needn't lie when they said they detected nothing.

With deliberate steps, Kevenor turned to survey the crowd and the council members who had lined up at a right angle to the platform. The only eyes he did not meet were Devron's. Kevenor faced the mayor and formally declared, "Nor do I find any cause for concern. Mayor Borchel, the Formers' Guild has determined that Former Devron has caused *no* harm to the city cavern or to the people of Jourendia."

Before the mayor could answer, Devron raised his voice to carry across the crowd. "There is another test that a former may request to prove innocence."

Kevenor hurriedly interrupted. "That is unnecessary. You are already cleared of guilt."

There was fear in his eyes, but Devron couldn't let himself be distracted now. "You and I know that because we are formers. Everyone else must take our word for it. I request this test, not for my own sake, but for the sake of every citizen, for they can judge the result themselves." Devron pointed to the side wall. "Bring me that broken chair, please."

Addressing the crowd again, he said, "It is well known that the substance gifts are granted by Ellincreo. He only withdraws a gift if it is used for harm. A harsh judgment, that would be, for my gift enables my purpose in life."

A streamer carried the chair forward, lifted it onto the platform, then handed Devron the two halves of a broken bar.

"Thank you." Devron inspected the pieces quickly. Ah, a scissor-type chair that opened side-to-side. Posts for a cloth back, which was missing. The broken bar was supposed to keep it from opening too far. "Could someone bring me a bucket of stone dust?"

A grower near one of the half-walls vaulted over it and sprinted toward the storage area. Devron ignored some grumbles that the stone dust shouldn't be wasted.

He lifted the collapsed chair so the crowd could see the damage. "This is made of slate, as is the broken support bar. I will now prove whether Ellincreo still grants me the gift of forming." He set the chair down as he looked earnestly over the waiting audience. "My responsibility to you is a matter of utmost importance. Indeed, if I have caused harm, I *ask* Ellincreo to remove my forming gift."

Well aware that he had harmed none, Devron expected to feel no change at all in his gift. Yet change, it did—breathtakingly—as he delved his forming sense into the bar and brought the severed ends together.

A thrill coursed through his body like it had on the first day of his gifting. The pieces snapped back to their original positions the instant they touched. The grains leaped to obey him, realigning across the crack. Had anyone ever been granted an enhanced gift before? This could only mean Ellincreo's approval of Devron's creations. A pity that no one else could discern it.

The man who'd fetched the dust put the bucket on the side of the platform, as Devron set the chair up facing the crowd and fit the support bar to hold it in proper position. So much creative energy was pumping through Devron that he didn't even walk to the bucket. The design was already clear in his mind. He commanded. Dust streamed from the bucket into his outstretched hand, coalescing into a rectangular panel as it moved.

Never had he summoned dust to leap across an open expanse and form on its way to him. It felt like showing off. Maybe not such a bad idea.

He held the panel above the posts where the back belonged, then curved it and commanded holes to form. The speed at which every grain obeyed him was stunning—even to him.

Those on the platform leaned forward, amazement clear on their faces. People in the crowd craned their necks for a better view.

Devron slid the backrest over the posts, then walked around in front of the chair and dropped into it. "Good as new. My gift is stronger than it has ever been."

He couldn't help smiling, almost giddy with newfound pleasure in his art. He stood and pushed the chair near to Chief Streamer Fezlie. "Would you care to sit down, ma'am?"

"Thank you, Devron, I would." She settled herself, saying, "Both the Formers' Guild and Ellincreo have approved Devron's work in bringing light to the city cavern. If anyone hasn't noticed, the Growers' Guild is ecstatic." She flicked a hand at the crowd. "This looks like two-thirds of Jourendia's adults. The very fact that we are present proves that we all still deem the cavern safe. It seems to me, Mayor, that a trial is out of the question."

"Not so fast," a council member shouted. Cadmore, of course. "We don't need chairs. We need the safety that comes from *all* citizens obeying the law, and we need soil. Devron defies law, and before our very eyes, he has just wasted a limited resource."

Devron tried to keep contempt from his voice. "I can get you all the rock dust you want."

"Now he's going to break another law and cut rock from our walls! We will never have safety if Devron can disregard…"

As the councilman ranted, an idea flashed into Devron's mind. Oh, yes! But he'd better not be too obvious. The rant was heading astray, so Devron interrupted. "I don't need to cut from the walls. There's a big pile of rocks in the center of the lake cavern." Surprise caused a momentary hush, so Devron continued. "Mind you, they aren't easy to get. It takes both a streamer and a former putting in a lot of work, but Fairlynn and I did it once with the help of streamers in training."

Voices erupted from the crowd. "Done without approval, no doubt…" "Mark my words, if Devron gets away with disobeying the mayor's dictates, no one else will obey them either…" "The mayor was in error. Devron has brought us light for food and—" "Makes no difference. *Every*one must obey, or *no* one will…" "Other criminals paid with their lives. Why should he get off…" "Devron cannot be executed. He's the best former we have."

The shouts continued, and Mayor Borchel leaned near Devron to murmur, "Why is it that every time you stand next to me on a platform, anarchy threatens?"

Devron softly answered the rhetorical question. "Because you work against me instead of with me. Please believe we are on the same side. Like right now. I want the laws of the kingdom upheld. I want your lawful word respected. Assign me a useful task for some duration as a penalty, and I will accept your decree." As if on cue, someone shouted about the rocks in the lake. "You can even grant the request of a citizen. How could I bother you if I'm pulling rocks out of the lake? Everyone will be happy."

Suspicion dripped from the mayor's sneer. "How will that make *you* happy?"

Devron's brows shot up. "To work without being hounded or criticized for a few months? That sounds lovely!"

The mayor waited a moment, then called for silence. That quick, he'd made up a speech acknowledging the value of daylight and reprimanding Devron for acting without approval. Since Devron was certainly knowledgeable and skilled enough to harm no one—and, indeed, help them—execution was too extreme a penalty. Yet his offense must be punished. "And thus," the mayor concluded, "I sentence him to withdraw rock from the lake for as long as that takes or until we have no need of more."

A beautifully vague duration, which Devron could use to his advantage. Before he could respond to the mayor, several well-wishers objected to the penalty. He held his hands up. "Let me speak." At least well-wishers were easily quieted. "In truth, I did what I believed I had to do for the good of Jourendia. But it disturbed me, too, because it might seem that I broke the ban on forming. Please understand that I still hold the kingdom's law in the highest regard, and I believe that is especially crucial to us now. To demonstrate my obedience to law, I accept the mayor's sentence. Tomorrow morning, I will be in the lake cavern to begin my work."

CHAPTER 24

If only Devron could quietly enjoy the city cavern's first true day. Impossible. Hecklers, he could ignore, but those who came to thank him for clearing the light shafts, he must acknowledge. The frustrated hecklers turned on his grateful supporters. Too many of them defended their belief that Devron was a hero wrongfully punished.

Mayor Borchel assigned four guards to escort Devron and Fairlynn to their home, then with several strikes of the gong and his booming voice, he summoned the crowd to reassemble to discuss another matter. Probably to keep them busy until Devron was away.

Heckling was worse in the settlement cavern, but a crier followed them down the slope, declaring that the city cavern had been proven safe and the mayor summoned the residents thither.

Devron closed his door on the strident repetitions and began to laugh. "Thither! Does anyone say *thither* anymore?" Fairlynn leaned into his arms, pressing her face against his chest. She shook along with him—in laughter, he assumed until she looked up at him with tears on her cheeks.

"It's really not funny enough to be laughing until I cry," she said.

"Relief, I suppose." He wiped a tear from her cheek with his thumb.

"I don't know. I'm both thrilled and furious. You should be honored on Savoring Day, not punished."

The muscles beside his mouth twitched. "That particular form of punishment was...my idea. Aren't you impressed by my cunning?"

"Is that what you were saying to him? I only caught a few words."

"Good. The fewer people who know I chose to be in the lake cavern, the better. I hate to ask you to suffer my sentence, but will you join me there? At least when I need to make a big show of how hard it is to draw a rock from the lake."

"Of course, I will. And if I remember right, it *was* hard."

"I have to make sure I can stretch the task out long enough for me to..." He still couldn't get those words out. He stepped back and rubbed his hands down his thighs. "For me to assess what might be possible with the dome."

She met his eyes. "What happened to you when you fixed that chair?"

Had it been visible? "What did you notice?"

"I've seen you polish before, Devron, but never like that. Never so fast."

He nodded solemnly. "Ellincreo increased my gift."

"Mm. Sounds like approval to me. He knows what you're considering. Obviously. It was his idea to start with."

"I still need to assess with utmost diligence," he said. "Now, more than ever." She must have heard concern in his voice, for she tilted her head in question. Did he dare to reveal the cause? Or dare to hide it? "This is something else you mustn't repeat. I hate to say it, but I think one other person must know. I watched the formers assess, er, *try* to assess the city cavern. None of them could reach the ceiling with their forming senses."

Her eyes rounded. "Not even Kevenor? Is he weaker than you noticed before?"

"He has either lost his gift or he didn't try. He cannot talk about it, for that would cost him his position. But that also means he may not know that the range of others is greatly diminished."

"But why? I've only ever heard of someone losing a gift if they used it for harm."

"Well, he abdicated his responsibilities, and he enforces a ban on large-scale forming. In this, he harms all of Jourendia."

"That's...not really the same as intentional harm."

"I thought at first that lack of use might be causing skills to weaken. But I noticed more today when they were all together and told to assess. Those who secretly helped with the gates—they were at least able to reach partway to the cavern ceiling. The staunch supporters of the forming ban..." He shook his head. "I couldn't feel them at all. Maybe refusal to use Ellincreo's gift will eventually negate it. I'm not sure if that means he withdraws it, or that the recipient discards it. Same awful result either way."

"This is terrible. Dirklan *needs* formers. That has always been the primary gift belowground."

"The tragedy has a silk lining, my dear. They won't be able to discern changes above the lake."

Her lips rounded. "None of them? Are you sure?"

"No. I'm not sure about Kevenor." Devron scratched his head. "After his father died and Bekta didn't return, he had the best range in Jourendia. If he simply wasn't trying to sense, then I really have no idea of his abilities."

A jiggle of the door handle interrupted them, and then a tap on the window. Ah, Talmarq. Devron opened the door to let him in. "Sorry, I think I'll be keeping this locked for a while."

"Probably best," Talmarq said.

"I'll give you a key and show you the sequence. It's a puzzle lock."

"No surprise there. Especially after the mayor 'sentenced' you to work in the lake cavern. How did you make that happen?"

"A subtle suggestion wrapped in the means to get me out of his way."

"They don't deserve you belowground, but I'm so glad you are here."

"At least someone appreciates him," Fairlynn said. "What did the mayor speak of after we left?"

"I had told him what happened in Crysalan, so he talked about that and used it to forbid fighting. He also forbids talking about whether the changes in the city cavern are good, because that might start fights. Things will be left as they are, and changes are still banned. Anyone involved in a fight will forfeit a day's wage to the city funds."

"Oh." Fairlynn wrinkled her brow. "Maybe that's not so bad."

"Depends on how far he takes it. Verbal arguments will be punished the same as physical fights. Stating opinions is now risky. Is it even safe to disagree with the mayor? Borchel's version of control might look more civilized than Sairtoka's, but he is still seizing control bit by bit." Talmarq dropped his voice. "We have got to find a way to contact the king."

Never in the past three months had the lake cavern been so busy. Well into the morning, Devron had barely found time for a quick inspection of the submerged rocks. Since only one set of gates was allowed to be open at a time, visitors arrived in groups. Every one of them had some excuse. They were checking whether the rock movement would alter the oystering schedule, or chatting with Fairlynn, or asking Devron about some minor repair work, or a dozen other excuses, before slipping in a soft word of thanks for what he'd done with the light shafts.

None of that surprised him. Other hints made his breath hitch. Comments about the need for a change in leadership, to one man's outright offer of support if Devron would take the reins in his own hands.

That offer spiked terror up his neck. "Don't speak of this," he murmured.

The inner gate began to open, which saved him from further discussion. The man whispered, "We'll keep you safe," and stepped away as though they hadn't even been talking.

Just as well since a council member entered. Ugh, Cadmore! Here to spew ignorant questions and demands at Devron. He bore it—no different than for the last three months, but would he never be free of this fool?

Chief Streamer Fezlie arrived and rid them of Cadmore by pointedly ignoring him. She'd brought Talmarq and began planning the streamer work needed to help Devron shift the rocks. The mayor arrived with one of his many appointees, this one being the new manager of oyster harvesting. A polite fellow who simply agreed with Devron.

Fezlie concluded the meeting. "It's decided then. I will assign two streamers a day to the lake cavern. Oyster gathering will be done in a straight swath wherever Devron specifies. When it's cleared, Devron and the streamers will bring a rock or two up from the pile along the bare path."

"Agreed," the oyster manager confirmed. "Where do we start today?"

"Wait a minute." Mayor Borchel looked around. "There are no other formers here. Has anyone else checked the rock pile yet?"

Not a single former had come all morning. Devron knew why, but apparently, the mayor did not. Nothing would make Devron touch *that* subject. "I expect Kevenor will be along soon, but I can specify the harvest area now. I won't be shifting rocks until late afternoon."

Borchel grunted. "I'll fill him in on what we decided." The mayor strode to the levers that controlled the gate motors. The lever for the outer gate was down, indicating that it was closed, so Borchel pulled the inner gate's lever up to start the opening motor.

Devron sensed its motion—the strain on gear wheels and shafts, the whispering glide of the gate panels in their grooves. Lovely! Everyone except Fairlynn and Talmarq left with the mayor. One of them pulled the lever down in the tunnel, and since it was connected, the inner lever lowered with it. The gears reversed and closed the gates. A moment later, the other lever rose, and Devron felt the outer gates begin their cycle.

He smiled. "Alone at last."

"Finally!" Talmarq turned to him. "Fezlie agreed to assign Fairlynn and me to stream the lake waters. For the most part anyway. She insists that we both get at least an hour of sunshine every day, but when it's time to move rock, I'll be here to help."

"Sounds good."

"How do we start?"

"Simply do your normal work. You two are streamers lowering water for oyster harvesting. Once we get a few rocks out, I will keep one on hand that I'm reducing to dust. We'll let everyone assume that's keeping me busy. Don't forget how words carry in here. If the inner gate is open, we can be heard in the tunnel, and even if the tunnel is empty, it contains air channels to the equipment rooms."

Talmarq looked nervously toward the solid wall beside the gate. Only the clear crystal was visible, for a faint light glowed through it. "How could anyone be in the equipment room?"

"The doors are locked, but obviously formers know their locations and how to open them."

"You're making me nervous."

"Forget the nerves. Just be cautious. At the moment, we are alone."

"Have you started?"

Devron closed his eyes in disbelief, and Fairlynn stepped in. "Talmarq, I think it would be best if you just let Devron check things over. He hasn't had a spare moment yet today, and we will have the first harvesters in here any moment now."

That provided Devron the time he needed to delve his forming sense into the dome and vast mass of rock surrounding the cavern before the gates opened again.

This time, only Kevenor entered. "Good morning, Uncle Dev."

"Good morning." His nephew looked more frazzled than usual, but it was a good sign that he'd spoken as family.

Kevenor grimaced. "Mayor Borchel thinks I should come and uh…" He glared over the water. "…*assess* a pile of loose rocks!"

Devron couldn't help laughing. He spread his hand toward the center of the lake. "Assess away."

"It's absurd! Insulting, even. I won't do it."

Hm. Did that mean he couldn't? And didn't want Devron to sense his inability? "Ah, but I think you should. Come." Devron strolled to the edge of the lake as he spoke, and Kevenor walked with him. "Unless you want to spend months explaining why you don't need to. Far less trouble to us both if we can say you assessed." Devron gestured again and sent his own forming sense through the pile.

And then he felt it. His nephew's presence and a great churning of emotion. Impossible to sort through that frothing mixture in the brief seconds he felt them. Frustration? Pain? Squelched anger? Was *this* why Kevenor didn't use his gift with Devron near?

"What d'you know?" Kevenor faked surprise. "There's a pile of grindstones out there!"

Since he'd made a joke of it, Devron mimicked his surprise. "Amazing. That's exactly what I sensed." Except his attempt failed. He couldn't jest while his nephew agonized.

The water lapped inches from their feet. Distant trickles laced the murmur of Fairlynn and Talmarq conversing near the storage closet.

Shoulders drooping, Kevenor shot a glance toward Devron, then stared into the water. "I've tried to do everything like my father taught me. Nothing works. No negotiation techniques. No strategies. No compromises. Nothing."

Devron put a hand on his shoulder. The best he could do, for what could he say? He didn't really know how Alverlee had instructed his son in private. It was true that Kevenor did sometimes remind him of how Alverlee used to talk—but it was different. Like Kevenor was trying to *achieve* strength, while Alverlee spoke *from* strength.

Kevenor whispered between his teeth. "I just don't understand why I can't make anything work. I'm actually glad my father isn't here to watch me fail. He was *so good* at this!"

"Don't forget that he led during prosperity, which is much easier. Alverlee gave decisions or advice from a position of authority. The mayor was his equal and could not order him to do—or not do—anything. Much as I admired my brother—well, there is a fine line between negotiating and placating. Patting the mayor's ego was unwise. I suspect it led Borchel to seize control of the formers as soon as the king was beyond reach. Of course, you're responsible for your own choices, but not *everything* is your fault."

Kevenor stared across the lake for a long moment. "What do *you* think I should do, Uncle Dev?"

It was on the tip of his tongue to tell Kevenor to recover the guild's autonomy. But could the guild still function? "At least encourage the formers—any of them who can—to keep forming." Kevenor glared at him. Had he touched a nerve? Which one? Best to be safe. "I realize that's hard for those gifted in heavy movement since we cannot drop ore now. But anyone who can do anything should continue using their gift."

Kevenor gave him a long look without an ounce of emotion. "Thanks for listening. I hope you don't get too bored down here." He produced a smile and joked again. "I did warn you."

Devron forced an answering smile. "That, you did."

The gates opened to admit a party of oyster gatherers, and Kevenor left.

By the end of working hours, Devron had decided on a routine, which he explained to the manager.

"Sounds fine by me." The man smiled like a boy. "Do you mind if I watch you bring up the first rock?"

Devron chuckled. "As long as you don some waders. I think that's going to be the requirement for spectators. It gets damp, to put it mildly. I may summon extra hands to work."

"I'm game. I always keep waders in the storage closet anyway."

Fairlynn and Talmarq got the flow started, and the men pulled on waders. The task went much like it had three months ago, but this rock was not hollow. Devron summoned a smaller, but heavier sphere from the pile's fringe. A lot of work, but they got it out.

"Roll it over this way." Devron pointed toward the folding chairs they'd used between streaming activities. He and the manager stopped beside the chairs, while the streamers calmed the lake.

The manager, still breathing heavily, frowned despite the restored quiet. "That is one crazy current you stirred up. How do we know it's not damaging the oysters?"

Fairlynn answered him with her classic composure. "I hold a layer of water stable over them. They have no idea that a current flows above it."

"Don't worry—I won't try to tell you your job. I'm just glad you can do it." The manager turned to Devron. "That was a *lot* of effort for just one rock!"

Exactly the response Devron wanted. He had used his gift sparingly, relying on muscle to make this seem barely possible. "Can't deny that," he said. "I'm going to have to make a sling or something if we're going to get all that rock out. But that's for tomorrow."

They left their waders hanging to dry and headed home. Fairlynn fed their remaining three ducks, while Devron and Talmarq picked a little produce.

"I'll bet those young duck hens brought you a small fortune," Talmarq said.

Devron nodded. "More than the drakes. Food prices are fixed now, but a hen is at the top. The trade I made for old Speckles over there was the best deal of my life. Let's go down and eat."

Their small meal was soon finished, and they left the kitchen table, which only emphasized hunger these days. In the welcome room, Devron closed the windows, then sat in one of the chairs, while Fairlynn settled on the couch.

Talmarq, who had been holding his tongue, took the other chair. "Well?" The lift of his voice revealed how hard it had been for him to wait.

"The dome is solid as ever." Devron tried to make himself say, *I will do it*. The words stuck, and his stomach contorted. If he did it wrong...

"You're going to...to..." Talmarq also fumbled.

"Hard to say, isn't it?" Devron scratched his forehead and realized his hand was trembling. "I'm just going to admit up front that it terrifies me to separate that dome into panels. All I'm agreeing to is that I'll etch the internal design. It's a lot bigger than my model, so give me a couple days before asking me if I've finished. You won't see a thing."

"Sorry if I'm a pest. It's just...you understand, don't you?"

"You needn't explain, but you do need to work on patience because this will take time."

"Not much choice in that, for we need the new year tides to open it anyway. Will..." Talmarq drew a shaky breath. "Do you think you can finish it in three months?"

"Probably. I'll know after I separate the first panel, but the gates I cut have given me valuable experience. So did the long-distance etching for the shaft to the new-found river."

"We still have the problem of secrecy," Fairlynn said.

"Yes. I sensed Kevenor's gift today for a few seconds. He still possesses it, though I don't know his range."

Talmarq's brows shot up. "Was that in doubt?"

"It was...*is*...but you absolutely must not repeat this." Devron hated how often he needed to say that. "No one actually assessed the city cavern roof yesterday. Some tried, but they didn't reach it. I must hang all my hopes on this—that they were *unable* to reach it."

"Do you suppose..." Fairlynn played with a fold of her skirt. "Don't tell any Keepers of the Writ what I'm suggesting, but might Ellincreo have lessened the gift within those formers so that you would be free to work undetected?"

"I don't know." Devron tried not to sound disgruntled. "It's not like I can write him a note or something and get a letter back." He cleared his throat and tried again. "There will eventually be visible signs on the inside of the dome. I'll wait as long as I can, but... I just can't see my way clear. The moment someone suspects—either a former who senses far enough or anyone else who looks at the dome—they'll drag me out and kill me."

CHAPTER 25

Devron steeled his nerve and etched the full design into the cavern dome. Such creative power flowed through him that he finished within a single day. An act of immeasurable joy. And so terrifying that he couldn't bring himself to tell anyone. Not even Fairlynn. All through the next day, he waited to be discovered.

Please, Ellincreo, don't let them kill me in front of Fairlynn.

Late that evening, Fairlynn pulled him into a tight hug in their bedroom. "You've been so tense, Dev." She pressed her fingertips along his shoulder blades. "Makes me wish I was a medic former who could loosen all these ipenrock muscles. What's wrong?"

"I finished etching the design in the dome. Yesterday, in fact. I've waited all day to be called to answer for it. To be hanged or beaten to death."

"Oh, Devron. You must ask Ellincreo for peace. You cannot live like this for three months."

"I prayed all day. Begged him not to let you see me being killed. I usually feel his comfort, at the very least, even if I don't get a clear answer. But he's been silent today."

"Oh." She looked thoughtful. "Probably because it was a wasted prayer. I already asked him to save your life, so there won't be any murder to hide from me."

Devron blinked, and his chest began to shake. "Fine. Ruin my self-sacrificing prayer then."

"Happy to."

"I guess, if I'm honest, there was more fear than faith in that prayer anyway."

"Put it aside, my brave husband. You are doing the will of Ellincreo, so let your courage stand. Tomorrow, that is. Lie down now, and I'll give you a massage."

He stripped his shirt off and lay prone on their bed, resting his forehead on his folded arm.

She rocked her knuckles down the sides of his spine, then pressed the heels of her hands in to knead muscles around his shoulder blades. "I think you should take a break."

"The break I took today didn't help." The mattress muffled his words.

"That's not what I mean. Do *pure* art. Not for function—only for the beauty and pleasure of it."

No time for that. He already worried over wasting today when he didn't know how much effort the dome panels would require. Nor could he take raw materials into the lake cavern where some scarcity-driven person would be bound to raise a fuss. No medium to work with except the walls, and that would—The dome! His breath halted. Geometric art.

His wife swept her hands up and down his ribcage. "*Now* what are you tensing up over?"

He exhaled a heavy load along with the air. "Fairlynn, you are a genius."

Three more suicides. All formers. The beckoning of his art died in the cool, dim reality of the lake cavern. Devron rubbed his forehead. Dealing with those three men had been thorny since the collapse, but still...he'd known them for twenty years. Colleagues. They had dropped tons of ore over the decades, fueling Jourendia's economy. Never again. Couldn't they have waited? Clung to hope a little longer? Despite his best effort to remain stoic, he sniffed.

Fezlie, seated beside him, patted his crossed leg. "Sorry to be the bearer of bad news. Again."

"Better you than...others." She would know whom he meant. Cadmore was over there bothering the oyster manager even now. It would be Devron's turn next. How was he going to bear it? Devron hunched forward, rubbing his thighs. Why had they done it? All three of them were among the formers who did not reach for the city cavern roof. Had they lost their gift? Or did they know something that he didn't?

Fairlynn edged closer, touching him without seeming to. A silent comfort as Fezlie moved away and intercepted Cadmore. That wouldn't work for long.

Kevenor stepped nearer. "Did she tell you? About the latest, uh, deaths?"

Devron didn't want to talk to him either. "Yes." He propped an elbow on his knee and leaned his brow against his splayed fingers. Would they all just go away if he refused to look at them?

Not Cadmore. "Devron, where is the rock you pulled out yesterday?"

"Give it a rest!" Fezlie hissed. "Can't you see he's grieving?"

"Leave me be, woman." Cadmore's footsteps drew closer as Fezlie's *humph* echoed across the chamber. She marched between the tunnel gates, which had just begun to close.

Cadmore spoke so brusquely that his words shocked even Devron. "We all honor the recent sacrifice of the formers, but we must still tend to resources for the living. Where is the—"

Devron bolted to his feet. "You sacrificed them, did you?"

Cadmore gasped. "No! They did it themselves. Suicide. To help others live."

"Stop repeating that lie. One of them still had children to finish raising. Now that he is dead, they will have *less* food, not more."

"Well, th—"

"It is despair that leads able-bodied men to early death. Despair that you foster."

Cadmore backstepped. "That is unjust."

"Is it? Do you not hound every former who is doing even the most trivial approved work? How many times did you rant at our skilled and brilliant architect, even while he churned rotting matter into soil? Do you think every former in the cavern didn't hear you? Didn't know your words derided them as well as him? That the contempt you throw at me rebounds to all of them too? More so, in fact. Those who have ended their lives know full well that you and your council have stolen their gift and their purpose. You have decreed that they are worthless."

Cadmore backed away as Devron advanced. "We have not."

"Do you not hound me every day?"

"Resources—"

"To demand a *rock*? Which I have already pulled out by my own choice. Even you cannot be that much of an idiot." The gates began to separate, but Devron didn't care. "You are here to harass me and nothing more."

Kevenor gripped Devron's arm and whispered, "Uncle, someone will hear. There will be trouble."

Mayor Borchel stepped through the opening. "Ah, Cadmore, I've been looking for you. Please come with me."

Cadmore jabbed a finger toward Devron. "He started a fight with me. You heard him. He must be fined."

"How dare you?" Fairlynn snapped. "You started it!"

Borchel held up his hands in determined calm. "Let's remember civility."

Devron pointed at Cadmore. "If this man comes into the cavern, I will not draw any rock from the lake."

"You see!" Cadmore bounced on the balls of his feet.

"Do be quiet." The mayor spiked his soft words with a sizzling look at Cadmore. He seemed to already know what was going on. Fezlie must have told him something.

Kevenor matched Borchel's calm voice. "I fear Cadmore was indeed rather crass and would not allow my uncle even one moment to grieve the loss of friends. Now that the cause is understood, there is no need for us to delay here."

Kevenor tried to get them moving toward the gate, but Cadmore blurted out, "How was I to know—"

Mayor Borchel gripped Cadmore's arm, fingers digging deep. "Devron, my sympathies may sound false in the midst of this heat, so I will show them instead by giving you and Fairlynn a few minutes alone." With that, he dragged Cadmore into the tunnel, and Kevenor strode along with them.

Fairlynn slipped a hand around Devron's arm, and he laid his fingers over hers.

Tromping feet halted beyond the sliding whisper of the gate. The mayor's words reached them an instant before the panels met. "No, don't open the other set."

Devron straightened. Why linger in the tunnel unless the mayor had more to say? "Shh!" He hurried to the equipment room door and led Fairlynn inside. A single light always glowed, but he dared not turn on others. He gripped Fairlynn's hand, leading her around the gear wheels that dominated the center of the room. Beyond it, they crept along a shadowed gap below the air vent into the tunnel wall. Muted voices reached them here, and he tapped his fingertip to her lips.

"Don't bother me with that again," Borchel snapped. "If common sense didn't tell you, the tears on his face should have."

Tears? Devron swiped his cheeks—they *were* wet.

"But he said—"

"Nothing that others aren't thinking." Kevenor's voice. "You have overstepped far too long. If you want proof of that, consider how you pushed Devron over the edge just now. If there is one former in all of Jourendia whom we *cannot* do without...it is Devron." Kevenor slowed his words. "You promised to heed me, Mayor. If anything, you should be giving Devron a safety escort between his home and the cavern—or anywhere else he needs to walk. And in the cavern...you've got your oyster manager, plus a streamer, plus the most skilled former in Jourendia. You don't need a council member disrupting their authority and driving our greatest asset to distraction."

Clueless as ever, Cadmore squawked, "But who's going to monitor him? Keep him from unapproved forming?"

Borchel sounded like he was grinding rock in his throat. "You mean like you kept him from polishing light shafts in the city cavern?" A grumpy sound didn't stop the mayor. "You stay away from Devron. When it's your turn for oysters, hire an out-of-work former to rake them in for you."

Someone shoved the lever to open the outer gate.

A muffled snort from Fairlynn drew Devron's eyes to her shadowed face. The way her cheeks bunched up above the hand she pressed over her mouth, she would have been crowing louder than the motor and gears if she hadn't stifled it.

He pulled her against his chest and held her until the motors fell silent. "Let's get out of here." He led her past the equipment again and out to the lake cavern. Thoughts churned as he pushed the door to fit seamlessly into the wall.

"Oh, Devron!" She was so excited that her clenched fists shook. "That couldn't have been better. No more hounding council members. No *Cadmore*!" She rolled her eyes at his name. "I'm even proud of Kevenor. He helped—in the right way this time—and he acknowledged you. How important you are." She tilted her head and stared hard at him. "Now why does that make you look so skeptical?"

"Why did he acknowledge me? He's never done so before, and now...he was awfully vague about my importance."

"Oh. Um...well, maybe he noticed that your gift increased, and he... You don't think that's it, do you?"

"No." He tucked her hand into the crook of his arm, and they walked to the lake's edge. "I think he knows that they lost their gift. And that others are losing it as well. Except for me."

"They? You mean the formers who died? You don't think it was despair after all?"

"Despair, yes, but not from the hounding council members. Those three who took their lives—they supported the ban on forming. Also, their skills were useful for big ore drops but not much else. They haven't formed in over three months."

Water lapped rhythmically at the rock platform. A long sigh escaped Fairlynn. "How sure are you that they actually lost their gift?"

"They were among those who should have checked the city cavern, but no forming sense rose from them at all."

"But you told me the same of Kevenor, and then later you sensed him reaching out to the rocks here in the lake."

"True, but Kevenor doesn't want me discredited. Those three resented me after the collapse. One of them even dressed me down in public for opposing the ban on forming. They could have used the assessment as a chance to find fault with me." He thought a moment longer. "Probably realized the loss of their gift right then and there. It would only be a matter of time until it was discovered by others. They'd be shamed, for all would assume they'd used their gift to harm. Even if mining is someday approved, they wouldn't be able to drop ore. So, what to do? Take a few days to make sure their affairs are in order, then commit the final act. The one false solution that makes every challenge in life...permanently unsolvable."

"So tragic," she murmured.

The worst of it was that others were in the same situation. But Fairlynn was drooping already and didn't need more to bear. He turned and took both of her hands. "There. I have spoken the true cause of my grief. A pity I couldn't have done that before it spilled into rage." His mouth twisted. "I haven't cried in anger since I was in my teen years."

"Too many emotions piled atop one another, I suppose. The funny thing is, your anger—which could have been disastrous—actually got Cadmore out of your way *for good*."

He chuckled. "For that, I don't even mind the embarrassment of losing control."

To Devron's surprise, a strange sort of peace grew from the event. It wasn't just the blissful absence of council members. A guard was assigned to accompany him around Jourendia, which seemed rather unnecessary—though he much appreciated it when the guard put a sudden halt to a snide remark directed at Devron.

But now he would never know the real meaning of the calm that hovered over the passing days. Had people come to accept that clarifying the light shafts had been wise? Or did word get around that criticizing him was costly? Was the calm genuine or forced by the mayor's decree that forbade arguments? He raised the question with Fairlynn one day after they returned home from the market.

"I know what you mean," she said. "Believe me, I'm glad to be able to shop without all the ranting, but I also feel like...I don't know...like the peace is very careful, so then it seems fake." Talmarq descended the steps as she spoke, and she asked him, "What do *you* think of how people are acting since Devron opened the light shafts?"

"Temporary truce, I suppose. It won't last once the stored food runs out." He turned to Devron. "Someone—whom I don't even know—stopped beside me and nonchalantly wondered aloud whether you might support an early election and whether you might consider running for mayor."

A shiver coursed through Devron. "What a horror! How did you answer?"

"That you've never mentioned either. Is any of it possible?"

"Me as mayor? I cannot imagine anything worse."

"I can!" Fairlynn sneered, probably thinking of Borchel. "You would have accepted the role of Chief Former, which would equal the responsibility of mayor. Or should, anyway."

"That, I am qualified for—as long as the guild is autonomous."

"What of an early election?" Talmarq asked him.

"I've heard suggestions that developments warrant it, but I'm not sure if it would make a difference. Fearful people seek control. They will elect whoever ensures control, which our current mayor does."

"Now that opinions are silenced..." Talmarq spread his hands. "It's impossible to judge whether public opinion is shifting. Or to encourage it to shift."

"Don't go there, Talmarq," Devron warned. "Change is not our friend during these critical three months. I need to be left alone in the lake cavern."

Talmarq's eyes widened, though he seemed to be trying to hide his urgency. "Have you..."

"I have begun, but it is a lot of work and I need moments when I can pull dust out of the dome. No one must see that. Nor must they notice that too much rock dust is coming from the lake cavern."

Kevenor sauntered over to sit beside Devron as Fairlynn followed some harvesters from the cavern. "How are things going, Uncle Dev?"

Devron gestured toward one of two carts that cycled between the lake and city caverns. "The sand from yesterday's grindstone is over there. Feel free to inspect it."

"If that's what I meant, I would have. I mean how are *you* doing? Is the boredom wearing on you?"

Ah, Devron could make use of this. To reveal without revealing. Perhaps even learn. He achieved a despondent shrug. "I do a little art to pass the time. It was actually the mayor who inspired me. He has started asking me whether I have noticed any changes in the dome." Kevenor exhaled loudly, but Devron kept talking. "It occurred to me that if I decorated the inside of the dome with a geometric pattern, then anyone at all can simply look at it and see that the pattern remains undisturbed."

"Please tell me you aren't altering the dome."

Devron chuckled as he stood. "It's entirely superficial, of course. I'll show you." He commanded one of the magnery lights, which were sealed behind clear crystals, to swivel upward on its mounting rod and illuminate the dome. High above, nine faint lines swirled down from the apex. As they spread, each one split to send another line angling away, crisscrossing into a diamond pattern. The lattice faded to nothing about halfway down the cylindrical walls of the cavern. No one would realize that some of those lines on the dome would one day become the edges of panels. At least, not unless they sensed deep within the dome.

Kevenor squinted at the distant ceiling. "I can hardly make it out."

No alarm marred his face, and no forming sense reached upward. Good, so far. "It's just etched outlines. I think I'll polish to give contrast between rough and smooth surfaces. Something to give it beauty while subtly portraying stability."

Kevenor snorted. "Maybe you should draw columns on the wall."

Devron's laugh echoed around the chamber. "I just might do that."

"How did it go," Kevenor asked, "with having Santear bring the children over for a visit yesterday?"

"A nice little variation. Fairlynn especially enjoys seeing them."

"Did Tebber mind his manners?"

"Within reason. I think Santear only had to remind him once that he had been told to obey Mama-Lynn and Uncle Dev. Perrie spent most of her time chattering to Fairlynn, so he really didn't get much opportunity to torment her. How is Santear adjusting?"

"It's hard for the poor girl." Kevenor shook his head. "She starts to tremble if Crilla gets short, and she melts into tears now and then. On the positive side, Crilla must watch her tone. I don't object to that change one bit."

Perhaps that was why Family Day dinners had grown easier. Thankfully, that trend continued. Devron suspected that the calm—both in his family and in his city—might be a brittle façade. That its ultimate shattering would slice deep wounds. But nonetheless, he made use of it. The tides would not wait for him.

D evron took a break from separating panels and did his best to impartially assess the completed work. He found no flaws. Little comfort—he longed all the more for another former to confirm it. At least he could find relief in having finished the initial set by the end of the first month.

He stretched and walked over to Fairlynn and Talmarq, who chatted by the lake during a quiet moment. The young streamer looked at him, an ever-present question in his eyes. "I've finished all nine of the fully recessed panels," Devron told him.

Talmarq whisper-shouted, "That is fabulous news!"

Devron gave him an understated smile. "I thought you might like it."

Talmarq ran stiff fingers through his hair and took a quick walk away and back along the shore. With some energy vented, he asked, "That means you're on schedule to finish by the low tides, right?"

"Probably. These were the smallest panels, but also the hardest to form."

"Why?"

"It's just so much work to get the loose dust out. With the next sets, I'll have some existing channels to pull it through."

"What do you do with the dust anyway?"

"Condense it into spheres and add them to the pile of grindstones—for you to drag out."

Talmarq tilted his head back and laughed. So good to see his smile stretch broadly across his face.

"I thought you made the stone trellises from it," Fairlynn said. "The ones Geon wanted for the city cavern gardens."

"That too. I've even used a little to create the shading in the swirls on the dome and the latticework coming down from it."

Talmarq got the worried look that usually preceded a question. "You say the rest are easier to form, but bigger—does that mean each set will take a month? That's pushing awfully close to the new year tides."

"Less than a month, I think. The next set is crucial though. Seawater touches about a third of each panel. When I separate along—we'll call it the wet surface—I want both of you here to watch for leaks."

"Certainly," Talmarq responded. "When will that be?"

"Today, provided I get enough time without harvesters." Devron sent his forming command into the dome and started the next phase. A few minutes later, he felt the outer gates part. "Here comes the next group." He kept working until the outer gates closed and inner ones began to open.

As usual, he ignored the harvesters and leaned back to rest, while Fairlynn went to the lake edge to set the water swirling toward the outlet channels. With Talmarq at her side, this step would go faster than usual.

A soft voice near his ear startled him. "The mayor and chief former summon you."

Devron's chair scraped as he jerked around to face the man. One of the safety guards who usually attended the mayor. Devron glanced toward Fairlynn to see if she had noticed, but the water and conversation masked the sound.

"Only you are summoned." The guard must have followed the direction of his eyes.

Devron's stomach plummeted so low that it felt like he'd leave it in the chair when he stood. He still looked toward Fairlynn, longing to call out to her.

"They want no crowd or fuss. Come along now." Despite the whisper, that was a command.

CHAPTER 26

The guard maintained a casual pace at Devron's side as they traversed the thoroughfare. Devron longed to ask where they were going, but what if his fear showed? This may have nothing to do with the dome. Raising suspicion was the last thing he wanted. They headed toward the city cavern, yet the guard had specified 'no crowd,' so that didn't make sense. All seemed quiet in the settlement cavern. They were nearing the rail terminal, which stood idle. What could this possibly be about?

The guard pointed left. "This way."

They turned and passed the vacant platform. Devron sensed along the rails, but they carried no vibration from a moving conveyance. Then he saw the backs of a few heads near the tunnel opening. The people stood at rail level, beyond an empty carriage. Hiding?

At the far edge of the platform, they turned the corner. The guard motioned him to continue on and took up a position facing outward.

The three at the tunnel acknowledged Devron as he approached. Kevenor, Mayor Borchel, and Councilwoman Byartur.

"Thank you for joining us," the mayor said.

Optional, was it? "Happy to be of service," Devron replied.

"We need you to cut stone panels to close the tunnel."

Devron was too stunned to speak.

Borchel continued. "In the manner you used in the lake tunnel, so no one can see the cutting of it."

When Devron only stared, Byartur added an explanation. "To protect us. As soon as it's known that our food production is increasing, we'll be overrun. We don't have nearly enough people to protect ourselves and our food."

Devron turned from her to Borchel. "Are you asking me to sever the rails?"

He looked uncomfortable. "Only if necessary. But you see, a gate cannot pass over them, for it would have no groove to rest in. A wall could have a notch carved out over the rails, but then...how to open it? Regardless, Kevenor says you are best qualified to separate the panels from the surrounding rock. Of course, if you have a design idea, we are open to it—so long as a person cannot crawl through the opening near the rails."

This made no sense. "Crawl? The entire purpose of the rails is to bring people and freight through."

"That's just it," Byartur explained. "With food so short, and Crysalan so unprepared and violent, we cannot allow anyone through. That's why several of us council members prefer a wall to a gate."

"Let me be sure I understand your goal." Devron dipped his voice. "No mail. No visitors. No trade of any sort ever again. Not even passing an idea between Jourendia and the rest of Dirklan? We won't even learn if a way is found to reach aboveground Welcia."

The mayor's gaze shifted awkwardly. "That last part is why other council members want a gate. You can leave that decision to us. Either way, we'll need you to cut the stone panels. Be sure to make them thick enough to withstand an assault. We'll make some pretext of why you are here instead of in the lake cavern, for we don't want to spread concern before we have protection ready."

Or before anyone realized they were being isolated? Permanently? Devron felt both hot and cold at once. Closing themselves off from the rest of Dirklan would be disastrous. Both his efforts with the dome and Talmarq's efforts with the rivers would become utterly futile. But he must not let his despair show. Nor could he explain his objections. To delay, he ran his eyes over the wall surrounding the tunnel, as though sensing it. If he obeyed the mayor, every hopeful attempt for survival would succumb to fear. But what could he say? Was his silence merely another form of fear—and just as damaging as their fear? But if he spoke, he couldn't finish the dome. He would be killed like Greehan and Wandermae. Their courage—wait. Wandermae. The air!

"I cannot cut it," Devron blurted out.

"Why not?" the mayor asked. "Kevenor assured us it was stable."

Fear sparked in Kevenor's eyes. Devron must be careful. Neither worry his nephew with exposure, nor worry Jourendians with instability. "It is stable, but the tunnel is a major air channel. If I cut a slab to block it, then I threaten to suffocate Crysalan at the very least, maybe all of Dirklan. I cannot use my forming gift to harm."

Byartur uttered a high-pitched snort. "If you don't do it, you're harming us. What good is a former who won't use his gift to protect his own city?"

He raised his eyebrows. "You sound much like Sairtoka while she instigated murder. Are you trying to dispose of another mouth to feed?"

"Don't be so paranoid. Just answer the question. What are you worth to your own people?"

Oh, to ask her what worth *she* provided! No, bad strategy. "The value of a former is to do the work that *you* cannot do, to explain solutions that *you* cannot see, and to prevent *you* from doing harm that you do not understand." He turned to the mayor again before she could respond. "I have heard the need for protection. Give me time, please, to devise a solution."

"That is wise, mayor," Kevenor said. "Taking a day to think through the design will save many days in forming it."

About time he found something to say. Chief former, indeed! Devron turned and walked away. He must keep his stride calmer than he felt. Firm without hurry. Oh, how he hated acting a part.

A soft voice murmured within. *Then don't. Simply rest within me, where your creations are true to their purpose. Like just now. You spoke words that overcame clamoring fear and retained hope for your people.*

Perhaps he had, blind though they were to it. Tension drained from him. If only he could remember more often how close Ellincreo was.

A familiar guard was sitting on the edge of the platform near the thoroughfare, and he jumped down to accompany Devron. "I was told to come and escort you back. What was that about?"

A few heads turned their way. Should he let the masses know about the coming gate—or wall? No, he must present a good solution before fear had a chance to sink another talon into them. "Just a question about the rails and tunnel." He grinned and added, "Yes, I'm old enough to remember their forming." His age...had it really bothered him so much? Almost laughable now.

At least his response had shifted attention away, allowing him to ponder as he walked. What sort of gate could be made that would allow both air and freight to pass through? People, too, one at a time. And formed without his presence or effort? They reached the outer gate to the lake tunnel, and Devron turned to his guard. "I need to talk with Earlman, but I can't run all over Jourendia searching. Could you find him and tell him, please?"

"Well...you're not going anywhere else, are you?"

"Not if you send him to me."

"All right then."

Devron returned to the lake cavern before the harvesters left with their oysters. Fairlynn raised her brows in a silent question, which he answered with a tight smile. The moment the crowd departed, he ducked into the equipment room and grabbed his design tools. Fairlynn was at the door by the time he stepped out.

"What's going on?"

"Not to worry. Just a terrible decision that would ruin everything, but I have a plan." He sat down and balanced the quartz design board on his knees. "I need to draw this before Earlman gets here." He sketched the tunnel shape over the scale grid that was etched into the board.

"What terrible decision?" Talmarq asked.

"They want to close off the tunnel. And pull me out of here to do the work."

"No!" he gasped.

"Agreed. They aren't planning to tell the masses until the deed is done. Don't share this yet, but in case your opinion is ever needed, remember that Wandermae told us the tunnel is a major air channel. Above all, it must never be blocked. Let me think now."

A couple hours later, Earlman sat beside him, intent on the drawing while Devron pointed and explained. "Don't suggest embedding anything in the wall. The two side pieces can slide on these rails, which will be mounted outside of the wall. These notches will just clear the rails and extend beyond them. The center will be covered by this gate, which can be lowered from above."

Earlman pulled on his lower lip. "I like the independent operations. We can open one rail at a time, or just the center to let a person through on foot, or a mailbag, or whatever. I don't know where you're going to get this much iron from though."

"Iron was being stockpiled for the city construction. I don't know how much, but that storage chamber has been locked ever since the collapse. No one locks an empty chamber. Iron and such came from somewhere when we needed it for components of the gate works here. The mayor claims he gathered the metals from non-critical uses, but if people complained about giving it up, I never heard them."

"No matter where it comes from, he won't be happy to part with all this iron."

"True, but it is strong enough to withstand force. Refuse to form a solid rock wall, no matter what. We need this fence-like structure that air can pass through. We need it easy to open and close, not massive stone slabs. You can also stress how much wider the rail tunnel is than the lake tunnel. The same design cannot work at that width."

"I agree with you," Earlman said, "but why talk me into it? Why not just do it yourself? It would get you away from this dim cavern and tedious work."

Ugh, a point Devron hadn't prepared an answer for. And he needed one that a former would believe. "I...want formers working. Those who are willing to anyway. Those who dare. You'll get paid. Who knows, Kevenor might even acknowledge your contribution."

Earlman snorted. "And the cavern roof might turn into blue sky. What's your real reason?"

"Well, no one seems willing to speak of it." When Earlman compressed his lips and resolutely nodded, Devron continued. "I suspect that the formers are losing their gifts. The only formers I can still sense are those who keep *using* the gift."

Earlman's facial muscles quivered. "I've been wondering who knew. Haven't dared to ask. What about Kevenor?"

"He still has some of his gift, but he hides it. I don't know how much he retains."

"He's no chief former," Earlman grumbled. "You are."

The words hitched Devron's breath. Comforting and unnerving at the same time. "Your confidence in me is a huge relief, but this isn't the time for outward change. For now, steward your gift by using it. I chose you for this task because I felt I could trust you to follow my plan. If you're pressured to change it, find a way to let me know."

Earlman actually smiled. How could he look so relieved when he would become the new target for ignorant council members? "I'll stop by your house around breakfast to pick up the final design." He left with a jaunty step.

That evening, Kevenor seemed ready to be convinced, but the mayor was the real challenge. He looked pleased while Devron presented his plan. "This design allows air movement, provides strong protection, and will permit deliveries and approved visitors to pass through." He kept smiling when Devron pointed out details on the design board. Then Devron explained the color coding for the required materials.

"That's iron?" Borchel demanded. "All of it? Absolutely not. Make it from stone!"

It took several minutes of insistence from both Kevenor and Devron to convince him that stone was not a suitable material. He kept resisting the use of iron, but he refused to state the quantity in storage. Probably didn't know, since miners had always managed the weighing and inventory.

Finally, Devron said, "I thought sure we would have enough, but if not, let's go to the storage chamber now so I can see what we have to work with and adjust the design accordingly."

"That's not the point," Borchel snapped. "Iron will become much more necessary as time passes."

What could he mean?

Fairlynn chimed in for the first time. "You aren't thinking about making money off of it, are you?"

"No, no! Although it may become possible to trade our iron for food."

"Why would anyone give up food for iron?" she asked.

The mayor hemmed for a moment but couldn't seem to find a way out. "We've never had to deal with it, of course, but we will someday." They all stared at him. "We'll need weapons."

Devron swallowed hard. He was so tired of the sick feeling that twisted through him at each new onslaught of insanity. The mayor blathered about Jourendians defending themselves against so-called outsiders, but the image that writhed through Devron's mind was of neighbors wielding blades against each other. He was putting every scrap of iron that he could into those gates. Now for a reason the mayor would like. Devron cleared his throat. "As Councilwoman Byartur pointed out, we don't have enough people to win a battle for our food. The best use for our iron is to keep raiders out. I will ensure maximum strength."

At last, he managed to convince the mayor, who left with Kevenor. But Devron knew full well that a gate couldn't prevent violence within. Not when starvation carved gouges between their bones.

Devron handed his wet waders to Talmarq, who hung them to dry. They were mostly for show in case anyone entered while he was summoning a grindstone to the shore. No one had, so they finished their work quickly before most people left their homes.

He didn't waste any time in starting his real work. The panel's division neared the space that Devron could not sense. The place where water lurked. An ocean of it. The closer he got, the more fear spiked through his mind. Slowing him. Conventional wisdom screamed at him to stop. The specter of starvation prodded him on. Either decision seemed compelled by fear.

Ellincreo, what do I do?

Did you feel fear when I showed you the vision?

No, but...this is the real thing.

The vision is the real thing. The dome is to become a copy of it. Work from the vision, not from opinions.

The vision... He pondered it again, eyes closed. Enjoyed its symmetry and movement. Remembered the peace and excitement he'd felt. Reached up to the dome again to envision its overlay. Traced the panel's edge, separating...realigning grains. The seam almost felt like it would race ahead of him. As though rock comprehended his desire and hastened to comply. He paused when the end joined to its beginning, then studied it with his forming sense. Delved the weight...the stability...the dome's immobile structure. Comforting to know it hadn't moved.

He became aware of Fairlynn's steady regard. With a tentative smile, he murmured, "What?"

"You don't often look so rapt, my husband. Have you formed a wet edge?"

"I have."

Talmarq, who had been loitering near the gates, hurried over. "What? Where?"

"Up there." Devron pointed to one side. "It's only the width of a hair, but quite long."

Both streamers grew intent and silent. He really ought to give them a more specific location. Devron walked to a magnery light, angled it upward, then using his finger to cast a shadow, he traced the line he had carved on the outside of the dome.

"That helps," Talmarq murmured. After a few minutes, he said, "I just can't make out any movement of water within the rock. Outside, yes, but not entering."

"It's so narrow that it may not be possible yet. I'll form the plane in this direction..." Devron wiggled his shadow finger to show them. "...and widen the gap today. Check it now and then, but only when none of the gifted are here to feel what you're doing." He returned the light to its normal position. "The outer gate is opening." He began shaving sand off the stone he and Talmarq had lifted into the cart earlier.

They all settled into ordinary tasks, letting harvesters think whatever they pleased. Really, Devron preferred when those who distrusted him came, for they didn't chat. He could work on the dome while they pointedly ignored him.

And so, he formed—carving out enough space for panels to move while leaving only a hairline separation where each panel nested against its neighbor.

Occasionally, he was forced to delay work to check on Earlman's progress with the rail gate, to smooth the iron until it glided like oil, and finally, to assess the finished construction. The mayor let its completion pass with nothing more than a quiet word of thanks. Probably because those who came to look at it just shook their heads and walked away.

Despite interruptions, Devron finished the second set of dome panels in less than a month and immediately started the third. These last nine would reach the apex. Again, his confidence faltered with the first severing. He soon regained it, for never once did Fairlynn or Talmarq tell him of drips reaching the interior.

But even while he assured himself that the dome was stable, in the back of his mind, he knew the deluge was coming. A flood that he could not imagine.

CHAPTER 27

"**M**aybe you should stop calling it an assessment," Fairlynn said. "Streamers don't assess. We test."

"Sounds like splitting hairs over terms," Devron replied.

"It isn't though. You formers can assess because your substance doesn't move. It will be the same in a day or a year. But the water is never the same, so yes, we must do it again, even if you think we should already know."

That arrested his glowering eyes, and he spoke milder. "It's not that. Having someone open the gates when your last test was in full motion was—unnerving. To put it mildly."

The memory sent a quiver through her. Only Santear and Perrie had passed through the gates, but if it had been Kevenor...ugh! The last grindstone in the lake was now split and hollowed out to match the cavern's shape. Devron had also fashioned three miniature containers that rested inside it. Fairlynn could sense their varied shapes only by the voids they created in the water. Out there in the middle of the lake, the stone looked ordinary. But to a former, it would be very hard to explain. "All the more reason to get this done," she said. "Talmarq, let's drain the lake."

Like last time, she gelled a sheet of water over the oysters and cylinder, then helped Talmarq drive water into the high channels, including the higher gaps scattered around the cavern. Not that they drained much, but when Devron told her of them, she and Talmarq started experimenting. Only by sending water down the gaps could they delve their pathways. They must know every possibility, for a full-scale whirlpool was beyond knowable.

They paused when the lake level mimicked low tide over the cylinder. Much like the level for oyster harvesting. Except oystering wasn't done on Savoring Day, so this would seem like theft if anyone came in. She looked to Devron. "The gates are still closed, right?"

At Devron's nod, Talmarq spun up a vortex and dipped it inside the cylinder. They watched the model containers rise up the vortex, then spread once the whirlpool dispersed.

Devron rubbed his hands on his thighs. "The models still bounce around a lot before the vortex gets ahold of them. I don't think we can send more than one."

She pointed at a model. "Let's go with that barrel shape. It rose a little better than the others, it's quite stable, and it's the most visible on the surface." Hopefully, that would be as true in the harbor as it was in the lake.

"Yes," Talmarq said, "and it has the most room for something of value, along with the maps and letters. Assuming they find it in time and send it back down, we can always hope they fill it with seed." He turned to Devron. "How much weight do you suppose a full-sized version will hold?"

"As much as they can stuff into it. I'll honeycomb the shell to lighten it and leave an air chamber at the top to seal the papers in." Devron looked over at the fat tub he had created from a large grindstone. It appeared to be a multipurpose furnishing—either a barrel-like container or the base of a table when they laid a slab across it, as they had today. Devron had claimed to be experimenting with a new design, so no one wondered when the tub changed shape. "Please tell me this is the last test and we can bring that thing in."

If there wasn't so much risk of discovery...but there was. Fairlynn spoke decisively. "We'd best do so."

She and Talmarq commanded a familiar current, and Devron summoned. They didn't even bother with waders this time. They simply grabbed the cylinder at the water's edge, let it drain for a minute, then rolled it next to the tub. Devron promptly sat down and altered it to look like a cover for the tub.

Fairlynn drew a deep breath. "Just over a week now." Both men nodded solemnly, doubtless understanding the message behind the obvious statement. A meaning that she couldn't put into words.

Talmarq had finished his maps. Devron had drafted a letter to the king. The only thing remaining was the container, and Fairlynn knew Devron could form and reform it a half dozen times between now and the fateful day of the new year tides.

He didn't even need to be in this cavern anymore, with all the grindstones cleared out of the lake's basin. Jourendians seemed to have forgotten Devron's infraction, and a guard no longer followed them around. Regardless, the three of them spent half of each day here. Easy enough for Fairlynn and Talmarq to get streaming duties, and Devron was putting the finishing touches on the decorative column etchings around the lake cavern. An excuse to be present. She had no doubt that his forming senses lingered in the twenty-seven panels of the dome.

She often reached there too, but she felt no seepage. Dry as a gem to her, for she still could not penetrate the stone to feel the harbor waters.

Light shifted up the walls as Talmarq used the recessed levers to angle the magnery lamps. Unless the gates opened, they had time enough for a long thorough check. As he turned each light, the swirling diamond pattern that Devron had crafted was revealed. Fairlynn now knew which grooves edged panels. No dark water stains marred the shaded diamonds lining their lower edges. Nor did streamlets flow down the recesses beside the false columns, which appeared to support a latticework dome.

Devron's study would take longer than hers, for every single day, he fully reassessed the entire dome.

Fairlynn strolled along the shore, then bent at her strong hip to pick up the model container that had come to rest there. She bade the waters to bring the others to her and gathered them up as well. They must not be seen. She tucked them into the basket they had brought, as though their only purpose was to eat their meager lunch by the lake. Once a common Savoring Day practice—before fears destroyed simple pleasures.

Talmarq's streaming senses reached and explored. An essence she could feel but not follow to its farthest extent. She folded the tablecloth she had spread over the stone slab, while his presence roamed to-and-fro.

"Olanni!" he shouted.

Fairlynn startled so hard, she grabbed the table's edge to steady herself. "What?"

Devron, half out of his chair, demanded, "Do you feel her?"

"Yes!" Talmarq jumped like a child, fists clenched overhead.

Devron paced, staring upward, his brow furrowed. "Where is she?"

"I don't know—I feel her streaming within the waters."

"From the port shore? From the cliff? From a boat? Where?"

"Why does it matt—oh!" Talmarq stilled and focused again. "Um, I think she's moving, so maybe in a boat." He waved his hands. "Roughly over there."

Devron massaged above his ears. He must be straining his forming senses to the max. Then a smile cleared the deepest creases from his brow.

Fairlynn knew that intent look. He was still working, and nothing would make her demand an explanation yet. Talmarq, too, watched Devron. Only the loosening and clenching of his fists revealed his boyish struggle for patience.

The moment Devron relaxed, Talmarq demanded, "What did you feel?"

Devron inhaled deeply. "The former who has so often helped me polish light shafts was there. Probably with Olanni. I'm guessing he was stunned by what he sensed in the dome, but at least he knows." Devron wrapped an arm around Fairlynn's waist and extended the other across Talmarq's shoulders. "You were right about Olanni. She didn't forget us."

Amazed gratitude swelled through Fairlynn. For this, she could even endure the hollow cheeks of her husband and this young man who had come to seem almost like a son to her. "Hope still lives. What a perfect Savoring Day gift!"

Everything felt different. On the way home from the lake cavern, Fairlynn had to explain away her joyous look by expounding on the purpose of Savoring Day to an acquaintance. The young woman soon looked like she regretted asking why Fairlynn seemed so happy. Apparently, a good mood was forbidden now, too. *I don't care! I'm keeping it!*

Easily done through an evening in her own home, and when breakfast left their stomachs begging for more, Fairlynn recounted how wonderful it had felt to know Olanni and a former searched for them.

A smile lingered in Devron's eyes, but he reminded her, "Hope calmly, my dear. I don't want suspicions following us to the lake."

Kevenor's family happened to come for oyster harvesting that morning. The children—so thin! Fairlynn's heart ached, but she gripped hope all the tighter. Her truce with Crilla still held, and Kevenor was clearly intent on oysters, not the dome. It didn't even bother her when one of the cantankerous harvesters griped about embellishment of the lake cavern—unapproved forming, according to him.

Perrie stamped a small foot and declared, "My Uncle Dev is an artist."

The man sputtered and came up with a pathetic retort. "Well, you can't eat art."

Crilla took her two youngest by their hands and prepared to depart through the opening gates. "You can't eat a kind word either, but I still prefer them to bitter words."

Kevenor picked up his oyster bucket and addressed the grump. "Get used to it. Devron has always been an artist, and he always will be." He motioned to the gate. "After you."

Fairlynn leaned against Devron's side, enjoying a rare moment alone with him.

He shook his head. "It's almost like our prickly family approves of us."

"Nice, isn't it? I really doubted Crilla's apology. Sort of felt like it was safe for her to offer it after I married you. But I do believe she has softened over the months."

He grunted. He had doubted it, too. Maybe he still did. Or maybe he was disturbed about the very things that had begun to trouble her.

She looked up at him. "Are you wondering how they will react after...well...after the new year tides?"

"No. Those worries will only torment me. I refuse to think beyond the lowest tides."

Devron opened the teal door of his home and motioned Fairlynn through.

Talmarq sat at the kitchen table, back to the door, head in his hands. Hopefully, he was only tired.

They rounded the welcome room furniture and entered the kitchen. Talmarq hadn't moved. His knuckles showed white where they peeked through his hair. Now what? If it threatened their plans... Devron sat down opposite him. "What has happened?"

"Do you know Ruby and Wendal?" His voice sounded awful.

"I don't think so."

"They're a young couple who live at the boarding house. Came here just before the collapse. They'd asked the council to meet to consider a request. Everyone thought it was going to be about permission to build a house in the city cavern."

Fairlynn slid into the seat next to Devron. "It wasn't?"

Talmarq finally straightened, shaking his head. "They're going to have a baby. They've just discovered it."

Oh, that heinous ban!

"They both swear they didn't intend it," Talmarq said. "Counting the days of her cycle and avoiding fertile times. But it happened anyway. They asked for the additional ration for pregnancy and that the baby be granted rations when it's born." His breath rasped. "The council refused."

"Oh, no!" Fairlynn moaned.

"A few women tried to speak on their behalf—saying that cycles could change without any way of knowing. That old guy on the council insisted it was still their fault because they didn't abstain entirely."

Devron sneered. "Easy for him to say, with his wife dead for years." Was there anything they could do about it? That was always the question. "What was the mood of the crowd?"

"Deathly quiet. And yes, I mean that both ways. Other than a few who wanted her to get the extra ration, everyone just sat there staring." His lips tightened over clenched teeth. "They will let her baby starve so they can live maybe one day longer."

The silence stretched. Devron wished he'd been present, but that would have sparked a different disaster. "Please tell me you stayed out of trouble."

Talmarq's fists whitened. "I did. Shamed myself to do it, but I held my tongue."

"That was wisdom, not shame. We *must* get a message and maps out to the king. That is the best way to provide enough food to feed her baby for a lifetime."

"I know." Frustration edged his words. "I've sworn not to breathe a single hint that help is coming—until after we've done it. We will do it, won't we?" His voice shook. "I mean, I know you've gotten the dome ready, but I've never heard you actually say that we will open it."

The menace of sand still troubled Devron, but they had come too far. Though his stomach cramped, he laid his hands over Talmarq's fists. "We will open the dome."

He nodded firmly, but his sniff and twitchy muscles made him look more like a haunted teen than a confident young man.

"I've separated the panels," Devron said, "but opening it is mostly up to the streamers aboveground now. Only they can get a strong enough whirlpool going. Nonetheless, I'll command the panels to move—give them a hard nudge in the right direction anyway. Formers above who are paying attention will sense it. You and I felt a former and a streamer up there, so we know they are at least talking. And watching."

Talmarq nodded like he was trying to calm himself. "I know we discussed putting a durable alloy in the capsule as the payload, but…" He licked his lips and stared hard at Devron. "I want you to put…*me* into it."

Both Devron and Fairlynn jerked upright, and she gasped. "*You?*"

"I can't stay here."

"That is not safe," Devron declared.

"I *cannot* stay here! Not where people starve babies and mothers."

"You would suffocate if the capsule wasn't found and opened in time."

"You're a former. Put a latch on the inside."

"If you open the top, it could flood and sink, taking the maps down with it. Or you might be unconscious and suffocate anyway. The ride will be violent, and we don't know how long it will take."

"If you cannot figure out a design that includes me, then we will send it as planned. But know this—I will throw myself into the vortex."

"No, no, *no!*" Fairlynn slapped her hands on the table. "We are sending only one object because of the risk of collision. You won't survive getting whacked by a stone barrel, and even if you miss it, you will drown."

"I'm a streamer. I'll—"

"Don't even think it," she snapped. "No one can swim out of a vortex. If you're still alive when it releases your body, you won't know up from down. You won't get air until you break the surface, which you won't be able to find. If, by one chance in a million, you *do* find it, then—battered and half drowned—you must swim to shore from the middle of the harbor. Have you ever done that, even in peak condition?"

Talmarq looked away—either in defeat or knowing better than to argue with Fairlynn when she let loose. The mulish look returned to his mouth. Devron could almost hear him repeating *I cannot stay.* He could have many reasons beyond the insanity belowground. His longing for home. A place where food was plentiful. Perhaps more than anything, his love for Adelle summoned him.

Fairlynn fidgeted beside him, no doubt seeing the way Talmarq's nostrils flared and his shoulders settled back. She broke the silence with a loud tsk. "Devron, you're just going to have to find a way to make a capsule safe for him."

Great!

"**W**hat in the caverns are you doing with that strange table?" the oyster manager asked as he hung up his waders.

Devron had tilted the surface toward a stool, his current technique for hiding the finished top or explaining it if a former looked closely. "It's more convenient this way if I'm drawing a design."

The corners of the manager's mouth did a weird quirk. "If you say so."

The last harvester paused by the inner gate and called to them. "Are you coming now?"

"Yes, hold it for me." The manager turned to the threesome. "That's the last group today. Aren't you leaving?"

Fairlynn answered him. "We'll wait for the lake to settle."

"I just can't figure you three out. Why do you stay here so much?"

The question Devron hated. Talmarq offered an excuse. "I can feel the harbor waters, and the tides interest me, especially so close to the new year."

The manager shrugged. "Suit yourselves." He hurried off through the gate.

They waited in silence until both sets had closed. Devron made extra sure that no one lingered between them or had entered the equipment room through the far door.

"We're alone," he said. "What's all that extra sloshing?"

"I kept lake water in the channels," Fairlynn replied, "and I'm pulling it back to refill quicker."

Despite his worries, a soft smile formed. "You're amazing!"

She angled a saucy look at him. "Aren't I, though?"

Talmarq was already gripping the tabletop. Devron grabbed the other side, and they lifted the slab and flipped it over onto the ground. A domelike protrusion stuck up from the underside, complete with a reflective pattern of highly polished alloys. The white squares had been easy, but the crimson had been a real challenge to fashion. Working together, he and Talmarq unscrewed it from the fitting on the underside of the slab. A configuration that exactly matched the fitting on its true base. A barrel, to everyone else, but really the largest section of the capsule. He'd carved a ring of arrows and the word *open* into the top's surface—instructions to whoever found it. This better be the final version. So little time remained.

They had tested floating a partial version with Talmarq sitting in the barrel end before the seal was made, but this was the whole thing.

Fairlynn fetched Talmarq's modified travel bag and helped him buckle it to his chest, while Devron rolled the base to the water's edge. Talmarq pulled on Devron's leather work gloves and climbed in. He sat on the flat bottom with his knees drawn up and his feet braced against the sides.

Devron had fused a strap into the stone, and Talmarq buckled it as low as possible over his hips. Only his head stuck above the edge. He ducked it when Devron and Fairlynn hefted the top third of the capsule, placed it over him, and screwed it down. With a scrape, the air vents around the top opened.

"How's it feel?" Devron asked.

Talmarq's voice was muffled. "A little crowded and dark, but nothing I can't handle."

"Ready for your first tumble?"

"Let's do it." Talmarq slid the vent cover closed, and it snapped into its sealed position.

Fairlynn and Devron met each other's eyes. Her lips worked in and out as Devron tilted the capsule and gave it a push into the water. It rolled down the slope in a wobbly spin. Then it reached deeper water and righted itself. A little off-balance but not bad. Devron released muscles held ready to dash into the water and retrieve the thing.

After a moment, the vents opened again and Talmarq shouted, "I'm still doing fine. Let's spin 'er up."

Streamer work. Talmarq would help as much as he could. That was part of the test—to see how well he could keep his wits and use his gift. He had promised to stop when he got dizzy. Devron went to get his waders and pulled them on while the streamers worked. They kept the spin tight to the center of the lake, but there just wasn't enough depth, even after removing the grindstones. No way could this mimic a vortex in an ocean.

After several minutes, Fairlynn cast the whirl into disarray. Water whooshed up over the entire platform that rose from the lake edge. The waves, both coming and going, parted to bypass her. Not a drop touched her shoes.

The capsule, which they both watched intently, submerged, bobbed, and righted again. Probably uncomfortable, but at least Talmarq was right-side up. Eventually, the vent opened, and he called out, "Are we done then?"

"Yes," Fairlynn answered. "I'll bring you back."

Devron thumped to her side in his waders and watched her draw a current toward shore, with the capsule in its grip. "Is he helping at all?"

"No, but I can feel him sensing the waters."

Once it bumped against the slope, Devron waded in to roll the capsule out of the lake. He set it upright on the shore and unscrewed the top. "How are you?"

"Nothing to worry about. Bumped a little, but I'm dry."

Fairlynn raised an eyebrow. "You're panting."

"Yes, well...it was...exciting." Gripping the capsule edges, he struggled to his feet and swayed a bit.

"Are you dizzy, or short of air, or both?" she asked.

"Dizzy. Not so much from the vortex, but crossing it sent me careening."

Devron gripped Talmarq's arm as he swung a leg over the capsule's edge. "How can that little vortex be any test at all?"

"Oh, not much." Fairlynn waved her hand dismissively. "We knew that. Mostly, we wanted to create turbulence that he couldn't predict." Her brows drew closer as Talmarq grimaced. "Did you get banged up?"

"My head is fine, but I think I'm going to make some elbow pads." He rubbed his left elbow as he straightened and bent his arm. "Not serious. As for the rest, air was fine, but I wasn't out there long. The seals all held watertight. I could make sense of the vortex, but not the turbulence until I stabilized the right way up." He looked back and forth between them. "I know it was like comparing a raindrop to a thunderstorm, but I'm going through with the real thing."

As though Devron had any doubt of that. "Well then, we're down to one problem."

They both angled a sharp look at him. "I thought the capsule was the last hurdle," Talmarq said.

"No. Sand. Let's turn this back into a table before anyone shows up." They hustled through the conversion, and Fairlynn bade the water to leave surfaces that should be dry.

"What's this about sand?" Talmarq asked from the rack of waders. He turned the nearest magnery lamp upward.

Devron braced his hands against his hips and looked up at the dome. "That ring isn't just decorative. It's the inner edge of a groove that all the panels rest in. I had to make the groove wide enough for the panels to tilt outward. The outside edge keeps filling with sand. I drive it out twice a day, but it just comes back."

"Is it there now?"

"Yes."

"Let me see if I can get rid of it." Talmarq focused upward. "The current is moving in the prevailing direction." Streamer fashion, he swung his arm in a circle several times. No doubt, the current beyond the dome followed the motion.

Devron sensed. "Sand is moving out with the current, but I think you missed the point. I can command the sand to leave. I just can't stop more from coming back. Let the current normalize again." They waited while he sensed. "It's coming back. You see, it's in the water, which goes everywhere. Once the dome opens, water will have access to every gap. Any sand it carries will likely get trapped. A little, I can deal with. A lot...not so much."

"When did you realize this?" Talmarq asked.

"Oh, back when I modeled with the stone egg. It's obvious, really. Alverlee even ranted about it...that time you overheard."

Fairlynn nibbled a fingernail. "He never mentioned that part to me. What did he say?"

"That it would all be back with the next wave even if I...fused it." Devron slowed on the final words.

"Fused?" Talmarq asked. "Is that significant?"

"Maybe." Devron reached up again. "Shh," he whispered when Talmarq started a question. Devron bade sand grains to connect...to form a thin crystal arc from the groove's edge to the nearest panel. When it was a few inches long, it broke away. "No, that's not working."

Fairlynn touched his arm. "What isn't, dear?"

"I tried fusing the sand into...kind of a glass sheath. There's too much movement. The current shatters it. So would moving the panels. That's not the answer either."

"What are we going to do about it?" she asked.

A crawling sensation crept down Devron's neck. "Well...Ellincreo has given me an answer to every other problem. Not this one though, so maybe that means it really *isn't* a problem." The crawling traveled across his shoulders. It seemed like an answer hovered, but he couldn't lay hold of it. "If it is, then I guess we rely on him to bring an answer in time."

Talmarq licked his lips. "Uh, the new year is *tomorrow*."

"I know." Devron made sure that his words sounded confident. "And you leave the next day. Let's go home." No point in telling them the obvious. He was as fallible as the next person. Just as apt to miss the prompting of Ellincreo. Just as prone to error. And that truth haunted him.

CHAPTER 28

This was the worst new year celebration Devron had ever attended. Half the people didn't even bother to show up, and the mood—if this was celebrating, he'd hate to see mourning. He smoothed his hand over Fairlynn's fingers, which rested on his bent arm as they watched the full moon illuminate the month marker. He shifted his gaze to the small moon's markers. Soon the upper half-circle sharpened to full brightness.

No cheering this time, though the mayor found some words to welcome the new year. Sweet memories from six months ago tasted bitter today. Alverlee making sure that Devron received commendation. Now, his brother was dead, and Devron was eyed with suspicion, no matter how much he helped. And they didn't know the half of it.

Under cover of the mayor's hearty voice, Devron whispered to Fairlynn, "It's so different than last half year."

"Different, indeed. You're a married man now!"

His breath halted for a second, and then his chest shook. Trust Fairlynn to take the opposite track. "With the best wife in Dirklan, no less."

The traditional shared meal was omitted for obvious reasons. First time ever. Mayor Borchel skirted the awkwardness of no one knowing what to do next by asking the musicians to begin early. What was this out-of-place tune? Starting with a slow-tempo ring dance?

Fairlynn blinked a few times, then propped her cane against a chair. "Let's join it."

They stepped in and wound arms with their neighbors. Were his shoulders as bony as those beneath his hands? Perhaps the slow tempo had been a wise choice. The hungry had little energy for dancing. Fairlynn's weak hip would be less obvious tonight, though they weren't planning to stay beyond accomplishing their single purpose anyway.

The musicians left a gap between each dance. Perhaps this was the new time to talk with friends since there was no shared meal. While chatting with Geon, Devron realized that growers were the only group well-represented. Even streamers outnumbered formers. His beloved guild—abased. So hard to keep acting the part of one celebrating the gift of another year. He led Fairlynn into a sedate couples' dance. At least with her, enjoyment wasn't pretense.

As the dance ended, Talmarq left his partner and went to get a drink of water from the central fountain, where Chief Streamer Fezlie dispensed. Good. He didn't delay. Devron and Fairlynn strolled near enough to hear without being too obvious.

Talmarq sat down beside Fezlie and spoke of tides while she held cups beneath the gurgling fountain. He was good at this. Streamer talk, but he let others overhear like it was nothing unusual that he planned to spend more than a full day in the lake cavern.

"Yes, starting before dawn," Talmarq replied to an incredulous question. "I'm watching three low tides near noon, midnight, and noon." He laughed at a comment, then to another responded, "Oh, I'll catch a few winks in between the tidal changes. Fairlynn has already promised me cushions and blankets. She fills in for my mother, you know."

"Will the oystering bother you?" Fezlie asked.

He shrugged but managed to look like it troubled him. "I'll have to make do, I suppose. It would be nice if it didn't start until after noon." He slightly inclined his head. "At the oyster manager's discretion, of course."

By the time he meandered away from the central fountain, a couple dozen people—the mayor among them—knew that he was going to bed down in the lake cavern. Another step accomplished. The three of them soon left the strained gaiety and returned home.

"Well done," Fairlynn said to Talmarq. "We can take anything we want to the cavern tonight."

He muttered something and rubbed his hair. "I'm too antsy to wait on packing." He ran up the stairs.

Devron drew Fairlynn against his chest. "That celebration was utterly surreal."

"It was." She leaned in, wrapping her arms around him. "I imagine our next one will be too."

Such determined hope. She might see the next one, but that word *our*... More likely she'd be a widow again. Why must saving his people hurt the one he loved the most? Best not to speak, for his voice would certainly crack. So, he held her tighter and rubbed her back, enjoying the subtle pleasure of her cheek resting against his shoulder.

The interlude ended as Talmarq ran back down the stairs with spare bedding over his shoulder and his travel bag hanging open. He had changed his clothes to a practical heavy shirt buttoned over a light one. Ah, yes, the weather aboveground must be on the warm side.

Talmarq tossed the bag onto the round table where the stiff portfolio of his maps lay. He slid it in between the dress shirt and trousers he'd worn earlier. One folded paper, he laid on the table. "I know you don't want to talk about this, but do the two of you have written wills?"

That was blunt. Devron nodded. "Written after our marriage and duly stored in the local archive."

"Good. I do *not* have a will in the archive, so I need you to witness this. I'll leave it for you to reveal."

Fairlynn looked steadily at him. "Are you expecting to die tomorrow?"

"No, though it is a risk. Either way, I won't be returning. I made that clear and gave my reason, too—that I will not live among those who starve babies. My ration is really the only thing of value that I possess here, and I bequeathed it to the child that will be born to Ruby and Wendal. I have no idea if the council will honor it, but I'm trying. The best I can do for them since I couldn't speak up." He opened the paper and pushed it near them. "See. Short and to the point. Please sign as witnesses."

Devron got pen and ink from shelves at the side of the room and complied. He handed the pen to Fairlynn. "I don't mind packing early, but we are still going to sit down to a meal. We'll stick with the plans we made and sleep in our beds until..." He quirked a grin. "...until that alarming clock of yours wakes us."

Wake them, it did. In the darkest hours before dawn, the three of them exited their front door, carrying a thick bedroll, food basket, and Talmarq's bag. A safety guard paced the area and nodded to them, clearly in the know. He followed them down the thoroughfare. Extra protection was nice, but now they would have two guards to deal with. Already off-plan.

Long shadows crossed on the stone, cast by magnery lamps ahead and behind. Footsteps and the tap of a cane echoed through the uneasy silence. They neared the lake tunnel, and the guard who kept watch by the gate reached for the lever.

"Hold a moment," Devron said. "We'll go in through the side door."

It was impossible to judge the guard's expression, for the magnery lamp glowed from behind, silhouetting the man. "Suit yourself."

The door tucked into an alcove a few yards away was supposedly secret. Which probably meant that everyone tried for a peek at it, but only a former could open its lock. Internal blocks must be slid aside, and no key could reach them.

As they turned left toward it, the guard who had followed them offered, "I'll wait here to escort you home." He only expected Talmarq to stay, of course. Not good.

"Don't bother waiting," Devron said. "Fairlynn wants to see if she can sense the tides while they are strongest."

The guard shook his head. "After three months stuck here, you should hate this place. What's the deal?"

"I don't see why." Fairlynn shrugged. "It's a lake, and I am a streamer."

Devron walked to the door and opened it as she spoke. Talmarq stepped through. Fairlynn was listening to the guard over her shoulder, but she kept walking. Devron put a hand on her back to guide her through. "Thanks for the escort," he said cheerfully and stepped within. He summoned the door to close without a sound and commanded the lock to fasten. Already his heart hammered, and they hadn't done anything yet.

Fairlynn turned on the nearest lamp. Devron handed the bedroll to Talmarq while sending a forming command past him to the far door. It opened at his invisible push. The cavern beyond was so dark that the window to it looked like a solid wall, but faint silvery light traced the door's edge. Moonlight—rarely seen here.

He whispered, "Go turn on the cavern lamps and check things."

As the two walked past the gate works, Devron went to the motor's emergency disconnect and shoved it down. He grabbed a heavy wrench from the tool rack, its long handle cold in his grip, and approached the main gearwheel for the outer gate. Not solid, of course. No sense in wasting metal. But only he realized how its holes aligned with its supporting framework. He slid the wrench through the gear and both sides of the frame. The harsh scrape of metal grated his nerves.

Talmarq returned. "No one is out there, and the capsule is untouched." His gaze caught on the out-of-place wrench. "Is it locked down, then?"

"The gate will not open by motor or by manual cranking." Devron returned to the door he had locked. Not good enough. "Give me a moment."

He commanded stone. The surrounding gaps sealed. From the outside, it would look like no door existed. The internal structure changed at his order. Deep and high, it merged with ipenrock. The door wasn't just closed. It had become a wall. He left the hinge and lock intact, but for good measure, he changed it to a puzzle lock—with no solution. Easy enough to fix later, and it would delay attempted intrusion. *If* anyone besides him could change a wall back into a door. Still quite possible, which troubled him greatly.

"That's the best I can do to lock us in. With luck, your hint to delay oystering might keep anyone from trying. Until after we have utterly terrified everyone."

Fairlynn pointed at the device below a bell that hung beside the door-turned-wall. "What is that?"

He pushed it in, then slid it aside to show her. "A talking slot. We'll leave it closed." He suited action to words. "Locking step complete. Let's keep going."

Trying very hard not to think beyond each step they had planned, Devron assessed the dome, sealed the inner gate, and helped the others stow away every moveable object. All except the capsule, which now waited beside the lapping water in the dawn of lengthening days. Devron sealed the doors of the storage closets. Every trivial thing seemed so significant. Even turning to watch his busy wife.

Fairlynn opened the food basket and spread her cloth on the bare platform. Talmarq extended a stabilizing hand to her, which she used to lower herself to the ground. A ray of sunlight from a light shaft caught the golden highlights in her dark hair. She glanced his way and smiled.

An invitation he never ignored. So amazing that he had been blessed with her through these difficult months. Would he have completed the dome if she hadn't encouraged him to follow the vision? He reached her side and sat down for breakfast.

"Are you sure?" Fairlynn asked Talmarq.

"Quite. The last thing I want in a pitching capsule is food in my stomach. You and Devron split my share."

They had mostly vegetables, but Fairlynn handed Devron a hard-boiled egg, which he began peeling.

Talmarq sat with them but looked toward the lake instead of food. "I wonder how long the oyster harvesters will wait."

"If word got through to the manager, he'll probably come first to check with you. Could be after his lunch but maybe before."

"Hopefully, I'm floating in the lake by then." Talmarq wrapped his arms around his knees, a lowered brow the only hint of his thoughts.

The cavern's echoey silence whispered while Fairlynn peeled the third egg. "Three laying hens are a blessing. If the council won't honor your ration bequest, we'll see that Ruby gets your egg."

"Thank you." Talmarq glanced to Devron. "Do you think we'll know when they figure out that they cannot get in?"

"Easily. I'm attentive to the gear. When the motor doesn't work, they'll try to crank by hand, which I will notice. And soon after that, we will hear the bell." He nodded toward the inner door of the equipment room, which he had left standing open. "Or possibly Kevenor shouting through the slot."

"Are you going to answer them?" Fairlynn asked.

"Depends on the timing. Near low tide, definitely not. Earlier...hmm...I suppose I could say that Talmarq finds the tidal currents odd, so I decided to lock everything down. Call it rational caution—who could argue with that?"

"Fezlie," Talmarq said bluntly.

"True." Devron lifted one shoulder. "But she cannot make me open. If anyone has that ability, we are hustling you into the capsule. Fairlynn and I will go into the equipment room and seal the other door. Because if the streamers aboveground have prepared like we hope, I may not be able to keep the dome closed, even if I wanted to. Can you tell if anyone is active with the harbor waters?"

"The swirl of the current is faster than six months ago." Talmarq raised his eyes as though he could see through rock. "Olanni is up there. Others too."

Ugh. Devron fought the all-too-familiar drop of his stomach. The option to call it off was truly gone. And he still didn't know what to do about sand. A fact he could not utter. Instead, he said, "We wish you and Adelle every joy."

Ah, what a pleasure to see that wide grin Talmarq used to flash. "Thank you! But don't worry. Even if my sweetheart is standing on shore, I'll go first to the palace. Well—I'll take her with me—but I *will* see the king and queen."

Fairlynn gathered the breakfast waste and tucked the cloth into her basket like she was trying to stretch every task as long as possible through too many minutes. Devron carried it to the equipment room, then returned to find their impatient traveler pacing. They had a couple hours to go, which they did their best to fill.

Finally, Talmarq ended the stressful monotony. "The tidal drop is underway, and the current around us is faster than I've ever felt it." He pulled the stuffed socks from his travel bag and tried to tie one over his elbow.

"Let me do that." Fairlynn took over and was soon strapping his bag to his chest.

Straining metal caught Devron's attention. "Someone is jerking the manual gate crank." He strode to the capsule top, and Talmarq ran to throw a leg over the base. "Pause and think," Devron reminded him. "The gloves. Protect your hands."

"Oh, yeah." Talmarq pulled them from a pocket and tugged them on. "You two have been wonderful. I don't know how I would have endured without you. I'll never forget."

They gripped shoulders as he climbed in—and not simply for support. Fairlynn kissed his cheek and offered her own, where Talmarq planted a loud kiss. "Don't tell Adelle," he joked.

When he sat to buckle himself in, Devron and Fairlynn lifted the capsule top, screwed it into place, and rolled him into the lake.

Intent, Fairlynn spread her hands, wide and low. "There, a blanket for our oysters." Whatever she did, a haze now half-concealed them in a broad ring around the lake, for they'd had no time to spread to where the grindstones once rested in the smooth basin.

The bell rang—pulled hard repeatedly.

Devron grabbed Fairlynn's cane from the ground and hustled her into the equipment room. He sealed the door. "Shh." He'd already turned off the extra lamps. With shadows behind them, their view through the crystal window was clear.

In a moment, the speaking slot opened, and Kevenor called, "Devron?"

He didn't answer.

Other voices spoke, which Kevenor tried to calm. Eventually, Mayor Borchel's voice and then Chief Streamer Fezlie's joined them.

"You're still holding the oysters?" Devron whispered.

Fairlynn nodded.

"The pressure on the dome has changed. It's beginning."

Devron drew on his gift. Rarely did he need to amass it, but this was different. He felt it arise, surging even more than at his trial. He focused his innate knowledge of the twenty-seven panels—and commanded. *Spread!*

Never had he heard such a sound. No crash like an ore drop. Nor the scrape of panels. Almost a throaty groan, as though the ipenrock spoke. There was no movement, but it felt like the panels were suspended. Hanging balanced between their own weight and a swirling summons above. Then a slow, choreographed twirl began.

Brilliant, watery light flashed into the lake cavern. Beside him, Fairlynn uttered a squeak, quickly muffled. A stream flickered in the sunlight. Narrow at first, it snaked like a ribbon spun by a child. The panels moved as though gripped by outside hands. The ribbon widened to a thrashing tentacle. Still it grew, turning into a massive beast that skimmed the walls.

"What have we done?" Devron rasped through a constricted throat. "It will kill him."

"Fear not. It's controlled." Worry bled into Fairlynn's whisper. "Mostly. How are the panels?"

"Steady, even motion." He explored them. Their strength awed him. A majestic inward curve, graceful within a lifting pressure. Whatever sand had been in the groove, had been swept away. With his relief, the outside voices penetrated. A woman shrieked. "Is that Fezlie?"

"Yes. She must sense the vortex."

Even he sensed the violent swirl, although it was outside the panels. How was it possible for him to sense water? *No!*

The swirl was sand. Scattered at the panel peaks, but a thick charging mass engulfed the seafloor. It drove into the panel gaps. Like a fluid. An outrage to a former. Devron rejected the movement and clutched sand at a panel's edge. *Seize!*

The grains gripped and held. A narrow crust formed, irrelevant to the whole dome. "Extend! Seal!"

He didn't even realize he'd hissed the words aloud until Fairlynn asked, "What's wrong?"

"The water drives sand between the panels, filling every gap. It will not close if jammed with sand." He was soaked with sweat already. "I can't seal it fast enough." *Uhf.* He collided with another's forming sense. The familiar one. Devron commanded more sand to fuse along a separation and seal the gap beyond it. He felt understanding. Then his friend was gone. But he knew. "There are other formers starting to help."

"Ellincreo be praised."

"What's the vortex doing?"

"It holds a gap the size of the capsule—about halfway up. Leave Talmarq to the streamers above."

He had closed his eyes against dripping sweat. A cloth swept his brow—Fairlynn's touch. His effort reached a high area where less sand entered. There would never be time to finish it all, so he dove low again and worked upward. Only one panel was mostly sealed so far. Someone else worked on the next. For a split second, he spread his awareness through the open dome. Several formers worked, but not enough.

His chest shook with despair. Tears squeezed through his scrunched eyelids, for even as he patched, he knew it was hopeless. And his fault!

"What's happening?" Fairlynn squeaked.

"We are sealing the lower part, but there's already so much sand wedged inside that it won't close." Guilt crushed his voice to barely audible. "I've destroyed the dome."

"If water carried it in, water can carry it out. Point at the panel that is sealed."

He did so. What could she be thinking?

"Protect your seal."

He sensed and gripped its length. Pressure wobbled.

"There!" she shouted. "I have found the seal's end. Hold tight."

The pressure stabilized. Pushing inward at one opening, suctioning at the other. The spin lengthened within until a narrow vortex of sand spun through the entire gap and out one end. Relief dizzied him. "It's working. Never mind the sand that's left in that one."

"A streamer above watched me. Keep sealing while I check wide."

That scrap of hope was enough. He worked faster in renewed strength. Beside his panel, another former and streamer cleaned sand from a gap. "Do you feel that? They're helping in pairs from above."

"Yes!" Tears wavered in her shaking voice.

"Don't cry, love."

"They're happy tears. Talmarq's capsule has entered the air cup of the vortex."

Devron opened his eyes to look. Shock. The window was submerged. The dome appeared to sway, but a tight funnel stood erect in the cavern. Only by forming sense could he find a hint of the capsule near the panel peaks.

He raced seals up the sides of another panel. Another gap rinsed. Supporting pressure was different now. Sand surged from two other gaps beside his.

"The tide—" Fairlynn panted. "I can feel it changing."

Devron explored another panel. Half-sealed. He zipped up the far side. "We may yet make it. How much water remains in the cavern—or can be sucked out?"

"I can't quite tell, but they are lifting out as much as they can. Like an ad hoc chorus of streamers trying for a single note of *Up!*"

Devron spread his forming sense wide, searching for trapped sand. A few gaps were still being drilled out. The water level crept down the window. "The panels are heavy."

"The streamers feel their pull too. Should I command water out of the gaps?"

"Hint if you like. I'm going to drop them." He drew a deep breath. "Close!"

With a great whoosh, the panels rushed to nest within themselves. Water spurted from the gaps, cascading into the lake. A rain so intense, the water edged up the window before it dropped again.

Devron wrapped an arm around Fairlynn's waist. His clothes stuck to his clammy skin, and she was just as sweaty as he. For several moments, he could only watch the water line on the window, slowing to a gentle lapping. "It looks like it's receding."

"Yes, the cavern's draining. The oysters are still covered."

"Can you check the tunnel between the gates?"

She tilted her head for a moment. "Nice and dry."

A booming voice—Borchel's—tried to defeat the muffling of the speaking slot. "Get over here and tell us what happened!"

CHAPTER 29

They eyed the slot. Somewhere along the way, they had stopped whispering. What had the others heard? Devron raised his voice. "Jourendia is safe. The dome is intact. The oysters are not harmed. All will return to normal." How was he going to explain this?

A mix of voices hissed outside, then Fezlie shouted over them. "I hear only Devron and Fairlynn. Where is Talmarq?"

"Not here."

Borchel spoke. "If he is the cause of this disaster, we will find him and publicly hang him."

Oh, for patience! Devron spoke slow distinct sentences. "Please listen again. Jourendia is safe. The dome is intact. More food will soon become available."

"Where is Talmarq?" Borchel thundered.

Typical. Devron couldn't get anything through to them like this. How to get to the real point? Fairlynn watched him, her mouth rounding in question. He touched her lips for silence, suddenly realizing its value.

Kevenor sounded distant. "Let me talk to him." Then closer. "Devron?"

He led Fairlynn across the equipment room to the speaking slot. "Fairlynn and I would gladly report to our guild chiefs, but we cannot do it with the mayor shouting about who he is going to kill next. I have just performed the hardest task of my life. I'm exhausted. I need to be allowed to speak *without* interruptions."

The mayor snarled, "Your disrespect is—"

Devron slid the cover closed. He smiled at Fairlynn and waited. It took a couple minutes for someone outside to slide it open again.

Fortunately, it was Kevenor's voice this time. "We're ready for your report now."

"Who is out there listening?"

"Mayor Borchel and Chief Streamer Fezlie are still here. Also, Former Earlman. No one else."

"All right," Devron said. "I will start with Talmarq. By now, I hope that he is climbing out of a capsule on the shore above us. He is on his way to the king and queen with the maps of the underground rivers he discovered, some container designs developed in Illia, and a letter from me to the king. We believe that this information will enable food to be sent from aboveground into Dirklan. That is the entire purpose of all that happens this day."

The others were probably reeling from that, but at least they didn't speak.

"Now, let me explain how this happened." Devron took a deep breath for the words they wouldn't want to hear. "I was granted a vision before the collapse. I prepared as Ellincreo instructed me."

"These three months…" Kevenor squawked—half question, half accusation. "You *planned* this?"

Devron continued. "I removed the grindstones to protect the oysters, for I realized that a vortex would sling the stones around the lake basin. Fairlynn only came with me to cover the oysters, lest they be swept up. As for the dome—I knew it well, for I watched my father form it in place years ago. If it was not prepared, there would be no way to close it again, so I implemented the design that Ellincreo gave me. It now consists of twenty-seven nested panels, which can open and *close*."

"You opened the dome *on purpose?*" There was no doubt this time that Kevenor accused.

"Actually, streamers aboveground opened it. The tide must be low and currents favorable. Back in that week between the visions and the collapse, I built a model of the dome divided into panels. Olanni and Talmarq saw it. He was convinced that she would report to the Streamers' Guild and King Tandorad. Obviously, he was right. We knew it because he felt Olanni streaming within the harbor currents. Searching for him, no doubt."

The mayor spoke with sharp precision. "So! You risked a man's life on this idiotic notion that food can travel through underground cataracts?"

That from the mayor—who encouraged suicide and starving babies? Unbelievable. "Our original plan was to send the maps and other papers in the capsule I designed, along with a durable alloy suggested for food containers. However, Talmarq was greatly disturbed by the decision to deny food to a baby yet unborn. He begged us to send him home. But allow me to finish my report, please." Devron left no pause.

"My part today was to ensure that the dome closed again. I know that I am as fallible as any other person. If I had erred in forming or overlooked a problem, I alone could fix it. Sand was indeed a far greater problem than I'd envisioned. I devised a way to seal it out, but not until much sand had filled gaps in the panels. Fairlynn discovered a way to flush the sand out. Formers and streamers above helped us as best they could. I fear the reach greatly taxed their strength. Now that I understand both the problem and solution, I can minimize it."

At least two gasps reached him through the slot. The mayor declared, "You will *never* open the dome again. You have placed all of Jourendia under enormous risk. You have proven you will not comply, no matter how you are punished. I hereby sentence you to death. Open this door."

Weirdest rant and demand ever! Though sentenced to death, Devron almost laughed aloud.

Fairlynn squeezed his hand. "Excuse me, Mayor, but you don't understand. The *streamers above* opened the dome by utilizing the currents. Devron *protects* it while it stands open, so that it can close under its own weight."

Apparently, the mayor couldn't restrain himself. "You're in trouble too, Fairlynn, for not informing—"

"I haven't finished my report," Devron half-shouted over him.

Fezlie shushed the mayor, and Kevenor returned to the slot. "Continue."

"This pertains to the future. First, I must know if the streamers here sensed the vortex."

"Yes," Fezlie replied. "I and a few others."

"Did you sense Fairlynn streaming to flush the sand?"

A pause, then Fezlie sounded a bit uncomfortable. "Not from out here, but we didn't understand what we were observing."

"A disadvantage," he acknowledged. "Kevenor, did you sense the dome opening?"

His throat sounded tight. "Not directly."

"Earlman, did you?"

"I sensed a disturbance, but not detail."

"Here is the situation," Devron said. "The lowest tide of the year is tonight. I expect the dome to open and hope to receive...at least a message through that passage. Maybe a little food if they can package it well enough. Before noon tomorrow, there will be another opportunity—the last for either six months or a year. My message to the king says that I will be here attending the dome in case they open it at either time. I will neither desert my post nor open this door until after tomorrow's low tide."

"You must find a way to stop them!" The mayor spat the words. "Seal up the dome or something. Kevenor, get the door open. We'll pry the gates if we must."

"Don't you see, Mayor?" Fezlie spoke deliberately as though he were slow-witted. "Devron built the gates to protect Jourendia from an opening dome."

Kevenor added, "All openings to the lake cavern must remain locked until tomorrow afternoon."

Silence. Then the mayor moved close to the slot, venom on his tongue. "Enjoy your final day." He scraped the cover shut so hard that it sang like a blade.

Fairlynn glared at the slot, her chest rising and falling. "I actually voted for that creature in the last election."

Much easier to talk about the past than the future. "So did I. Too bad no one can see what pressure will bring from a person until after the fact." As they turned, she slipped her hand within his arm. He bent it, realizing he was her only support. "Please don't tell me we left your cane out there."

"No, it's on the floor by the window."

They walked to it slowly, for all they could do now was wait. He picked up the cane for her, then stared out over the lake at the level of his chest. "It all looks especially dim after seeing blue-tinged water above." A delayed quiver coursed through him. "I hope I can enjoy the sight a little better the next time."

"It was terrifyingly beautiful, wasn't it?"

"Indeed." He kept a firm grip on her waist, holding her tight against his side. "I need to start assessing the dome."

She was silent for a moment, then pointed. "There is a slow leak up that way."

"I'm not surprised. That's the only panel that settled askew. Most of the loose sand was ground to powder, but one side of that gap wasn't cleaned as well as the others."

"Can you get the debris out?"

"I'm already pulling it through. Don't be surprised when it starts splashing. How long until the lake is low enough for us to open the door?"

"Oh, roughly an hour, I suppose."

Plenty of time to clean the gaps and rest a bit. And try hard not to think about tomorrow.

As the hours passed, the silences between him and Fairlynn stretched longer. With no work left to do, waiting was that much harder. They settled on the shore, staring across the rippling lake. The briny scent reminded him of that long-ago visit to Regissa with his father. But ever and again his thoughts returned to his vision and spiraled down through every detail of his creation.

Finally, Devron said, "I think I've figured out why Ellincreo didn't show me the solution to the sand."

"Do tell."

"I would have deemed it impossible. The quantity and movement of sand..." He shook his head. "I would have believed it was a warning and done everything I could to hold the dome closed. Once the formers realized I was holding it, they would have helped me. This would all have been for nothing."

"Ah." She stretched the syllable. "The solution took many streamers and formers, but there was simply no way you could expect them to be ready. You could never have known it was even possible." She nodded sagely. "Ellincreo was wise and kind to *not* answer your question."

He hugged her tighter against his side, his heart too filled with gratitude to express it in words.

As night crept over the light shafts, Devron turned on the magnery lamps. He kept his senses fixed on the dome. Without Talmarq or daylight, his only hint that it was time would be subtle pressure changes against the panels. What if he missed it? Maybe they should get to safety now.

Fairlynn lifted her eyes, a look of wonder filling her face. "Oh, Dev, I can feel it."

"What? The current?"

She nodded. "Not like Talmarq, I'm sure, but now that I have known it with the dome open, I recognize the lowering and the tightening swirl." She uttered an exultant laugh. "I think it won't be long."

They returned to the equipment room, and Devron sealed it again before the outer lift of the dome prompted his command to open. No brilliance greeted them this time. Silver etched the descending vortex. It seemed determined to thrash while it strained to reach the lake. Then it touched and straightened like a taut string while sheets of water swirled around the cavern walls.

Naturally, the external seals had shattered when the dome closed, but this time Devron and the formers above immediately started resealing the panels the moment they fully opened.

After a few minutes, Fairlynn told him, "There are fewer streamers. We aren't tripping over each other's streams this time."

"I'm glad I didn't know you were tripping before. There's an object swirling in tight over the lake."

She wiggled like Perrie expecting a gift. "Ooh, I can't wait to see what they sent us."

"Focus first on flushing out those gaps."

The process went a little easier this time, perhaps because it was far less frightening.

A descending object, however, was another matter entirely. Streamers had dealt with the ascent, but apparently, they expected him to grapple this—what? Sphere? If Fairlynn's claw-like hands were any indication, she was trying to clutch the base of the vortex. At least they slowed its fall.

The sphere struck the bottom of the lake basin and shattered.

"No," she whimpered.

Center, he commanded to the solid pieces. Would the fragments tear open Fairlynn's barrier above the oysters? "Keep it in the middle."

She must have some control over the vortex, for debris swirled around each other. Five objects were larger than the others—cylinders with rounded ends.

"The sphere was a shell," he said. "We can save some of the contents. Once I've got the intact goods isolated at the bottom, can you cover them?"

"Yes. Tell me when."

Thus, they saved five cylinders, tucked away on the lake bottom, while they got the dome closed. Then they waited like a couple children on Gifting Day until the lake drained enough to let them retrieve the treasure.

Finally, they rolled the cylinders into the equipment room and propped one up on end. It stood about four feet tall with engraved instructions for opening the seal. They both twisted it, fingers trembling. The rounded compartment contained papers, and the rest of it held a cloth bag full of raw, shelled nuts. They stared. Food, but it could be planted too.

Fairlynn licked her lips. "Is it wrong to take one?"

Devron picked one out and held it before her mouth. "We have both worked hard enough to claim a bite." She didn't hesitate to let him lay it on her tongue. He also ate one, but though he enjoyed his own taste, watching Fairlynn slowly chew with that blissful look on her face was even sweeter.

He tied the bag again and straightened to check the papers. "This one is planting instructions for several crops." He slid it to the bottom. "This one...looks like news of aboveground Welcia since the collapse." Fairlynn leaned in, so he handed it to her. "And this..." His voice suspended. Devron flopped against the wall for support. He devoured the words, both reading and sensing the precious paper and ink. He must find his voice. "He made it," Devron rasped. "Talmarq made it to the king."

"What's it say?"

Too choked by emotion to read clearly, he handed it to her. He must get control and figure out what to tell those beyond the far door. He'd best see what was in the other cylinders. A task quickly accomplished while Fairlynn reread the letter through her tears, murmuring, *Oh, Devron*, again and again.

When she wiped her sleeve over her cheeks, he said, "There are duplicates of the king's letter in every one of these. Also, news and instructions, with different types of produce in each."

She sniffed and blinked hard. "We must tell them."

"Yes, at once." He strode to the speaking slot and slid the cover aside. "Who is out there?"

"Earlman here." No surprise, for he'd found a moment to let them know he would remain by the door. "Also Chief Streamer Fezlie and a guard."

Excellent. Two that he trusted and one he could send away. "Guard, please fetch Mayor Borchel and Chief Former Kevenor."

"Right away."

The instant he was gone, Devron softly addressed his friends. "King Tandorad has sent us duplicate letters promising help. Take them as I push two of them through the slot. Don't even look, just hide them quick." He bent, watching for faint light to clear the slot as they pulled the papers out.

Earlman whispered, "Why hide th—"

"Ah, Mayor, Chief Former," Fezlie said loudly. "Devron has news."

"Let's have it," the mayor snapped.

"We have received a container through the passage. Since—"

"Did it close?"

Devron took a second to figure out what he meant. "Yes, the dome closed. The container, though—since it was a first attempt, its outer surface shattered, but we were able to recover five canisters that it held. They contain nuts, flax seed, and three types of food grain. Also, a letter from the king, which I will now read."

Devron cleared his throat and held the paper to the light of the nearest lamp.

> *From King Tandorad and Queen Dizelle,*
> *To our Welcian family in Dirklan.*
>
> *We must write in haste, for we have just received word through the passage, which was masterfully created by Former Devron and traversed by Streamer Talmarq, who arrived safely. We extend our highest commendations for their bravery and skill.*
>
> *We do not know if this first attempt to send you word and food will reach you, but we trust these eight small canisters will give you hope for what is to come. Rest in the assurance that we will spare no effort or resources to utilize the rivers discovered by Streamer Talmarq. Prepare to receive provisions by them.*
>
> *Take heart, our family belowground. You are not forgotten. You are citizens of Welcia, entitled to the protection of the crown. Though separated, we will find means to communicate. At the next turning of the tide over Passage Lake of Jourendia, we will send letters to every city in Dirklan.*

Devron cleared his tightening throat. "It is signed by the king and queen and sealed with the royal signet." He folded the paper. "I will pass it through the slot to you, Mayor."

The letter was snatched out, but the mayor didn't take even one second to glance at it. "He wrote of eight, but you counted five. What of the others?"

"They must have shattered with the shell, but—"

"An unreliable passage—as any sane person would realize."

"This first provision is the promise of what is to come. I know it is late, Mayor, but please send a crier through the streets. Read this at once to all of Jourendia, for—"

"What nerve is this, that a criminal orders the mayor to awaken a city?"

"This news," Fezlie declared, "must be read to all, beginning at dawn."

"*After* the noon hour," the mayor growled, "assuming we are still alive. I shall discuss this with the council tomorrow." The slot cover snapped shut, no doubt by the mayor's hand.

Devron leaned against the wall. Was it too much to ask that such unparalleled news be received with joy? "If ever I needed a reminder, that was it."

Fairlynn rested her hands on his shoulders, her words soft. "Reminder of what, my dear?"

"That the praises of man are of little worth. What one approves, another condemns."

"The praise of the king and queen is of much greater worth than the opinions of a foolish mayor."

He traced his fingers down her cheek. "I know you mean to lift my spirits, but... All right, I admit, you do have a point, and I am grateful." He touched his forehead to hers for an instant. "But a fact remains. I have refused to think on it this whole time. Afraid that I might waver in fulfilling the vision, because I cannot bear to bring you more pain. But from this moment until the next low tide—"

The slot cover stealthily opened and admitted a whisper. "Devron?"

He straightened and put his mouth to the gap so he could answer just as soft. "Who speaks?"

"Earlman. I see why you wanted the letters hidden. So they can be revealed if the mayor conceals the news."

"Yes. Has there been an uproar about the dome?"

"None. People only know that oyster harvesting won't resume until the tides have stabilized. He threatened Fezlie and me with imprisonment if we did not agree to keep the secret. She and I settled between ourselves to wait until the third successful close. Then we'll tell all if the mayor does not. But I fear delay and lost opportunity. The mail courier arrived this past evening and leaves at first light."

"Ah." Devron considered. The courier often criticized Sairtoka and Pondarro. Of course, he groused about everything. Reliable or not, there was no other means to send word. "I'm giving you one more copy." He pushed another one through. "Give both of your copies to the courier. Bid him take one to the Keepers of the Writ in secret. The other, he should carry to—"

"Shh," Earlman hissed, then spoke loudly. "I must take a break, but I will return by first light."

"Yes, Fairlynn and I must sleep too. We need nothing else until morning anyway."

Another voice passed through the slot. "Well, if you do chance to need something or want to send a message, there will be two of us guards here all night."

"Understood," Devron replied.

Fairlynn stepped near and infused her voice with trembling excitement. "Were you close enough to hear when Devron read the king's letter?"

"King's letter? This little slot...hard to make out much when we're always being pushed out of the way."

She made use of the opportunity to relate what had happened.

A bit of awe crept into the guards' voices, but one said to the other, "You know we'll lose our jobs if we—" The sliding panel cut off his words.

Once again, Devron flopped back against the wall.

"You see?" Fairlynn squeezed his hand. "There is still hope. The word will spread."

He sighed. "There is hope for Dirklan, but we have to face reality. The mayor will still demand my immediate death the moment I step through this door."

She licked her lips. "Maybe we should wait just a bit...enough for word to spread."

"We cannot wait long enough. It will take time for the rivers to be prepared for transport. Also, we'll probably be the last city to get any of it." He sneered. "If Sairtoka gets her claws in our share, we'll starve anyway. The mayor will not be the only person who considers me the greatest threat to Jourendia. An uncontrollable threat."

Fairlynn bunched her fists. "It's not right!"

"I know." He held her head gently between his hands. "I can bring food to Dirklan—some of it, anyway—but I cannot bring justice."

Tears crept down her cheeks.

He took a breath. "I waited as long as I could to say all this. We cannot have it on our minds while the dome is open. We must commit every thought to clearing sand from the gaps, and to soft-landing whatever they send through. Before that, we must sleep." He slid his hands down to cradle her face. "So right now, in this moment, I must tell you that even though the last three months have been the most difficult I have ever lived through, they have also been the happiest months of my life. All because of you."

"Oh, Devron." Her breathless words squeaked amidst flowing tears.

"I love you," he whispered, "and I am so very sorry that you must suffer loss again."

"You have nothing...*nothing* to be sorry for." Her voice broke, and she buried her face against his chest.

He held her. Would hold her no matter how long the tears flowed.

Quite suddenly, her lungs stopped heaving, though she still gripped his chest. Then she leaned back to look into his face. "I have not clung to hope to throw it away now. If—and mind you, I am only saying *if*—we have just hours left, then they shall remain as happy and hopeful as the last three months." She kissed him so firmly, it almost felt brusque. "Let's make our bed beside the lake, my husband."

They arranged their bedroll on the platform. One magnery lamp shed a subtle glow across calm water. A trickle in the darkness sent wavelets to lap at the shore. They snuggled close for warmth. Any doubt he'd had of being able to sleep fled with her love. They knew peace again until two bright rays of sunshine woke them.

CHAPTER 30

Who would have thought that opening the dome could ever approach normalcy? Yet Devron felt like he knew what he was doing. He'd better, for this time he was determined that the next delivery would not shatter, even if they'd packed it in glass. Fairlynn planned to get control higher up the vortex, and he...well, stopping a falling object was not his expertise, but he'd at least command strength to the shell.

"I feel an object in the surface vortex," Fairlynn said. "A little smaller than the last, I think."

Not his problem yet. The sooner he got the open panels sealed, the sooner he could focus on the container.

"Ah," he murmured when the time came. "They copied my design—same size and shape." He swept another wide check of the panels and gaps, then focused on the container. "Wait a minute. That's no copy. It's the one I made."

"It's possible that some of the debris from their last attempt reached the shore. They'd want to be sure this one works."

"As do I," he murmured, focusing his awareness throughout the capsule he'd formed, while careful to leave its payload untouched. Challenging with the twirl, but he soon felt the regular motion that meant Fairlynn had control. Nothing could wrest the capsule from the vortex's grip, but its power obeyed her, bringing the capsule down at a regular pace.

Once it was fully submerged, it seemed harder for her. She panted, and beads of sweat stood on her lip. "I have no idea what's happening with flushing the gaps, but the capsule is in the lake. Close the dome when you can."

Streamers above had cleared the sand. The current's lift was negligible now, so Devron summoned the panels together. "That's the earliest and smoothest closing we've had yet. How's the water level?"

"No higher than before." She wiped sweat with the back of her hand. "I sensed Talmarq at times. There were flows both rising and descending throughout the cavern. Can't tell you if he was just learning them or trying to control, but... Shew!" Her shoulders drooped, but after a moment, she straightened. "I hope it's not so hard the next time."

"You sound better already."

She pulled the hairpins from the messy roll she had twisted and shook out her long curls. "Of course. Now I'm down to my own little lake with drain channels I know."

He stared out the water-covered window. "Is it slowing faster? Er, I mean..."

She laughed. "Yes, and dropping faster. I'm using up the high energy of the water to make streams leap to the higher channels."

Wow. Streamers still amazed him. "If you can, bring the capsule over by the window. I'll help you keep it near, and we should be able to set it on the platform as the water recedes."

By the time it approached, the water level was nearing the bottom of the crystal window. "It's bobbing at a *tilt*," Devron murmured. Could it be...?

"Why surprised? It did that before."

"It held Talmarq then. Off-center weight." He angled this way and that, trying to see the vents. By the time the capsule bumped gently against the wall, he was sure they were still closed. If someone was indeed inside, they were either unsure if it was safe to open the vents or unconscious. Might even be dead.

Devron stabilized the bobbing movement, then twisted the vent covers with a forming command. He felt the capsule jerk. His knees jellied. "There is a person inside it. Alive, at least. Possibly hurt." He looked at the door and raked his hair. "How long till the water is low enough to open the door?"

"I'm hurrying, but it takes time. Can we—why isn't there a speaking slot on this side?"

"The water... I never expected anyone out there."

"Right. Of course not. We must just do what we can do. Keep the capsule near, while I drive water up the walls."

That poor person. Waiting with no idea what was happening outside. Devron side-stepped to the wall between window and door. He envisioned a slot, sliced the outline, then drew the separated plug inward. He grabbed it and tossed it aside. Mouth to the slot, he shouted, "Can you hear me?"

He pressed his ear to the hole. A muffled shout of, "Yes," reached him. To Fairlynn, he said, "Male voice. Not Talmarq." He shouted again. "Are you all right?"

"I...think so."

What had the man endured? "We must lower the lake before we can reach you. Rest. You are safe now."

"Thank you!" By the unusual emphasis, he'd been in need of some reassurance.

Devron braced his hands against the wall, feeling helpless. "I don't know why I used the word *we*. You're the streamer."

She darted a quick smile his way. "I'd say this feels very much like *we*. You have panels to tend anyway."

He took a quick check of the other speaking slot. Still closed. Good. He reached to the dome. More relief. "The panels are in good shape and well-seated. I'll drop stray sand if it doesn't interfere with your work."

"Not at all. Tell me when the capsule makes contact with the raised platform."

"I will."

If only that had happened before Borchel opened the far slot. "What's going on in there?"

Could the gifted discern that something was different? What did they tell the mayor? Devron couldn't deal with this yet. He shouted across the equipment room, "The dome is closed, but we're still working. Leave us be." For good measure, he commanded the cover to slide shut.

Fairlynn whispered, "Are they trying to get through?"

"It's too soon for that attempt. I'll know if they try." He kept working stray sand from the gaps, amazed again at how swiftly he acquired new skills. No matter what others thought—good or bad—he knew that Ellincreo worked through him. And that was enough. It *had* to be enough.

Soon, he felt the capsule bump against the leveled platform. "It's coming to rest."

"All right. I'm going to drive the water off the platform. I'll be holding it back for a bit, like when I drain the lake. We can at least get him out of the capsule. He can rest in here while we finish."

Devron halted his reach for the door. "Out of the capsule, yes. In here, no."

Fairlynn glanced at the far slot. "Oh. Right. Let's take the bedroll and a chair out there."

When Devron opened the door, she dried a swath a couple yards wide along the wall. He flipped open one of their folding chairs, threw the blankets onto it, then closed the door almost to latching. He and Fairlynn hurried to the capsule.

Devron spoke loudly. "We're right next to you now. We'll turn the top and lift it off, so duck your head."

"Understood."

They opened the capsule and then set the top on the ground. Only the back of the man's head showed until his arms emerged and he clutched the capsule edge. Since he was clearly trying to stand, Devron gripped his torso below his arms and lifted.

"Ugh. Thank you." The man turned to face them. "A most uncomfortable journey."

Devron's jaw went slack. "You're...aren't you...Prince Queltin?"

"Yes, or Judge Queltin as circumstances require." It was doubtful whether he saw their hurried bow and curtsy, for he swayed and tightened his grip on the capsule edge. "Though, at the moment, I'm too dizzy to judge up from down."

"Let me help you, please." Devron stepped near. "If you would put your arm around my shoulders."

With Devron's aid, he climbed out, then opted to sit in the chair rather than lie down on the blanket. "My thanks for your assistance." He closed his eyes and leaned back. "Let me know when you have finished whatever your tasks or gifts demand."

Not what Devron was accustomed to. Not at all. Fairlynn nodded, still speechless. Devron spotted her cane, lying beside the capsule, and picked it up for her.

"Carry on, my dear," he murmured with a gentle touch on her back. He finished the dome before the lake settled, then went to form a sliding cover for the slot he'd cut. The bell was clanging, but nothing would make him answer yet.

"What is that noise?" Prince Queltin asked.

"A bell to let me know that someone wants to talk with me on the far side of the equipment room. I need to finish covering this slot first so it can be sealed." He looked to the prince. "I just cut the opening a half-hour ago when I realized there might be a person in the returned capsule."

"It was a comfort to hear a voice. You needn't hurry with the covering now. I assure you, no further attempts will be made to open the dome until the half year—and even that one is debated."

"This is my last chance to put everything in order. Once I leave the cavern..." How to phrase this? "The mayor has sentenced me to death."

"Has he, indeed?" the prince said in a conversational tone. "How convenient."

Devron turned back to his task to hide his expression. *Convenient?* What did—no, he must focus. While his stomach thrashed, he slid the slot cover back and forth a few times, then snapped it into its sealed position. What else needed doing? The storage closets. He unsealed their air vents, turning toward them as he did so. The movement brought him to face the prince, who was watching him.

Fairlynn's slow steps approached. A night sleeping on padded stone had been hard on her. "The lake is low enough to finish draining on its own. What do you have left, Devron?"

"I need to get the gates working again, then I must open the far door."

"Leave those for a moment." The prince unbuckled a large leather case that was strapped to his chest and shifted it to the stone floor beside his chair. He rose, steady on his feet now. He wore a leather coat, which he unbuttoned. "As a judge, I always prefer facts confirmed. Am I correct that I address Former Devron and Streamer Fairlynn?"

"Yes," Devron said. "We are honored to meet you."

"I, too, am honored to meet those who have accomplished near impossibilities in the face of extreme opposition." With considerable difficulty, he worked one arm out of its sleeve. A wadded sock fell to the ground. "As you can see, I took travel advice from Talmarq, another remarkable acquaintance." The next sleeve was easier to shed, and he bent to open his travel case and stow his socks—which seemed rather unprincely. He extracted a portfolio, and from that, a document. He held it ceremoniously at the top and bottom edges, then read it with weighty pauses and intonation.

A Royal Decree,
Announcing a Chief Former of Dirklan.

Seeing that the previous Chief Former of Dirklan is
deceased;
Seeing that Dirklan requires a Chief Former with the
wisdom to discern safe forming and the courage to
implement his decisions;
Seeing that Former Devron has demonstrated uncommon
skill, foresight, and integrity;
Seeing that he has aided his people despite great opposition
and personal risk;
Seeing that he has remained steadfast against both the
powerful and the fearful;

Now therefore, in accordance with the vote of the Formers'
Guild of Welcia, I, King Tandorad, do hereby announce
Devron as the Chief Former of Dirklan, answerable first to
Ellincreo and second to the Crown and the Formers' Guild
of Welcia.

Devron swayed, his breath firmly stuck.

The prince stepped forward and clapped his shoulder. "It is my honor to be the first to congratulate you on your appointment."

How could this be possible? Fairlynn's cane clattered on the stone as she threw an arm around his neck. He could only stare past her at the paper. "Does it really say all that?"

The prince's lips twitched, though he maintained a solemn demeanor. He turned the paper toward Devron, displaying the words and royal seal. "That and more about your authority, wages, et cetera."

Fairlynn whispered vehemently into his ear. "You *so* deserve this!"

He hugged her, which was probably improper, though no worse than his ridiculous question or gaping jaw. The prince had turned back to his case, so Devron hastily collected himself, positioning Fairlynn at his side with her hand formally resting on his arm.

"I thought you'd want to hear that," the prince said, "before I rush through everything else." He extracted a velvet coat from the case and put it on over his fine white shirt as he talked. "I should mention that I was present when Talmarq gave his report in the king's court. A rather extensive report, including the state of society in Dirklan and your heavily resisted attempts to use your forming gift to prevent starvation."

He fastened the waist buttons of his expertly tailored coat and tugged his sleeve cuffs down. "If that obnoxious bell is any indication, we have little time before someone does something stupid." He picked up the cane and handed it to Fairlynn. "Ma'am, I have no appointment for you, nor can I claim to know anything about the streaming you've done over the past day. However, Talmarq is impressed, so I offer you the crown's commendation and gratitude."

It was her turn to be stunned, and Devron's turn to swell with pride. Suddenly—for no explainable reason—he could face what was coming next. It was probably going to be stunning, but he would not stand around slack-jawed and blubbering.

The prince had turned to pick up something he had cast aside. "Talmarq gave me these to wear on the way down and asked that I return them to you." He placed work gloves into Devron's open hand.

Stunning? Not! Devron shook with silent laughter.

The prince faintly smiled, pulling his sash over his shoulder and pinning it with a golden royal crest. "Didn't expect to see them again?"

Devron cleared his throat. "No, I didn't."

"Sorry for all the pomp..." the prince flicked a hand at his clothing. "...but I think the sight of it may be useful." He bent to his case again.

"Quite likely. Do you know that the mayor is supported by a fairly large group of guards?"

"Yes. Miners by profession, I understand. Will they be pleased by an offer to safely mine again?" Frowning, he pulled out a judge's skullcap with the added embellishment of a thin gold circlet.

"They probably would," Devron answered. "Is the circlet bent? Oh, yes. I can repair it for you." He accepted the headgear, enjoying the curious, expectant look in the prince's eye. An easy matter to coax the two bends to reverse. "I am thrilled that you are here, of course, but still amazed. Do you mind me asking *why* you came here? One of the sons of the king and queen—to a land teetering on the verge of starvation."

"Did you receive any of the previous shipment intact? The letter from the king and queen?"

"Yes, only five canisters intact, so five copies of the letter." Devron formed the gold band into an oval.

"They meant what they wrote, and I am to fulfill their words. The royal family takes its duties seriously. Food, of course, is your greatest need, but a state of chaos could still cause starvation and all manner of abuses. I have come to restore order and justice."

A surge built through Devron's veins. Like his heart was daring to beat in full strength for the first time in months. He handed the skullcap back to the prince. "Position this where you like it to rest." When he did so, Devron commanded the gold to an exact fit.

"Thank you. That feels perfect." The bell clanged as it had far too many times. Prince Queltin half closed his eyes and spoke through his teeth. "I need to know what has happened since Talmarq left. Can you tell me while taking care of the gates?"

Devron angled his head. "I must go into the equipment room. They've probably got the speaking slot open and may hear our discussion."

"Hm." The prince pursed his lips. "Tell them you'll be done in...however many minutes you need. Say nothing else."

Devron led the way inside and complied. Or tried to.

The mayor shouted over him. "Your meddling has brought a throng from Crysalan to our gates. Open this door now! Fairlynn will suffer more for every minute you delay."

Prince Queltin's mouth curled into a dangerous smile. He closed the slot and braced his hand against the sliding peg to keep it shut. "Who was speaking?"

"Mayor Borchel."

"Disregard him. Just tell me what has happened."

Devron related it succinctly. As he pulled the wrench from the gear wheel and reset the motors, Fairlynn packed their few things and tied the bedroll.

"So..." The prince looked thoughtful. "Apparently, the king's letter reached Crysalan. Yet the mayor still threatens here, likely keeping Jourendia ignorant." He narrowed his eyes. "Which entrance will give us the broadest audience—this door or the gate?"

"The gate. No more than a half-dozen can fit near the door."

"Leave it sealed. We'll exit through the gate."

Devron frowned, then slowly smiled. "The mayor and guards will be at the alcove to arrest me. Would you like him slightly delayed in reaching the gate?"

"Please."

Devron nodded, "You two go out, and I'll be right behind you."

They departed, and Devron opened the slot. "I just need to test the motors, and then I can open this door. It will be hard for us to hear each other while they are running." He used a forming command to shift the lever mechanism, which started the inner gate's motor. He hurried to the lake cavern and locked the equipment room door in time to join the other two as they traversed the tunnel. Devron wouldn't even wait for the inner gate to close. Better to let those who stood beyond see straight through the tunnel to the cavern. To let them see the lake as they used to. If they bothered to look.

Who would even be there? What if it was a mob, bent on execution? Would they recognize Prince Queltin? It wasn't likely that many had ever seen him, but they ought to recognize the royal garb. His name, however, most would know. Devron raised the outer gate's lever. "Should I introduce you?"

"Please do." The prince positioned himself at the exact center of the parting gates.

The first sound from beyond was a gasp and Fezlie's incredulous voice. "Prince Queltin?"

That was a good start but too soft. Devron tried for the loudest, declarative pitch he could produce. "People of Jourendia, I present Prince Queltin, a judge of Welcia, sent to us by King Tandorad."

Jaws dropped, but the curtsy that Fezlie offered got people moving into the proper show of respect. Someone at the side stumbled from a bow as the mayor pushed through. Oblivious. Had he not heard? Or did he not believe it? He just stood there, staring where the crowd had split enough to allow him and Kevenor through. At least Kevenor had the sense to bow.

Devron continued introductions. "This is Chief Streamer Fezlie." The prince nodded to her but didn't speak, so he must want it kept short. "This is Chief Former Kevenor, and this is Mayor Borchel." Devron swept his open palm across the rapidly growing crowd. "The council members are here also."

"I shall meet them by name," Prince Queltin said, "after I have addressed all of Jourendia. Clear a path up the thoroughfare to the rail platform."

He must have had a detailed conversation with Talmarq.

Some guards toward the rear started directing people back and aside, but the mayor stepped into the space between the trio and crowd. "I'll conduct you to the settlement hall to meet with Jourendia's council and guild chiefs." Perhaps the prince's immovable expression worried him, for he added, "No one will be able to hear you at the platform, for Devron incited a mob to come from Crysalan."

CHAPTER 31

The threat of a mob made no impact on the prince. "I am pleased that the king's letter has been read in Crysalan. Has it been read here?"

Mayor Borchel spoke over the crowd's murmurs. "It arrived too late. There has not been time to—"

"Nonsense," the prince said. "I shall read the king's letters from the rail platform. Former Devron and Streamer Fairlynn will escort me there. Guild chiefs, mayor, and council members are summoned to attend. Town criers are to spread word at once through all of Jourendia." He stepped past the mayor, for the gap in the crowd had widened enough by now that the mayor could no longer block it.

Devron hurried to place Fairlynn's hand on his arm and accompany the prince, who seemed to favor a brisk pace. He couldn't accommodate both.

Behind them, the mayor hissed the word *Guards!*

Prince Queltin halted and spun to face them. "Guards, be aware that you will be held responsible for following any illegal orders."

The two beside the mayor already looked perplexed, and now they shifted ever so slightly backward.

The prince must have caught sight of Fairlynn's struggle. He angled his head toward her. "Forgive my unnecessary haste. There is no hurry."

They strolled up the thoroughfare, the crowd on either side keeping pace. Few had run ahead, for it seemed that no one could take their eyes from the one who had journeyed here from aboveground.

In the distance, a crier's voice rang out. "All Jourendia is summoned to the rail platform to hear letters from the king read by his emissary, Prince Queltin." Three strikes of a hand gong punctuated each repetition, demanding attention.

Running footsteps approached—not good. People were beginning to push through the nearest onlookers. Earlman, who had kept pace with Devron, was barely able to maintain position, and a guard who was rapidly losing patience shoved someone back.

"I need Earlman nearby," Devron told the guard.

The man practically grabbed Earlman and thrust him into the procession before bellowing, "No one breaks this line."

Other shouts from the guards, "No running! No pushing!" half drowned out Earlman's whisper to Devron. "My gift is...just like it...reach the dome...told no one."

Much as Devron wanted to confirm this apparently good news, he feared trampling in the crowd. "Sir," he said to the prince, "you need to get up into view."

They had nearly reached the steps that spread along the length of the platform. The prince seemed to understand but turned on the first step to assist Fairlynn. Thus, Devron and Fairlynn reached the platform at the same time as Prince Queltin.

He swept his gaze over the crowded street along the platform and all the way to the tunnel gate beyond the far end, where guards with sharpened stone rods couldn't decide which direction to look. People still hurried up the thoroughfare, or clustered in the windows of the nearest houses, or leaned over the half walls of the roofs across the street.

The hard soles of the prince's abovegrounder shoes struck the stone as he took up a central position on the platform. Shoulders firm, he lifted his hands. "Peace. I will wait for all to assemble. You will hear your king's words in a few minutes. Is there a wind weaver who can spread my voice?"

Fezlie reached the top step. "There is one recently gifted, but only a few of us know whom, lest the fearful try to kill her."

The prince shook his head and scanned the assembly. "Young lady, you need not reveal yourself until you are ready, but I honor Ellincreo's gift within you. Please use it to spread my voice."

Some guards now lined the lowest step that ran along the platform to keep anyone from climbing. No such order reigned in the tunnel, where people still shouted for a share of the food while rattling the three portions of the gate.

"Earlman?" Devron glanced around and motioned him nearer. "Assess the gate." To the prince, he added, "Earlman is one of our best formers—he constructed that gate."

Earlman halted his turn toward the tunnel and pointed at Devron. "*He* is the best former, and he *designed* the gate. We *need* him."

The prince's smile flickered. "Yes, I know. All of you, stay on this end of the platform while I talk with Crysalan for a moment." He strode toward the tunnel. "You near the gates—stop shouting. You will be heard soon. Is Mayor Sairtoka or Chief Former Pondarro among you?"

A cacophony answered first, then Sairtoka's voice crested above the others. Had a wind weaver dared use her gift to lift it? "Yes, I am here. Guards, clear this rabble and let me through." In a bad temper.

She seemed to be following a huge personal guard whose head extended above everyone else's. He didn't hesitate to injure citizens to clear a path for her and Pondarro.

Sairtoka shouted past her guard. "Mayor Borchel, I hold you responsible for this chaos. If you could control your own people, this never would have happened." A feminine hand gripped a bar of the central gate, and Sairtoka craned her head to see through. "Now open this ga—" She stared, dumbfounded, at the prince. "Who are you?"

"I am Prince Queltin."

"Pondarro," she hissed, "is that true?"

His sneer in her direction did not improve his harried expression. "Yes."

"People of Crysalan..." Authority resonated in the prince's voice. "Be assured that I will attend to your concerns soon. For now, please back away thirty paces so the gate may be opened."

His voice echoed down the tunnel. Within seconds, it clarified. Definitely, a wind weaver hiding in that group. Had she, or he, heard the king's letter and taken courage?

The crowd that had shouted over the guards now shuffled back. That could have been due to the hulking guard and an equally cruel helper who turned to drive them, but awestruck murmurs suggested otherwise. Mayor Borchel seemed to be trying to pass a message down the string of guards, telling them not to open the gate. Why must he make it hard for them?

The prince paid them no heed and, in due time, said to Earlman, "Open the gate."

Devron sensed Earlman's forming command, strong and sure as ever it had been, triggering the mechanism to open the narrow, central portion. His restored gift sent a rush of immense relief down Devron's arms.

As the gate lifted, the prince ordered, "Sairtoka and Pondarro, come through and onto the platform."

Devron half-dreaded a mass charge, but that did not happen. Sairtoka started speaking as the gate descended behind them but only got two words out.

Prince Queltin pointed to a spot on the platform several yards from where he stood. "I grant you permission to stand there and listen. You will not speak until I address you."

The local wind weaver seemed to be trying. The prince's voice carried, though it echoed about oddly. Nonetheless, it held authority quite different than the two mayors could achieve.

Devron felt an indescribable energy pulsing through the crowd. Uncertainty, yes, but expectancy quivered through it. Perhaps rumors had spread of the grain canisters, but that could not account for the stirring. Jourendia had not simply received food from aboveground, but a *person*. And not just any person, the king's son. A dense pause held them. A question hovered over both crowds. What would happen?

The prince spoke toward the tunnel. "If any residents of other cities are in the tunnel, I ask you to make your way near to the gate. I will need to speak with you before you return to your homes." He strode back toward the local crowd. "Mayor Borchel, you were given a letter from King Tandorad, which you failed to read to Jourendia. Give it to me." He held out an imperative hand.

The mayor fumbled with a pocket. "I—"

"There are other copies if you refuse to comply."

The mayor, a tad pale, gave up on whatever he'd planned to say and handed over the letter. Devron watched faces in the crowd as the prince briefly explained that Devron had created a safe passage in the lake cavern, which Talmarq had traversed. He then read the king's first letter and told of his own journey through the passage. He slipped the letter into his portfolio. "I'm sure you have many questions about how the passage works and how the rivers will bring you food. All will be answered in due time. First, I must address the breakdown of law."

Sairtoka abandoned restraint. "So! You think you are going to become a king to rule over us, do you?"

The prince did not even glance at her. "Most of you probably know that I have served as a judge for twenty years now, specializing in all cases pertaining to Dirklan. I was appointed as one of the high judges of Welcia three years ago. I shall now read a royal decree." He opened his portfolio. "Chief Streamer Fezlie and Chief Former Kevenor, come to either side so you may affirm that I read true. Confirm first that the king's seal and signature are present."

They both agreed it was so, then the prince began to read.

A Decree to Establish the Province of Dirklan in the
Kingdom of Welcia.

Seeing that Dirklan lost direct access to the king and all
courts of law due to the collapse in LourEstelle;
Seeing that order and justice are required to maintain
peaceful and prosperous freedom;
Seeing that some leaders of cities within Dirklan are
accused of usurping authority over the substance guilds, of
unlawful executions, of raising armed forces against their
own people, and of sundry other crimes;

Now therefore, the king and queen of Welcia decree,

Dirklan is hereby created as a province of Welcia with
entitlements and responsibilities equal to all other
provinces of the land.
Prince Queltin shall act on behalf of the king to establish
the Province of Dirklan with a constitution ratified by the
population, and to oversee the election of officials.
The constitution is to be presented to the king no later than
the beginning of the next new year.

Until that time, all security forces in Dirklan answer to
Prince Queltin.
Prince Queltin is hereby appointed as High Judge of the
Province of Dirklan.

*As Judge Queltin, he shall hear accusations and try cases,
beginning with the crimes committed by elected officials.
Those found guilty are forbidden to hold office again.
Judge Queltin shall establish lower courts in the cities of
Dirklan.
The appointment of a high judge shall remain in effect as
long as the incumbent is able to fulfill his or her duties.
Thereafter, the king or queen of Welcia shall appoint a new
high judge.*

Prince Queltin paused and looked to the two guild chiefs. "Do you concur that I have read the decree accurately?"

They both agreed.

A princely smile softened his expression as he gazed over the crowds before him and down the tunnel. "It is my great delight to offer these first congratulations. You are now recognized as the Province of Dirklan." He paused as a whispery sound swept the crowd. "I suspect that you don't yet realize the significance of your new status, but I assure you, a cheer is in order. You are no longer buried as though dead." He deepened his voice. "Dirklan, arise!" He turned to the tunnel and shouted it again.

A few local people uttered it in off-tempo unison. No one seemed to know how to join a cheer anymore. A few tilted their heads back and readied a shout. Devron joined them. "Dirklan, arise!" A musician grabbed a gong from one of the town criers and beat a cadence to encourage several more repeats, then ended it with a flourish.

Fairlynn leaned into Devron. "Oh, Dev! Hearing the cheer come down the tunnel like that. There's hope for my old home."

He could only nod, for there were no words for all the ideas and questions that raced through his brain and set his stomach to fluttering.

"Plenty of hope," Prince Queltin said. He addressed the crowd again. "I have multiple copies of the documents to be mounted behind crystals in all cities. But for now, I have another decree to read." He withdrew it from the portfolio, made sure his witnesses were attending, then read the decree appointing Devron as Chief Former of Dirklan. Since Devron's name was mentioned halfway through, the prince had to raise his voice over a growing clamor. Even then, he wouldn't have succeeded without the hidden wind weaver's help, her vocal lift beginning to steady.

By the time the prince finished reading, Geon let out a yell so loud no one could understand it. His message came through anyway, as he leaped with raised fists and an enormous smile. All the growers and many formers joined in. The streamers contented themselves with smiles and clapping.

Perrie darted up the steps between guards and flung herself against Devron's legs, squeaking, "I knew you would bring the light back!"

Ah, that was the best cheer of all.

It was impossible, of course, that everyone would be happy, but the disgruntled sort couldn't stir up enough noise to drown out the cheers. They made do with scowls. Some council members tried to climb the steps, asserting that the king didn't know about the law Devron had broken and other such absurdities.

The prince looked down on them, his eyes half closed but his voice neutral. "The king knows about unwarranted accusations made against Provincial Chief Former Devron. He also knows about the mayor and council of Jourendia usurping authority over the Formers' Guild. Nonetheless, you are welcome to state your accusations in a formal hearing if you believe that kingdom law was broken."

The prince didn't wait for an answer, instead turning to Devron. "It is my understanding that the current chief former of Jourendia was not chosen according to kingdom law, so convene your guild soon to legally appoint whomever the guild selects."

Devron faced the crowd. How could he invite formers who'd lost hope, without sowing dismay elsewhere? "All in Jourendia who have ever known the former's gift, meet with me in Settlement Hall for our guild meeting during the last work hour today." It wouldn't be an easy meeting, but they were going to talk about what no one wanted to say. And they were going to face the need to prove their gifts.

Prince Queltin clearly didn't like long gaps in proceedings. His voice deepened into mournful gravity. "The king and queen—and I, too—are deeply grieved by the death of Wandermae, Chief Wind Weaver of Dirklan. Though she now rests in the joy of Ellincreo, we realize that losing her below has thrown her entire guild into disarray. I will ensure that a meeting of all wind weavers in the province is convened as soon as possible. Until that time, I assure the wind weavers that your gift is still valued, it is critical to our well-being, and it will not be threatened in any way. Continue to practice it as Ellincreo has gifted you." He left a rare and weighty pause, moving his gaze slowly over the crowd as he walked the platform and ended near the tunnel. "Carry those words to all of Crysalan."

The prince returned, looking over the guards as his heels struck stone. "The guards of Dirklan must serve me willingly. I doubt it will be a lifelong duty. I hope to soon release most of you to...mining or whatever profession you prefer. Until then, I need your choice. You may decline service by laying any weapons, accoutrements, or insignia on the platform. Those who intend to remain, raise your right hand so I may clearly see your commitment."

Devron didn't know the ever-increasing number of guards, but so many hands went up...were any declining?

"My thanks for your continued service," the prince said. "It is time for arrests. Guards near the platform, prepare bindings." Prince Queltin executed a sharp quarter turn. "Borchel, you are under arrest by the king's warrant, with the primary charges of illegal executions and usurping authority over the Formers' Guild."

Borchel had grown steadily paler. No sound passed his sagging mouth. Nor did he move when a guard mounted the steps and tightened a leather strap around his wrists.

The prince spun to face the other mayor. "Sairtoka and Pondarro, you are both under arrest by the king's warrant for inciting the murders of Wandermae and Greehan—both of them honorably using their gifts for the good of Dirklan. Other accusations include extortion from other cities and individuals, bribery, and sundry crimes."

"No!" Sairtoka snapped. "You have no knowledge—no understanding of what has happened here. This is an outrage."

"You may give your defense at your trial. Guards, bind them."

"You'll regret this. I have support. Pondarro, defend me."

How could she be so foolish? Her struggles only brought more guards around them.

"Break through the gate!" she shrieked.

Her massive guard bellowed from the tunnel with a throaty bass. "Let them go or your little kingdom ends right at this gate. And not a scrap of food that comes down those rivers will ever reach Jourendia."

"You see," Sairtoka snarled.

The gate clanked hard as her guard's arrogant face smashed against the iron bars. He thrust back, but something looped his neck and pulled taut. A second man was thrown backward against the gate, his head striking hard before his knees buckled. Several people pressed against the walls of the tunnel, but in the midst, guards wearing the same armbands as the giant, fought to subdue him.

One of them shouted, "Prince, if you want the guards of Crysalan, you must arrest these two."

"So, I shall. Subdue and bind them."

One was unconscious, but the big man had no escape and fought like he knew it, using the gate for rear protection. The prince motioned to the Jourendian guards who held stone spears. "Use those if you are sure of your mark."

A guard pierced the giant's back where it pressed against the bars. The big man howled, then toppled. Blows still struck him.

"Cease fighting," the prince commanded.

Some guards continued, but others straightened. One with a swelling ear and bloody hair yelled, "Halt!" That ended it.

Moans from the giant rumbled through the tense silence. He lay in a pool of blood. By the look of the fighters, not all of it was his.

The one who had shouted *halt* asked, "Please forgive them for the delay, sir. He was as much to blame for...for Wandermae and other killings as...as those two." Though stiff from injury, he gestured toward Sairtoka and Pondarro, who lay prone and bound on the platform.

"Nonetheless," Prince Queltin said, "he shall have a trial. The days of mob killings are *over*."

Devron sensed the crowd's anxiety, for they could not see the tunnel mouth directly. As the prince tended matters at the gate, Devron gave the local crowd a summary of what had happened and reassured them that the gate remained stable. He closed with, "Even though this last bit was harsh, take heart in knowing that justice has returned to Dirklan."

No one spoke at first, then someone mumbled, "That's only a few taken down from their army of bullies."

Fairlynn stepped to Devron's side. "True, but it is good news, just the same. I have friends in Crysalan who still write to me. Many there have been longing for the end of this tyranny. The leaders..." She smirked. "...including the captain of the bullies, have been taken down. Even among those in the tunnel, I heard cries for justice and cursing of the tyrants who oppressed them. I grew up in Crysalan, and I have faith in my people that they will grab hold of peace and justice more swiftly than they lost them." Her lips twitched into a risky smile. "For the first time in six months, I can imagine gathering in the sacred chamber for the next Gifting Day. Just think how we will rejoice."

Perrie, clinging to Fairlynn's skirt, shouted, "And feast!" Childish though her voice was, it carried through the cavern, drawing out several chuckles and lighthearted chatter. What a precious sound.

Those arrested were being led away as the prince returned to Devron's side. He dismissed the crowd with kind words and the promise of a town meeting the next morning. After conferring briefly with Fezlie, he returned to Devron. "You seem to have done well at calming your people while I was occupied with the fringe of Crysalan."

"Oh...thank you. I hope I wasn't overstepping."

The prince's brows rose a notch. "You realize, do you not, that you are the highest-ranking resident of Jourendia? As for the Province of Dirklan, only I outrank you."

"I...suppose so. I'll have to get used to that."

"Indeed. I hear you have a spare room, and I really should be staying with the highest-ranking official."

"Ah. You are most welcome, and I am sure we could all use a break." Devron stepped back. "Earlman, the prince's travel case and our night things are in the equipment room. Please take a guard and fetch them to my house."

"Right away."

A guard hurried to join Earlman, and Devron realized that the man was responding as to an order. From him. Weird beyond grasping. As were all the guards hanging about to escort them as they descended from the platform.

Kevenor waited at the base and took Perrie's hand. Devron licked his lips, but Kevenor leaned in to grip his shoulder and whispered, "No words right now, Uncle Dev. Just know that I am immensely relieved, and I will see you at the meeting this afternoon."

Fairlynn gave him an encouraging smile and extended it to Crilla, who stood a few feet away with her sons and niece.

Prince Queltin frowned at Fairlynn's heavy lean on her cane. "Do you have a household servant?"

Where did he think he was? As Fairlynn murmured *no*, Crilla urged her niece forward. "Santear can help you."

"That would be lovely." Fairlynn smiled. "I'll pay you, dear."

Santear blinked and gulped as she joined their entourage for a slow walk home. Clearly, a great many people had forgotten what work they had to do, all keeping a close eye on events while trying not to stare too blatantly.

Devron led his guests through his teal door. Much as he was longing for home, nothing was over yet.

Fairlynn did manage to give it a homey feel, though. "The ducks are hungry, Santear. Please feed them and bring the eggs down."

"Of course." Santear was already halfway up the stairs when she answered.

Fairlynn exhaled long and slow, watching her disappear. "I have this odd feeling that life just got a lot easier in the same moment that it got a lot harder."

"No doubt it will require adjustments," the prince said. "Talmarq told me that you have a troublesome hip, but I didn't realize how bad it was."

She shrugged off his concern. "It will be better in a few days. It's only worse now because I slept on stone last night."

Devron stroked her hand on his arm. "I'm so sorry, love."

"None of that. I wouldn't have missed it for all of Dirklan."

He grinned wryly. "That just might be what we would have lost if you *had* missed it. Speaking of which, I'm tired of the clothes I slept in." Devron unceremoniously pointed out a few things to his royal guest and invited him to make use of whatever was needed. Then he led his wife to their bedroom.

For several long minutes, they just stood holding one another in silence.

Eventually, she murmured, "Everything has changed. Everything!"

Her breath tickled the base of his neck. "Far more than I ever expected." He switched to irony. "I was just trying to get us some food." They leaned back and laughed together, though probably more than the quip deserved. "We are going to have so much to do."

"At least we don't have to hide *any* of it! Or sit in the same dim cavern for months."

"That is a plus. *Busy* is going to start—or resume—in a few minutes." They separated and grabbed clothes from the closet and drawers. "There is going to be travel," he said. "For the rest of our lives. Tiring for anyone, but I'm worried about you."

"Well, you can stop that, right now. We'll get used to it, though I imagine we should hire someone for a permanent position here. Don't forget that a provincial guild chief is the best-paying job in Dirklan. You're the one who is going to have the most to do. A guild meeting this afternoon, for instance, which you haven't had time to plan."

He shed his shirt and grabbed another. "Planned enough. I'm telling them up front that I know all their gifts are diminished. Oh, by the way, Earlman's gift is fully restored, so I think Ellincreo really was keeping the others from stopping me. I can use that to silence the shame and give hope that their gifts will return. Then I'll explain why range is no longer the most critical aspect of our gift. The essential skill of a Chief Former of Jourendia is now the ability to control the passage. That will provide the excuse for insisting that they all must prove their skills again. And last, I send them home with orders to *work* for a change." He met her eyes in the mirror, humor narrowing them. "I think they'll like it."

Her smile bloomed. "Oh, I bet they will." She sat down to pull on leggings below her second-best dress. "What next?"

"After I resurrect Jourendia's guild, I'll have to see what damage was done elsewhere and get formers productive again. Especially with those underground rivers, which are certain to contain obstacles. We'll need to coordinate timing and location with Prince Queltin's travels." He shook his head. "I can't believe I'm saying that. Do you realize that he's here *permanently?* Dirklan's own representative of the crown. And I...we..." He spread a hand, at a loss for words.

She grabbed his hand and squeezed. "It's crazy, isn't it!" With mock chagrin, she rocked her shoulders. "And I just can't seem to get away from being a chief former's wife."

He took her face gently in both hands and kissed her. "You're so good at it, after all. Come, we'd best get back to all this official-ness."

He really didn't think it would confront him the moment they stepped into his welcome room. But it did. Earlman had arrived with their belongings—and the oyster manager, who must have brought a problem.

"Continue your scheduling role," the prince replied to him, "but report to the chief streamer, at least for now. As for the gates, that is the chief former's decision."

"The lake gates?" Devron asked. "What of them?"

"You left them open when you came through. People are arguing over them. Er, they're used to them being closed and all that."

Open or closed—it made no difference. Devron had been forced to cater to fears for so long that he almost gave in. No more. "Leave them open."

Earlman looked like he was going to shout for joy. The manager looked like he was swallowing a bucketful of raw oysters. "I'm...not sure...how to deal with all the fuss."

"Mm. Earlman and I need to finish a little work there. I will come now."

Devron set out at once, Earlman at his side, and the oyster manager trailing. "The work," Devron explained, "is to turn a certain wall back into a door." He grinned. "I also modified the lock."

Earlman laughed. "Yeah, I saw that! I believe I can separate the door. May I try?"

"Absolutely. Then assess the dome." The outer gate was already in view. Closed. That didn't take long. "We'll go in through the gates."

The crowd was not dense enough to block his approach. Devron strode to the levers—both down. He raised one, and the outer gate began to open. No comment so far. Then he grabbed the other lever and pulled it up, both gates now separating. He turned to face the onlookers, who were already voicing opinions. Well behind them up the sloped thoroughfare, the prince stood with arms crossed. Watching—listening.

"Quiet." Devron spoke the single word with authority, then closed his lips.

It took a moment, but enough people repeated him to gain silence.

Devron calmly enunciated each word. "The dome is safe. Therefore, the gates remain open."

He listened to the questions and demands shouted all at once, then raised his hands for silence. He waited until he had it before answering them. "I did not form these gates because I feared collapse. I didn't even form them because *you* feared collapse. I formed them *only* so that I could open the dome. During the low tides of the new year and half year, they will be closed. That is their only purpose. Guards, you will stand watch at each end of the tunnel to keep the gates open until everyone complies with my decision."

A guard promptly strode down the tunnel as ordered, but someone in the crowd whined, "What would it hurt to close them now?"

"I do not make this decision lightly," Devron said. "Fear is a far greater risk than collapse. We have placated fear, making it grow ever stronger. It bred despair, and that killed some of us. It delayed light, robbing us of desperately needed food. But collapse in Jourendia..." He shook his head. "It never happened. It was never even likely. Fear is the one true danger. From this day on, we will *starve* fear, not *placate* it. We will walk unhindered to and from the lake, and we will trample the fear beneath our feet."

A quaking voice rose. "LourEstelle is crushed. You cannot say that a collapse will never happen."

"I am not saying that. But I have seen Jourendia crushed too." He sneered. "Crushed by *fear*. Nothing but a weightless choice—killing us. I will not bow to fear. I will not pander to it. And I will not feed *your* fears by closing these gates."

He let the words hang in silence. "We hold the gift of life. Let us live it. Remember our custom, how we often rested by the lapping waters while light from afar danced through them. I invite you to return with me, and savor peace again."

He turned and strolled down the tunnel. Some footsteps followed. Others did not. But as for him—he would savor the gift of life. And he would use it.

EPILOGUE

Devron led Fairlynn through the waning light in the sacred chamber, her long skirt swishing against his leg. With the crowds gone now, the chamber echoed only to the tune of water. They stopped one tier up from the pool before the golden vision wall.

"I love this sound," she murmured. "Like the steady flow of life behind the sudden tragedies and triumphs. The whispery song behind celebration that lingers after everyone has gone home."

"You like it better than the sound of a vortex?"

She gave a dramatic shudder. "Oh, by the caverns, yes! A vortex is a rude, demanding thing." Her smile suddenly bloomed. "Of course, I will never forget the sound of that first canister splashing from the inbound river, while all of you formers stood around debating options for a receiving chute."

He chuckled. "I've never been so happy to get drenched—even with that floury muck from the broken one."

"I know I shouldn't have laughed," which she was again trying to suppress, "but the looks on your glue-speckled faces..." She gave up and let her mirth bubble out.

He savored the new memories that replaced moments of anguish and months of frustration. All of Dirklan had been giddy with relief as the aboveground food canisters rode the cataract into Northeshur. And from there, loaded onto rail carts, they'd sped to every city's rail terminal. "I'll bet there wasn't a dry eye in any city of Dirklan when their first shipment arrived."

Her voice trilled. "Arrived day after day!"

Reliable. Sufficient. With the promise of more. At last, three months after the opening of the dome, they had dared to plan a feast. Ordinary portions, in reality, but compared to tight rations, it *felt* like a feast. Children ran laughing and playing amidst the tables, and no adult uttered one word of restraint. Festive clothes may still hang loose from shoulders, but joy sated every heart.

Even though Jourendia had been chosen as the new capital city, only Crysalan could hold so many celebrants. So here, they'd converged, in a city once proud, now humbled. Devron doubted it would have been possible if Judge Queltin had not dispensed prompt justice. After that, healing began. Forgiving Crysalan may have been the first unified act of love that Dirklan produced since the collapse.

Besides, only in Crysalan could they assemble before the vision wall. A gift that so many had mocked on that fateful day. It had, indeed, been necessary to return to this chamber. A little humility was in order.

The new Chief Keeper of the Writ had spoken of the need to honor all gifts—even those that one did not understand. He offered a quiet moment, suggesting that those who disdained the visions could use it to acknowledge their error in the privacy of their hearts. His next prayer was of gratitude for the visions that had saved those who escaped and also those who lived through the disaster.

As Devron pondered, the seeming disparity faded. Though some visions had been dire warning and others hopeful creation, all flowed from the same source. From a love that spoke true even when the message was unpleasant and unwanted. Oh, how crucial it was to follow love instead of fear!

The golden wall glowed before him and Fairlynn with the ruddy light of a distant sunset. A garden now surmounted it. A few vines had strayed to the top of the wall and peeked over the edge. It held no vision for him today, but it did whisper hope. A vision would come if he needed it, either here or in his heart, ready for him to create.

Fairlynn tilted her head to look up at him. "What do you see in that wall?"

Perhaps he should not stare at it so fixedly. "It holds no vision today, my dear."

"And here I was hoping that it showed you a tunnel route." Her vibrant mood made the words sound like a tease, but they were still true.

Always the tunnel...even though everyone knew of the persistent issues near Mount Estelle. He'd ordered all fringe caverns of LourEstelle and the access avenue to be permanently abandoned and sealed. A hard decision, but necessary. Considering the chances of quakes and flooding, a safe tunnel route seemed inconceivable. No one wanted to hear that. Not even his wife. "I will search, but I cannot promise that we will see a tunnel in our lifetime."

"Well then..." She swayed in a dance motion, and sang out, "Gardens forever!" She giggled at the absurd echo. "They're not a bad thing after all—as long as they are not our only food source."

Yes, the import river was the solution, but few seemed to realize it was also the single point of failure. If anything went wrong before Dirklan had a tunnel, hunger would swiftly attack. An almost forgotten twinge made his stomach flip. Not that awful feeling again! It hadn't troubled him since the day he'd opened the dome over Passage Lake. Clearly, fear was a subtle beast, slithering out of hiding when one least suspected.

Fairlynn slipped her arm around his waist, and he hugged her close. Her pleasant scent was back—thanks to her favorite hot spring. The highlights of her hair were tinged with pink in the twilight. Her smile beckoned. He kissed her welcoming lips, long and slow.

Several timeless minutes later, they settled into a sweet embrace. Realization wove through Devron. Even though he still knew the risks facing his people, fear had lost its grip on his gut. Why?

Love again? Placed in the forefront where it belonged. This time it had emerged through his wife, but he'd found it in other places too. In the eyes of a child, in the help of a friend, and—even amidst the darkest, loneliest impasses—in the heart of Ellincreo. Whenever love was allowed to flow, its power revealed fear's weakness. No disaster could overcome them, as long as they remembered this truth.

SHARE THE ADVENTURE

I hope that you found something in these pages that made your life a little richer. If you liked this story, maybe others would too. You can help them find it by leaving a brief review or even by clicking some stars wherever you like to purchase or review books. Those star ratings and reviews help me, too, and I greatly appreciate all of them.

Would you like to read more stories like this one? If so, I invite you to join my newsletter. I will send you some free short stories, share a little about life, and let you know about new books and an occasional sale. I won't overload your inbox or share your email address with others. You may unsubscribe at any time. Sign up at SharonRoseAuthor.com. I hope to hear from you!

THE NEXT ADVENTURE

TO WEAVE THE WIND
ARTS OF SUBSTANCE – NOVEL 2

Only the powerfully gifted new ambassador can save the underground province.
Or so they believe until she arrives.

Dirklan Province is owed a royal ambassador. What they desperately need is a powerful streamer to restore the trade cataracts. Fanteal should provide both, for they've heard of her amazing gift.

Fanteal soon discovers that she will be more of a pawn than an ambassador. Worse yet, as crowds cheer her arrival, she collapses from a mysterious illness. Rumors spread that something is wrong with her gift. Had their old prime minister lied? Why?

The new prime minister's son, Jaikon, becomes Fanteal's unwilling champion. He alone saw her gift manifest. Didn't he? His already shaky reputation will never recover if she possesses the wrong gift.

Fanteal must learn what secrets the last prime minister took to his grave. What did he know about wind weavers and this so-called illness? But her visit to his private library just spawns more questions, and it ends with a disastrous public challenge of her gift.

Now everyone knows the truth—or thinks they do. Trade will fail and severe poverty will follow. Yet Fanteal and Jaikon know there is a far more dangerous truth lurking in their underground world.

BOOKS BY SHARON ROSE

FANTASY

Arts of Substance

To Form a Passage – Novel 1
To Weave the Wind – Novel 2
To Stream an Ocean – Novel 3

Castle in the Wilde

A Castle Lost — An Early Days Novella
A Castle Sealed — Prequel Novella
A Castle Awakened — Novel 1
A Castle Contended — Novel 2
A Castle From Ashes — Novel 3

SCIENCE FICTION

Diverse Similarity — Novel 1
Diverse Demands — Novel 2
Agents of Rivelt — A Novel in Short Stories

More titles are coming. Find the full list at SharonRoseAuthor.com.

ACKNOWLEDGMENTS

There's so much to be grateful for! Where to start?

Small? That would be Sheba, the furball who keeps my lap warm while I write.

Difficult? That would be editing (shudder) and Bridgett makes it bearable.

Typos? Beastly little things! Laura, Tori, and Michael helped stomp them out.

Art? I'm always amazed at how Kirk turns my imagination into a book cover.

The long haul? This heavy work is supported by so many. Realm Makers, Write Now at Living Word Christian Center, friends who know nothing about writing but still listen to me, and of course, my wonderful family.

Ideas and comfort? Father, Friend, and Spirit. Yes, I'm talking about God, but hey, I'm a writer! A single word is not enough for the one who loves me so deeply.

Readers? That's probably *you*. Whether you read in advance, or you found this book long after I write these words, thank you for imagining with me. I hope you found some treasures to keep.

I appreciate all of you more than I can ever say!

ABOUT THE AUTHOR

Sharon Rose has been weaving stories since her second-grade masterpiece, titled *My Life as a Flying Squirrel*. No publisher snatched it up, but her classmates loved it.

After creating home and family, Sharon pursued her dream of creating stories for people like you. To date, she has published ten books, with more in the works. She writes fantasy and science fiction because they offer vast spaces to explore the realities that we all face. Her stories blend cultures and characters into adventures with mystery, romance, and hope.

When not writing or reading, Sharon may be traveling, enjoying gardens, or searching for unique coffee shops with her husband. She lives in Minnesota, USA, famed for its 10,000 lakes and vibrant seasons.

To find out more, visit SharonRoseAuthor.com.
Follow me on:
Amazon, Goodreads, BookBub, Facebook, etc.
Find all of my links at: https://linktr.ee/sharonrose.author